For my frien... ...

Enjoy

A CANOPY OF STARS

BY

STEPHEN TAYLOR

First printing October 2010

Copyright © Stephen Taylor 2010

A CANOPY OF STARS

ISBN-10: 0-9552315-9-0
ISBN-13: 978-0-9552315-9-9

Cover design by
Nicholas Brown

NEW WRITERS BOOKS
An Imprint of DSC Publications

Published and Distributed by
DSC Publications
20 Wreake Drive, Rearsby, Leicester, LE7 4YZ, England

Printed by
IPS
59 Winchester Road, Countesthorpe, Leicester, LE8 5PN

Dedication.

For my daughter Helen and for Sian with much love.

Also by Stephen Taylor

No Quarter Asked No Quarter Given:

A Georgian romp of a story; of rousing achievements and
acclaim: but eventually betrayal. A story of an unlikely friendship,
destroyed by disloyalty and by treachery

Short listed for the 2010 Brit Writers award

Foreword
A Canopy of Stars.

In this absorbing tale of persecution, grief, injustice and love
Stephen Taylor has captured the essence of how it must have
felt to be on the wrong side of the law in Georgian London.
This is an intricate story with many intriguing strands, the
historical detail lending a depth and richness that kept me
engaged from beginning to surprising end.
**Historical Novelist Jo Field, author of '*Rogues & Rebels'*
and freelance copy-editor**

PROLOGUE

The power of emotions can be overwhelming. For now; now there was only annoyance; quite low, it would hardly act as a counterweight on the other side of the scales that measure such things. There was no hint in Julia's mind of the more powerful emotions that lay in wait for her; that would ambush her, change the way she thought, the way she behaved; that would change her very being in the weeks, the months to come. Emotions that would be both, at the same time, pleasurable and vindictive; emotions that she had no comprehension even existed, yet would bite into her, savage her. Her sheltered life had so far protected her from the force of them, she was little more that an emotional virgin to match her virginal physical state. But now; now was just another day – or so she thought: but that was not to be.

CHAPTER 1

London 1823

Julia looked forlornly out of her carriage window as it rattled past St Paul's Cathedral, the din of the iron clad wheels and the clatter of the hooves on the cobbled streets hardly registering in her mind. She was angry with her father. He was sat facing her but she did not want to look at him. George Carmichael was a renowned lawyer and barrister. His head was bowed studying the papers on his lap; the rocking carriage making them difficult to read.

'It's no good being angry at me,' he said without looking up from his papers, 'I don't make the rules. All court personnel, from the judges and juries to the lawyers and court officials, are *men*.'

'I know; the only women allowed are the witnesses. I have to be a spectator in the gallery.' She recited it back to him the way he had said it to her many times before.

'I shouldn't have indulged you and let you study under me. It's given you expectations that I can't fulfil.' His tone was philosophical.

'I'm the best student you have ever had; you've said so yourself.'

'That's true, my dear, but the best I can do is let you clerk for me.'

'So why can't I do that from the courtroom?'

'Sorry my dear, but you just *can't*. You'll have go into the public gallery and take your notes from there.' He reached into his waistcoat and took himself a pinch of snuff. Julia turned her head away; the aromatic smell of it was not one that she liked.

The carriage turned onto Old Bailey Street and Julia looked back out of the window. She sighed as they passed the semicircular brick wall immediately in front of the courthouse. They went around the rear to the covered colonnade for the carriages. George Carmichael held out his hand as his daughter stepped down from the carriage steps. He kissed her on the cheek affectionately and she smiled back, but only out of politeness.

'Will you be alright in the gallery?' He wanted to indulge her as he often did, but was unable to, 'You'll have quite a wait for my case.'

'I'll be fine,' she said, 'I find it interesting sometimes to watch the other cases. The poor souls who can't afford counsel, doing the best they can to represent themselves.'

'The 'Judge is there to help them,' said her father matter-of-factly.

'Sometimes; but sometimes they are convicted and leave the court without even knowing that.'

'Aye, the lack of education is a terrible thing.'

She gave him a wry smile. 'I never know whether you really care or not,' she said as she walked away.

'Julia,' he called after her. She turned and stepped back to him. 'You are twenty-two now, my dear. Isn't it time you put all this lawyer nonsense behind you and found yourself a nice husband.'

'I'm too plain for that. A husband won't take me.'

'Now stop that talk at once,' her father wagged an admonishing finger and frowned, 'you are a most attractive young lady.'

'Bless you Father, but you see me through a father's eyes. I know I'm too tall and too plain.'

'Nonsense,' he snapped, hurrying away, but in his heart he knew what she said was true. Julia had inherited his physique rather than that of her petite mother. She was unfashionably tall and towered over other women, but she had a natural elegance. Her features were angular rather than delicate; even so, she was a handsome woman, if not a beauty by the standards of the day. It irritated him that she could not see that.

Once in the gallery, Julia perched her portfolio precariously on her lap and lifted the lid. In the corner was a hole purposely made to take an ink well; she opened the hinged stopper and placed her pen in the groove next to it. The gallery was not busy today and there was an empty chair beside her on which she placed her satchel. She would need to balance that on her lap as well if the gallery filled up. She looked down over the courthouse; it had only one courtroom, but it was vast. Four large brass chandeliers hung from the ceiling to add majesty to the auditorium and she thought to herself that it must frighten the wits out of the prisoners. Searching the room beneath her she could see the large semi-circular mahogany table provided for the counsel to plead from, but her father was not yet there, his case was much later.

The business of the session got underway, and Julia took the opportunity to scribble some preparatory notes in her portfolio. The commissions were read and the justices seated. She didn't look up as the jury was sworn and they started to examine the bills of indictment as produced by the clerks, but the shuffle of feet broke her concentration when the prisoners, chained together at the ankles, were brought into the court to await their arraignment. They were, in the main, a rag-bag collection of the low-life of London, but Julia still had a compassion for them. She was an inherently compassionate person. She was a Christian and that coloured her view of humanity, but that in itself made her different from the majority of her fellow worshippers, who seemed only to pay lip-service to the concept of forgiveness. It annoyed her that, when it came to it, so many had so little charity in their hearts. Julia shivered as she contemplated the fate of many of these poor souls. She knew the laws were made by the rich with the purpose of protecting their property. But worst of all, she knew that nearly two hundred offences carried the death penalty. If found guilty, the best these poor wretches could hope for was transportation; the worst was the hangman's noose

The prisoners had been brought from the cells in the basement and before that from the disease-ridden dungeons of Newgate Prison, which was attached to the courthouse by a brick-walled passage. Their ruffian clothes were now even more dishevelled, but one man stood out from the others. Somehow he had managed to keep himself reasonably clean. His clothes, although dirtied, had quality that the others didn't have. He was taller than the others too and Julia found herself looking at his handsome face; he had such a noble aspect. Then she chided herself for being silly and returned to her scribbling. The Clerk then called for anyone to give evidence against the accused. The witnesses who came forward for the Crown were sworn to tell the truth. The jury then gave its verdict.

Julia took little interest as the cases sped by, many lasting no more than a few minutes, perhaps half an hour for a felony. Still scribbling she became aware of some confusion below her and looked up from her papers. The name 'David Neander' had been called and the tall, handsome man, his shackles struck off, was brought to the bar. He was indicted for the felony of stealing, on the 10th of December, a wether sheep to the value of forty shillings, being the property of Herbert Bond. The confusion had come about because the accused was a foreign Jew and despite the same jury having sat for several cases, Judge Harcourt Cardew now ordered a jury of half English and half foreigner. There was a buzz of noise as the old jurors shuffled out and the new ones took their places. Saul Hugeunnin, sworn in as the interpreter, asked the prisoner how he was to plead. The normal response was not forthcoming and Julia, looking at the interpreter's face, could see he was confused. Amused, she put down her pen and craned forward to watch the proceedings below.

Clearly irritated, the Clerk snapped, 'How does he plead?'

'He doesn't,' said the perplexed interpreter, 'he says that Yiddish is not his first language, sir.'

'So what is his first language?' asked the Clerk, an expression of increasing exasperation crossing his features.

'German, sir, but he says he is fluent in French and Latin as well. He would like an interpreter in one of these three.'

Laughter broke out around the court, and Julia also smiled at the accused man's colourfulness. The gallery was to his right, above the jurors, and she could see them turning to each other enjoying the amusement.

Judge Harcourt Cardew clearly considered the man's request impertinent. He scowled and called out for order, his full-bottomed wig swishing from side to side as he shouted to each side of the court. 'Did he impart that request to you in – err, Yiddish?' he asked Saul Hugeunnin when the noise had died down.

'Yes, Your Honour.'

'Then that will suffice; let that be an end to it.' It was his ruling and he emphasised it with a dismissive wave of his arm.

Julia thought to herself that the prisoner my have inadvertently made a great mistake; the Judge may take against him. Justice might be hard to find this day. She unexpectedly felt concern for this unknown foreigner, although she could not have explained why. She looked across at the Judge, his elevated position and his scarlet, ermine-lined robe emphasising his importance, and saw the contempt etched large on his features. And then she understood why. The prisoner's request for a different interpreter should have told the Judge that this was an educated man; not just another ignorant vagabond, but Judge Harcourt Cardew saw only a Jew before him and he was making no attempt to hide his displeasure. Julia leaned forward in her chair and listened intently; she wanted to know this man's fate.

CHAPTER 2

Frankfurt 1816

When I was 14, I first became aware of the animosity towards my family. No, that's not quite true. I was *aware* of it from my very first memories of childhood consciousness. Even though I couldn't articulate exactly what it was, I knew it was there; that somehow we were different from other people. For a start we were Jewish, but German speaking Jews; Papa insisted on that. So we were not German and not quite part of the Jewish community either – they spoke Yiddish, or to be more precise a variation called *Judendeutsch*. It was my responsibility to see my brother Moses and my sister Henriette safely home from school. We attended the Jewish school on the main road, the *Allerheiligen Strasse*. Papa taught at the school but he stayed behind to work after our lessons. It wasn't a long walk; we turned onto the *Bornheimer Strasse*, which led onto the *Judengasse*, and then cut through to the *Kiostergasse*. We lived on the corner of the *Kiostergasse* and *Nonnengasse*. It was no more than six hundred metres.

At eleven years old, Moses was three years younger than me and Henriette was two years younger than him. They were both difficult to control; after spending all day at their studies cooped up in the classroom, all that energy wanted to explode. They wanted to run and jump, but Papa had told me that we needed to be as inconspicuous as possible until we were home. This particular day was not exceptional, it was like any other, we were on the *Allerheiligen Strasse*; but there was a German on the path coming towards us. He yelled out, '*Dud mach mores*', which roughly meant, 'Jew pay your dues'. I ushered Moses and Henriette into the street out of his way and then I took off my hat and bowed as I had been taught to do. That's what Papa had told me. But there was a mule, harnessed to a cart, on the road. It was a fiercely hot summer's day and the animal stank. Dozens of flies danced around it and the occasional ineffectual wafting

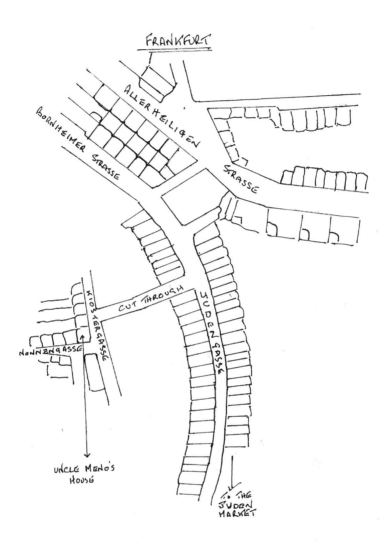

of its mangey tail did little to dissuade them from getting at the main attraction: its festering foul-smelling droppings. The animal was obviously parched and uncomfortable in the heat of the burning sun, it snorted at us for getting in its way, irritated, although it was going nowhere without its master.

'Loeb, why do we have to walk in the street?' asked Henriette.

'Because we're Jewish,' I answered without really thinking about what I was saying and that seemed to be enough to satisfy Henriette and Moses. I was their big brother Loeb, and I knew what I was talking about. But for the first time the animosity towards us troubled my mind and I realised that the fact that we were Jewish was no answer – it was merely a statement of fact. As we walked home that thought began to bother me. I had been taught about the *Judenstattigkeit*, the Jew's Statute. It imposed severe limitations on our freedoms, banned us from owning land, said what commodities we could trade in, where in the city we could go and even had a clothes ordinance saying what we could wear. All this started to trouble my mind.

We turned onto the *Judengasse*, the Jewish Alley, and suddenly we seemed to be in darkness and our eyes needed time to adjust. The street was cobbled but there was no sunlight to pick out the individual cobbles. I shivered, despite it being high summer the *Judengasse* seeming to be several degrees cooler that the rest of the city. That should have been pleasant and yet it wasn't; there was an open sewer that ran in shallow ditches. The air was foul and you could smell the street well before you got there. Papa had told me all about the *Judengasse*. It was originally located outside the east wall of the medieval city. It was long, about 330 metres long, but just three to four metres wide, with three town gates. These gates used to be locked at night as well as on Sundays and Christian holidays. For hundreds of years it had been the home to all the Jews of the city; the city authorities demanded that of them – they had created a ghetto. The population grew, of course, but the city senate refused to allow the ghetto area to expand. The place had been massively overcrowded, but then, as Jews we were non-citizens; we were at the mercy of the Lutheran senate of aristocratic families and rich merchants: I realized at that moment that they hated Jews.

I didn't like the *Judengasse*, it gave me the creeps. It was as though all colours had been banished; it was all shades of grimy grey through to demonic black. The people had been forced to build upwards. Four stories tall, the brick, wood and slate buildings towered above us, and there they were topped off by garrets overhanging at their tops so that they were nearly touching the houses on the other side of the street. The semicircular road snaked round, a mass of terraced buildings arching into the sky above us, leaving the road in permanent twilight. Our footprints suddenly echoed back at us and it always made us involuntarily quicken our steps until we could cut through onto the *Kiostergasse* and back into the light. Moses always made a point of saying he wasn't scared, but I knew he was only whistling in the dark.

Papa had grown up in the *Judengasse* with Uncle Meno until they were both sent away to the *Freischule* - the Free School - in Berlin. They weren't in the city twenty years ago. In July 1796 French revolutionary troops besieged and shelled the city. I had learned all about that at the Jewish School. The northern part of the *Judengasse* was hit and started to burn, destroying about a third of the houses. The ghetto was at an end, despite the anti-Jewish city senate, which was now forced to allow the Jews to leave the Jewish quarter.

We cut through an alleyway onto the *Kiostergasse*. We could see our house as soon as we entered back into the brilliant sunshine. I cupped my hand over my eyes at the sight of it. It was only a matter of metres but it was a million kilometers from the isolation of the *Judengasse*. I would painfully learn later, however, that the sensation of isolation was still fixed in the psyche of German and Jew alike.

We lived on the corner of the *Kiostergasse* and *Nonnengasse*. Our house was quite a big house. It was three stories tall and we lived on the third floor with Mama and Papa. I say *our* house, but it was really Uncle Meno's house. He was rich, or at least I thought he was at the time. Uncle Meno was a doctor. It was one of the few professions that Jews were allowed to follow. He was very successful, not only with rich Jewish families but also the rich German families. Papa had told me that the German's looked distastefully on our religion as being ritualistic and superstitious. But in some paradoxical sort of way that view seemed to assist Uncle Meno. Jewish doctors were somehow seen as having mystical powers that Germans didn't posses. It made Uncle Meno chuckle and he did nothing to dissuade his patients of this. I liked Uncle Meno; he indulged us. He had no children of his own and he liked spending time with us – well, especially me, and I helped him in his pharmacy making up the potions.

When Moses and Henriette saw our house they ran ahead excitedly. I was happy to let them go now. They ran into the open side door and up the stairs pulling themselves up by holding onto a braided rope that worked as a banister, their footsteps thudding against the steps so that they echoed around the house like a drummer pounding away at a kettle drum.

'Children, Children!!' I heard Mama saying as I followed them up the stairs. 'Uncle Meno is at work downstairs. Be a little quieter can't you?' She said this every day, but there was such a release of energy after being at school that they couldn't help themselves. As I entered the kitchen, Mama was stood with her hands on her hips but she was hiding a smile. She was glad to see us home again.

The front door was reserved for patients. The whole of the ground floor was Uncle Meno's place of business. He had his office and a consulting room and a room at the back which was used as his pharmacy. His office fascinated me. It smelled of leather and beeswax. All along one wall was a bookcase filled with large medical textbooks. I was allowed to look in them when Uncle Meno was with me. He would look at me over his spectacles and chuckle when my face contorted at the sight of the gruesome drawings that assaulted my senses. He used to chuckle a lot, Uncle Meno. That's what I remember of him.

Mama gave us something to eat and drink, and then sent us out to play. She knew we needed to get rid of all that energy before the evening meal. I was still troubled, however, and I just sat on the step by the side door. We had been in Frankfurt for just over a year by then, but we hadn't made many friends. When we did play in the streets with some of the neighbourhood kids, they didn't always come back to play the next day. That was disappointing but I hadn't really thought about the reason for it until now. The Jewish kids dressed and spoke differently to the German kids, but we didn't. We dressed like them and spoke German.

Moses and Henriette were playing a game of dare. Henriette had dared Moses that he wouldn't run down the full length of the Judengasse and knock on the front door of the Rothschild's house, No.148, on his own. Believe it or not, old man Meyer Amsell Rothschild still lived there in the *Judengasse*, despite having built a banking empire, which he now ran with his sons. He was one of the richest men in the world, we all knew that. People said the Rothschilds had built mansions all over Europe, but he still lived here where he had always lived.

Our Moses was a plucky little so-and-so. No matter how frightened he was he was always up for a dare. Henriette, on the other hand, had worked that out and could play him like a fiddle. Although she was only nine she was somehow the dominant one of the two. She was clever at her studies as well, nearly as good as I was. She was the apple of Papa's eye. I was a bit jealous, if truth be known. I knew that Papa loved me; it was just that he seemed to expect so much more of me. If she wanted his attention, she just climbed onto has lap and snuggled up to him. No matter what he was doing or who he was talking to, he gave her his full attention. She was good at getting everything she wanted, our Henriette.

I should have stopped Moses running off to the *Judengasse* but I was too absorbed in my reverie. I saw him set off and disappear around the corner of the cut through alley, but I wasn't concerned for him. He was gone about four or five minutes, but then came running back, his pounding boots announcing his return long before we could actually see him. His face was crimson; he was panting heavily and the thumping of his heart was evident from the tremor in his voice, but he pumped out his little chest in pride. 'See, I told you I wasn't afraid,' he lied.

That evening after the family meal, I was desperate to talk to Papa, but I had to wait. Papa had a visitor and they were talking politics as usual. Papa was a journalist as well as a teacher and he edited a political journal, much to my mother's displeasure. Moses and Henriette had gone to bed; I was allowed to stay up longer than them, but the man seemed to stay forever and I knew that I too would be sent to bed before too long. Papa and the man and Uncle Meno were arguing, or it seemed to me that they were, but then Papa liked a good argument though he called it 'debating'. Eventually the man went and I saw my chance, but before I could say anything, Mama spoke.

'Papa, you should be careful,' she always called him 'Papa'.

'Stop fussing Mama, I know what I'm doing,' he always called her 'Mama'.

'The city authorities don't like the journal and the elders at the Jewish school don't like what you're doing either. You need that job, Papa.'

'And we need that extra money, Mama.'

'Where is this extra money, I never see much of it?'

Papa went quiet for a moment. I think Mama had caught him out in his fib. I was surprised as I thought Papa knew everything about everything, but I saw my chance.

'Papa,' I said, 'why does everybody dislike us?' Suddenly I was aware of the atmosphere changing. Papa looked round at me, but at the same time so did Mama and Uncle Meno. I thought I had said something wrong and I felt myself blushing.

'You're a good boy, Loeb,' interrupted Mama, 'nobody dislikes you.'

'I don't mean that, Mama,' I said.

I realize now that the atmosphere had changed because I had asked one of *those* questions. Those questions in life that, on the face of it, are very simple, but yet are the hardest to answer; they tap into so many other difficult and disparate concepts. But it was also a rights-of-passage question, a question that a young boy asks when he advances to being a man. In my case I needed to establish my sense of self, but that was not so easy, we were not a normal family. I heard Papa sigh heavily; he knew it might be a long night.

'You ask a good question my boy,' said Papa, 'and it's true that maybe it would be easier for us if we were strict in our religious observance.'

'So why aren't we, Papa?'

'Because the old orthodoxy comes with strict ritual and superstition and we have taken the decision to educate ourselves. I don't like the ignorance of the common Jew. They dress and speak differently and contribute to their own isolation.'

I think I understood that; Papa believed in reform, I already knew that. But it was not the answer I was looking for. 'But where are all our relatives, Papa? At the Jewish school all the other kids seem to be related to each other one way or another, but the only relative that Moses, Henriette and I have is Uncle Meno.'

'Ah,' said Papa, sighing deeply. 'Yes, our family never forgave your grandfather for sending Uncle Meno and me away to be educated at a German Free School. They look on us as bad Jews. Mama's family doesn't speak to her either.'

'So our own people don't like us and the German's certainly don't,' I said. 'You dress and speak like a German, but you are still barred from most professions, aren't you?'

'Yes, Frankfurt is the worst of the German cities; it's the most anti-Semitic.'

'So why did we come back here, if you knew that?'

Papa looked at me intently for some moments. Then he looked down at the floor and he seemed to drift away from us. He scratched the nape of his neck in contemplation. It was as though my words had revived a long lost memory; a very painful memory. I looked at Mama and I could see the concern on her face. I had seen Papa like this before and we kids knew better than to bother him when he was like this. Melancholy was a frequent visitor to him and it upset Mama because she didn't know how to deal with it. The silence seemed to go on forever and I felt that I needed to do something.

'I'll go to my bed,' I said. It was the best I could come up with at fourteen. I headed for the bedroom that I shared with Moses and Henriette, but Uncle Meno took me by the arm.

'After school tomorrow,' he said, 'you come and help me in the pharmacy, yes?' He winked at me as if to say, *I'll explain it all to you then.*

CHAPTER 3

London 1823

Julia Carmichael took a blank piece of paper from the back of her portfolio. She placed it on top of her other working papers and wrote down two words that would stand as a heading – *David Neander*. Then she wrote down a note that said, *Judge won't allow the prisoner access to a proper translator.* Then she put down her pen and listened intently.

Herbert Bond was the prosecutor of the charge and he was called and sworn. The Clerk called upon him to give his testimony.

'I am a butcher in the Strand; I lost a sheep on the 10th of December, out of a field at Mary-le-bone. I swear to the skin of the sheep that was found upon him.' He spoke as though he had been rehearsing it for days, which he probably had, thought Julia, as Bond pointed at the accused.

'Have you seen the side of the sheep?' asked Judge Harcourt Cardew.

'Yes, my mark was across the loins. I marked it down the head and across the shoulders, and there were two crosses besides across the loins, which is the mark that the salesman puts upon them.'

'I suppose the salesman puts his mark upon the whole lot that he is to sell that day?'

'Yes sir'.

'Was your own mark so particular that you could venture to swear to it?'

'There was my own mark upon it, a cross with red ochre. Butchers generally mark different marks. I can venture to swear to the skin from that mark.'

The next witness was the Watchman, John Henry. He was sworn in and gave his story. 'I am a shopkeeper on Oxford Road. The 10th December was in the period when it was required of me to act as the Watchman for the area. I met the prisoner between seven and eight in the morning, at the top of Oxford Road, towards the fields and I saw that he had a bundle on his shoulder. I retreated after he passed me, about ten or fifteen yards, then I went forward and laid my hand on his bundle and perceived it was some animal. I then followed him for about two hundred or two-hundred-and-fifty yards, but he realised that I was following him and he threw away the bundle and endeavoured to escape. I then laid hold of him and he told me he was promised a shilling by a farmer, or some man in the country to take the bundle to Oxford Road. I asked him why he threw away the property and he answered me in French - he said he could not speak English, Your Honour - that the property had only been delivered to him, to take it to Oxford Road.'

Julia picked up her pen again, and jotted down another note. *How did the Watchman know what he said? Can he speak French?*

The Watchman continued. 'I brought him back to the bundle, but he would not take it up any more. I asked him where he lived. He said he had no abode. I asked him again to take up his bundle and go with me but he said he would not, so I, with two or three more young men, put the bundle upon him and went with him to the Watch-house, where we opened the bundle. It was the hind part of a sheep with half the skin on, which belonged to that flesh. It was cut right through and was the hind part - the two hind legs. We examined the thief, but he would not speak English, any more than now. He insisted that this bundle was given him by a man in the country, to take it to Oxford Road. He did not say what particular place; just that he was to take it to Oxford Road. Mr Bond then came and said that he owned the skin.'

A juror stood and asked, 'Had the prisoner a knife?'

'We did not examine him at the time,' said the Watchman, 'but when we did, which was about four hours after he was taken, he had no knife upon him.'

He was not armed and did not resist arrest. Julia jotted down the note.

The Clerk to the Court then called on the prisoner to give his defence and David Neander came to the witness box. Julia looked down at what seemed to her such an exotic figure. He looked around the courtroom in bewilderment, then up at the gallery and she caught a glimpse of his eyes; they were large and dreamy blue, and his whole persona seemed to radiate from them. This pale-skinned, lean man was not what she expected a Jew to look like; he was so tall. His well-groomed hair was dark, almost black, brushed back to reveal a high forehead; the hair then fell away in waves to his shoulders. She wondered how he had managed to stay so tidy having been kept in a cell for weeks. His black jacket was not of a fashionable English style and she assumed it be Continental; the only thing she recognised was the open, loose Byronic-style collar. He held a wide-rimmed, high felt hat in his hands, his fingers curling it anxiously by the rim. Although this anxiety was also etched across his face, he nevertheless seemed to have a dignity that was so unusual to see in a felon.

His first words were to answer the Clerk to the Court's request that he state his name, address and occupation; he spoke in short sentences in Yiddish and the translator then conveyed his words to the court.

'My name is David Neander and I lived temporarily in St Giles,' he said. 'I am a poet.' Saul Hugeunnin looked sheepish as he spoke the translated words. Laughter again broke out in the court and the Judge winced in annoyance: prisoners were, commonly, not men of letters. If such a man came before the court he would most likely be before the King's Bench as a debtor, not charged with a felony. The people in the gallery now viewed the case as a comedy and this was spreading to the minor officials in the courtroom. This man was being viewed as an entertainment, Julia thought to herself, intrigued. He had the presence of the poet Byron himself; a hint in his appearance of that famed handsomeness and flamboyance.

The Judge interrupted, making no attempt to hide his irritation. 'Are you a published poet, sir?' he asked. 'Do you earn your living by such activity?'

'Yes sir,' Neander answered through the interpreter. 'Writing *is* my chosen profession. But it is true that at the present time I have to meet my living expenses by other means.'

'Well perhaps you would like to tell the court what those other means are?'

'Before arriving in England, I worked as a translator but I also fought as a pugilist to supplement my income.

'You are a fighter?' said the Judge, whilst waving away the attempt at further laughter from the gallery. There was disbelief evident in his voice.

'That is correct sir,' said David Neander.

'And have you done any fighting since you came to England?'

'No sir. I had only been in England for two days when I was arrested. I came with funds that I had saved, but my money was stolen from my lodgings on my first day in this country. I had then resolved to rely on my youth and strength to offer my labour to anyone who would employ me.'

The Judge wrinkled his nose as though there was a bad smell under it. He looked down on the accused through narrowed eyes, his fingers toying idly with the file of papers on his bench. After a moment he shrugged and looked away. Watching his body language, Julia could tell he was wondering if there was any truth in what the strange man in the dock was saying, dismissing him as a Jew and a liar. She, on the other hand, was convinced she saw truth in Neander's eyes. It was as if she and the Judge were viewing the same man from opposite ends of a telescope such was the difference in their perceptions. The thought troubled her. How could anyone receive justice in the face of such prejudice?

The Judge shot a look to the Clerk as if to tell him to proceed. The Clerk nodded, viewed the prisoner and told him to continue with his defence

'I was alone, when a person offered me a shilling to carry a parcel. I was to carry it into Oxford Road, but I did not know where that was. The man gave me directions, but I was still not sure that I understood them as I had so little of the English language. He said that it did not matter because he would be following fifty paces behind me. I had no particular place to deliver it to; the man was to direct me. At each corner I turned to look at the man and I followed his hand signals for the directions. When I came upon Oxford Road, another man stopped me, but I did not know what he was saying and I did not know that he was a law officer. I looked around for the man that had offered me the shilling, and I saw that he had turned and was running away. So I threw down the bundle and started to run after the man.'

He was not attempting to escape. Julia jotted down another note.

'I tried to explain to the man that had stopped me that the other man was running away, but I have only a few words of English. I told him I could converse in French if they could find someone to translate, but they did not understand me. This man then called on the assistance of several others and they put the bundle back on my shoulders and took me to some other place that I did not know. I continued to try and explain in French, but they did not bring a French speaker to assist me. Nobody would listen to me.'

The watchman didn't investigate the prisoner's story. The transcript will show that the Judge has said nothing wrong, but his tone and inflection throughout has been negative to the prisoner. Julia jotted the comments but then kept her pen in her hand, putting the end to her lips pensively, as the Clerk set the case over to the jury.

The jury huddled; the case had been put to them to consider their verdict. Julia noticed the Foreman was becoming agitated as, in hushed voices they debated for a considerable time. Finally, the Foreman stood to inform the court that eleven gentlemen were of one opinion, but that the twelfth gentleman wished the jury to go out of the court. The Judge set them to do so and the jury filed out, withdrawing at twelve o'clock.

In a state of obvious confusion, David Neander looked around the courtroom. He leaned sideways from the dock to try to get the attention of the interpreter, but the Dock Officer pulled him back forcefully. It was clear to Julia that he had no idea what was happening; his incomprehension was evident in his features, his eyebrows knotted and those large blue eyes gazed beseechingly around the courtroom looking for a friendly face to help him, but he saw no one. Julia felt a pang of compassion for this man; he was alone, so totally alone. She knew she could have helped him, but was not allowed to do so. The minutes ticked by slowly, as if time itself was taking a rest. Eventually, the interpreter remembered his duty and advised the prisoner that the jury was considering its verdict. Julia took to scribbling again. She wrote the names of the law cases that she thought would have precedence and the errors in procedure at this hearing.

At twelve-thirty the jury returned. The Foreman was called to stand and give his verdict. He stood and coughed to clear his throat, his gaze darting to the prisoner and back to the Judge.

On the edge of her seat, Julia realised she had been chewing on her pen, but then put it back into her mouth, her attention focused entirely on the Foreman as he opened his mouth to deliver the verdict.

'GUILTY.'

The word rang out as if a bell was tolling. It echoed in the vastness of the chamber. Julia's heart sank. Her compassion for this man was now overtaken by her anger; justice had failed to be done. The Foreman continued. 'Sir,' he said, 'the jury wish to recommend him strongly to his Majesty's mercy

All eyes now turned to look at the Judge. His shoulders hunched as he placed his elbows on the bench at which he sat. From his high perch much of his robe was obscured, but his face was clear for all to see. Julia saw only his coldness as he stared down at the prisoner: two cold eyes sat in judgement atop sagging, ruddy cheeks, criss-crossed with red, snake-like veins.

Judge Harcourt Cardew sniffed before he spoke. 'David Neander the Jew; you are new to this country but this did not stop you committing this crime within days of arriving in this fair country of ours. Your kind must realise that this will not be tolerated by the citizens of this city.' So saying, he drew his black cap onto his full-bottomed wig. There was a sharp intake of breath around the court and then it went silent.

Oh my god, thought Julia, *he's going to disregard the jury's plea for mercy.*

'Prisoner at the bar,' the Judge intoned, 'it is my painful duty to pronounce the awful sentence of the law which must follow the verdict that has just been recorded; that you be taken to the place of execution, there to be hanged by the neck until you are dead, and may God have mercy on your sinful soul.'

CHAPTER 4

Frankfurt 1816

That next day was also baking hot. I went through the front door into Uncle Meno's surgery as soon as I got home from school, but he had a patient with him and I started to wait, but he told me to come back in an hour. Mama gave us some apple-spritzer and I took mine to the side door and watched Moses and Henriette playing. They were playing soldiers and were pretending to be cavalry officers. Moses was using a broom handle as a lance. He told Henriette that she couldn't be a soldier because she was a girl but she could still play and they would rescue her from the Frenchies. Henriette was having none of that; she decided that if Moses could pretend to be a soldier then so could she. Dieter saw them playing and came to join in. He was a German boy and lived down the street; he played with us sometimes but I don't think his father approved. Moses waved at me to come and play. At 14; I thought their games were far too childish for me, but there was something about playing soldiers that a boy just cannot resist. I sprang to my feet, mounting my invisible charger in one movement and set off after them, hacking at invisible French infantrymen with my imaginary sabre as I ran.

We were Prussian cavalry officers in our game. I now realise how incongruous that was. Napoleon had defeated Frederick William III of Prussia in 1806. Although Frankfurt was a city state and not part of Prussia it was still German, and from Dieter's point of view it made sense to pretend to be Prussian. But we were Jewish kids. Under Napoleon, Jews were given full citizen rights. But even Prussian Jews fought in the Prussian army in the subsequent war of liberation. It was a strange form of patriotism but it was no less strong for all that.

We charged up and down the dirty street shouting our battle cries, our boots stirring up little eddies of dust that we then ran through so that grime clung ever upwards on our legs and collected on our faces and in our hair. Four doors down from our house lived Fraulein Breitner. She was the meanest woman on the street. I was never quite sure if it was because we were Jewish or that she was just plain mean all the time. An outsized, rotund woman with large hands; her calloused skin seemed to be stretched tautly over them so that they appeared like bony crab claws. We normally gave her house a wide berth, but in the excitement of our game we ran past it. She came out wielding her broom at us, telling us to keep away from her house and to take our noise elsewhere. Moses took this as a personal challenge. She was now a Frenchie and with his own broom handle, now converted into a sabre, he made a thrust at hers. *'Die, French dog,'* he said, but this particular French dog didn't take kindly to the name or the challenge. She reached out, her eyes bulging in incandescent rage, her free crab-like hand trying to grab him by the hair, and I could see that Moses was in for a whipping. I grabbed him by the collar and pulled him back out of her reach just as her skeletal fingers clawed at him. Her impotent fury now raging out of control, she rushed into the street swinging wildly at any of us that came near her, and so the cavalry decided to retreat back to their lines, which were outside our own front door. Frau Breitner continued to rail at us from down the street, in particular threatening to give Moses a good whipping when he wasn't expecting it.

If we couldn't be cavalry officers in our game then we decided to be gunners. In the Napoleonic wars the artillery had proved to be a battle-winning force and we knew all about that,papa having read it to us from the newspapers. We now loaded our imaginary cannon, pushing a wad down its long barrel and then ramming home the shell with an imaginary large wooden ramrod. I was to light the fuse and I told the others to move out of the way so they wouldn't be hit by the recoil, but Moses wasn't happy about the target.

'Not yet! Not yet!' he shouted. He scurried around the side and then swivelled the imaginary carriage so that it was facing

Frau Breitner's. 'Lower the trajectory,' I yelled, because the target was now much nearer, and Henriette turned the wheel so that the unseen barrel descended. I reached out with the touch paper and lit the fuse; everyone retreated as I had commanded to avoid the recoil and then we all collectively shouted: '*Booom!*'. The ball exploded from the barrel reducing Frau Breitner's house to rubble and we cheered at the destruction of the hated Frenchie.

Uncle Meno chuckled when he saw me. '*What!*' I said, not understanding his amusement. He directed me towards the mirror and I could see at once the problem. My hair and face were covered in brown dust, but large rivulets of sweat had run down my face leaving trails that revealed glowing bright pink skin beneath. I looked like a dishevelled clown.

'I can't let you into my clean pharmacy like that,' he said.

'I'll go and wash,' I was anxious not to miss this opportunity. He saw the disappointment in my face.

'Come on', he chuckled, 'let's take a walk down the *Judengasse*. It'll add perspective to what I'm going to tell you.'

I wasn't sure what he meant, but I jumped at the opportunity. I wanted to talk even if that meant going down the *Judengasse*.

I shivered as we entered the sun-starved alleyway; Uncle Meno saw my unease. 'I hadn't realised before that you find it uncomfortable,' he said and then he wrinkled his nose; we both did. 'Yes it does smell a bit doesn't it,' he chuckled. 'We grew up here – your papa and me; it is perfectly normal for us. It was all we knew, until of course we went away to Berlin to the Free School. Did *you* like the Free School in Geissen?'

'Oh yes,' I said, 'much better than the Jewish school. We learned German, French, Latin, Greek - and German history and literature as well,' I added, 'it was the best.'

'German, French, Latin and Greek,' he repeated nodding his head. 'Is not your Jewish education interesting then?' Uncle Meno looked down at me sternly and I thought I had said something wrong. Then his face broke away from that sternness and I saw that he was teasing me. He gave his usual chuckle as he spoke. 'Go on then, tell me what's wrong with the Jewish school?'

'Well,' I said trying to put my thoughts in order, 'If I'm Jewish then I suppose that it's good to learn Hebrew, it's just that...'

'It's all that reciting,' he said, helping me out.

'Yes,' I said, 'and speaking Yiddish. It uses those strange Hebrew characters. When they are chalked on the board instead of the alphabet, I don't always follow them.'

'Don't always follow them?' I realised that he was repeating everything I said; he did that, Uncle Meno; it was like a game with him. He saw my irritation, but I don't think he could stop himself teasing; it was what he did. 'You are a very bright boy, Loeb; you will learn it well in time.' He patted me on the head; I took it as affection rather than that he was patronising me.

We walked along for some moments with only the echoes of our feet keeping us company. Then Uncle Meno stopped and looked down at me. 'What do you know about your father?'

The question took me by surprise. It wasn't a question that anybody asks a person. I looked up at him. Uncle Meno was in his late forties; taller than my father but somehow more Jewish looking, although he too was clean shaven in the German style. He had large dark eyes, a little sunken but expressive and always a little mischief in them.

'Well,' I stumbled, 'he was a lecturer in German Literature at Geissen University, but he lost his job when the edict of citizenship was suspended after the defeat of Napoleon.'

'The defeat of Napoleon?'

'Are you going to keep repeating everything I say, Uncle Meno?'

'Repeating?' And then that chuckle emerged again. That was usually enough for me join in the humour, but today was different.

'I'm sorry my boy,' he said, putting his arm around my shoulder and hugging me towards him as if to reinforce his words. We walked on in silence for some moments and I could see that he was deciding what to tell me. A yelping dog somewhere in the distance broke into his reverie and he turned to look at me earnestly.

'Yes, that's true my boy, you have learned your history well, but did you know your father was regarded as a great *German poet?*'

'What! Papa?' I was incredulous.

'Oh yes; your papa, Felix Ephraim. He was widely published and read by all the German intellectuals. He is not just your papa – he is a great man.'

'Papa a great man?' We stopped walking and I stared at Uncle Meno, but I didn't know what else to say. I just continued to look at him, my expression asking him to tell me more. That chuckle emerged and he started to walk again; I followed him, keeping close to catch what he was saying.

'I need to take you back thirty years or so. Your father and I were sent away to the Free School in Berlin. Your grandfather was an enlightened man for his time and he wanted us to better ourselves. He wanted us to have an education and then become doctors. The free schools were something new. They were for poor young men, not only the privileged rich. It enabled us to get a general education but also to mix with non-Jewish students. You know that for yourself, of course. I was two years older than your papa and I did what your grandfather wanted; I went on from school to study medicine. But going to the Free School was like coming out of a dark tunnel into the light; like walking out of the *Judengasse* into the summer sun. Studying German, French, Latin, Greek, German history and literature – I don't think your grandfather ever realised the immensity of sending us to the Free School. It opened up a new world to us; especially your papa.'

'Especially Papa?' I saw Uncle Meno look down at me; there was a twinkle in his eye. He was being serious but he could not let this humour pass him by. I then realised that I was now repeating what he was saying. He started to chuckle but then stopped himself and went on.

'Oh yes, especially him. You see he fell in love with German literature and he started to write poetry. And then he abandoned his medical studies and changed to study German literature. But there was far more to it than just that.'

'I'm not sure I follow, Uncle Meno.'

'No Loeb, you won't. Let me try and tell you about that time in Berlin. There was something very special, very new going on there. It was a city that was nothing like Frankfurt. It was a time of open-mindedness, and it was a time of the growth of literary salons.'

'What were they?' I asked eagerly.

'They were just gatherings, usually at somebody's house, where you could go to meet writers and poets, and talk and join other people who loved literature. It doesn't sound so much does it, but I promise you that it was a remarkable time. The salons were about the promotion of the arts, but it was also a time of free thinking. Your papa wasn't the only Jew who loved German literature. There was a large Jewish middle class who shared his love. Some of these salons were run by Jewish ladies, but the meetings were not confined to just Jew or just German. The love of literature was common to both.' He paused for a time, looking ahead purposefully as though in his mind's eye he was seeing those times again. He suddenly snapped back to the present. 'Felix, your father, became a favourite of Rahal Levin. She ran a very successful salon, and she championed your papa's poetry. She was instrumental in getting it published and once it was, his fame spread. He became recognised as a great German poet, even though he was Jewish. For a time the Germans seemed blind to his Jewishness.'

'I didn't realise all that.'

'Why should you? You weren't born then, and then you were a child, but now you are a man. I think that now you need to understand.'

'So why can't Papa tell me all this?'

'Ah - he will Loeb, but in his own time. It's very painful for him.'

We reached the end of the *Judengasse* and paused for a few seconds and then we just turned instinctively and started to walk back.

'I want you to put yourself in his position. He is a young man in Berlin, not much older than you. He is among other young enlightened Jews who mix socially with the German intellectuals and are accepted by them as equals. He is educated in the language and culture of the country in which he lives and he wants to be part of it. Many of these young Jews hated their Jewish background and some of them converted to Christianity, but your papa resisted. He was a free thinker and his philosophy was of an enlightened Judaism not strict ritual and superstitious observance. He believed that Jews contributed to their own isolation. He was a reformer and he wrote extensively about his vision. It was a wonderful time and he was one of the prophets of change. He was a follower of the great Moses Mendelssohn – your brother is named after him. Your sister is named after Henriette Herz, another Jewish salon hostess, she was said to be the most beautiful woman in Berlin. Oh, but it was a great time; a time of hope, a time of optimism, my boy.'

'So what went wrong?' I asked naively.

'The victory of Napoleon in 1806; that's what went wrong.'

'But Napoleon gave the Jews emancipation. Surely that was what Papa wanted.'

'Oh yes, that's exactly what he wanted, but that defeat stung the Prussians and the other German states. It released the patriotism in them, but it wasn't a good patriotism; it was a very nasty form of patriotism aimed at anybody who was non-German, and that included the assimilated middle class Jews who lived among them.'

'Is that what Papa was then?'

'To all intents and purposes, yes; he had his doctorate in German literature, and he was accepted as a lecturer at Guissen

University. He took a wife and started a family. He continued to write and his published work was eagerly anticipated. He was one of the country's great free thinkers.'

'But it all went wrong, didn't it?'

'Yes it did. You are very perceptive, young Loeb. After the defeat of Napoleon, all that pent-up patriotism that had been festering burst forth. First the edict of emancipation was revoked, but then there was opposition to your papa's position as a lecturer at the university; those patriots didn't want the German youth educated by a Jew. So your father did what a lot of Jews had done; what he had said that he would never do – and this will shock you my boy.'

'Shock me!' I said, 'Why? What did he do?'

Uncle Meno paused for a moment as he wafted away a fly; there were always flies in the *Judengasse*. 'He converted to Christianity, that's what he did.'

'What! Papa is a Christian?'

'He was, and he did it to try to preserve what he had achieved. But even that didn't work. He was a non-practising Jew before conversion and then he became a non-practising Christian. He was being pragmatic, or so he thought. But then the students began to embrace all that fanatical patriotism - the *bierkellers* were full of them singing their patriotic songs - they became disruptive in his classes and many of them refused to attend. His position became intolerable, and eventually they took his job from him.'

I was stunned. We walked nearly all the way back up the *Judengasse* without me saying anything else. I know now that Uncle Meno was being quiet deliberately. He was letting it all sink in, and I needed that. *Papa a Christian! Papa a great poet!* To me he had always just been my papa. My mind was in a whirl. Uncle Meno pushed me to the side of the road; a cart was coming but I hadn't heard the mule's hooves clip-clopping or the heavy wheels clattering on the cobbles. Uncle Meno watched the cart rattle on down the *Judengasse* and then he put his arm on my shoulder again and we started to walk on. We went down the side alley back onto the *Kiostergasse* and from there could see our house. We stopped outside the front door, Uncle Meno's hand still on my shoulder. He still had something to say.

'When your father lost his job, he only had his literary fees to fall back on but then even they started to dry up as the oppressive patriotism deepened. He became a journalist, but his free thinking was becoming increasingly unpopular. So I asked the elders of the Jewish school to offer him a job and you all came to Frankfurt to live with me.' He put his other hand on my other shoulder and looked down intently into my eyes. 'So my boy,' he said, 'do not be too hard on your papa when he has the melancholies. He has had to give up virtually everything he has strived to achieve; he finds himself back in Frankfurt where he started and you know how he hates this city. As he says, it may call itself a "free city", but it is neither independent nor tolerant; it is the most unenlightened of all the German cities. But it's more than that. Everything that he has worked towards is gone; all that anticipation that things would change has evaporated; all that enthusiasm for change is no more. It's something that you need to understand my boy.'

He patted me on the head again and then went into his front door. I glanced down at myself and brushed some of the dust off me. I realised that I looked like a child; I had been playing childish games. Uncle Meno had given me a nudge into manhood. My narrow world had been substantially enlarged; I would never look at Papa in the same way again.

CHAPTER 5

London, 1823

'They're going to hang him, Father!' Julia was in full flow. The carriage wheels rattled on the cobbled streets on their way home from the Courthouse.

'Well at least the poor wretch had a fair trial.' Her father sat behind his paper catching up on the news that he had not had the chance to read on his way to court.

'You've not been listening to me, have you?' She reached across the carriage and put her hand on the top of the paper lowering it gently as she did so. 'Father?' She initially saw only irritation on his face; he didn't want to be bothered about this unknown man.

George Carmichael looked at the passion in his daughter's eyes and realised why he loved her so much. He couldn't deny her anything within his powers. He put his paper down and smiled back at her. 'Rogues are hung all the time my dear. Hanging is a matter for the legislature not lawyers; if you don't like it, petition parliament.'

'*They're* more anti-women than the law,' her eyes flashed annoyance. 'But that's irrelevant; he's not a rogue. He's not an uneducated ruffian. He speaks four languages; he's an educated man.'

'But he's still had his day in court and was found guilty.'

'Yes, but it was all stacked against him. He didn't have a chance.'

'Look, we have the most advanced legal system in the world my dear. You should be proud of it.'

'Yes, if you're rich, but what chance does a poor man have? There's no right to a defence counsel. The only defendants who have one are the rich who can afford it.'

'You don't expect us lawyers to work for nothing, do you?' said her father. 'If there was a *right* to counsel who would pay for them?' George Carmichael shook his newspaper to show that in his mind he had won the debate, and then disappeared behind it.

Julia sighed heavily to herself. Newspapers, of course, cannot look smug, but somehow this one seemed to.

Later, at the evening meal Julia returned to the discussion. 'There was little care and deliberation,' she said, 'it was all done with undue haste. And now the poor man is to hang.'

'Julia!' said her mother, 'hanging is no subject for the dining table.'

'Quite right,' said her father. 'Julia; remember your mother's sensibilities.'

'I'm sorry, Mamma.' She turned to her mother, contritely aware that she had broken the rules of polite society.

'All this lawyering is not right for a young girl; it's most unladylike,' said her mother in response. 'You shouldn't be filling your head with it all.'

'What should I fill it with then; embroidery?' There was pique in her tone.

'Julia!' said her father pulling her up. 'That will do.'

'I'm sorry Mamma; it's just that I'm not the sort of girl who can be content with embroidery and the boredom of a young girl's existence. What do they do all day? Immerse themselves in cheap romantic fiction to fill the long hours of boredom that they are forced to endure, that's what!'

'I blame your father for indulging you. You should be thinking about marriage at your age.' Julia's mother turned to her husband. 'Did you speak to her as we discussed, George?'

'Aye, I did but the girl has no interest in marriage it seems.'

They both turned to look at their daughter. She met their gaze and knew that she was a disappointment to them, but she also knew she was loved. She was the second of two sisters. Her elder sister Emma had been married off at eighteen and now, aged twenty-four, already had two children. What was even more galling for Julia was that Emma seemed perfectly happy with her life. She had accepted what society required of a young girl. Julia was the different one and she knew it. She had no brothers and she succeeded in manipulating her father because he had no son to take into his business.

'I'm going to see this man in prison,' she said suddenly, knowing her father would be outraged, but at least it took the subject away from marriage.

'Oh no you are not,' he said. 'The prison is definitely no place for a young, innocent girl.'

'Then come with me.'

Her father had raised his spoon to his lips and was about to drink the soup from it. He froze in motion but shot a look across the table to her. 'I'll be damned if I will,' he said.

'George! Language at the table if you please,' said his wife.

CHAPTER 6

Frankfurt 1817

When I turned fifteen I remembered Mama reaching up and cupping my face affectionately. 'You have grown so much in the last year,' she said to me. 'Look at you; you look like a man.' She rubbed the back of her hand softly against the skin of my cheeks and she could feel the newly sprouting stubble. 'I'll get you a razor when I go to the Jewish market.'

'Will they sell razors at the Jewish market?' I said playfully. 'The Jewish men all wear beards.'

'Oh yes, don't worry about that, 'you can get nearly everything at the Jewish market. Just because their husbands don't shave it does not mean the wives don't.' Mama's eyes twinkled as she saw my face flush. I was a little shocked to hear that these ladies needed to shave like men, and not a little shocked also that Mama would confide this fact to me. She was beginning to look at me differently, I suppose. In the last year I'd had a growing spurt. I was now nearly as tall as Papa and I looked down on Mama. I was a bit on the gangly side as my build had failed to keep up with my sudden growth, but I had clearly lost that appearance of childhood. I was a good student and what I failed to learn at the Jewish school Papa taught me at home. The hours of study were long and difficult, particularly in the winter months huddled over a flickering candle, but I was not a reluctant student. It opened up a world to me that was tantalising when viewed against the restrictive existence in the Jewish community. I'd had a glimpse of something outside of it, which the other students had not, and I was hungry for more. I saw an education as a passport to something different, although I did not know what. Studying in winter by candlelight was tiresome but I overcame it – it was summer that was more of a problem for me. An opportunity to be outside was a great temptation. Although I was a natural student I was no recluse; I longed to be outdoors. I was athletic and I seemed to have endless energy. I needed that release valve that the outdoors provided. Frankfurt was a restricted city and the air quality was not good, but at least I could get out of the house. I would take my books into the fields at the edge of the city and study there for hours. And I ran everywhere. I suppose I was that strange mix of an athlete with an academic mind.

The *Judengasse* curved from North West to South East, and at the southern end was the Jewish market. Henriette usually accompanied Mama on her shopping trips, but this day she was playing in the street with Moses and when Mama went to call her, I said that I would go with her instead. As we emerged from the gloom of the *Judengasse* the vibrancy of the market assaulted our senses. The piquant smells of spices and the sweet smells of fresh fruit mingled to produce a profusion of aromas. There was a wall of noise. Stall holders barking out the cost of their wares and customers bargaining with them to get the best deals. Mama came everyday so that everything we ate was fresh, if not always of the best quality as our reduced circumstances began to bite. When it came to bartering, Mama was the best. The greengrocer would say to her that she would put him out of business, but then he would laugh as he emptied the produce into her basket from his weighing tray. That's how I remember it; it was a bewildering place but there seemed to be happiness about. In many ways it was more the centre of the community than the synagogue. Our family were outside the mainstream Jewish community, but here we seemed to belong.

Mama was deep in negotiation with another stall holder trying to save a few gulden when I became aware of a high-pitched cry. I recognised the voice and Mama did too and she turned from the stallholder instantly to look for it. It was Henriette.

'Mama! Mama!' she was crying and running round the stalls in a state of panic because she couldn't find us.'

'Henriette! Henriette!' Mama cried back and Henriette stopped immediately as if frozen, but then headed towards her mama's voice as if it was a direction finder. She ran into Mama at full pelt and Mama knelt, holding her daughter by the shoulders, a cold fear directing her actions. 'What is it, Henriette?' she asked forcefully, emphasising each word deliberately.

'It's Moses, Mama.'

'What about Moses – what has happened to him?'

'Oliver Breitner's got him.'

I saw Mama's alarm visibly lighten. It was no more than a boyhood fight and that was something that she could handle. 'All right Henriette; calm down now – I'm coming.'

'I'll go and sort it out Mama,' I said and immediately ran off. I heard her call after me but I didn't listen. I thought I was being helpful, but Mama knew that if I got involved then the conflict would only escalate. All she had to do was rescue Moses and then clean his wounds. I couldn't see that of course.

Oliver Breitner was Frau Breitner's son. He was not around when we moved to Frankfurt. He had gone to sea at the age of fourteen as a *Marinejüngsterer*, a naval cadet. He was now seventeen and he was on leave visiting his parents. He had brought two friends with him. When I rounded the corner onto the *Nonnengasse*, our street, I saw the three of them in their smart blue and white naval uniforms. They were out in front of Frau Breitners' house; Oliver had Moses by the back of the collar and was shaking him about like a rag doll. The others were laughing and egging him on. His mother stood in her door leaning against the frame. Her arms were folded over her ample bosom and there was a self satisfied look on her face. She was probably behind all this. If she couldn't catch Moses to give him a good whipping then she was happy to see her son do it for her.

I was out of breath when I arrived but I ran straight up to Oliver. 'That's enough,' I said and I tried to wrestle Moses free of his grip. I expected him to let go. I saw myself in the role of the authority figure and that he would release him now that his fun was over and that would be the end of it. I was wrong. He just swivelled round putting himself between me and Moses. Each time I tried to grab Moses to free him, Oliver just turned away. All the time Moses was kicking and punching out, but Oliver held him at armslength so that he only pawed at thin air. 'Come on let him go; he's only half your size,' I said. It was the worst thing I could have said. I couldn't see what Mama had instinctively known.

'But you're not, are you Jew boy?' said Oliver.

'No I'm not,' I said foolishly. I went forward and met his stare determinedly to show that I was not afraid. Actually I wasn't afraid; it had all happened so quickly. As we stood face to face I could see that I was as tall as him but he was two years older and his navy training had filled him out. He was much thicker set than me. He let my brother go and Moses ran around behind me. 'Go home, Moses,' I said but he had no intention of doing so.

'Get him Loeb,' he said. He had faith in me but I'm not sure why.

Oliver brought both his hands up and then thudded them with all his force into my shoulders. The weight difference between us became immediately apparent to me. His larger bulk gave him a distinct advantage; I was flung easily backwards, off my feet and onto my behind. I looked up at him towering above me and saw the perverse pleasure standing in his eyes. At that moment I knew that I was in for a beating. His naval friends laughed at my sprawling attempts to get up. The palms of my hands were grazed where I had taken the weight of the fall and I looked down on them and at that moment the stinging entered my brain. I got to my knees, but when I tried to rise, Oliver walked forward and just pushed me back again. This happened time after time, and with each fall his friends laughed at my discomfort. Then he turned to acknowledge their laughs and I took my opportunity to scramble to my feet, moving away from him to put some distance between us. I had the chance to run away and I should have done so - but I didn't; something had happened to me.

It seemed important to stand up against him even if that meant a good beating.

And then Mama arrived. I recognised her bandana; Papa had taken her away from her orthodox Jewish life, but she still always covered her hair as married Jewish women were required to do. She walked straight up to Moses and told him to go home and take Henriette with him. They turned and walked away, but they stopped about half way to our house and looked back. Then she started towards me. Her intention was to put herself between Oliver and me, at which point the fight would effectively be over. Oliver would not try to get at me through her. But then his fellow navel cadets blocked her way. Wherever she tried to go they just moved in front of her. Mama looked towards Frau Breitner. 'Will you stop this please?' Frau Breitner met her stare but there was a sour expression on her face. Their gaze locked for several moments and then I knew, and Mama knew, that Oliver's mother would do nothing to help us. She was a mean woman by instinct, but added to this there was now something else; we were Jews. This was to be just another Jew beating.

I raised my fists for the first time. I saw the look of pleasure on Oliver's face. His fun was to be allowed to continue. He again thudded his right hand into my left shoulder, but this time I just turned slightly so that I didn't absorb the full force. This happened several more times, but I didn't do anything to fight back. Then he swung his right fist at my face and my nose seemed to explode with a stinging pain. My eyes poured with tears and I felt the warm flow of blood down my chin. I put my hand to my nose and then looked down at the crimson liquid that dripped from my fingers.

I'd had fights at the Free School, but they were nothing serious; nothing more than heads down and throwing punches that landed on the arms and the shoulders, and these scraps were quickly broken up by the masters. I'd had some rudimentary boxing training, however, from the sports master; we all had - the art of self defence. It sprang into my mind and I took up the 'attitude' that I had been taught. I was left-handed so that I put my right leg and right arm forward, bending at the knees, my fists clasped under my chin. When Oliver and his friends saw me they burst out with mocking laughter as if I were some runt mimicking a real pugilist. My resolve doubled; I flicked out a right hand and caught Oliver a blow to his mouth. There was little power in the punch, but it did cause a tiny trickle of blood to start to flow from his lip. That look of amusement immediately deserted his face to be replaced by anger.

'You little Jewish turd,' he said and immediately came after me.

I threw another right jab at him and again connected, but he just walked through it and grabbed the collar of my coat. He whirled me round using my collar as the pivot and sent me sprawling to the floor. Then he fell on top of me and put his big sweaty hand on the side of my head, forcing my face into the dirt road.

'You're a little Jewish turd – what are you?'

I felt all his weight on top of me holding me down and no matter how much I struggled I didn't seem to be able to move. My lips had been parted by the force of his hand and were now scouring the dust and dirt of the road. I was literally eating dirt. He wanted me to say that I was a little Jewish turd, but I would not. I looked down into the dirt and saw beginning to form a congealing pink puddle of mucus and blood from around my nose and mouth. It was at that moment that I discovered something about myself. I discovered that I had reserves of determination that I didn't know I possessed. I would be damned before I would do what he asked.

'Come on Jew boy, let's hear you say it.' But there was no way that I would.

I heard Mama like a voice in the distance shout out to Frau Breitner, 'He's had enough now. He's been beaten fair and square.'

Fair and square! This isn't fair and square, I thought to myself. He's older and bigger than me. I was pinned there for several minutes. Oliver then looked up at his mates to... well, accept his acclaim, I suppose. They looked back at him and somehow their expression seemed to tell Oliver that he had won and now it was time to let me go. There was still belligerence in him, however. He put his knee on my neck using me to help lever himself back to his feet. He was the victor and my humiliation was part of his spoils. That knee really hurt and I rubbed my neck as I too got to my feet, spitting out the dirt from my mouth. I bent over and put my hands on my knees and although I was hurt I suddenly felt that I had plenty of energy left. I straightened up as Mama came and took my arm.

'Come on, let's get you cleaned up,' she said, looking at the torn pocket of my jacket, 'that will need mending as well,' she added. I took off my jacket and gave it to her, at the same time I pulled my arm free. It was an exaggerated movement motivated by my own defiance, which was continuing to grow within me.

'I'm not going, Mama. I have something to finish.'

She pulled me back to her. 'If you go back to the fight you will get *really* hurt.' Her eyes gave me the full force of her look. It was that look that mamas have when they are not to be disobeyed. I could see it clearly; but disobey her I did. I pulled away again and walked straight back and confronted Oliver. I saw his face sneer; it was a sneer of pleasure. His onlooking friends had denied him the satisfaction of a full beating, but now I was giving him the opportunity he wanted.

He came towards me and I took up my stance. I jabbed out my right and then crossed a left. It came quite naturally to me and both punches landed. It seemed to double his anger. He threw a round right-hand punch at me, which hit me on the side of my head and I was sent sprawling, my ear ringing painfully as I fell. His punches were harder than mine and I did not have the punch resistance to take them. Each time he hit me I went down to the ground - but each time I got up again. I was in some sort of a zone; a zone that did not let pain enter. And then I learned something else about myself: alongside that stubborn determination I had reserves of stamina to back it up. I saw the sweat appear on Oliver's face; it was reddened with effort and his mouth had fallen open as he gasped for air. *He* was out of breath but I *was not*. Without rationalising that in my mind, I reacted to it. Instead of walking onto the punishment I started to fight on the defensive. I stayed out of range tempting him to come and get me. He obliged and lunged at me throwing powerful swings and then I just moved away from the punches so that they scythed through fresh air.

'Come on fat boy,' I said. I was tormenting him. It did not occur to me that it might make my beating worse. It made Oliver wild and he lunged at me again like a feral animal, but his attack was clumsy and uncoordinated. Suddenly I felt like a natural fighting machine; able to use my strength to the best advantage. My strength, of course, was not my power, but my agility and stamina. I stepped to the side and he lunged past me. I pivoted as if I had done it many times before. It was, in truth, totally new to me but it seemed so natural. And then, equally naturally, my left hand came down in an arc and I hit him on the side of the head behind his ear. I had put my whole strength behind it and that power, together with his momentum, sent him sprawling to the ground. The cheering stopped. This was not supposed to happen.

His friends looked at each other and then at Frau Breitner, who had been leaning against her doorframe; she suddenly stood up in alarm. But I was as surprised as any of them – and then a realisation took me. If I got involved in a brawl with Oliver I would get a beating, but if I used my brain and my athleticism, then maybe, just maybe....

I watched Oliver get inelegantly back to feet. He turned and looked at me and I held his stare. For the first time the look of contempt had gone from his gaze; now there was fear. He was facing humiliation and that was far worse than a beating. I was a kid and he was nearly a man; his humiliation would be doubled. This fear released adrenalin within him and he came at me swinging, but I just backed away and then to the side. I was playing him like a fish on a hook. And then he stopped; he had used up the last dregs of his stamina. He had nothing left and he just stood awaiting his fate. He brought his hands up to his face for protection, but other that that he was a sitting target.

I walked forward to take my prize. I felt no sympathy for him at that point; I just wanted to teach him a lesson. By covering his face he had left his body exposed and I sunk a powerful blow under his elbow and I heard the air hiss over his teeth as it left his body. Adversity seemed to have taught me in a matter of minutes what a professional pugilist trains for years to learn. Oliver's hands came down exposing his face and my eyes flashed as I saw my opportunity. I recoiled from the hip to unleash as powerful a punch as I could. I was like an archer homing in on the bull's eye. But it was not to be. His sailor-friends came to his aid. I was taken in a firm grip on either side and pulled away from him. 'He's beaten,' said one of them. I was suddenly fearful that they would take over from Oliver, but that was not their intention. I looked back at my victim; he was gasping for air, the blow to the midriff leaving him defenceless. I had won.

'Am I a little Jewish turd now,' I taunted back at the pitiable figure before me. I suppose that I was on a high, but Mama would not let me enjoy it. She came and took me by the arm and pulled me away back towards our house. I went with her, but I continued to look back over my shoulder the whole way. I was not an aggressive child who was constantly fighting; I was the academic child with his head in a book, but I had just stood up to the bully and bested him. Me! - I knew how to fight. I did not know how I knew how to fight, but fight I most certainly could.

CHAPTER 7

London, 1823

Julia put her scented handkerchief to her nose; she baulked at the nauseating stench of the gaol. The further they walked into it the more offensive the stinking odour became and her nose wrinkled in response. Her father noticed her hesitant reaction.

'This is a pretty state of affairs. I warned you that a prison is no place for a lady, didn't I?'

'Yes you did, Father, several times.' It annoyed her that he may have been right but she was not going to be seen to acknowledge that fact.

They followed the gaoler. Julia looked intently at him. She wasn't sure what she had expected but the man had a villainous face. He was unshaven; his teeth blackened; his clothes soiled and much of the smell emanated from him as it did the gaol. Fat, sausage-like fingers fiddled with the oversized keys, swinging them on the large rusted ring as he walked, so that they rang a rhythmic out-of-tune air. He whistled a counterpoint accompaniment that was neither tuneful nor in time, but it was enough to show that he was happy in his grimy work.

Julia peered in at the ashen, hollow-eyed, fearful faces of some of the inmates as they leaned against the bars of their cells and she thought that the gaoler looked more of a villain than they did. She knew it was only those awaiting trial or under sentence of death who were incarcerated in this overcrowded, disease-ridden gaol; the place was rife with gaol fever. Three prisoners were held in each cell, but when they came to David Neander's cell he was the sole occupant. The gaoler looked back at Julia, his black-toothed grin seeming to indicate that it was an achievement merely to find the right cell, and then rattled keys in the lock to open the heavy iron door.

The cell was a dim place, the corridor lit by lanterns enclosing stinking tallow candles, that provided little light to invade it, but added to the cocktail of stench: Julia shivered even before she entered the dank, dark confines. She could also smell if not see mould on the walls. David Neander was sat on the floor, there was no furniture. Neither was there a bunk to sleep on, only some soiled straw in a corner. In the ten days since his trial the last semblance of good grooming had gone from him. He had several days' dark growth on his face and his shirt was now grimy and sweat-stained. He looked up and stared at them, his face showing his extreme surprise. He got to his feet and carefully took up his jacket. He had turned it inside out and placed it away from as much of the dirt as he could. He righted it and put it on; it seemed important to him that his appearance suggested he was a gentleman. He ran his fingers through his hair and then stood to show himself in the most presentable and well-mannered way that he could in the circumstances.

'Good day, Mr Neander,' she spoke to him in French, 'my name is Julia Carmichael and this is my father, George Carmichael.'

He reached out and took her hand gently although she had not really offered it and she steeled herself not to snatch it away. He nodded respectfully to her as he did so; then he turned to her father and did the same, this time the nod bordering on a masculine bow.

'I fear that this is no place for a lady,' he said, answering her in English. He saw the look of surprise on her face. 'I spend my time learning English, Miss Carmichael. I need to understand what they will do to me.'

'You are right sir,' said George, 'this is no place for a lady.' He made no attempt to hide his displeasure.

'Father!' she said, her irritation plain in her tone. Then she turned back to the prisoner. 'Do forgive my father; he is only trying to protect me.'

'It is the way of a father to his daughter,' said David empathetically. He had reverted to French.

'Perhaps French *will* be better, Mr Neander,' said Julia, 'we have important things to discuss.'

'Yes, I am learning English only slowly; I have only the gaoler to talk to and his vocabulary is limited to grunts at times. But surprisingly he can read and write; the other turnkey cannot.' David stared at her, seemingly at a loss for words, his eyes asking the question: *what important things?*

Ignoring her father's 'tut-tut' behind her, Julia looked back at those eyes. They were bright, big, clear, penetrating and most of all, brilliantly blue. She demurred, looked away, but then her eyes were drawn back to him as though to a magnet; she gazed at him for what seemed like a time without end. The words formed on her lips, but they came hard. It was as though those eyes were boring into her very soul. She caught herself; scolded herself for her foolishness; forced herself to speak.

'I was in the gallery at your trial.' She heard a tremble in her voice and embarrassed, coughed to cover it, but did not succeed. She felt her face begin to colour. 'I fear that you didn't get justice that day.'

'Justice is not something that I have come to expect in my life; I am Jewish,' he said as if that was explanation enough.

George Carmichael came to his daughter's aid. 'Did you understand sir, what happened to you in court? Do you understand what the verdict and the sentence mean?'

David nodded; his body language displaying his resignation. 'The gaoler took great pleasure in making it very clear to me. They will hang me. They would have hung me already, but it seems that it is cheaper to dispatch justice collectively. They will keep me here for some weeks or even months until they have enough other poor souls to dangle. The gaoler tells me that this makes a better spectacle for the baying masses. But, in the meantime, at least it qualifies me for a single cell and it is less likely that I will die of gaol fever and cheat the hangman.'

Julia put her hand to her mouth. She felt a pang of apprehension in the pit of her stomach at the mental images that surfaced like leaping salmon in her mind. She saw him dangling on the end of a rope; his eyes bulging, his lips blue, urine running down his legs and cascading to the floor as the crowd bayed and jostled for a better view. And then lifelessness, flaccid, a soulless corpse being cut down to be fought over by the body-snatchers, who would sell it to the anatomists to dissect in the name of science. Julia caught herself, forcing herself to dispel these thoughts; she needed to be professional if she was to help this man. She needed the detached skills of a lawyer and not the delicate sensibilities of a silly young girl.

'That's why we are here, Mr. Neander, I hope we will be able to help you.'

He took a step backwards frowning in puzzlement, but the sudden spark of hope in his eyes invited her to continue.

'I have some knowledge of the law and my father is a practising lawyer and barrister,' she said.

'But I have no money to pay you.' The look of puzzlement was still on his face.

Julia felt a movement at her back and turning to her father, saw him nodding in agreement at David's comment. Her eyes narrowed and she shot him a fiery glance before turning back to the prisoner. 'I am aware of that, Mr Neander, but perhaps we should not put a price on justice.'

'Ah, a noble thought,' he shrugged, 'if only that were true the world would be a better place.'

'You see,' said her father, 'Mr Neander understands the way of the world, even if you don't.'

'I see the way of the world, sir,' said David, 'but that doesn't mean we should not aspire to make it a better place. We should not censure your daughter for being a visionary; a reformer.'

'But you would say that sir, wouldn't you,' said George Carmichael, 'you are facing the hangman after all.'

'Ah, the cut and thrust of intellectual debate; determining the proposer's point of view; where the argument is centred. At another time I would be happy to debate it with you sir, but for now I must concede that you are right. I am in no position to reject any help from anyone. I am powerless to help myself at the moment.'

'Then you will accept our help, Mr Neander,' said Julia.

David bowed nobly to confirm.

'Then I need to go over your story with you, in detail. I have a transcript of your evidence, but I want to make sure I have the full picture.' She opened her portfolio and held it precariously with her left arm whilst the pencil retrieved from her pocket hovered expectantly in her right hand. Still standing, she angled her portfolio, towards the lantern in the corridor to catch the little light that was available to her then screwing up her eyes, she scribbled down his words as he described the circumstances of his arrest, translating them into English as she did so.

'How do we challenge this verdict, Miss Carmichael,' asked David when they had finished.

Julia sighed and then marshalled her thoughts. 'There are three substantive questions to be asked: firstly, have you been charged with a known crime? That would be difficult to challenge since the trial clearly established that a crime took place and that you are properly charged with it.'

David nodded thoughtfully, 'And the second?'

'Did the jury act perversely when they brought in a verdict of guilty?'

'That would also be difficult,' interrupted George Carmichael. 'It is not unknown for juries to bring in a verdict that is perverse on the evidence. But, having read the transcript, I think this would be hard to establish.'

'So that leaves us with what?' David asked, looking expectantly from Julia to her father.

'That there was an error in the proceeding,' said Julia. 'I think we may have a case there.' She waited a moment, added, 'Although that too is going to be difficult.'

'And what would you claim was the in error in the proceedings?' asked David.

'Well, you were not armed, you did not resist arrest and, as the Watchman testified, you were not attempting to run away. The Judge failed to reiterate these facts to the jury.'

'Is that an error of the court?'

'No it is not,' interrupted her father intolerantly, 'there is no requirement for the Judge to do so; no requirement for him to sum up the evidence.'

'Well there ought to be,' Julia said petulantly, reacting to her fathers negativity.

'Until the law is changed in that respect, my girl, that argument will not succeed. Have I taught you nothing? The jury heard Mr Neander's explanations in his defence and are perfectly at liberty to accept or reject them. They chose the latter; there is no error there.'

She turned towards her father and held his gaze. 'You are not helping at all, Father.'

'Perhaps that's exactly what I *am* doing. I'm not giving Mr Neander false hope. He seems to have been given a fair trial and was then convicted by the unanimous verdict of his equals.'

'Nevertheless,' said Julia, being just as combative as her father, 'the system is not perfect and has convicted an innocent man.'

'Unfortunately that is a matter of opinion, and in law it is the opinion of the jury that counts and not yours, young lady.' George Carmichael folded his arms across his chest, his body language suggesting he had had his say.

Julia looked at him for a heartbeat, and did not attempt to hide her annoyance. Then she turned back to David and held his gaze, her own expression softening as if she was apologising for her father. 'I will not lie to you, Mr Neander, this is not going to be easy, but the law does recognise that judges and juries do make mistakes.' She turned and shot a look back to her father, 'isn't that right, Father?' He did not initially respond, '*Is that not right*, Father?' she said again, emphasising each word succinctly.

'Yes, yes,' he said irritably.'

'Believe it or not, Mr Neander, I have discussed this with my father before we came, when he was much more accommodating, and he has suggested a course of action. Judges should not pronounce on a question of fact. I believe; that is, *we* believe, that we might be able to show that the Judge somehow... *blurred* the difference between fact and law.'

Julia saw David's brow furrow. 'I am not sure that I follow?' he said.

'We need to show that he was not completely objective; that he did not convey a neutral approach.'

'Does the transcript support that?' asked David eagerly.

Julia sighed; her father's words suddenly hitting her in a delayed reaction as she saw the hope rise in David's expression. Anxious not to give him false hope she spoke cautiously. 'Well no, and that is our problem here, the transcript doesn't support that contention, but I was in court and I heard the Judge's remarks. What we have to show is that he was not completely objective; that the inflection in his voice or his facial expression meant that he was, in effect, leading the jury and pronouncing on matters of fact. Fact is for the jury, his role is to pronounce on the law.'

'And is this contention a common form of appeal?' asked David.

'No it is not, sir,' grunted George Carmichael. He looked at his daughter, his eyes instructing her to come clean.

'No sir, it's never been used before,' she said sheepishly, 'we will be looking to create a precedent.'

'Ah,' said David, but then he became introspective as he began to understand the enormity of the task before him. 'It is not a big hope,' he said eventually, 'but it's a hope I did not have before. I must be thankful to the Lord for that. He has sent you to help me.'

Julia looked at his anaemic face; the lack of sun had made his skin milky-white, but it was those eyes, those blue, blue eyes that took her full attention so that her gaze never dwelt on anything but them.

Seeing his daughter's mesmerised expression, George Carmichael shuffled his feet in irritation and coughed. 'There is another course of action that is a possibility, Mr Neander. You must tell him, Julia.'

Still held by David's gaze it seemed to Julia that his grimy, unshaven appearance dissolved away, as did the sound of voices in the distance. Even the acrid smell was somehow cast from her mind. She blinked, looked away and brought her mind to bear, aware that she was blushing and grateful that it was too dark for him to notice. 'Father is referring to a plea for clemency, Mr Neander - to the Home Office.'

'Is that your recommendation?'

'Well it's certainly my father's,' she said.

'But not yours?'

'Well no... it's not.'

David looked at her intently urging her to go on.

For a moment Julia hesitated, then said, 'The Home Secretary receives thousands of such pleas – heart-wrenching cases, but very few are granted, even when it's the first offence. And then only when there are family dependents. You have no family dependent on you, no starving children; no aged parents to look after. And how do we prove that you do not have a history of criminality abroad? I fear we would be raising your hopes to no purpose were we to go down that route.' She saw the look of despondency return, and knew she had to do something. 'Is there anything else we can do for you in the meantime, Mr Neander? I could leave a few shillings with the gaoler for some better victuals for you.' She realised it was an inadequate response as soon as the words escaped her mouth.

'Thank you kind lady, but no; I am sure that I can survive on the bread, water and gruel, but...' he hesitated, 'perhaps a few coins would secure me a desk to work at, and...' he hesitated again.

'Go on, Mr Neander,' said Julia.

'Some reading material so that I can learn English - and also a copy of the court transcript, and perhaps a law text book?'

Looking back at her father, Julia saw his eyes roll at the request, but *she* saw no impertinence in it. She feared that she would not be able to save this educated man from the hangman, but at least she could do this for him. She smiled, 'I'll see what I can do, Mr Neander.'

CHAPTER 8

Frankfurt 1817

When Papa came home, Mama was still cleaning me up. My face had continued to swell and the bruising was coming out. My left eye was just a slit in a blackening engorged mound. My right eye was similarly puffed up but I could just see out if it. The whole left side of my face was distended so that my features were uneven, like a knobbly potato. I hurt everywhere and that hurt intensified every time I moved. I loved it. If I had been a beaten pup then the pain would have been unbearable, but I was wearing my wounds like a badge of honour.

Papa looked at me and I saw his dismay as he took in the evidence that I, his son, had received a beating. To be assaulted was a fact of life of being Jewish and his immediate reaction was that the reality of it had come early in my young life. He came and bent over me; kissed my dirtied hair. I could see the look of impotence on his face; a kiss was all he thought he could offer me. The fact that he could not put it right hurt his perception of himself as a father. And then Moses came to my aid. He blurted out what had happened.

'No, you don't understand, Papa. Loeb won; he won the fight.' The words cascaded from his mouth, not always in the right order, his excitement getting in the way of the telling. 'You should have seen him Papa, he wouldn't give up. He just kept getting back up until there was no fight left in Oliver Breitner.'

'Frau Breitner's son?' It obviously registered in Papa's mind that Oliver was older and bigger than me.

'And he has taken a beating for all that,' interrupted Mama, trying to calm Moses's enthusiasm.

Papa leaned over and kissed my head again, but this time I could feel that it came with a different emotion. This time there was pride with the kiss; the pride of a father in his son's achievements. Mama saw it too and I think that it awakened a fear in her, a fear that next time I would not be so lucky.

'Loeb fought like the pugilists we saw in the park, Papa.' Moses's enthusiasm was unrestrained.

'Hush, Moses!' snapped Mama, 'that's enough of that.'

'But Mama?'

'But Mama nothing! You hold your tongue now.'

I was cast in the role of hero to Moses; which was ironic because I'd always thought that would be *his* role in life, he was such a free spirit. *He* would be the one to rise to a challenge, not me – I was the book-learning member of the family. But Moses just could not hold his tongue. Enthusiasm was cascading out of every pore of his excited young body like water from a breached dam; he just had to tell his papa of the hero that had been discovered amongst us. But our mother was forbidding him and that frustration was just too much for his young mind to bear. It burst forward in a childlike tantrum of petulance – but then he *was* still a child; a child caught up in something more that he could comprehend. He saw only his side of things.

'Shan't!' Why must I always be the one to hold my tongue?' The words spurted out of him. 'I'm going away from here and you'll all be sorry. I'm going to throw myself in the River Main. You'll all be sorry then.' He slammed the door theatrically as he left.

'The boy was only excited, Mama,' said Papa.

Mama knew that of course, but I think that fear had got the better of her. She sighed to acknowledge that Papa was right. Henriette, who had been standing open-mouthed watching what went on, went after Moses but came back a few minutes later.

'He won't come back, Papa,' she said as if she believed it to be true.

'He'll come home when he is hungry,' said Papa knowingly. He was not worried. He was right; Moses came and sat at the dinner table sometime later, just as the evening meal was being served, without any words of explanation, as though nothing untoward had taken place.

Papa blessed the meal. We were basically non-practising Jews, but there were still parts of Jewish life that we embraced. That was Mama's influence; Papa disliked much of what he perceived Judaism to be, but now I think that, deep down, he was much more Jew than German, even if he would not have admitted that to himself. Mama respected Papa; she was a good Jew in that. She also realised what a great man he was, but she had given up so much of her Jewish background to support him, and she had no intention of allowing her children to be totally divorced from their Jewish roots. I can hear her now, saying, *'Honour your father and mother for they are the representatives of God.'* She said that all the time to us, reminding us of the obligation that Jewish children had to their parents.

'I named you well, Loeb,' said Papa as we ate. The words were somehow imbibed with satisfaction. I did not understand; I stared at him with my spoon poised halfway between my soup and my bruised and throbbing lips and he saw that he needed to explain. 'None of you children were given names by accident. Henriette was named after Henriette Herz, and Moses after Moses Mendelssohn.'

'And me, Papa?'

'You Loeb; you were named after Loeb Baruch.'

'Who?' I had never heard of him.

'The greatest man I have ever met, Loeb; and the bravest.'

'Stop teasing him,' said Mama.

Papa's face broke out into a wide smile. 'Loeb Baruch was his Jewish name. You will know him by his German name; Ludwig Börne.'

'Ludwig Börne! You knew Ludwig Börne, Papa.?' Even I had heard of the famous journalist, Karl Ludwig Börne.

'Yes, in Berlin. We met at the literary salon run by Henriette Herz. But he came from the *Judengasse* in Frankfurt just like Uncle Meno and me, and he had also been sent to a Free School; his was in Halle.

'What was he like Papa?'

'He was a fearless writer, my boy; they couldn't censor him, even when they threatened to send him to prison. He was a free thinker, he opened my eyes and the eyes of many others; he was my mentor in the early days. He recruited me to write for his magazine, *Die Wage*. He taught me to write directly to the people, and not the establishment.'

I could see the pride in his past resurface briefly as he spoke. I saw Moses's features in his face; I had never seen that likeness before; that sense of enthusiasm was there on his face, just like Moses when he accepts a dare and runs through the *Judengasse*. We all felt very close at that time. I was in pain but I had never felt so good. Somehow, something as grubby as a street brawl had raised our spirits; and why? Because I had won! It was so childish, so immature and yet even my papa embraced it. Humiliation was something that Jews had to learn to live with; humiliation on so many different levels. As children we even had to get off the street to let the Christian German pass. But for this brief time, this evening behind our closed door, we didn't have to. Mama could see the danger in this reaction but I think she also, deep down, was pleased. To the victor the spoils - and our spoils were so very limited; it was a negative; the absence of humiliation. Somewhere, Oliver Brietner would be consumed by humiliation; but tonight it wasn't us, and we were so very grateful for that.

That evening I went for a short walk in the balmy summer's night; there was too much going on in my young mind to sleep. When I returned to our side door something made me look up. A canopy of stars had emerged; horizon to horizon. I suddenly felt insignificant, the vista dwarfing our little house and street and making it seem so unimportant. Yet I was full of ambitions and I remember wondering what life had in store for me. I felt enthusiastic about my future.

CHAPTER 9

London 1823

The gaoler jangled his keys as he unlocked the cell door. He pulled it open and in a display of unexpected manners, gestured for Julia to enter. His behaviour was prompted by the few coins she had been giving him for his favours and he now viewed her as a source that needed to be protected. She gave a slight nod to acknowledge him as she entered. He gestured his hand in the direction of the cell to indicate his work; she looked at the desk and stool that he had acquired for David Neander. The desk was tiny and the surface threadbare and chipped so that it would not function as a smooth writing surface, but the gaoler was obviously pleased with his efforts. She pressed a copper coin into his clammy hand, glad that she was wearing gloves.

'Thank-ee, Ma'am,' he said through a black-toothed smile, touching his knuckles to his forelock in gratitude. The two words rode on a waft of putrid breath that made Julia recoil and momentarily she preferred the sullen non-gratitude he had exhibited on her first visit. She smiled a greeting at David, but it was as much to turn away from the gaoler's stench as it was of politeness.

'Could you also find *me* a chair or a stool to sit on gaoler?' she said, forcing herself to look back at him. He touched his forelock again and scrambled away enthusiastically to undertake his commission. There was a brief commotion at the far end of the corridor where he was obviously taking a stool away from another prisoner. He arrived back triumphantly a moment later to present it to Julia. Clutching another coin, he left the cell walking backwards as if he was in the presence of royalty. When he had gone Julia looked back at David and saw him smile and she too saw the humour in the situation.

He had stood politely when she had entered and now he gestured for her to sit before he could do so. 'Please,' he said in English, 'do sit down, you have come alone?'

She raised her eyebrows in surprise; it had been only a week since her last visit, and she had sent the books the day after that, but his English was so much better. 'Err – yes, I have, Mr Neander,' she said, seating herself on the grubby stool.

'Is your father in court today?'

'Ah – well yes he is, but I have to confess that he doesn't know I am here.'

'He will be very angry, Miss Carmichael. This is no place for a young lady to be without a man to escort her.'

She knew he was right on both counts but she did not want to acknowledge it, so changed the subject. 'You are keeping your spirits up, Mr Neander?'

'Yes, now that I have something to do, my spirits are rising.'

'Your English, Mr Neander! It is so good.' There was astonishment in her tone.

He smiled a satisfied smile; pleased with her reaction. 'It is only a week but I have spent very many hours studying; I have nothing else to do, and besides, I have a natural aptitude for languages.'

'You certainly seem to have, Mr Neander.' He acknowledged the compliment with a smile. 'But the law books,' she said, 'they must be very difficult to understand. They are difficult enough for English speakers.'

'That is true. But there is also a lot of very precise language which helps me to learn.'

Julia found this hard to believe. 'Perhaps we may have to revert to French to help you with the difficult legal parts; that is if my French will cope with it.'

It was then she noticed his eyes again; those penetrating blue eyes; drawing her attention away from everything around her. Like a figure disappearing in the mist, the stench of the place drifted from her consciousness. His eyes held her gaze, and for some moments the two of them were locked in a silence of unspoken words. Then he looked down, his gaze darting to her bosom and back again.

Julia's heart fluttered. Nobody had ever looked at her this way before. She was consumed by a cocktail of conflicting emotions. It was thrilling, exhilarating but it was also disturbing. There was pleasure but there was also alarm. She felt herself colouring the way she had done the last time they had met and she reacted in the same way: anger grew within her - anger with herself. This man had drawn her into his world from across a courtroom – anonymously; but now that they had met, the intensity was escalating out of her control. He was releasing emotions within her that she had never encountered before. He was seeing her as a desirable woman; there was now no doubt about that in her mind. What she would not at this point admit to herself was that she liked it. She was vaguely aware that there was an addiction growing within her, but she did not understand it and so dismissed it from her mind.

'Will you call me "David"? I would like us to be friends.'

'I'm not sure that that would be proper, Mr Neander,' she heard her voice tremble.

'Ah – the rules of society; the rules that say we must be formally introduced, must be of the same class, the same religion - but I have no time to follow these rules. I fear the hangman will come for me before long.'

'Oh, please don't say that Mr Neander.' A fear had suddenly taken her because of his stark words. She caught herself in full flow, put her hand to her mouth and then withdrew it self-consciously. Making a big effort to calm herself, she said, 'We are far from defeated, Mr Neander.'

'Kind words, Miss Carmichael. I hope you are right, but in the meantime I would still like you to call me "David".'

It was a simple request and a few moments ago she would have readily agreed, but now she was flustered, afraid that this was a further escalation that she could not cope with and she resolved to decline.

'Yes, I would like that, David,' she said. In disbelief Julia heard these words escape her mouth, which seemed to have taken no notice of her conscious reasoning and had in turn overridden her impulse to refuse him. She was astounded by herself, and even more so when she heard herself adding, 'And please David, do call me "Julia".'

'I would like that very much, Julia,' he held her gaze for a heartbeat.

Julia's mind was suddenly completely blank. She forced herself to speak but the words would not come. When they did they burst forth, the words unrelated to their previous conversation. 'I have brought you small beer to drink and candles to work by,' she said, handing him a flagon and a brown paper parcel. 'Oh! And inks and pens as well – you'll need them.'

He took them from her, touching her hand as he did so. He heart raced at the contact and she tried hard to regain control of her emotions. 'You must tell me something about yourself, David. Am I right in thinking you are German?'

'I am and I am not.' There was resignation in his tone.

'I'm not sure that I follow...'

'I speak German, I am a German poet, but because I am Jewish by birth no German state will allow me citizenship.'

'But that can't be so, David, surely not. You are an educated man; you have so much to offer.'

'And yet it is, Julia. The educated middle class Jew is more despised by the German than the orthodox Jew and because the middle class Jews live amongst them, they fear that.'

She thought for a moment about what he had said. It offended her; if she had been German she would have railed against this injustice, but she was forced to let it pass. 'But your religion will be a comfort to you in you hour of trouble, will it not?'

He looked down as he thought of his response, 'Perhaps, but it is not *my* religion; that is to say, I am not an orthodox Jew; but yes, I have my own relationship with God and I do look for comfort from that. In the night, with only anxious thoughts for company, I pray to Him.' Embarrassed, suddenly, he changed the subject. 'And how is my case coming along?'

'Ah yes, the case; we intend to enter a *Writ of Error.*'

'Which is what exactly?'

'We shall ask that the court record be sent to a superior court for inspection.'

'And what are the chances that they will agree?'

'That is difficult to judge. We have two options. We can either show that there is an error in the court record or that we can provide new evidence consistent with the record, but that now requires examining in court.'

'I take it that the production of new evidence is our best option.'

'Father thinks so, but I was appalled by the way the Judge dealt with the case. My instinct is to discredit the way he handled the proceedings.'

'No, no, you must not do that, Julia.'

'Why ever not?' Julia's brow wrinkled in puzzlement.

'That would mean a loss of dignity for him,' he explained.

'Well good,' she retorted, 'he deserves it.'

'No, Julia,' he sighed, 'you don't understand. I am Jewish! The English legal system will not allow a judge to be humiliated to right an injustice to a *Jew.'*

'But the English legal system requires the court to discount your Jewishness, David.'

'You are an idealist like me, Julia, but you must not be blind to the reality of the world. They will not allow a judge to...err...' he struggled to find the right English phrase.

'Yes,' she said. There was resignation in her voice as she finally understood what he meant, 'We say: *"to lose face".*'

'Ah yes – that is what I meant. They will not allow the Judge to lose face. A single Jew has no importance to them.'

Julia suddenly squealed and jumped to her feet. She had felt a louse creep up her leg; she turned her back on David so that she could raise her skirt, patting furiously at the crawling tickle in the hope of squashing the offending insect. She turned back to him, flustered, put her hand on her chest. David had stood, concerned, and she saw the look of bewilderment on his face. 'I beg your pardon sir,' she said, 'it was just...'

She did not complete the sentence, but now he understood. He smiled a knowing smile and gestured her to sit again. 'I fear they are many in this place,' he said apologetically.

Still flustered, Julia brushed aside the incident and forced herself to go on. 'We were talking about evidence; we simply must find *new* evidence to present.'

'I think I can help there,' he said thoughtfully. 'If I can show that I only arrived in England on the Saturday and was then arrested on the following Monday, how could I have known the city and where to take the carcass? The ship's manifest will show me as a passenger disembarking on that day, and a member of the crew can testify to my identity. That will be new evidence to demonstrate that I was not lying.'

Julia jotted down his words with enthusiasm, 'That's good; I'll go to see the Harbourmaster. The Ship's Master will have had to present his papers when he docked. That's a good start, David,' she was relieved, she feared she had come with little of encouragement to tell him.

Emboldened by her evident enthusiasm, he asked, 'What is an "Action of Attaint"?'

Julia frowned, gave a small shrug, 'I have to be honest and say I don't know – why do you ask?'

He grabbed up a large legal volume, already open at the relevant page, and ran his finger down to the appropriate paragraph, tapping it to show her where to read.

As Julia leaned in to him, her scent entered David's consciousness. Savouring it, he became acutely aware of his own position and he wondered how badly he smelt. He moved away slightly, disappointed that he felt he had to, but after all these weeks in this wretched cell he must surely reek.

Removing her bonnet and gloves, Julia cast around for somewhere to put them. He took them from her and placed them carefully on the desk. 'Oh, I see,' she said, reading out loud the paragraph he indicated, '*An action can be brought against the jurors for bringing in a false verdict.*' This means that if we were successful then the verdict would be quashed. I must confess that I've never seen this before, David, but it's certainly a possibility. I'll talk to my father about it.'

Julia looked up at him in disbelief and wondered at his intellect. A week ago he could hardly speak English and yet here he was, taking a legal volume running to many thousands of words and working out a possible route of appeal that neither she nor her father had considered. It added to her appreciation of him.

Their conversation lightened and they began to talk freely of more inconsequential matters. They talked of poetry, of literature. They talked of politics, of history, of religion, of humanities, of reform. He was interested in her past, her childhood, her family, whilst all the time deflecting her enquiries about his own past; deflecting so successfully that she did not then realise it. She saw in David everything she wanted her father to be; the father who had gone such a long way in indulging her, who was universally regarded as a man with an open mind; but that was never enough for her.

Julia now began to re-evaluate everything in her life based upon how David perceived it. She was drawn into his web, and she went without hesitation.

CHAPTER 10

Frankfurt 1818

'I won't do it,' said Henriette, 'you can't make me. I'll tell Mama of you.'

We were making the short journey home from school. Moses and Henriette were arguing; they seemed to be doing it more and more. They didn't mean anything by it, but it could be tiresome. It was just a combination of too much energy and not enough chances to release it.

'That's enough of that,' I said, 'Mama's got enough to worry about without you tittle-tattling to her, Henriette Ephraim.' She looked at me perplexed, her expression questioning why I had said it. I didn't want to lie to her, but neither did I want to burden her with the truth. I turned to Moses, hoping that would deflect the unspoken question I didn't want to answer. 'And you can stop teasing your sister as well, Moses Ephraim.'

'Sorry Loeb,' he said. I could see Henriette was amazed; Moses would not normally apologise like that. He was thirteen now and was aware of things that Henriette, at eleven was not.

I was big brother; they listened to me - well more than they used to when I was a child like them. I *was* big brother now, not just in name. I had surprised everybody by growing so tall and athletic. In the year 1818 I was sixteen, going on seventeen. I was one metre eighty - almost six feet tall; I had started to fill out and my whiskers needed shaving every day, for I had decided not to grow the customary beard. I was taller than Papa and Uncle Meno; in fact I seemed to be taller than almost everybody. I looked older than my years as well, and I did not look Jewish. I dressed and appeared to be German, and most people accepted me at face value, well at least until they learned my name, when some would then realise that I was not one of them. I could see it in their faces as the realisation took them; they would somehow shrink back, it was almost imperceptive, but I could see it - it was there.

Although I was relieved that I didn't look Jewish, I don't think I was ashamed of being a Jew – well I hope not at least, but I wanted to be accepted as a German: that I have to confess. And there was the route of my problem. 1818 was a year when the attitude of the Germans towards us Jews worsened. That is what Mama was so worried about. I wanted to be part of my country; to belong and to contribute to it with my education and my skill. The fact that my country did not seem to want me was a thorn in my side, it pricked at my sense of who I was. But then, at sixteen did I really know who I was? I don't know, but I thought I knew what I wanted to be: a German first and a Jew second.

Mother on the other hand was not worried about such intangible concepts. She was just worried for our safety, worried that violence might burst into life and threaten her family. Young men in their drinking clubs singing their nationalistic songs were taking their brand of patriotism into the workplace and into the universities. Papa had seen it emerging when at Geissen University and had told us about what he had seen; it was a reaction to the defeat by Napoleon. Napoleon was now gone but that German nationalism was still about, eager to undo all the social changes the French had introduced. Even our little city state of Frankfurt was not immune to this nationalism.

It was over a year since my fight with Oliver Breitner. In Moses' eyes it had signalled a change in the balance of power with the formidable Frau Breitner. He had never really been afraid of her, he was such a naturally brave boy, but he had always been wary of the fact that this vinegary Frau might give him a good beating. But now even that possibility did not deter him. He taunted her at every opportunity. It was her custom to come out brandishing her broom whenever the children were playing outside her house. She would hold it in her bony hands at arms' length, wielding it from side to side trying to whack them with it. It was no idle threat; if she had managed to hit them it would have been with considerable force. Moses, Henriette and whoever they were playing with were usually shoed away, but one day last week, Moses had unexpectedly stood his ground. That broom did indeed whack him for his trouble, the backhand stroke catching him around the left ear. It was a tactical deployment on his part, however. He took the blow then raised his arm and trapped the broom beneath it. Frau Breitner was now enraged and she tugged and tugged to get him to release it. She was stronger that Moses of course and she tried to swat him away as if he was some insignificant little fly, but he had the broom's head anchored under his arm like a nut held firm in a spanner. Neither was our Moses the swat-away type. He clung on for dear life as she pulled him from left to right, right to left, backwards and forwards. He fell to the ground but still he held on; he was not going to take that thwack for nothing. And then she started to gasp for breath, wheezing at the strain of manhandling this impudent little Jew boy. She let go with a screeched yell. Moses fell backwards as she turned to the comfort of her doorway, muttering anti-Jewish obscenities that Moses did not understand. He now had the miscreant broom; it was a spoil of war. For the next hour he walked up and down outside her house, the errant broom playing the part of a soldier's musket across his shoulder. Frau Breitner's house was under siege, and he was the commanding general and also the foot-soldier keeping guard.

That is what he was teasing Henriette with. He wanted her to march up and down outside Frau Breitner's house before supper to taunt the old woman as *he* had done. But Henriette was not like Moses; she was too shrewd to risk a beating just so that Moses could have the satisfaction of continuing the taunt.

After the evening meal that night we played cards whilst Papa was busy writing an article for a magazine - Mama, Henriette, Moses and me. It was a summer's evening and the long day had not yet turned into night. The low sun burst into our living room through the small mullioned window, drowning us in warm golden light. The living room was also the kitchen where Mama cooked and the dining room where we all ate at the kitchen table. Papa was at one end of the table and we were squeezed together at the other end. We were playing *Doppelkopf*, a team game where each team consists of two players. Mama loved playing cards and we loved playing with her. Henriette was cheating; she always cheated, but the game was quite complicated and she did not always keep up. It was about scoring points, so Mama always played with Henriette so that she could work out the scoring for her, and to stop her cheating. I always played with Moses; I used to keep score for him but he was now old enough to do it for himself. We got quite rowdy at times and Mama kept hushing us as it was obvious that we were disturbing Papa. From time to time I saw him looking up from his papers to attract Mama's attention. They would exchange glances and then she would hush us, but she also laughed out loud with us a lot of the time. In the long summer nights she wasn't as strict about bed times and we looked forward to playing cards with her.

When the game finished Moses and I had won; we got more than the 121 points needed to win, and that was the signal for Moses and Henriette to go off to bed. They did not want to go, but Mama was aware that Papa wanted some peace and quiet to finish his article. She had tuned into his irritation that the children were still up well past their bedtime.

'One more game; please Mama?' Henriette pleaded.

Mama paused for a moment; I think she wanted to play on as well but knew that Papa would not like it. I thought I would help her; I had been shown a card trick at school and was eager to try it out.

'Look,' I said, 'I'll show you a trick if you'll go to bed straight afterwards.'

'Oh yes please,' said Henriette, she leaned forward across the table, her elbows taking her weight so that she could get a better look at what I was doing.

I took five cards from the deck; two pairs, tens and nines, and an odd one, a queen. I held all the cards together with the queen in the middle of the five. I showed the faces of the cards to Henriette and then turned them over so that she could only see the backs of them. I asked her to put one of Mama's hair clips on the middle card. She grabbed at Mama's hair to find a clip, but Mama told her to wait, taking one out for her. Carefully, Henriette placed it over the middle card, but when I turned it over the clip was on the first card. Henriette looked at me and then at Mama and then back at me. She was obviously dumbfounded by the trick. She looked at Mama again.

'How did he do that, Mama?' she said.

'I don't know,' said Mama, 'its Loeb's trick.'

'Again, again,' she said, and I did it again. The hair clip seemed to jump to the first card each time I turned it over.

Moses then wanted a go and I repeated it for him; he was equally as dumfounded as Henriette. 'How's it done Loeb,' he said, his eagerness showing in his raised voice.

It wasn't even a trick. I didn't have to perform any slight of hand; it was just an optical illusion. The hair-clip didn't move at all. If I had turned the cards back they would have seen that it was still over the middle card when viewed from the back. But I was now playing the part of the magician, and I proudly proclaimed, 'It's magic!'

It was an innocent enough remark I suppose. It was to illustrate a card trick; nothing more than that. But Papa didn't see it that way. He jumped to his feet his face suddenly reddened with anger.

'We are not ignorant Jews,' he yelled, 'we are educated Jews not consumed with superstition. There will be no mention of magic in this house.'

'Papa!' said Mama. Her voice was quiet and delicate but yet there was no doubt there was admonishment in her tone, 'The boy meant no harm. We're just playing games.'

'Even those sanctimonious Germans think that Jews are an ignorant and superstitious people,' Papa snapped. 'Jews just fuel their self-righteous attitudes.' His rage was undiminished. 'I'll have no mention of magic and the mystical in my house; do you hear me?'

We were all frightened, even me, or should I say even Moses, for I looked at his eyes and there was genuine fear there. It was mirrored in Henriette's eyes as well. We knew that Papa could be intense at times but we had never been afraid of him before; he seemed to be out of control. I looked across at Mama and saw a different reaction in her eyes. There was resentment there. She was a mother reacting to a threat to her children, even if that threat came from her mate. Papa was an intellectual, a brilliant man. Mama was neither of those, but she had her own intelligence; she was a very able woman in her own right. Nobody was going to frighten her children.

'Papa!' she snapped. It was just one word, but her eyes spoke thousands of others and they cut through his rage even if they didn't diminish it. He sat down as if commanded to by those reproachful eyes. Unable to express his rage, his impotence manifested itself physically; he started to tremble. I saw his hands shake. He forced his voice down; his words were quiet but there was no gentleness in them; they were strained.

'Have I taught you children nothing? We are not ignorant superstitious Jews.'

I now know what was behind his outburst. His whole world, everything that he believed in, everything he had striven to achieve was crumbling around him. All that expectation he'd had as a younger man was receding into the distance. He was a reformer; he wanted Jews to change and be assimilated into German society. He wanted a well educated Jewish middle class to lead that change. But now he saw all around him the opposite beginning to happen - alienation not assimilation - and his dreams were in tatters. And all that pent up frustration had been released by one innocent word – 'magic'. Mama understood that but we did not; we were just bewildered. Even though she understood, Mama was not going to make allowances; nobody was going to frighten her children. Papa sat there shaking with unreleased rage but she held his gaze with a steely stare, her eyes narrowing to reinforce her meaning. Our fear mounted. We had never seen Papa like this before, but we had never seen Mama like this either; something had to give.

And then Henriette seemed to know what to do. Little Henriette, who intellectually had no comprehension of the events behind the scene that was unfolding before her, knew what to do to diffuse it. She got off her chair and walked round to Papa and crawled up onto his knee. She didn't say a word. She just put her arms around him and buried her head deep into his chest. Papa's hand instinctively came around and stroked the back of her head; still shaking at first but it calmed quickly as he stroked. He bent forward and kissed her head gently. And that was that; it was over. Little Henriette knew more than all of us. Little Henriette! Who would have thought it?

CHAPTER 11

London 1823

George Carmichael's chambers were practical rather than sumptuous. The walls were panelled with dark oak and the solitary window of his office lifted the gloom hardly at all, and then only at the height of a bright summer's day. Long before dusk he was obliged to burn expensive candles, despite his irritation at the cost, but he was able to charge them to his clients and that reduced his concern. His desk, facing the door so he could call for his clerk when he needed him, was covered in legal papers: some wrapped in ribbon, others loose. To the casual observer it was without apparent organisation, but this was George's domain, the place where he was master, and he knew exactly what was where. Today, however, his troublesome daughter was being more that usually annoying and distracting him from his busy workload.

'An Action of Attaint?' He looked up at her, surprised at the suggestion.

'Yes,' said Julia. 'Do you think it would work in David's case?' She sniffed and the aroma of his office took her attention; it smelled of musty papers, snuff, pipe tobacco and furniture wax; it was a smell that reassured her; it was the smell of her wonderful father.

He raised an eyebrow at her, discomfited by her familiar use of just the forename, 'David', but he let it pass. 'I have many other more important cases to consider, Julia,' he said as he returned his gaze to the papers he was attempting to study, irritation apparent in his tone.

Julia flashed her father a fiery look, which was wasted as he did not look up from his papers. Her mounting anger prickled in the air. 'More important?' she snapped. 'By more important you mean more wealthy! Are any of your wealthy clients on trial for their lives?'

George Carmichael put down his pen and sat back in his seat. Steepling his fingers before his mouth he mentally counted to ten. His own anger was mounting, but he suppressed it, knowing that when the passions ran through his daughter there was no use in opposing her.

'Actions of Attaint have been obsolete for years,' he said. 'They're a relic; not used any more, haven't been used for years,' he repeated, returning his attention deliberately to his papers.

'But would it work?' she persisted. 'Won't it avoid challenging the actions of the trial judge?'

'Well that's certainly true,' he said, retrieving his pen without looking up, 'but there will be a price to pay.'

'I'm not sure I understand, Father.' She waited while he finished reading a sentence, but her body language suggested that she was not going to leave this matter there.

Once more, George put his pen down and sighing, gave her his attention. 'You are effectively putting the original jury on trial.'

'Well what's wrong with that, if we get a retrial?'

'Think about it, Julia; if the action was to succeed there would be consequences for the trial jury.'

'You mean they will effectively be found guilty of an offence, and that could mean they suffer a severe sentence?'

'Not effectively but *actually*.'

'So it's not just a case of getting David's case back in court?'

'No it's not, and that's why it's never used. It can't succeed.'

'But I don't understand, why can't it succeed?' she said.

'Because you won't get the new jury to find against the old jury; there but for the grace of God and all that. They are not going to condemn other jurors to possible transportation.'

'So where do we go from here?'

'You tell *Mister* Neander to leave the legal matters to me.' Too late, he bit his tongue.

'Then you *will* help, Father?'

He had painted himself into a corner and suddenly realised it. 'Well fine; so be it. But we enter a *Writ of Error* as we originally thought.*'

Julia went around his desk, stood behind him and put her arms around his neck. She kissed his cheek lovingly and he put his hand affectionately on hers. 'You play me like a fiddle, girl,' he said, 'don't think I don't know you do.'

'Why Father,' she said impishly, 'would I ever do such a thing?'

'You know very well that you would. I indulge you far too much, my girl. Your mother is always telling me so.'

'But I wouldn't be "Daddy's girl" if you didn't, would I?'

'Never mind all that nonsense.' He removed her arms from around his neck in an effort to regain control. 'Why is this David Neander so special anyway?'

'Injustice, father,' she lied, 'it's so very difficult to take.'

'Are you sure that is all it is? I don't want you getting hurt; and you will, mark my words.'

Julia did not answer. She had not admitted her true feelings even to herself; she walked to the door, turned and just smiled at her father.

CHAPTER 12

Frankfurt 1819

The August of 1819 brought very troubled times to all of us, German and Jew alike. There had been a drought in 1816 and the people had endured high bread prices ever since. Many went hungry and there was discontent everywhere. I was seventeen and was well aware that somehow Mama and Papa had managed to protect us from the agonies of aching, hungered stomachs. I now know that our larder was often filled by Uncle Meno. He earned a good living as a doctor and he was happy to support his extended family; he had no children of his own. What I don't know was how Papa felt about it; he was a proud man, but if his pride was bruised by Uncle Meno's generosity, he never showed it.

By the time I was coming up eighteen I was a strapping, lean, athletic, well-nourished boy. I was now one metre, eighty-three - a full six feet tall - to the amazement of everyone. In general, Germans were taller than Jews. It was one of the things that distinguished them at a glance. Even the middle class Jew, dressed in a smart German frock-coat, normally did not have the stature of the German, but I did.

I desperately wanted to study at a German University, like Papa and Uncle Meno had done, but times were now much different from when they had attended. We hatched together a plan, however, and Papa wrote to his old friend, the famous Ludwig Börne, so that I would have a letter of introduction to present to the Rector. I applied to Papa's old university at Gießen; the letter of introduction, which Ludwig Börne had written in glowing terms although he had never met me, seemed to have done the trick. I was invited to attend an interview. Gießen University was fifty-eight kilometres away from Frankfurt; it was a twelve-hour walk and I made a six a.m. start so that I would be there by early evening. I had enough money to pay for two nights' lodgings courtesy of Papa, but also a fine black frock-coat that Uncle Meno had lent me together with a pair of his knee breeches that mother had carefully washed and ironed. She had also purchased a new pair of extra long stockings, which were long enough to camouflage the fact that I was taller than Uncle Meno and a gap needed to be bridged. I was not allowed to wear these for the journey; they were neatly packed away in my hip bag, along with some provisions for the outward journey and a few extra marks from uncle Meno to purchase some victuals whilst in the town and for my eventual return.

The journey did not take the expected twelve hours. There was nothing wrong with the estimate; it's just that I ran much of the way. I ran to most places; I always did. I arrived in Gießen just after two p.m. and spent the afternoon looking around the town and its university. It looked wonderful to me and I wanted to be a part of it again. I had attended the Free-School here of course, and Papa had been one of the University's lecturers. The buildings were elegant and impressive and the town had a magnificence that turned my youthful impressionable head. I looked at the young gentlemen students carrying their books and scurrying to their next lectures, and I pictured myself doing the same thing in a few months' time.

I was in a state of euphoria by the time I went to an inn to purchase the two nights' lodgings. I was accepted instantly as a young German student and shown to a large, clean, if sparsely furnished room. There was a bunk for sleeping in, but apart from that there was only a small table holding a bowl and a pitcher of water. Nevertheless, I pictured myself at study; a candle burning into the night, an ink well in the corner, text books open for reference, a half completed essay, a quill lying across it as I studied German literature.

I went back down to the inn. I was ravenously hungry after my long journey and I ordered a plate of *der Sauerbraten*, a traditional dish made by steeping a joint of roast beef in a sweet and sour marinade for two days. It was not the sort of dish I would have eaten at home, but in my mind I was not a Jew today, I was a German. The portion was huge but I devoured it to sate my hunger, all swilled down by a large earthenware stein of beer. My thumb flicked the tankard's hinged lid open and closed as I sat back in my chair, my belly feeling bloated but satisfied and I felt at one with the town, the inn, the University.

I wasn't used to alcohol, but I continued to drink. Young German men, whom I took to be students, began to arrive and it wasn't long before they started to sing. I was encouraged to join them and eagerly took up their offer. I explained that I had to attend an admissions interview the next day and I was patted soundly on the back to show their encouragement. I gave my name as Loeb which caused no hesitation and there seemed no need for surnames. I was helped with the words of the songs and picked them up easily. Some I knew as traditional songs that I had sung at the Free School. My naivety was total. I swung my stein to the rhythm of the songs, as they did; I was in a state of enchantment. It was a glimpse of the life I wanted for myself. But then the nature of the songs changed. They became nationalistic; they became patriotic; extremely patriotic. I'd like to say that I saw through them, that I rose above them, that I saw the dangers in them. I'd like to say that, but it would be a lie. I sang them with my new German student friends with as much gusto as they did. My father would have been ashamed of me if he had seen my behaviour.

What can I say in my defence? My behaviour was alcohol-based; that was undoubtedly true. There is an urge in all of us to belong and I pursued that urge without restraint. But at the end of the day I have no defence; my life as a young Jew should have prepared me with more insight. I didn't even have the good grace to be contrite the next morning.

I awoke with my head throbbing, the alcohol giving me a hangover; the first I had ever had. But even though I felt physically terrible my spirits were still on a high. My elation overcame my queasiness and I breakfasted on black-bread, eggs, salted meats and cheese with strong black coffee to wash it all down. I looked resplendent in Uncle Memo's black frock-coat. It was the one he wore when visiting the houses of his very wealthiest patients. Today would be the day that I entered the German world as an equal.

'This is quite a testimonial, Mr Ephraim,' said the Rector, reading the letter from Ludwig Börne. He was small and slightly built man with sad, life-worn eyes. Those eyes looked at me like a bloodhound; they were pulled down by the rest of his ageing, sagging face so that there was a half moon of blood red where the bottom eyelid was detached from the eyeball.

'Thank you, sir,' I was being as polite as I could be.

He fiddled with his spectacles; his unease was apparent. 'But I suppose I should have expected nothing else from the son of Felix Ephraim. How is your father by the way, is he well?'

'Yes sir, he is well enough.' The sentence was incomplete and the professor looked at me over the top of those spectacles, which he had now replaced on his face. He understood the words that were not said as well as the ones that I had used.

'Yes, I was most saddened to see him leave us.' His tone was reflective, 'A man of the highest calibre; we shouldn't have to lose such good men. And we should jump at enrolling students of your calibre as well.'

'Thank you sir,' I said, thinking that the interview was going well. It wasn't; I just couldn't see it.

'No, no, my boy.' The Rector corrected me. 'Things have got worse here since your father was forced to leave. We didn't take even one Jewish student last year.'

'Papa will be saddened by that news.' The statement was correct but I used it more for tactical reasons as the first signs of a problem were becoming apparent to me.

'Is he often melancholy – your father I mean? He was always a reformer but his reformations have come to nothing haven't they. It must be very difficult for him.'

'It is, sir,' I said, 'but he carries on writing. The Frankfurt authorities often censor his work, but they are sometimes smuggled out and published in full elsewhere in the German confederation.'

'I know. I have read some of the magazines. I admire his bravery Mr Ephraim, but he should also be careful.'

'I'm sure he will be, sir.'

I had been here for fifteen minutes now, and the interview had not yet come around to *me*. I didn't know whether this was a good thing or not. But then the reality became apparent.

The Rector sat up in his chair as though resolve had suddenly taken him. 'Look my boy; I had hoped I could use your application to reverse the unpleasant trends of the last few years, but...' He paused and I waited for his negativity to subside: it didn't. He sighed heavily, 'But the events of yesterday make this impossible. I fear this is not a good time for you to come to Gießen University.' He must have seen the puzzlement on my face and realized that he needed to explain. 'Wurzburg in Bavaria - you have seen the morning papers young man – haven't you?'

'No, sir.' My puzzlement only increased.

'There has been rioting in the streets for two days now. They are targeting the homes and businesses of Jews I'm afraid - looting, demolishing. It's all out of control; the mob are running amuck, shouting something odd, *Hep!-Hep! Jude verreck*, death to all Jews.'

I did not know what to say. I was still clinging to the hope that the University would accept me. 'But Bavaria is a long way away?' It was the best that I could come up with.

'Not so far my boy, that the ripples won't reach us here. The rioting is already spreading to other German cities. It's as though we are back in the Middle Ages; I'm ashamed to say that it started at the University in Wurzburg.'

'The University?'

'Yes the University and it shames me to say so. They should be places of enlightenment not dens of Medieval prejudice.' He was agitated as he spoke. 'The newspapers say that it started when an old professor was teaching the students about the 1816 Congress of Vienna when the Jewish representatives called for emancipation. The old man had apparently suggested that it should indeed be extended to the Jews. They ran the poor old fool out of his lecture room. Some of the other professors supported the students and then they took to the streets. They were joined by shopkeepers, tradesmen, unemployed workers; anybody on the streets.'

'And has the riot been put down.' I was suddenly anxious.

'It appears so, my boy. The army was called out but the Jewish population has taken flight.'

'I must go home.' I got up without really thinking what I was doing. It took the professor by surprise but I glimpsed some relief in his eyes as I was effectively terminating the interview and it obviated the need for him to turn me down formally. He stood and held out his hand and I shook it instinctively but my thoughts were running ahead of me.

'It's a pretty state of affairs,' he said not releasing my hand, 'now you take care, my boy.'

'I will,' I was at the door as the words escaped my lips.

'And remember me to your father.' His voice was raised to catch my attention. I was already in the corridor eager to get away.

Back at the inn I toyed with the idea of setting off home that evening but it would be dark in a few hours' time. I would have an early night and set off at first light. I took a meal of *Handkäse mit Musik*, a strong cheese made from curdled milk with a dressing of vegetable oil, vinegar, caraway, salt and pepper and sliced onions; served with rye bread and butter. It fought a digestive battle in my stomach in the night and I remembered why they called it *'with music'* - flatulence was sometimes a by-product of the dish. But the gas was the least of my discomforts. I slept fitfully and lay awake for long periods contemplating my folly of the previous evening. How could I have been so self-centered? My need to belong had overridden my sense of self; of who I really was. Reality is a difficult pill to take; I was consumed with shame and when I did drift off, my dreams were disturbed and horrid. I was away from my family at a dangerous time and all I wanted to do was to run home; run home as fast as I could.

I rose a good hour before dawn, finally accepting there was no more sleep left in me. I poured the cold water from the pitcher into the bowl and immersed my head as deeply as I could to chase away the last of the sleep. It made me shiver right down to my toes, but I think it was as much a release of a fearful tremble as a reaction to the cold. My family needed me; my pulse was racing as a consequence. I needed to go to them.

It was still dark when I hit the street. I had taken no breakfast and my only sustenance was a few gulps of cold water. There were no candles burning in the houses; the streets were deserted. I started to run. My feet pounded the cobbles. I passed a baker's shop and saw the hint of candle light escaping from a back room but other than that I seemed to be the sole person alive in the town. I had already left behind the city limits when the first rays of the sun breached the horizon. I was still running. Something told me there was something wrong; that something terrible was about to happen. There was a nagging urgency in my mind harassing me with every step. I was desperate to get home.

It was just after noon when I entered the village of Eckenheim. My exhaustion suddenly hit me. My running had become mesmeric; somehow the cadenced rhythm of my pounding, metronomic feet had cast the fatigue from my mind, but my body told me to stop. I had run on and off for over six hours, but each time my body had stopped to recharge itself, my insistent mind had started me running again. That natural stamina that I seemed to have was my ally but now I needed to stop. I needed to refuel; I needed to eat. The village looked friendly, its half-timbered houses and winding alleys somehow welcoming. Eckenheim was a place of farmers and gardeners who sold their products to neighboring Frankfurt and it reassured me that I was nearing home.

I quickly found the village inn, ordered some black-bread and cheese, and washed it down with a mug of *apfelwein*. I saw the landlord look at me as I ate ravenously and gulped at the cider, my anxiety to get on with my journey fueling my ill manners. I made an attempt to calm myself. I slowed my eating but the meal rapidly disappeared as my body demanded sustenance: I ordered more. I told myself that I was being silly and panicking unnecessarily; the fact that there was anti-Jewish rioting in Wurzburg did not mean that my family was at risk in Frankfurt.

'You're going to Frankfurt, young sir?' The landlord placed the second portion before me and gazed at me not troubling to hide his curiosity.

It suddenly entered my mind that I must look decidedly odd; my face was probably beetroot-red from my exertions and I was sweating profusely. A large drop of sweat dripped from my chin as I looked up at him. I took my handkerchief from my pocket and wiped my face. The cloth came away soaking wet. I had not realized until that moment what I must look like and embarrassment now took me as I spoke. 'Yes, Landlord, Frankfurt,' I said shortly.

'Then you need to be careful when you get there, young sir, a horseman told me this morning they have called out the Militia to keep order.'

I remember that I was gripped by fear at his words. The sweat on my fatigued body felt suddenly cold against my skin. There was a chill under my arms, down my back, down my thighs. The hair on the back of my head prickled and I knew that my instincts had been right. 'The Militia? Why have they done that?' was all that I could say.

'Riots in the Jewish community yesterday,' he turned to go away adding over his shoulder, 'the Yids deserve all they get if you ask me.'

I stared down at the bread and cheese temporarily paralyzed with fear. Then the need for action grabbed me. I broke off a hunk of cheese and put it in my mouth followed by a piece of bread, then emptied the remainder of the plateful into my soiled handkerchief and tied it up; there was no room in my mind for considerations of hygiene. Standing, I frantically gathered up my belongings; reaching back I drained the last of the *apfelwein,* threw down some copins and then walked briskly to the door. I saw the landlord looking with amusement at my swollen cheeks as I tried to swallow the excessive mouthful.

I had another twelve kilometers to go. My feet started to pound again but my mind raced ahead. I had no recollection of the route I took, the tracks that I covered. It was just a blur and didn't enter my conscious mind. Kilometer after kilometer disappeared beneath my feet as if sucked into some avaricious void. But as I entered the city limits that cerebral zone was punctuated; I stopped running instinctively. Burning! I smelled burning. Smoke was on the air. I looked up at the sky. There were several plumes of smoke over the city. It must have been two hours or so after noon and the sun was burning fiercely in a cloudless, windless sky so that the smoke hung lazily over the cityscape. My fear mounted.

I heard a commotion nearby and ran in the direction of the noise. As I turned the corner I was horrified at the sight that befell me. There was an old Jewish man being accosted by a dozen or so rioters. He was clearly not a wealthy Jew. His black clothes were traditional and of poor quality; his beard long and graying matching the ringlets that hung down beside his lank hair. His appearance had obviously singled him out as a target. He had been trying to get home, I supposed, to the relative safety of his house, but had been spotted.

Cries of '*Hep! Hep!*' rang out. It was a traditional herding cry of German shepherds and more and more people were answering the call. I stopped as if paralyzed, just looking on in impotent observation. I was bumped from behind, a young German

man trying to get to the entertainment. 'Sorry,' he said as he looked back at me, and then urged me to join him, waving his arm for me to follow. I realized at that moment that I was safe from the mob. My stature and my blues eyes pronounced me as a German, whereas this unfortunate rotund old man with his bearded features and his bulbous nose had the badges of Judaism stamped on him.

The horror of the scene intensified before my eyes. Children were running with the mob. Their parents, instead of hiding them away for their own safety, were encouraging them to witness the savagery that was unfolding. The children were laughing and giggling without any admonishment from the adults. I walked slowly forward to the place were the old Jew was held as if I were being drawn reluctantly into the lair of the Devil himself. The victim was being held by a tall man wearing spectacles and a smart frock-coat with a splendid six-button waistcoat; he was clearly not an aggrieved unemployed worker, nor a trader anxious to blame the Jews for the bad economic conditions. This was a professional man of some sort. But worst of all, he was holding the old Jew so that somebody else could beat him - and that somebody else was woman. This toothless, large-bosomed little woman held a broom handle in her hand and was using it as a truncheon, the blows raining down on the old man so that blood was running from several reddened contusions on his face. The poor old man was being prevented from falling to the ground or to shield his face from the blows by the restraint of the professional man. And the entire time the crowd bayed, '*Hep! Hep!*'

Later, the newspapers suggested that this was the traditional rallying cry of the Crusaders, *Hep,* being an acronym for the Latin, *Hierosolyma Est Perdita,* 'Jerusalem is Lost'. But I was there; it was nothing of the sort, nothing so grand or respectable. These people were clearly anti-Semitic, but they were a mob; they did not have the education to know such things. They were just herding Jews as they would animals.

I didn't know what to do, but knew that I had to do something. The idea of just walking away never occurred to me. I don't know whether that counts as bravery – I think that you have to overcome fear to be truly brave and I didn't feel fear at that time. But neither was I going to be foolhardy. I realized that just wading in to try and protect this man was never going to be allowed by the crowd. Instead I'd use guile.

'Over there!' I shouted out and then began to run to the next corner. I looked behind and saw that I had the attention of some of the rioters. 'Another Jew!' I shouted again and waved my arms for them to follow. They started to do so. *'Hep! Hep!'* I now shouted and the mob took up my cry, my deception was working.

The professional man and the little woman looked up to see the mob running away from them. They released the old man, who, now only half-conscious, fell heavily to the ground. This odd couple took off after the mob anxious not to be left out, but they were now at the back of the pursuing pack. As I ran, three of the mob came to my shoulder.

'Where is he?' one of them said.

'There,' I said, pointing with all the cunning of a hunted fox, 'he's just gone round that next corner.'

They passed me running, eager to apprehend the non-existent Jew. I slowed to allow them to go; others followed them. I slowed to a walk as I neared the corner. The professional man caught me up and as he ran by he looked over his shoulder at me, puzzlement on his face. He clearly didn't understand why I had given up the chase. I stopped and looked back. The little woman brandishing the broom handle was the only one left. She was wheezing, her face bright vermillion with effort; her pendulous breasts swinging before her as she ran on her short fat legs.

'Do you know a short cut?' she wheezed, stopping as she reached me, assuming that I had halted for a purpose. I had; it was a contrivance, but not the one that she assumed.

I didn't answer her. I just set off in another direction. Anxiety told me to run, but then I stopped, dithered. I didn't know whether to run home or go back and help the old man. I started again; the old Jew would now have to fend for himself. I ran towards the *Judengasse*. The Jews now lived all over the city, but that was still the heart of the Jewish community and we lived so close to it. I ran onto the *Allerheilig Strasse* and then onto the *Judengasse*. I was suddenly in semi-darkness and my eyes took a moment to adjust. It was eerily quiet and for a moment I was reassured by that, but then I looked around at the debris all about. The mob had obviously been here and had then moved on.

I walked the *Judengasse*; it curved round to the right, the buildings overhanging. The fear that had made me run now made me walk tentatively, anxious of what I might find. I took the cut-through alleyway which led onto the *Kiostergasse*. I could see the bright light that marked the end of the *Judengasse* coming towards me and it was then that I heard them. It was only muffled to start with; the overhanging buildings dampening the noise as well as the light. But it was unmistakable – it was the mob. As I emerged back into the bright summer sunlight, the muffled sound turned into a roar; it made me jump. I froze with heightened dread. I looked to my right down the *Kiostergasse* to where the road crossed the *Nonnengasse*. Our house was at that corner and that is where the mob was.

I ran towards them and then tried to disperse them, shouting wildly as I did so. But they assumed that I was with them; another rioter just anxious to get his share of the spoils. The mob was not at the front door, which was the entrance to Uncle Meno's surgery. For some reason they were encamped outside the side entrance - that was the entrance to our apartment. Stairs led up to the third floor and the mob was climbing them squeezed in like frenzied sardines, their sheer numbers stopping their progress. Then there was a cheer, and the snake that was the mob began to come out backwards to let others down.

A large unshaven man now appeared at the door. He had loot in his hands; our meagre possessions, mostly books but books were valuable. He held them up to the mob displaying his booty like a conquering general and the crowd cheered again. He stepped out into the street followed by others similarly brandishing their booty; our belongings - and then I saw *her* following them; Frau Breitner. She looked at me sheepishly at first and then a sneering smiled erupted across her features. For some reason that I will never understand, she did not reveal my identity to the crowd; that contemptuous smile seemed to suggest that she had already sated her vengeance. It was all I could think.

I burst past her, barging her out of the way, but I noticed the sneer didn't diminish. I bounded up the stairs two at a time, pushing stragglers aside.

'There's nothing left!' one shouted back up at me.

'Mama! Papa!' I called as I reached the landing not caring if anybody heard me. 'Henriette! Moses!'

There was no answer and I prayed that they weren't in there. The door was half open but I couldn't see very much of the room, just the side wall. I was suddenly cold and I shivered. I put my hand on the door handle and I said again, 'Mama; Papa,' but this time quietly. I pushed tentatively at the door; slowly crept into the room. With each tiptoed step my dread mounted. And then I stood, transfixed, a nightmare scene from hell before me.

Death; death lingered in the air. He had left, but his presence was still echoing in the prickling atmosphere. The first body was just inside the door. It was Papa. He had obviously been trying to protect his family. I turned him over. He was still warm. There was blood coming from his nose; his mouth; his eyes. I felt for a pulse frantically, but there was nothing. His lips were blue. I think that he had actually died from asphyxiation, been forced to the ground by the sheer weight of the mob and then suffocated underfoot as more and more people had forced their unwanted presence into the tiny room. I bent to kiss his forehead, stood and then looked around. I cannot describe how I felt; there are no words.

Mama was at the far end of the room. She was lying on her back in a pool of blood, her eyes wide open staring fixedly at the ceiling, but without seeing anything and I knew that they would never see anything again. Bruising had started before death had kindly taken her. She had received a terrible beating. Blow after blow must have rained down on her. The safety of her own home had turned out to be her place of execution, her executioners being her fellow citizens. I leaned over her and gently closed her eyes with my two splayed fingers then I fell to my knees before her and dropped an affectionate kiss on her forehead as I had done for Papa.

I looked round then for Henriette and Moses. They were not here – oh thank God, they were not here. 'At least you managed to save your children, Mama,' I said out loud to her lifeless, broken body. Grief took me strangely. I didn't weep; it was as though I was drained of all emotion. At that moment I was just an empty, non-functioning husk. I don't know how long I knelt there, comatose, staring but seeing nothing. But then the terror returned.

I heard the slightest of movements from beneath the wrecked table as it shifted downwards beside Mama's bloodied body. Sobbing, I grasped the broken corner and lifted; I knew instinctively what I would find. Henriette and Moses must have been hidden under there by Mama, who had then thrown a large tablecloth over the table. But the legs had given way under the weight of the mob. I stood and carefully removing the cloth, I lifted the table. There beneath it were two crushed little bodies. They looked so insignificant. Moses was wrapped around Henriette. He had been big brother to the last of his breath. I felt for a pulse, but Henriette was lifeless, her fragile little body had been easily crushed to death. I kissed her forehead as I had done to Mama and Papa then I felt for Moses's pulse. There was something; the faintest whisper of movement beneath my fingers.

I moved from his wrist to the side of his neck as Uncle Meno had shown me. Again I thought I felt something, but then it stopped. Frantically I searched, pressing my fingers to his neck, please God; please God.... Nothing; whatever I thought I had felt had disappeared. I cradled Moses in my arms and started to rock backwards and forwards. Vomit rose up from the pit of my stomach, seeping, foul tasting into my mouth, but I swallowed it back.

I don't know how long I sat there, it must have been for hours, but that last spark of my little brother's life had gone and never returned.

CHAPTER 13

London 1823

It was the first time that George Carmichael had appeared at the new second courtroom at the Old Bailey – it had been opened only a matter of months. He sat at the seating specifically provided for Counsel. He looked around and liked what he saw. It had been designed to address the inadequacy of the main courtroom; there was space for attorneys, law students, jurors in waiting, prosecutors, witnesses and officers of the court. He placed his legal papers, neatly wrapped in ribbon, before him on the table and then unwrapped them, setting them out in order; sat back in his ample chair and surveyed the impressive room. It was certainly striking yet it was almost deserted. The Judge had not yet entered and apart from himself, the only others present were three officers of the court who sat idly, like himself, waiting in anticipation. George took his pocket watch from his waistcoat – seven after three-of-the-clock he noticed. The hearing was scheduled for three, but judges were notoriously well wined and dined when sitting in court and were often late.

He looked up at the public gallery. It was also deserted except for one spectator. He smiled and nodded imperceptibly to his daughter. He went over in his mind his opening statement and was pleased with how it sounded. This was a type of submission that he had never made before and despite his initial reluctance to get involved, he was now rather taken by it all. But the minutes dragged on, counted by the rhythmic ticking of the large wall clock, its long pendulum swinging backwards and forwards inscribing an imaginary arc in the air and then erasing it with each backwards swing. George's fingers began to drum on the desk before him. He looked up again at his daughter and just shrugged his shoulders. Twenty-two after three. It must be a particularly fine Burgundy, he thought to himself.

He reshuffled the papers set out before him, for no other reason than to pass the time, and then put them back to their original positions. He took out his pocket watch again and checked it against the wall clock. He was a minute slow against it and he pulled out the winding knob and moved the minute hand forward, then wound it unnecessarily until it would go no further. He put the watch to his ear just to check that he had not over-wound it.

It was twenty-eight minutes before four when the sonorous voice of the usher called for everyone to rise. The usher's expression said it all: he had been here before and he sighed audibly; judges running late because of their over-indulgence and then not listening properly to the submissions before them, anxious only to settle the matter speedily; justice relegated to the whim of scheduling and gastronomic requirements.

The Judge waved his hand dismissively at the usher, who announced the case before the court. George Carmichael got to his feet, looked at the Judge for permission to proceed and was granted it by an almost imperceptible nod in his direction.

'My Lord, this case was originally heard some months ago in the January session of 1823, before Justice Lord Cardew, under reference T17900113-7.'

'Yes, Yes,' interrupted the Judge, 'do get on with it Mr Carmichael.'

George glanced up at his daughter. Her face was taut, a frown creasing her brow, her fingers clenched white-knuckled on the rail in front of her. He could tell what she was thinking: justice was absent at David Neander's first trial and it seemed it was going to be absent again. But at that moment, a stratagem entered George's head. He was by nature a very straightforward sort of man – not a man given to devious thoughts. And yet this was a very devious thought indeed. What if he delayed the proceedings at every opportunity – how would the Judge react? It was a dangerous tactic: he wanted the Judge to grant in favour of the submission and he might, just might, do that to avoid the case dragging on. On the other hand he might just react in the opposite way. This errant thought stung him, but he had no time to think it through or use his analytical thought processes as he had been trained to do. And yet it was a thought that seemed to take him over.

'Your Honour will have read the submission papers and will know that this is a very complicated case involving a myriad of legislation and case law.' He raised his eyes and threw an inquisitive look at the Judge.

The judge, realising he was expected to respond, thought for a moment and then nodded his agreement.

At that moment, George Carmichael knew the Judge had not read the papers, for this was not a complicated case - in fact quite the opposite; it was very clear cut. He shot a look into the gallery and saw his daughter's puzzlement. Giving her a surreptitious smile, he cleared his throat and began to recite the statute on which his submission was based. He quickly ran out of legislation, so started to make it up. He threw totally fictitious statute and case-law at the Judge and saw bewilderment enter the ponderous features. If he overdid it then the judge would realise he was being duped, but George gambled on the fact that the better part of a bottle of Burgundy had gone down the Judge's gullet with his lunch and befuddled his senses. Out of the corner of his eye he could see that Julia was leaning forward, mouth agape; he dared not look at her, but continued unabated.

He was in mid-sentence when the Judge raised his hand, his palm facing outwards as though he was halting traffic. George's heart missed a beat; had he pushed his stratagem beyond its boundaries?

'I'll stop you there, Mr Carmichael. I have already read the papers and studied the statute on which the submission is based. I am satisfied that it is soundly based in law. Very well, you may have your retrial.' He stood immediately and the usher called out for everyone to rise. George Carmichael bowed sycophantically. He knew that in the cold light of day the Judge would realise he had been duped, but the man could do nothing about it without admitting his own foolishness and his failure to read the papers beforehand.

As he disappeared through the Judge's doorway, George swung round and winked delightedly up at his daughter.

Her face was jubilant. She sent him a beaming smile and mouthed, *'Oh well done, Father, well done indeed!'*

CHAPTER 14

Frankfurt 1819

Time had stood still for me. At the very edge of my consciousness there was the sound of footsteps running up the steps to our rooms. I noticed that it was still light and became aware of Uncle Meno standing at the door. I turned my head slowly towards him, but I hardly acknowledged him; understanding of my surroundings was still denied me. I looked down at the doctor's bag he was carrying, his knuckles white as he took in the sight before him. I saw blood on his hand; his intense grip was causing his nails to bite into his palms as they wrapped venomously around the handle.

My awareness began to return at the sight of that black bag. I thought to myself that it was redundant, too late to be of any possible use, but I didn't say anything to Uncle Meno. He went down on one knee to take the pulse of Papa, but the body had already begun to go cold. He did the same with Mama and then Henriette, but their broken bodies were lifeless. He came to me and tried to prise Moses from my arms, but I wouldn't let go. He felt for the pulse at my brother's slender neck whilst I still held him tight – again, nothing.

'I've been out to see a patient,' he said. It was supposed, I think, to be an explanation of some sort, but neither of us saw it as anything more than useless redundant words. After a few silent introspective minutes he added, 'My patient was a wealthy merchant; he suggested that it would be wise to stay off the street whilst the mob was running.'

'He was probably right.' My words were as involuntary as were Uncle Meno's. I didn't look at him as I spoke.

'He offered me his home as sanctuary.' Uncle Meno didn't look at me either.

'That was good of him,' I mumbled at the floor.

We were both overtaken by a sort of torpor. There were practical things that needed to be done, but somehow we were both helpless in the face of what had happened. Neither of us could speak of it; we sat there on the floor for... well, I don't know how long we sat there; the shock of our sudden bereavement and the unimaginable violence that had caused it produced a kind of inertia in us.

Eventually, Uncle Meno spoke. 'I don't understand,' he turned and looked at me intently for the first time, 'the front of the house is damaged but there is no indication that they forced an entry. All my valuable equipment is still here. So why did they do this?'

'You're a doctor. Perhaps it was at the back of their minds that they might need you and your equipment at some time.'

Uncle Meno nodded as I spoke, but he wasn't convinced. 'When I walked back I saw much of the damage, Loeb. It's been about vandalising property. Some homes have even been burned down. Those of us caught on the street have been beaten, some very badly. I attended some on my way back, but nobody else seems to have died after their homes were invaded. It's because Felix was seen as an agitator, isn't it? Somebody has specifically led the mob here to find him.' His words were calm and laced with impotence, but he nodded again, this time in recognition that his thoughts, his reasoning, were correct.

I turned and looked back at him, equally as intently. Revulsion was growing inside me. His words had made me assess what had happened and I knew he was wrong. At that moment hatred was born within me. 'It was nothing to do with being an agitator,' I spat the words, 'the answer is much nearer home.'

'What do you mean, Loeb?'

'I mean Frau Breitner.'

'Surely you can't be serious. She's a caustic woman, I'll grant you that, but it's no reasons to suspect that... that she could do anything like *this*.'

'I saw her leave with the mob,' I said, 'and I saw the self-satisfied expression on her acidic, vengeful face. She was behind this, she was the instigator; I am sure of it. She fired up the mob, led them up our stairs, set them on...' I couldn't complete the sentence.

'What are you saying Loeb?'

'I'm saying she has taken her revenge.'

'Revenge? But this is *murder*. It's not some neighbourhood squabble!'

'Nevertheless, this is her revenge. For my beating her son, for Moses taunting her; for us being Jewish and having the temerity to live on the same street as her.' I looked up at Uncle Meno, saw the look of disbelief on his face, but I knew I was right. 'You don't believe me, but she was at the heart of what happened here today. I saw her. Someone tipped the mob over the edge. They were intent on wanton wreckage, vandalism, causing as much damage as they could. But then it was converted into a bloodlust. Someone manipulated that mob to do this terrible thing, and that person was Frau Breitner.'

Uncle Meno looked down at the floor, the magnitude of what I had said consuming him. His eyes stared blankly, as though by looking inward he could pierce his tumultuous thoughts. I started to rock, Moses still in my arms. I did not want to let go of him. If I let go then I knew that I would be alone in the wicked world. It was as if Uncle Meno and I were suddenly separated from each other by an invisible wall; as if we were not even in the same room.

Backwards and forwards I rocked; I think I went into a trance. But then fatigue came to my aid. I had run a distance more than that of the legendary Pheidippides, the Greek messenger who was sent from the town of Marathon to Athens to announce that the Persians had been defeated. Why does that stray fact now enter my mind as I try to explain what happened on that terrible bloody day? Ah! Perhaps because it is a fact that Papa had told me, a story he had taught me. Fatigue now overwhelmed me; the fear and the adrenalin that had kept me going were gone, there were no reserves left. I was now as empty physically as I was empty emotionally. I was a husk. I drifted away into a fitful sleep, a black swirling darkness of disturbed images of death, of body-twitching anguish, of tormented suffering voices, of cries of anguished fear.

When I awoke I was covered by a blanket, it was light again and I must have slept many hours. It was a new day. The candle was burnt out; just a congealed dribble of molten wax to remind me of the horrors of the day before. I lay there for a few seconds not quite sure where I was, but then a second wave of anguish hit me; the brutal events of the previous day returning to torment me again. I sat up, looked around, but the bodies of my dead family were gone. Even Moses had been taken from my sleeping arms. Uncle Meno had done what he had to; he was a doctor and doctors know about death and what to do. He was being supportive, but I resented him for it; I resented him with all the substance of my being. To deal with the bodies was part of my grieving process and he had robbed me of that; he was little more than a thief in the night. At that moment he had driven a mammoth wedge between us, and he did so without knowing it. I felt utterly alone in the world, a cruel and vindictive world. We should have been able to help each other, but I denied all access to my lovable, kind Uncle Meno. The world was now a bleaker place, without beauty, without hope, without humanity. It was a dark ugly place, a place unfit for the likes of good people; good people like Mama and Papa, like Henriette and Moses. Perhaps, that was why God had taken them from me.

CHAPTER 15

London 1823.

Happy to be the bearer of good news, Julia could barely contain herself as the gaoler led her through the dark corridors. She hardly noticed the stink of her surroundings, tapping her foot as she waited for the door to be unlocked and pushing passed her obsequious escort into the cell. The moment she saw the prisoner, the words burst out of her, 'Oh, David! David! You have your retrial. You should have *seen* Father. He was *wonderful.*'

'Now calm down Julia; why don't you begin at the beginning?' David laughed, his English near perfect now. He had been both reading and talking extensively, the latter with a sickly man in the next cell, though they had to speak into the corridor through the doors of their cells to be heard.

Julia realised she was gushing and felt her face suffuse with warmth. Blushing, she put her hand to her bosom and swallowed hard, forcing herself to take off her gloves, then her bonnet and finally her cape, her fingers fumbling with the tie. David took the garments from her, folded the cape neatly, put it on his desk and offered her his stool; it was again the only one available. She wore a brocade gown that was really much too grand for a visit to this gloomy, grimy gaol, but she had chosen it without any rational thought – deep down she had wanted to look attractive for him.

The gaoler lingered outside the cell rattling his keys, his sparse-toothed grin anticipating a small coin for his foul-breathed attention. Julia was too excited to respond to him. He knuckled his forehead anyway and with an exaggerated sigh disappeared down the corridor, mumbling to himself in disappointment.

Arranging herself on the stool, Julia nodded her thanks and said, 'I must tell you; it really *was* wonderful. I was there, David, I saw it all!' She knew she was gushing again, but couldn't help herself. It was as though a starting pistol had gone off in her head. It was not even the best place to start her story, but she continued anyway.

His face alight with eager anticipation, David moved to sit on the corner of his rickety desk and looked down at her intently, his lips lifting in a smile as she told him of the hearing, her father's strategy and how he had duped the Judge. She spared no detail and he listened, nodding encouragement each time she paused for breath.

'I couldn't understand what Father was up to, but then the Judge just seemed to lose interest and ordered the retrial; it was wonderful,' she said again.

David put his head back and laughed; his darkly handsome face almost boyish with relief. 'That is wonderful news indeed! I will sleep easier knowing the hangman is not waiting round the corner for me after all.'

Julia shuddered; the spectre of a hanging abruptly stealing her elation. She saw again in her mind's eye the terrible image of David swinging on the end of a rope, his eyes bulging, lips blue, engorged tongue, black, protruding from his lips as the strangling noose tightened ever more firmly round his neck. She felt her heart pounding, the blood rushing in her ears; heard the sound of keys being turned in a lock somewhere deep in the gaol, and then the sound of a cell door being slammed shut. There was a moan from an inmate further down the corridor. Julia's excitement evaporated as caution overtook her. 'We have not won *yet,* my dear.' She reached up and put her hand on his.

David's reaction was ambivalent. That mere touch was both tender yet arousing; it was something he had longed for, to feel her touch on his skin, but then he became aware of his own condition. Months without bathing, the weeks of accumulated sweat acrid and powerful on his body, the dirt ingrained in the skin of his hands. He had grown used to the foul smells of urine and faeces; it had not registered in his mind now for weeks, but her soft, intimate gesture brought it all back to him with repellent clarity. She seemed such a fragrant creature, while he was hesitant, unworthy. Regretfully, he pulled his hand away, painfully aware of the affect of his rejection sparking in Julia's eyes.

They sat silently for some moments, uncomfortable, until Julia suddenly remembered what she had brought with her. 'Oh, I almost forgot,' she said, unfolding the napkin she had been holding on her lap. 'I have brought you a slice of game pie with some boiled roots. They're both cold by now I'm afraid, but it is good fare.' She placed the bundle on the small desk, shuffling his papers to find room, and urging him to eat. He did so, reluctantly at first. Using the fork she had brought, he started to pick at the pie and the roots, embarrassed that she should see him this way, but then his hunger took over and he started to devour it.

'Oh, and some cheese and bread for later,' Julia retrieved from her satchel a second folded napkin and placed it on the desk on top of his papers, there being no other room. 'Is the food so bad here, David?'

He put his head on one side in contemplation, but continued to eat, saying between mouthfuls, 'It's not too bad; bread and cocoa for breakfast, bread and soup for dinner and bread and gruel for supper. I think there is supposed to be meat in the soup, but the money for it is probably stolen by the prison warders.'

When he had finished eating, he wiped his mouth with the napkin in a deliberate display of good manners then returned to their earlier conversation. 'It is only a *stay* of execution, I realise that my dear Julia, but I do believe the nights will not be as disturbing as before.' He smiled at her to reassure her.

That smile was welcoming to Julia, but it was overshadowed by those large dreamy blue eyes of his. They took her attention as they always seemed to do. For a moment she just lost herself in them, but then realised they were prompting her to respond. She smiled up at him, some of her initial enthusiasm returning to her. 'Oh yes, let us hope so,' she said.

Sliding from his perch on the edge of the desk he leaned towards her until they were almost touching then immediately leaned back again, his reticence being dominant.

Julia flushed, her heart missing a beat at the expectation that did not materialise, a small gasp escaping from her lips.

'So where do we go from here?' he said.

'We need to work hard, David, to prepare your case.'

'I'm sure that I can help with that – what can I be doing?'

'We need to show that your alternative version of events is credible; that is, we need to show that you are of good character, a man of honour, a man to be believed. We want the jury to believe what you say to them. Character witnesses would be very helpful. Is there nobody in this country who will stand and speak for you?'

'No – I know nobody here.'

'What about in Germany. Is there somebody who would come to England and speak on your behalf?'

'I have not been in Frankfurt since 1819, when I was just seventeen years old.'

'But your family are there are they not? Your brothers and sisters; can they not help?'

There was a silence that lasted for some moments and she saw that his thoughts were far away. When he turned and spoke, his voice was small and hesitant. 'No I have no family, no family at all.'

Julia's eyes welled with compassion, 'None at all?'

'No; none at all,' he confirmed.

She stared at him appalled, her sympathy for him mounting. Without thinking, she once more reached out and put her hand on his, but this time he cupped it with his other hand and the significance of the gesture manifested itself to her. Gently she withdrew her hand from his grasp and moved the conversation along, 'Then where were you after Frankfurt? I had not realised you had not come direct from there.'

He looked down as if some forgotten thought had taken him and entering a reverie he recited:

'From here I must depart,
My wondering staff in hand,
To Holland or to England,
In search of a free land.'

There was silence for a few moments as Julia assimilated his words then she spoke, 'Is that one of your poems, David?'

'No, it's by Adalbert von Chamisso, a German poet, surprisingly, but he was an intellectual. He was commenting on the options available to the Jewish intellectuals in Germany.' David's words were quiet, as if taken by this unexpected memory; then he returned to the original question, his voice more assertive, 'I was in Hamburg for the last year; before that I just travelled around Europe.'

'I could send an agent to Hamburg. Can you think of anyone who would stand for you from there?'

'I don't know.'

'What about an employer?'

'I will have to think hard about that.'

I think you should David,' she said, aware that for some reason he was being evasive. 'It's important.'

CHAPTER 16

Frankfurt 1819

'If you must go, leave it a few days, Loeb. At least until after the funeral and all this trouble dies down.'

Sitting in Uncle Meno's consulting room I looked up at him and saw the concern in his face. Those large sunken eyes that had always had the hint of mischief in them were now just deep pools of anxiety. The orthodox Jewish members of our family had long since rejected us, and Papa in turn had rejected their version of Jewishness. The two of us were all that was left of our family. He was the only family I had, but I was rejecting him. We should have been a support for each other, and looking back I probably let him down. He was a widower; his wife had contracted scarlet fever and died when it turned into pneumonia. He had no children of his own and had been part of our extended family for years. In his way, he must have been as devastated as I was, yet I was leaving him alone to face the rest of his life in abject isolation. But I was only seventeen coming up eighteen; not only had my family been killed, but everything I had been brought up to believe in had been wrenched away at stroke. I wanted to be a German Jew and contribute to my country as such, but that country had made it brutally clear that it did not want *me*. Everything that had underpinned what made me *me* was gone. I did not know who I was anymore. I was just overwhelmed with a feeling of emptiness and a desire to leave everything behind me; to get away from Frankfurt; to leave this awful city that held such indescribable terror and devastation; to run away. I knew Uncle Meno would deal with everything properly and the thought of attending the funeral was more than I could bear. I had said my goodbyes yesterday, weeping over the bodies of all that I held dear. Now, those doleful eyes looking down on me made me feel traitorous and for some moments I was tempted to reconsider my decision.

I stood and went to the window and looked out on the street, not really seeing; my thoughts elsewhere. Uncle Meno came and stood beside me, put his arm on my shoulder but he did not speak. He must have desperately wanted me to stay, but he must have also sensed the turmoil within me and afforded me the respect to make up my own mind. But then I became aware of something strange happening outside. There were people walking by our house. Nothing unusual in that, but it was as though it was a Sunday and the Lutherans were going to church, or just out for a leisurely walk in the city on their day of rest. I looked at Uncle Meno and he looked back at me, puzzlement in his face, gesturing that he too had sensed something unusual.

Herr Muller, the blacksmith rode by in his carriage. 'You know he hates Jews, don't you?' I said.

'No, my boy, he hates everybody, because they won't pay their bills. People pay my bills on time because they want to make sure that I will be there to treat them if they are ill, but the blacksmith is not so lucky.'

I had not thought of it that way before.

Herr Schwarzkopf passed by. He worked at the City Hall, and should have been at work hours ago. He looked in the window and saw us looking out at him. He nodded back at us, but it was more in embarrassment than courtesy. 'You know that he is drunk by the time he gets home of an evening,' I said.

'I know, he stops off at the tavern straight from work. He consults me about his liver. The man will die young, I'm afraid.'

Three *fräuleins*, whom I did not recognise, came into view chattering profusely amongst each other, their bonneted heads bobbing in the summer sun. They stopped as they reached the front of our house, as if they were holding their breath, and then the chattering burst out again as they passed us by. They were wearing their Sunday best clothes, silk dresses - *trachts* as they were called - hand embroidered, decorated with beads and with lace trimmings, each a different shade of blue; out for a relaxing walk in the summer sun.

And then the reality of what was happening hit us both at the same time. We looked at each other. They had come to gawp. We were the celebrity family, the place where the Jews had been killed. It probably was not anti-Semitic, just that we were news. The word must have gone around like wildfire and people had come merely to stare. A combination of pity, embarrassment and hatred had enticed them, but most of all they had that need to look, the way people stare at an awful accident, like when a runaway cart knocks down a child in the street and even when you didn't want to see it, you just couldn't look away. But we were no accident! I felt uncomfortable, as if we were in a goldfish bowl, but the water in our particular bowl was scarlet from the spilling of blood. Rage grew within me. I was so angry I could hardly breathe. How dare they, I thought to myself. I swung away from the window, made to set off out of the house to confront these gawping people, but Uncle Meno grabbed me by the shoulder.

'Let time pass a few days before you...' his words tailed away, his advice was sound but I was not in the mood to listen.

'They think we got what we deserved, don't they, our German neighbours; that's what they think don't they? That we were getting above ourselves, living in the same neighbourhood as them. That we belong back in the *Judengasse?*'

'Some, my boy, but not all; most are just silly people letting their curiosity get the better of their wits.'

But then came the final insult: Frau Breitner, her heavy-bosomed gait unmistakable. For her there was no pretence to be 'just passing'. She was wearing her house clothes not even her street clothes. She stopped in front of our house, turned and looked in. It was not a sideways glance as she passed. Hands on her hips, it was a challenging presence as if she had come to take her prize – and that prize was that she wanted us to know her culpability in the events of yesterday.

My red rage and repulsion at the sight of her ugly features were so intense I almost vomited. It was at that moment that my resolve returned. I turned back to Uncle Meno; the sight of Frau Breitner had overridden his mournful look imploring me to stay.

'I will go today; I have to,' I announced. I didn't have to, but it seemed a perfectly rational thing to say at the time.

Uncle Meno sighed heavily and looked down at the floor in resignation. He fumbled in his waistcoat pocket and took out a bunch of keys, selected one and with a small shrug of his shoulders went to his desk, which had miraculously escaped the attentions of the mob. He opened the bottom drawer and took out a heavy mahogany box. He then selected another key to open it and counted out most of the contents of the box, putting them in a purse for me.

Shaking my head I moved away from the window, 'I can't take all this money from you,' I said.

'And who else will I leave it to?' He spoke forcefully, making it clear that rejection was not an option. 'Take off your frock-coat,' he said.

I gave it to him, unsure of what he had in mind, and then I watched as he searched out a surgical needle and thread and began expertly to sew some of the coins from the purse into the lining of my jacket; he was more comfortable with the surgical needle than a sewing needle.

Leaving him to it, I went upstairs to my room and packed a few items of clothing into the same hip bag that I had taken to Gießen. Two extra pairs of breeches, two pairs of stockings, two pairs of drawers, and the razor that Mama had bought me the day I fought with Oliver Breitner. I left room for the best frock-coat, when Uncle Meno had fished sewing the coins into it. I then sought out a small travel chest from Papa's and Mama's room. The intention was to put all my other belongings in it and then send for it at a later date. It was less than half full when I had gathered together all my things and I realized how little I actually owned.

I took some lunch with Uncle Meno, black-bread and cheese washed down with *apfelwein*. We didn't say much to each other.

There was so much to say, but neither of us could say it. I remember that my mouth was dry and the rye grain bread was so hard to swallow and that I needed to gulp it down with the *apfelwein*. The silence was deafening and the minutes crawled by, marked by the ticking of the wall clock. I loved my Uncle Meno, but I just wanted to get away and I think he sensed that. I finished eating before he did, the last few mouthfuls gulped down noisily. He saw that I had finished and he pushed his plate away, his meal only half eaten.

'Do you have a consultation this afternoon,' I asked, not looking at him as I spoke. I wanted to avoid his eyes. It was a crass thing to say. It was transparent and exposed my impatience to get away - but he was already aware of that.

'Yes, a wealthy merchant's wife, with bunions,' he paused, 'but I expect that she won't want to visit the home of a Jew in view of the riots - she won't come.'

I stood up. It was a gesture that I intended to leave and he followed by standing as well. 'Well, I'll need to go if I'm to put the city behind me by the time it gets dark,' I said.

'Have you decided where you are headed, my boy?'

I nodded, 'England, eventually. That country has a reputation for tolerance, but in the meantime I'll head north and make for the coast. See if I can get some work on the way.'

'Look, my boy,' Uncle Meno came and stood before me deliberately, put a hand on each of my shoulders and gazed intently into my eyes, forcing me to look at him. 'Now you take care of yourself, do you hear me?'

'I will.' My words were hollow, no more than a mumbled, unthinking response, a reflex.

'No, I mean it, Loeb. Now you take care.' He pulled me towards him and embraced me warmly. I could feel that he was trembling. I embraced him back and we stood for some minutes just holding each other. 'And don't let pride keep you away. If things don't go right for you, then you come straight back. There will always be a home for you here.'

'I will.' I said it without conviction.

'No, you must promise me.' He was insistent.

'I promise, Uncle Meno.'

'Good.' He released me from the embrace, reached into his pocket, took out his fob watch and pressed it into my hand. It was a parting gift and I knew better than to question him again. He ruffled my hair forcefully as if I were a young boy again. It was an odd thing to do, yet somehow it was more communicative that any of the words we had spoken that day. It brought a smile to both our faces and temporarily cast away the countenance of bereavement that had taken us.

I set off with a sense of purpose; walking down our street I passed Frau Breitner's house. I stopped outside; I cannot say why I did it, unless I was just carrying my anger with me. Oliver Breitner came to the door and leant against the doorframe. I did not know that he was home; perhaps his mother had sent word to him of what had happened. He looked at me with a self-satisfied expression on his face as if revenge was a sugar-sweet delight. I had not just beaten him in a fight I had humiliated him before his friends. I felt that anger rising within me and wanted to beat him again. He must have sensed that for he stood upright and went back into his house the smirk still fixed on his face as he did so.

I wanted to get as far away from the city as I could. I made my way through the side streets and the alleys thinking there would be less trouble that way. It was a miscalculation on my part, however. The Militia was patrolling the main streets; it was away from them that those intent on mischief were gathering. It was not that far to the city limits even by this circuitous route and I expected to be away and putting miles between me and Frankfurt very quickly. I emerged from an alley and came, unexpectedly, upon a mob of about twenty strong. I stopped, startled; was looked up and down by those immediately in front of me, but I wasn't afraid. I was tall, blue eyed, not dressed in the traditional black of the Jew. And then a cry went up, '*Hep-*

Hep and the mob took off away from me. Those near me started to follow but one youth turned, looked back at me, puzzled. He stopped and came back.

'Are you not coming, friend? It looks as if they have found a Jew,' he said.

The anger within me was not far below the surface and it overrode my sense of self preservation. 'You have found one too, my friend.' I shouted. My meaning seemed at first to pass him by. He was unsure of what I was saying, but then my words crystallized in his mind.

'You?' It was all he could say.

'Yes me. I am a Jew – so what are you going to do about it, eh?'

He froze and looked about him at the mob running away. He seemed to sense his own personal danger at that point and I saw him open his mouth to cry out to them. I think that he was going to shout '*Hep-Hep*', but before he could I was on him. The impact of my body forced him backwards, off-balance. At the same time I swung my arm and my fist hit him powerfully in the face on his way down. His nose exploded in blood and then he hit the back of his head on the ground. He was groggy. I stood over him and I could see that, but the anger in me made me want to hit him again and again whilst he was down. It was transference – it was Oliver Breitner who I wanted to hurt, but I had transferred that to this poor lad. As I bunched my fist, I heard a cry from down the street; my assault had been seen. The cry of '*Hep-Hep*' was now coming back towards me. My sense of self preservation returned to me and I started running again. I knew I was an exceptional runner and I did not fear being captured. I believed that I could outrun any of them.

I was weighed down by my hip bag but even then I was easily outpacing my pursuers. The cross-strap across my shoulder affected my equilibrium, but I was still confident. The sound of the '*Hep Hep*' cry carried ahead of the pursuers and was taken up by others. I ran into a group of men. There was surprise on their faces but I pulled free and changed my direction. They realized that I was the subject of the cries–and immediately took off after me; they were fresh and only a few paces behind. I had adopted a long range gait but they were sprinting to catch me up. I had to respond and did so to put distance between them and myself. At the next corner, however, the scenario happened again. A new bunch of pursuers entered the chase and I had to sprint again. I looked over my shoulder and for the first time fear took me. They were gaining on me and I knew that eventually someone with a fresh pair of legs would catch me and hold me until the mob caught up.

And then I felt a hand clasp at my left shoulder. I swung my left arm violently and my elbow connected powerfully with the owner's face. I tried to continue to run through this; I heard a yelp as the man stopped. I was fearful of looking round; panic was keeping me going. Breathing deeply, I listened intently for a few seconds for the sound of footsteps behind me, but I could not hear any. As quickly as I could I turned. My pursuers had stopped to help the man I'd hit, but he was waving them on. It was a small respite. I had to continue running. I could see the end of the city ahead of me and the fields beyond. But then the 'Hep Hep' cry was taken up again and a new bunch of fresh pursuers lurched after me. I ran into a field hoping that I was clear and that they would return to the city, but I continued to hear the cries behind me.

My mind seemed to acquire the cunning of the fox. I needed to outrun them and hopefully, now I had left the city behind, no new pursuers would join in. Good as I was at running, however, I couldn't maintain this pace. I needed to go to ground – yes that's what I needed. But then a sharp pain pierced my consciousness; I found myself on one knee. A warm sensation was apparent on my scalp moving slowly down my forehead. I put my hand to my head; looked at the bright redness of my bloodstained fingers. I felt slightly dazed; realised I had been hit. I looked backwards down the field and saw just one pursuer. I had outrun them all but him. He too had now stopped; he must have picked up a stone and thrown it at me then, seeing me fall, he set off towards me again, shouting, using noise as a weapon, shrieking as he came closer – probably also trying to convey to his gang members that the chase was still on.

I shook my head in an attempt to shake the dizziness from my brain and rose to my feet in one movement, still groggy but the need to defend myself was intact. *Go! Go!* My mind said to me, *Get yourself out of here.* My legs at first were reluctant to obey, but that instinct to flee overrode them.

What happened next will probably never be totally clear to me; I have no more than a vague, disjointed recollection of events. Voices shouting, 'He's over there!' I was desperate to get away but unable to do so; diving into the undergrowth, heart pounding. I heard footsteps running towards me then diminishing in the distance. Crack! A stick whacked into the canopy of foliage above me. Silence, *I'm safe*, but then... men's voices, raised in anger. Incoherence. Cries delivered in annoyance that their quarry had escaped and me, cowering beneath the foliage while danger receded, only for it to return. My senses muzzy, yet somehow my brain responding to fear, able to growl silent instructions to my body, *Wait here, wait here.* Holding my breath, *Stay here, be quiet! BE QUIET!* Silence again – waiting - still silence; then coming out into bright sunlight from my heavily shaded hiding place. *Get out! Get out! Run like hell! Wait here. Be quiet, be quiet. Yes! yes! I think I'm safe now;* heart continuing to beat, thumping against my chest. Gulping for air as exhaustion gripped my tired body, but still having to run. *I must be out of sight of them now, I should be safe. A hiding place - good God, yes a hiding place. There - a copse, run for it!*

As I think about it now, years later, I see the images in my head as in a shattered mirror: the ground speeding beneath my feet; I hear again the chomp of last year's autumn leaves, semi-decayed beneath my pounding steps, disturbed from their silent resting place in the middle of the copse. The bright sunlight suddenly dimmed as if I were back in the *Judengasse*. Then I saw a fallen tree, the roots exposed, standing vertically, the soil unearthed by its fall so that a dark void had been created beneath it; a God-given hiding place. I remember thinking, *I don't know if I can get there? I need to rest. Need to sleep. No! Must stay awake, alert – must keep going; run for the fallen tree. Must keep going.* Slithering in between rotting roots – down, down, down - it's warm, it's dry, *I'm safe, I can rest now - can't I?*

CHAPTER 17

London 1823.

'Have you thought of someone to stand for you in court?' Julia took off her bonnet without invitation and then handed her cloak to David. It was wet, the day outside drab and overcast, and what little light permeated down to the cells was diminished even further. David had lit a candle, and she peered at him through a small arch of yellow light.

'No, but I have started to write poetry again.' It was a blatant piece of diversion but it went unnoticed.

'Poetry, but that's wonderful, David. May I read it?

'I thought that I might read it to you, if that's alright?'

'Of course it is, but I have no German to understand it.'

'I have written it in English; especially for you,' he added.

She looked at him expectantly, adjusting herself on the solitary stool to signal that she was ready. He lifted a pile of papers from the corner of the crumbling desk and started to speak the words. The stool was far from comfortable but soon that discomfort passed from her mind, the rich tones of his voice having a mesmerising affect on her. On the wings of his beautiful words she was transported away from the filthy, grimy conditions of that unspeakable place. Julia knew it was quite common for young women these days to spend hours reading poetry or romantic fiction to fill the long hours of boredom. She had never subscribed to this; to her own mind, she had spent her time constructively, learning the law and helping her father. But now, in the same way as those empty-headed young women that she so despised, she was transported to some magical place. She gazed at David as he spoke and his words seemed to emanate from those large, dreamy eyes. She was transfixed by them. It was as though they were in sharp focus at the hub of her vision, whilst everything else was increasingly diffused the further they were from those deep blue pools. The words were familiar to him and the text was necessary only as a reminder, so that his gaze spent longer on her than on the paper he held. Previously, she had found the effects of his stare alarming, but now she just let his eyes caress her.

When he reached the end of the first poem she let out a long, deep sigh. For some moments no words formed on her lips; it was a sigh of pure contentment. But his eyes were asking her to respond and she eventually realised that. When the words formed they were superficial and gushing. 'That was wonderful, David.'

'Wonderful?' The word was not enough for him. He wanted to know why she thought that.

'I didn't know you wrote romantic poetry, David?'

It was not the response he wanted but he answered anyway. 'I do not,' he said abruptly. 'I normally write about the wrongs of the world, but this took me by surprise.' He shrugged, said with a shy smile, 'I don't know where it came from.'

He read some more of his poems to her. Julia wallowed in every phrase, immersed herself in every word; every syllable. Her name was not mentioned, but she accepted every word as if it was directed at her, as if it was about her.

David could see she was rapt and was delighted by her response. He knew she was unaware he was being dishonest with her; that he was reading the poetry because he did not want to discuss his past; it was a tactic. Now, in doing so, he was forced to ask the question of himself. Why did he feel the need to write romantic poetry? He had only met this young woman a handful of times, yet he now realised he had feelings for her; feelings that went beyond mere affection. She was a fragrant breath of spring in his filthy existence in this festering hell-hole. It was love born out of adversity; much as a seriously ill patient struggling for his life falls in love with his nurse, so he was falling in love with Julia. Whatever its genesis, it was real and he now acknowledged that fact with a shiver. Life had been such a horrendous struggle for him, there had been no opportunity for the simple love of a woman. He had not admitted to himself at the time of writing what now seemed so obvious to him; he had written the poems exclusively for Julia and what had begun as a tactic changed into a brief idyll of pleasure as he read them all out to her.

When eventually he came to the end, they began to talk. They talked for hours: about life, about injustice, about the world. As they conversed, Julia started to re-evaluate everything in her life based upon how David perceived it, so profound was his effect on her. He was tall, he was handsome, he was educated, he was passionate and he was compassionate; he was everything that she could possibly want in a man all rolled up into this David Neander.

And then the bitter pill of reality broke into their temporary transportation and forced them to swallow hard. The jangling keys of the foul-breathed gaoler poked at them from off canvas, jabbing at them until they were once again aware of the festering place in which they sat. They looked at each other and sighed heavily as if playing a disheartening duet.

'We haven't talked about your case,' Julia said. There was no commitment in her tone. She desperately wanted to return to that blissful place she had occupied just a few moments ago. 'Have you thought of anybody who can stand for you in court?'

He let his guard down temporarily. 'There is a Rabbi who could stand as a character witness for me, but I'm not sure that it would help.'

'Why ever not?' she said.

'Because that would bring an orthodox Jew into court: the beard, the ringlets?'

'But if he can confirm your character?'

'Character? The court will care little for my character; it has already found me guilty on the evidence of merely being a Jew!'

'But surely...'

David's cut across her, his lips twisted in a grimace of contempt, 'What good would sympathetic words from the mouth of a Rabbi make?'

His words were so full of bitterness that Julia, who had started to challenge him, thought better of it. 'But we must start to build a strategy, David,' she said instead.

'Yes, dear Julia, you are right and I have been thinking about that too. Tell me; am I correct in thinking that the theft of a sheep is commonly a crime of the uneducated criminal classes?'

She nodded thoughtfully, her eyebrows raised in query.

'Then I must distance myself from that perception, I think.'

Again she nodded, 'But how?'

'Do you think you could get me some translation work to do? I'm sure I can work from here. If I can show the jury that I can earn a living as a translator, even while I'm in gaol, then they will see that I had no need to steal a sheep, that I am an educated man able to earn an honest living wherever I may be.'

'Yes, yes,' Julia cried eagerly, 'of course.' It seemed so obvious to her now he had suggested it and it raised her spirits; it was something positive to do. 'Yes,' she said again, 'leave it to me. I'll use my father's contacts.'

CHAPTER 18

Frankfurt 1819

It was dawn and another day when I emerged from my hiding place. I was stiff, having slept contorted amongst the roots. I was still clutching my hip bag. I had kept hold of it tightly all the time that had I had been pursued, grasping it as I ran. The irony then hit me and I wondered to myself if my life was worth more than the thalers, the silver coins that were sewn into the lining of my best coat. Should I have discarded the bag and saved myself more easily? I started to walk, but without any great purpose. After about half an hour, I came upon a stream that was reduced to little more than a trickle by the summer drought. I crouched down to drink, my head pounding as I bent over. I lifted the water in the palm of my hand; it was cold and refreshing on my tongue, invigorating in my mouth. I touched my forehead gingerly with a delicately probing finger, felt the congealed blood by the hairline. I cleansed it with the running water, then sat back on the bank of the stream and looked around.

I was now out of sight of the city; the place was deserted, not a soul was in sight. I reached into my pocket for Uncle Meno's fob watch and was relieved to hear it still ticking as I opened the cover – it had not been broken. It was only twenty minutes after six and there was nobody at work in the fields yet. I wound it and fastened the fob to my lapel buttonhole so that the watch was allowed to rest in my breast pocket. I stood, feeling a little better, not as light-headed.

I set off to walk. There was no destination in mind, other than to just head north. I walked and walked, but most of the countryside passed me by without it registering in my mind. My thoughts swirled vindictively around and around in my head, horrible mental images of the lifeless bodies of my family stung my senses, making me weep. I suppose that I was grieving -

grieving in the only way that was open to me. Walking and walking; my emotions moving from despair to anger from despondency to anguish, thoughts fighting with thoughts. Copious tears flowed down my face as the full depth of my misery overwhelmed me, but then that was chased away by those vindictive feelings of revenge. I was devastated, but I continued to walk. Hour after hour I walked, and then the hours turned into days. I ate at taverns along the way. Sometimes I slept rough, but at other times I converted some of the thalers into marks and used them to buy me a room and some vittles for the night. I did not speak to anybody intentionally, but the rural folk were friendly to me and after a few days I began to respond to them in the same way. My hatred at that appalling time for all things German was lessened slightly by these kind-hearted people; their small acts of anonymous generosity probably stopped me from turning into a rabid vengeful creature. With each step, I put more distance between me and that awful city of Frankfurt and those grotesque events - that was the intention; to leave those nightmare memories behind. If only it was as easy to wipe them from my mind.

On one night I remember that I awoke with a start after a tormenting dream, where the face of Moses had swirled vindictively before me asking why I had not come to save him - the way I had previously saved him from Oliver Brietner. I was sweating despite being in the open air, sleeping rough. I did not want to close my eyes again in case the dream returned so I rolled over on my back and stared at the sky. It was cloudless and there was that canopy of stars; horizon to horizon. I thought again about my future, but now there was no ambition left in me, the optimism of that young boy had gone, cast away by those awful events.

I walked past Friedrichdorf, Gießen, Siegen, and Hagen, mostly by-passing these towns and stopping in villages. And still I walked, mile after miserable mile, hour after wretched hour, day after desolate day until I eventually entered Dortmund. The bustle of the city temporarily snapped me out of my reverie. I became aware that my feet ached. I looked down at my shoes and realised that they now had holes in them. I sought out a cobbler's shop to buy a new pair and caught a sight of myself in his shop window. It was a shock: initially I did not recognise the unkempt, bearded man looking back at me in his dirtied shabby clothes. The cobbler chatted to me and I took the opportunity to ask him about the riots. They had spread to many of the German cities but Dortmund, it seemed, had not succumbed to this crazy, rampant anti-Semitism.

I began to notice that Dortmund had a different character to Frankfurt; it was less pretentious. Frankfurt considered itself privileged because it had been an important city state of the Holy Roman Empire, but although Dortmund itself was part of the Hanseatic League and had special status as a Free Imperial City, it seemed to me to be more down to earth, more honest. It was a wealthy trading city and a centre of the brewing trade - and beer was important to all the Germans. Now part of Prussia, it had industry that was immediately apparent to me. I don't think I made a conscious decision to stay in Dortmund, it just seemed to happen that way. I took a room, again spending Uncle Meno's money.

For days I hardly emerged from the room. I had no cooking facilities but I neglected myself, emerging only irregularly to eat. I was still in a state of turmoil, those awful memories having pursued me. I seemed to have lost my identity. My mind challenged everything I had been brought up to believe. Papa had put us in a unique position; we were Jewish by race but not entirely by creed. But it was even more subtle than that, we were *still* Jewish by creed but we were dissenters, reformers and that had put us outside the main family of Judaism. I needed something to help me make sense of what had happened to me. I was adrift without anything to cling on to.

I must have turned eighteen by myself in my room, but I didn't notice at the time, and even if I had there was no one to celebrate it with. I was utterly alone. I remember that the silence in my room was deafening; I had been used to noise; to always having my family all about me while trying to find some privacy to do my studies. Now I had that privacy and it was overwhelming.

I started going to the synagogue, believing that the answer to my abject loneliness lay in returning to the fold. I talked for hours with the Rabbi: Rabbi Baum. Baum means 'tree' in German, but he didn't match his name, well not in stature anyway. He was a tiny man, bald but with just enough hair for his ringlets to hang down the side of his face. Unshaven, of course, so that his long white beard seemed incongruous compared with the taut suntanned skin of his pate. But in other ways perhaps his name was apt. I was amazed how knowledgeable he was. He knew all about Jewish history. It was as though he had put down his own long personal roots extending into the combined knowledge of the faith. We talked about the Torah, the Holy book of Judaism; the Talmud, the source of Jewish Law; the purpose of the Universe; the gift from God to man of free will. Rabbi Baum was a wonderful little man and I grew to love him.

He knew of my father and surprisingly he had read a great deal of his work. It should have been an anathema to him but he was such a rounded man that he read it to understand a different point of view. He tried to help me come to terms with my loss and bereavement and, more complexly, the nonsensical manner of it. 'Suffering is a part of God's plan,' he told me.

My father had not neglected my Jewish history; the Rabbi would need more than simple words to reach me. 'I know,' I said, 'Jews have a history of suffering – in slavery in Egypt, in captivity in Babylon, the Romans raising the Temple to the ground.'

'Then you know that what happened to your family in Frankfurt is part of that history of suffering.'

But my faith was not strong enough for that explanation to be comforting to me. It made God seem a vengeful God. I think that Rabbi Baum saw in my eyes that the pain was undiminished. He tried to explain further to ease my troubled mind.

'The Jews have a covenant with God; He told Moses in the desert, if people would obey His law he would make them His chosen people.'

That did not help me at all. 'So the price I have to pay for being part of the chosen race is suffering?'

He smiled a kindly face at me and put his hand on mine. I think he too realised at that point that simple explanations would not be enough for me. I was not an uneducated man with a strong faith that would enable me to accept everything I was told without question. I was a problem to him. I had been brought up to challenge what I could not accept; such a temperament was incongruous with the nature of faith. He ran his hand across his bald pate in contemplation.

'God demands a sacrifice,' he said.

'So God's purpose is to test me by suffering?'

'God's purpose is a not always clear to us.'

I hated that as an answer. I thought it was intellectually bankrupt. When you have no reasoned argument left, you revert to the *God works in mysterious ways,* explanation. I was not going to let that go.

'If He is testing me, then I can understand that,' I said, 'but why did He punish the innocent; Henriette and Moses.' My voice cracked when I said their names. 'What sort of a God does that?' I wept.

'Ah Loeb, He is truly testing you,' he said. He stood and put his arms around me in a comforting embrace. I buried my head in his shoulder and wept uncontrollably. I remained seated but I was still as tall as he. I felt that I had won the intellectual debate, but the victory left me hollow. There was no comfort in it, because deep down I did not want to win. I wanted to be comforted by wise words.

'He gave us the gift of free will,' Rabbi Baum said quietly into my shoulder, 'but know He will punish the wicked.'

There was further debate in those words, but I did not continue, because paradoxically they gave me some perverse comfort. The thought of Fraulein Breitner being punished by a vengeful God was strangely satisfying. It went some way to sating my thirst for revenge.

He invited me to study with him. 'The study of the Torah is above the commandments,' he would say, 'and Torah study is compulsory for every Jew.' I did so willingly for a time although I was not ignorant of the things that I was being taught. Father had schooled me well, even though we had not been members of the synagogue. I remained argumentative but deep down I was searching for something that would make sense of what had happened to me.

Rabbi Baum got me some work as an interpreter. Working for Jewish merchants, I translated Yiddish to German, even though my Yiddish was not fluent, but also German to French. Occasionally I translated some Latin to German for some legal gentlemen, but mostly it was commerce. As the months passed I became desperate to rediscover the Jew in me; I wanted that foundation, I wanted the stability it would give me. I stopped shaving and grew my hair in the Jewish style; wore a *Kipa*, the skull cap. I dressed formally and wore a black hat when out. I was identifying myself to the world as a Jew; I wore the uniform. Despite being one meter, eighty-three tall, and blue-eyed, I now looked to be what I was: a Jew, and I was proud of it.

CHAPTER 19

London 1823

Julia approached the two great and imposing wrought-iron gates of a London residence, its splendour proclaiming to the world the status of its owner. She stood for a moment, head and eyes raised, as she looked through the railings to the lavish property within and felt insignificant before it. This was London's fashionable West End, and this property was part of the very beating heart of it. There were few, if any, residences finer than this. This was the London residence of Nathan Rothschild.

Julia had been busying herself arranging for translation work to be undertaken by David. It was a task at which she had been very successful. Initially, much of the work had been obtained as an indulgence to her or her father, but the completed work was of such a high standard that she had little difficulty in finding repeat work for David to take on. She was pleased about this; it would establish his character in the eyes of the court when his case again came to trial. It was part of her plan. She was delivering and collecting the work herself, much to the dislike of her father who still thought that she should not be visiting the gaol by herself; in fact he thought she should not visit the gaol at all. But her visits to the gaol were no ordeal in her eyes; they were now her reason for living. It was only there that she could revel in David's intellect; it was only there that she could engage in his poetry; only there that she could feel herself to be fully alive. She had even admitted to herself that she was totally smitten by him, even if she would have denied it had anyone suggested that to her.

It had been David's idea to write to Nathan Rothschild; he had given her a letter and asked that she arrange for it to be delivered to the Rothschilds' business address. Julia had disregarded this request, not out of any deception, just that she wanted to maximise his chances of getting help from such an important person. Her actions were pure; motivated by noble thoughts, but she had inadvertently set out on a path that would acquaint her with a part of David's past life that he had striven to keep from her.

She had written a short letter to Nathan Rothschild, saying that she intended to call on him to discuss a matter of some delicacy. She had arranged for its delivery on Saturday evening after six-of-the-clock, saying that she would call at eleven-of-the-clock on Sunday morning, believing that he would not have chance to decline the visit. She had heard of Nathan Rothschild of course; who had not, but she had also done her research to find out as much about him as possible. In less than a generation and a half, the sons of Miah Amshall Rothschild had made themselves the most powerful figures in the financial world. They had even been financiers to Wellington at the battle of Waterloo. Their job had been to convert the British Government bonds into gold and deliver it to Wellington and his army in the field. Nathan was the founder of the London branch, but there were also his brothers: Amshall in Frankfurt, James in Paris and Carl in Amsterdam. They were so wealthy they had built stately homes all over Europe and were so powerful that they dealt with Governments and Kings.

Julia looked up again at the imposing building and was momentarily intimidated, but her innate courage reasserted itself and with her portfolio case tucked under her arm, she opened the gates and walked boldly up to the commanding front door where she pulled on the bell, hearing it sound back to her from within.

The door opened slowly to reveal a footman in the finest livery of bottle green and silver braid. He gestured an unspoken question with the merest inclination of his head.

Julia answered without further prompting, 'Miss Julia Carmichael to see Mr Rothschild.'

The footman seemed to adopt a condescending stare as he looked her up and down. He did not speak for a heartbeat then just said, 'You are to wait here,' and closed the door in her face.

Julia suddenly felt she may have made a dreadful miscalculation. There was no doubt she had been deliberately snubbed. It was an obvious rudeness in a society that prized manners above almost all else. To add insult to injury it had been delivered by a servant. She realised that while she was left standing here, that servant would be reporting back to his master. Would she be deemed suitable for admittance? She sighed at her own stupidity in expecting such a powerful man to see her without an agreed prior appointment, but then the door opened again and the footman spoke, 'Would you come this way, Miss Carmichael?' He swept a white-gloved hand from her direction towards the interior of the house.

She was led into what she assumed to be an office. It had the look of a library, she thought, there being bookcases against three of the walls. On closer inspection she saw that many of the books were ledgers rather than literary works, so discounted that thought. There was a big mahogany partners desk in the far corner of the room, its polished surface catching the light from the tall window behind it. The footman bowed with the merest oblique movement of his head and left, closing the large double doors behind him. There was no one in the room and Julia, feeling awkward, stood alone for what seemed like several minutes, although it was in fact only a few seconds, marked by the distinct ticking of an elaborate desk clock.

The doors opened again and in walked a diminutive fat man, a small pair of gold-rimmed spectacles pinched on his nose. He strode towards Julia and held out his hand. She took it and he bowed extensively, clicking his heels slightly as he did so. His demeanour suggested that he was very busy and that he wished to waste as little time as possible.

'Good day, Miss err,' he paused for a second, 'Carmichael; and what can I do for you?' His voice was high-pitched with a heavy accent. The words it seemed were rhetorical and he did not wait for an answer before continuing. 'Is this a business matter, for if it is you should know that I do not deal with such matters from my home?' His words were a lie; Julia knew by repute that he worked all the days of the week except the Sabbath and regularly worked from home. He would even work on the Sabbath if business matters demanded it; Friday was a normal day of commerce in London.

'It is only partly business,' she said, her tone as conciliatory as his was abrupt, 'but also a matter of some delicacy.' She had chosen the phrase carefully in her letter and she now repeated it hoping to intrigue him. It seemed to be working.

'Go on,' he said.

She opened the portfolio case she was carrying and gave him David's letter, 'perhaps this letter will explain and then I will answer any questions you may have.'

He took the letter from her and then went and sat down at his desk reaching for the paper knife as he did so. He gestured for her to sit also. She looked about her; there were several upright chairs facing the desk; plush velvet seats, handsome, expensive. For a brief moment she did not know which to choose then opted for one in the middle of the row. Mr Rothschild did not break the seal, just slit the envelope with one quick movement and took out the letter – there were four pages and he scanned them rapidly. He shuffled each page to the back as he completed it, but when he was on the third page, Julia saw his eyebrows rise in surprise and she thought to herself that David must have done very well in composing his letter. When he had finished he put it down and looked up at her.

'I have read much of Herr Ephraim's father's work,' he said. 'I was a great admirer of him. I am saddened to hear of his death.'

Julia looked at him in total confusion. *Herr Ephraim? Who is Herr Ephraim?* What on earth was the man talking about? She was hoping for the promise of a position when David was released from prison; something that her father could present to the court.

Nathan Rothschild sensed her bewilderment, but mistook it for sensibility. 'I'm sorry,' he said, 'were you very close to Herr Felix?'

'Err – no.' There was little comprehension in her response; she was merely answering automatically. They looked at each other from what seemed like opposite ends of incomprehension.

'And how is young Herr Ephraim bearing up in prison?' he said eventually. 'Prison must be a daunting place for a sensitive man of letters.'

She made an assumption - it seemed the only one available to her – that the 'young Herr Ephraim' to whom he referred must be David Neander. 'He is a remarkable young man,' she said. *He certainly is*, she thought to herself, wondering why he had not mentioned this to her.

'Like his father before him, no doubt, although I never actually met him; and I certainly did not know that he had been a neighbour of my father's in the *Judengasse*.'

Julia was now even more confused. *What was the Judengasse? WHAT IS IN THAT LETTER?* She looked down briefly at her hands to conceal her confused thoughts as he continued.

'There is no mention, however, of your name in this letter, Miss Carmichael?'

I'm not surprised she thought to herself, still not meeting Mr Rothschild's eye.

'How do you know young Loeb?'

Startled, Julia looked up. *Loeb? Who is Loeb? Does he mean David?* Again she assumed that he did. 'Merely by chance, I was in court on the day that David's... err, I mean Loeb's case came to court. I was taking notes for a case of my father's and I saw the injustice that was done to... Loeb.'

'Your father? Your father is George Carmichael?'

'Yes – you have heard if him?'

'Yes, he has done some legal work for us.'

'I know, but I assumed that you would not have been personally involved.'

'I know everything about my business, Miss Carmichael,' he said proudly, but then paused – there was puzzlement in his eyes. 'But I'm still not sure that I understand, Miss Carmichael, just how then are you connected to Loeb Ephraim?'

'There is no connection, other that a belief in *justice*, Mr Rothschild.'

'So you are helping him purely for *altruistic* reasons?'

She looked up and saw the merest smile of disbelief at the corner of his mouth. 'Why yes! Of course,' she said, stung by his insinuation. 'But having met Mr Ephraim I also realised what a remarkable man he is, and…' She did not finish her sentence, her words tailing away as she realised that Nathan Rothschild had seen through her attempt at justification.

'His father was a remarkable man as well,' he said with a smile, 'probably gets it from him.'

Aware that Mr Rothschild was being kind in not challenging her motives Julia nodded, but remained silent.

'Do you know that Felix Ephraim's writings put his life in danger many times? His books were often banned, but published abroad then smuggled back into Berlin, into Prussia, into Frankfurt. His death is a tragedy, of course, but not totally surprising; he took risks you know.'

'No, I did not know that,' Julia murmured, shaking her head. Her voice sounded timid in her ears and realising that introspection was beginning to overtake her, she resolved to bolster her tone. She coughed, sat up straighter in her chair and added forcefully, 'I know little of… err, Loeb's family and background.'

'Then we are in the same boat there, Miss Carmichael; although I admired Felix Ephraim's writings I did not know him or his family personally.'

The words were clipped and there was finality in the little man's tone. Julia was unsure of where she should go from here. She was even unsure as to what David had asked in his letter. Choosing her words carefully, she said, 'Is there any way that you can help Loeb at this terrible time, Mr Rothschild?'

'I'm not unsympathetic, Miss Carmichael, and I am aware that my name will carry great weight in court. This young man is very astute in realising that, but I cannot in all honesty go into the witness box to swear to Leob's character. I simply do not know him sufficiently well –

117

not at all, in fact. I'll have a letter to that effect sent to him by way of reply.'

'Then is there anything else you can do for him, if not that, Mr Rothschild?'

He looked at Julia questioningly over his spectacles. 'What would you have me do?'

'Perhaps some translation work; if he could tell the court that he does such tasks for you, it might show his character in a different light?' Again, she chose her words with care.

'But I already employ translators for such tasks. I really have no work that I can put his way.'

'Is there a vacancy that you could offer him, when he is released?'

'Offer him a job without meeting him you mean? I have not been successful in running my business by doing things like that. And anyway, I have no vacancies for poets Miss Carmichael.' He stared back at her, his eyes blinking rapidly as if he were becoming bored by the meeting. But then his demeanour seemed to soften did his voice when he added, 'And unfortunately it is *"if"* he is released, Miss Carmichael, not *"when"*. You have to accept the gravity of his situation.'

'I'll not accept any such thing, Mr Rothschild. I'll do whatever it takes to get him released. I'll go to the King if necessary!'

'I should be offering *you* a job, Miss Carmichael, not young Loeb!'

He stood and smiled at her, offering his hand to indicate the meeting was over then ringing the bell for the servant. Before she knew it, Julia had been shown out and was in the street looking back at the great house.

Her mind racing and unsure of what had just happened, she wandered away in total confusion.

CHAPTER 20

Frankfurt 1821

I took a short cut through an alley. I was beginning to find my way around Dortmund; I was even beginning to feel at home in the city - I had been here for about fifteen months. It was a quarter after the hour of five and the light was beginning to go, the sun being low in the autumn sky. I had finished my day's labour translating French to German for a Jewish salt merchant. My spirits were unusually high, I was taking a meal with Rabbi Baum; our meetings were stimulating and I was looking forward to it. There were two Germans coming down the alley towards me, but they hardly registered in my mind, which was elsewhere at the time. The alley was narrow, but there was just enough room for the three of us to pass without anyone giving way. I was not being provocative; at least I do not think that I was. Papa had taught us to give way to Germans on the street, but that was for our protection. I was now a tall, athletic man and I suppose I felt that I didn't need anyone's protection any more.

What I had failed to consider was that until now I had not looked Jewish, my height and blue eyes proclaiming me, wrongly, to be German. That must have affected my behaviour and to the Germans at large I was committing no social error. That had now changed: I was sporting a dark beard and dressed in sober black. I had proclaimed myself to be a Jew despite my non-Jewish looks.

As I made to pass them by, the two Germans stopped and looked at me. I turned in surprise and saw the meanness in their faces. I had failed to give way to them in the street.

'*Juden*', growled one of them, and then he worked his mouth and spat a gob of spittle at me. It landed in my hair and I smelt the sourness of it. I looked them both up and down. They were dressed in work clothes and wearing heavy boots. They must have just finished work, probably on their way to the tavern to quench their thirst. I think that they expected me to concede to their perceived dominant position, but I had been through too much to do that. I was being foolhardy and such rational thoughts had not crossed my mind.

'Yes, Jewish,' I said. There was a challenge in my tone; I could see from their faces that they did not expect it.

'Then you need a lesson in manners, Jew-boy,' sneered the second man.

'I need no lesson from the likes of you.' I was in no mood to back down. I had escalated the confrontation in a matter of moments.

They walked towards me separating as they did so. My gaze darted from one to the other, wondering where the first attack would come from. That fighting cunning that I had discovered when battling with Oliver Breitner returned to me - it was as though it was a hidden, but a natural part of me. I had little room for manoeuvre in the narrow alley. That was a disadvantage and I sensed that. I also sensed that I needed to put one of them out of action quickly so that I was not fighting both men at the same time. I moved quickly to my right. In that simple movement I had put the three of us in a line, but more importantly one of my antagonists was now behind the other; he would have to get round his friend to get at me.

The nearest man walked towards me and I could see that he did not expect me to fight back. When I took up a pugilistic stance, at first he seemed puzzled then a smile of derision crossed his dismissive countenance. I put my fists before my face, the right hand and the right leg forward, the left hand back and protecting my head. I felt the wall at my back and knew that I couldn't move backwards out of range when the attack came; this was not good so I resolved to strike first. I led with my right hand and it homed in on the man's nose. I doubled it up and struck again in quick time, once more landing on his nose. Neither punch was landed with much venom, but I saw his eyes water at their stinging effect.

The second man tried to get passed his friend to get at me, but the first man would have none of it gesturing that he would be the first to attack me. He lunged forward, throwing a crudely round-right hand in the direction of my face, but the punch was slow, his fist marking a wide arc in the air as it came towards me. There was no sense in my trying to back away with the wall still behind me. Back-alley fighting was unknown to me, but I seemed to sense the dangers naturally. I pivoted from the waist and moved my body to the right. My feet were firmly placed so that the lateral movement was just of my upper body, but it was enough. The punch missed me easily, but its full force hit the wall at the side of my head. I heard the knuckles in his hand crunch at the full impact, followed by a scream of pain. That was not enough for me though. I righted myself then dropped down slightly to my left, bringing my left hand up from the hip and sinking it with as much force as I could muster just under his rib cage to his right. I heard the cry of pain interrupted by the belch of wind as it left his lungs and whistled over his teeth. Gasping for air and holding his broken fist he sank to the floor. I stepped over his fallen body disdainfully, moved towards his companion and stared at him. I saw fear enter his features: he had realised suddenly that I was not just another Jew to be beaten without any reprisals.

I think he would have run, but a small crowd had begun to assemble. Later in life I would learn that spectators are drawn like iron to a magnet by a fight, but at the time I was surprised by how quickly they had gathered. My adversary was local and the loss of face kept him there. He was smaller than his companion, but more muscular in build. I probably had five or six centimetres in height advantage over him and my reach was correspondingly longer as well.

I jabbed out my right hand into his face as soon as I came into his range and followed it up again and then again. He swung a right punch at me, but now I was well away from the wall and I just stepped back. 'Pah!' I growled, as if to show contempt for him as his punch fell short.

But there was still fight in him. He could see that he couldn't out-fight me so he tried to out-wrestle me. He put his head down and charged at me. I punched down with my left hand and it landed forcefully on the top of his head, but it did not stop his momentum. He hit me in the midriff with his shoulder and then he clasped his hands round my back pushing me backwards. I continued to punch downwards but he gave only the top of his head as a target and my punches had little effect. I honestly did not feel fear even at that point. That cunning had returned to me and my mind was sharp and focussed, unencumbered by any apprehension.

My back hit the wall again, this time with some force, but I could see that it gave me a support. I used it as a prop, wedging my shoulder blades firmly against it. He was using his energy in trying to push me backwards, but that was wasted and I knew it would just tire him out. He tried to lift me off my feet and throw me, but I was wedged tight by the wall. I needed to do little to maintain my equilibrium. And then I felt his thrusting begin to wane, it was coming in small spurts now and each one with less effort than the last. I knew that this was my opportunity to retake the advantage

I brought my knee up powerfully – I nearly lifted him off the ground, but he kept his hold tight. I repeated the move vigorously again and again and heard his gasp of pain each time my knee connected with his ribcage. I took a short rest as much to asses the situation as to regain my strength. I realised that this was the right tactic. I brought my knee up again, but this time put all my effort in a single powerful blow. I felt his grip on my back release and then he frantically grasped to re-engage, which he managed to do. I knew now what to do. I waited a few short breaths then vigorously brought up my knee. I felt his grip go again and at that moment I pivoted, grasping his shoulders and sweeping at his legs with my other leg, moving him off balance and throwing him to the ground. His companion still lay moaning where he had fallen; they were now both down

For a moment my concentration was broken and I thought I heard a voice shout out. 'Bravo young fella!' I looked round quickly, the spectators were now about twenty strong, but I realised that I had a job to finish. I stood over the second man so that when he tried to get up I just punched down at him. The blow hit him forcefully behind the ear and sent him crashing to the ground. Each time he attempted to get up I did the same – I had learnt this from the fight with Oliver Breitner some years before. He tried to grab my legs, but I just sank down with my knees into his ribcage and he let out a pained yell. I knew he was beaten. I backed away.

'Get up and fight,' I shouted at him. 'Come on, fight; I'm only a Jew boy. You can beat a Jew-boy can't you?'

He got to his hands and knees and spat out a bloodied gob of spittle then looked down at the vermillion specimen he had produced. He turned his head sideways to look up at me.

'Are you bested,' I shouted, but he didn't answer.

'Can't hear you,' I goaded him, my voice booming to the gallery.

There was still no answer and inwardly I was pleased; I wanted to continue inflicting pain on him. And then I felt an arm go round my shoulders. I jumped with alarm, afraid that I now needed to defend myself against the crowd. I turned and saw an affable stranger. There was no anger in his face, just appreciation. He smiled a benevolent smile at me. His voice was low, rich and soothing.

'Your work here is done for the day, lad,' he said, patting my shoulder.

'But he has not cried "*bested*"' I kept my arms raised in my fighting guard, but I think there was some bewilderment in my voice. I had been operating on pure instinct but now reason was creeping back to me.

'His voice has not cried "bested", but his face surely has, lad. Look at him.'

I looked down at my opponent and only at that moment did I see that it was all over; that he had no more to give. And then a spontaneous round of applause broke out. Why were they clapping? I wondered. My new companion must have seen the confusion on my face. 'They're showing their appreciation,' he said, 'you should raise your hand to acknowledge them.' I did so, but to this day I don't know why I took that advice because I still didn't really know why they were clapping. My new companion seemed to sense that I needed to be told. 'It's because you have given them fine sport, lad,' he said.

'Sport?' He must have thought I was an imbecile, but I was grappling with a concept that was entirely alien to me.

He nodded, 'Street fights happen all the time my friend and they always draw a crowd. German men see fighting as sport, whether it is the fine gentleman with a sword or the common folk with a cudgel or with bare fists.' He paused for a moment, 'And that's why there is money to be made from this.'

'Money?' In my bewilderment I was operating on single words only.

'Yes, money,' he nodded emphatically. 'And if you are any good then lots of it.'

I looked at him closely for the first time. He was a big man. He was no taller than I, but he was extremely broad of shoulder. He had a bulk that I didn't have. I looked down at his hand on my shoulder; it was a giant's hand, but scarred and gnarled. This was a chance encounter, but it was to be one of those pivotal moments that would change my life; it was just as pivotal as the murder of my family, although I did not know it at the time.

'I'd take you to get you cleaned up, lad, but to be honest you don't need it. There's not a mark on you - remarkable. Where did you learn to fight – who taught you?'

'Nobody taught me.'

He shot me a look of incredulity. 'Are you telling me the truth, lad?'

'I don't lie!' I snapped. There was aggression in my voice and I shrugged his arm of my shoulder as I spoke.

'Good enough! 'He put the palms of his hands up to emphasise that there was no challenge in his words. 'Let me introduce myself. I'm Bernd Hartman,' he held out his hand. I took it and it engulfed my own fist as we shook.

'My name is Loeb Ephraim.'

'Well then Loeb Ephraim. Will you take a tankard of beer with me at the tavern?'

I don't know why I went with him to the tavern, but I did. We sat down in a cubicle and I could see that all eyes were looking at us. I felt uncomfortable. The serving frau brought the beer steins and I gulped down half of it in one go. The fighting had somehow left me with a raging thirst. My companion smiled at me as I put the tankard down.

'I always have a thirst when *I've* been fighting too,' he said.

'You're a fighter?'

He laughed out loud, his deep voice booming around the tavern, 'Then you don't know who I am?'

'Should I?' I said innocently. His laugh boomed again.

'Well maybe not. But have you noticed that everybody is staring at us?'

'Yes, I'm sorry,' I said.

'What have you to be sorry for?' he was clearly puzzled.

'Well they obviously don't get many Jews in here. Your reputation will suffer.'

'They're not staring at you lad – they're staring at me. And I promise you that my reputation is not at stake.'

'You? Are you famous then?'

'Only a lot!' There was a low growling chuckle as he spoke. 'I was a famous pugilist, I was a champion. I think everybody in here will have seen me fight.'

'I'm sorry; I didn't realise,' I said contritely.

'Nothing to be sorry for lad; it will do me good to be unrecognised by someone, keep my feet on the ground.'

'Bernd *Hartman*? Is that your real name?' Hartman was German for tough or strong man.

He boomed another laugh. 'No it's not lad, but you know that you are the first person brave enough to ask that question?' He leant forward conspiratorially, looking from side to side, 'Now don't ever tell anybody, but my real name is Bernd Klein, but that would never do for a pugilist would it?'

We both laughed together this time, for *Klein* in German means 'small'. Then we drank deeply together. He wiped the froth from his mouth with the back of his hand and then shuffled closer to me on the bench. 'I have a proposition for you lad,' he said, lowering his voice for privacy. 'I run an academy. I teach young gentlemen how to defend themselves.'

'I don't understand,' I said, unsure how this affected me.

'I also train a stable of professional pugilists. I could train you to be one of them.'

I shook my head, 'I don't think I could be a professional fighter.' There was incredulity in my tone. It was not something I had ever envisaged.

'Well not yet, of course. But have you any idea what you have done today? You have bested two men at once. They were not professional pugilists, but they are known around this neighbourhood as hard men, and you have beaten them – and may I say beaten them well. You have a natural ring craft, Loeb Ephraim, which it is difficult to learn. And I can teach you the rest; to block and parry, to ride with the punches. I can build up your muscles to enhance your power. I can enhance your lung power and control your diet. What do you say, Loeb Ephraim. Will you come and join me?'

CHAPTER 21

London 1822

Julia had played this scene in her mind many times over in the last few days, but now that she was face to face with David, in his cell, the words came hard to her. She turned and gave the gaoler a small coin and he knuckled his forehead with his usual gap-toothed, foul-mouthed grin, and then the cell door clanged shut behind her. She waited until the gaoler was out of earshot and she heard his whistling disappearing down the corridor. Then she turned back to David, shot him a fiery look and she saw his eyes narrow in confused response. Words formed on her lips, but although she had rehearsed them in her mind all through the carriage journey to the gaol, she was suddenly too afraid to speak them. She sighed heavily and mentally composed herself as she did so. She opened her mouth, but before she could speak a paroxysm of coughing started from the next cell. She waited; but the convulsions continued as the owner tried in vain to retch up the irksome phlegm. Spasm after spasm followed; the sound cutting across her efforts to speak. It seemed that it would never end and as the scene before her began to degenerate into a farce her irritation increased.

'He is a sick man,' said David seeing her frustration, 'his constitution is not strong enough to cope with this foul place. The consumption will take him in a few days I fear.'

'Poor man,' she said. The words came from nowhere overriding her rising anger.

'Poor man indeed. He is reduced to skin and bone I'm afraid, and his fever rages. He is not long for this world.'

The retching finally succeeded in dislodging a gob of phlegm. Julia heard it splat on the cell floor and almost retched at the thought of it. Her fear for David's safety now took precedence in her thoughts..

'Take care David,' she said fervently, 'we don't want to fight for your acquittal only for the consumption to take you as well. You must stay away from this poor man.'

'There is a wall between us; we have had to talk through the cell doors into the corridor to speak to each other.' His words were matter-of-fact, 'but, anyway, he has little conversation left in him. His lungs are gone. At least he will be spared the hangman.'

That awful word again - hangman. It hit her like a thunderbolt, the mental images filling her fevered mind. She inclined her head, looking introspectively down at the floor. David moved towards her and gently grasped the collar of her cape and she allowed him to take it. Without thinking, she undid her bonnet and gave it to him also and he put both down carefully on the desk.

'You had better tell me what troubles you?' he said, offering her the solitary stool.

She sat and arranged her skirts, staring at him stony-faced. 'Who is Loeb Ephraim?' she asked, but as she spoke, her anger left her, the rancour gone from her voice. She was just desperate for answers.

He held his breath for some moments as if trying to hold back the inevitable. When he spoke at last, he refused to meet her gaze. 'He is someone I never want to think of again,' he said with an air of finality.

But Julia was not going to let it end at that. 'Are *you* Loeb Ephraim?' she burst out, exasperated.

Turning his back on her, David went to the cell door and looked through the bars. He did not answer her; head bent, he grasped them in his clenched fists with such force that he rattled the heavy door. For a moment Julia thought he was going to shout for the gaoler, but he just stood and stared blankly down the dimly lit corridor. There was another bout of retching from the next cell and this seemed to start somebody else coughing at the far end of the corridor. Julia was now barely aware of it, her attention focused solely on David's stiff back 'David? Are you Loeb Ephraim? Tell me, please,' she pleaded.

He turned to face her again, but this time met and held her gaze, 'Does it matter?'

It was not an answer she had expected, nor did she know how to respond. She repeated his words, exasperation evident in her tone, 'Does it matter?' For a moment it was all that she could say, but then the words cascaded out of her like water thrusting from a breached dam. 'It matters that you do not lie to me; it matters that I can trust what you say. Is everything about you a lie?'

'I have never lied to you,' he said, those large dreamy blue eyes holding her in an intense stare. 'You must believe me.'

'Why must I believe you? It seems that you are not the man I thought you were.'

'I hope I am the man you thought I was, but I am not the man I used to be.'

These words made no sense to Julia. She seemed to be caught between one thing and another. 'Then you had better tell me who you *were* and then perhaps I can see that for myself,' she said tartly.

Unable to face the disappointment in her eyes, David turned away again and stared down the filthy corridor. There was little natural light to illuminate the passage; it was as dark as his thoughts. He was being asked to dig up all the memories he had buried for the sake of his own sanity and with them all those destructive, painful feelings that he feared would be unleashed like wailing demons from the bowels of hell itself. He would rather dig a hole and bury himself than do this. He turned back and looked at her, 'You do not know what you ask of me.'

'I know that I deserve to be told the truth.'

Her words were forthright; he could see the pain of betrayal standing in her eyes. Helplessly, he held out his hands towards her, but could not speak.

She gazed at them for a moment and then looked up into his eyes. When she spoke her tone was gentler, as though she had read in them his pain. 'Is the truth so bad then?'

He nodded, but how could she, a young, beautiful girl with no experience of the world and its inherent evil, ever understand what his problem was. He knew from the frozen atmosphere between them that she believed his reluctance to be rooted in some deception; that there was something untold that would ruin their burgeoning relationship forever, something that would hurt her deeply. Yet he knew he must speak of it. He drew a breath, his outstretched hands curling into fists as he thrust them into the pockets of his trousers.

'Yes – the truth *is* so bad. I took a new name so that I could start a new life; a new life free from the pain of the old. "*Neander*" means "new man". I chose that name deliberately; it was a statement of intent. I was born Loeb Ephraim, but I was no longer he, I was David Neander. Can you understand that?'

'Of course I can, David.'

He sighed at the naivety of her response, yet how could she possibly comprehend his suffering? 'Can you? You have been sheltered from the cruelty of the world by your middling-class upbringing, by your mother and father. What can you know of evil?' Still holding her gaze, he enunciated each word deliberately and saw her flinch as though stung.

'That may be so, but I have sat many hours in the courtroom assisting my father. I am much more experienced in the ways of the world than you might think; certainly more so than other women of my age and status.'

'Certainly that is true, and I admire you greatly for your belief in justice – it is what initially attracted me to you.'

Julia dropped her gaze, an involuntary flush staining her cheeks at his words. Wearily, David turned away, moving to lean against the desk. Julia's demeanour only served to prove his point. If she had any notion – any comprehension of what he had said, she would have been too involved to succumb with a blush to his flattery. Facing her, he cried out, 'But I am *Jewish*, Julia! You *cannot* know what that means.'

'Then tell me David; tell me!'

'What do you know of the "*Hep Hep*" riots in the German states in 1819?' He saw the puzzlement in her eyes. Before she could speak, he said, 'You see; you know nothing of them, nothing of what happened!' His voice rose as he spoke and he saw at once that it affected her sensibilities. He had never raised his voice to her before; her eyes widened and he knew she was both hurt and alarmed; the man she was falling in love with was not a man who would raise his voice to her. In some irrational way this minor pain he had inflicted on her made up his mind for him. He would tell her his story; he would revisit all those terrible memories; he would accept the pain they would cause him – and he would do this because it would be his penance for hurting her. The crime and the penance were, of course, out of balance, but that was the power of love. He chose not to rationalise this in his mind at the time; knew only that he was falling in love with her and the sight of her taut, white face and bewildered expression was more than he could bear.

He walked towards her and took her hand gently. 'Julia, my dearest Julia; I don't know who is going to be the most distressed by what I am going to tell you – you or I.' Releasing her hand, he sat on the floor before her. He hung his head, his arms resting loosely on his knees and tried to talk, avoiding her eyes as he did so. The words of the story came to his lips, but they were reluctant to be spoken. And then, when the story came, there was no stopping it. He started when he was a child in *Gießen* and then told of his whole life as a Jew growing up in Germany. He painted a picture for her of a loving family, but that made the shock of what was to come even more traumatic. He talked for several hours sparing her no detail. The full horror of the murder of his family was told in matter-of-fact words, but that did not diminish their terror-crazed impact. All the time he avoided her eyes, speaking downwards, staring at the floor. He was barely aware of her, only when from time to time she gasped, did her presence pierce his consciousness. It was as though he had wrenched the scab off an old wound to reveal once again the festering beneath and once he had started, he could not stop.

Julia listened, appalled; biting her lips until they ran red with blood, her silent tears running constantly down her face. He was right; she had not comprehended the magnitude of his suffering and was totally unprepared for the grotesque and terrifying story that unfolded. Revulsion gripped her and she became more and more distressed. She struggled to avoid breaking down before him and that was *her* penance for pushing him into telling his story. This story had not been the one she feared; there was no secret wife left behind in Germany. That fear now dissolved and seemed insignificant and unimportant. In the face of David's anguish, Julia felt ashamed that she had allowed such trivia to enter her mind.

When he finished speaking, David remained staring at the floor. Julia looked away from him afraid he might look up; as if eye contact would defeat the resolve she was trying so hard to muster; the resolve not to take him in her arms. But then she heard a strangled sob and looking down saw his shoulders start to hunch, then to convulse. His head was still bowed between his arms as if to hide his distress from her. The story had been horrible but yet, paradoxically, nothing he had said had diminished her admiration for him; if anything it was enhanced by it. The sight of him sobbing somehow released her from the restriction of social conventions. She jumped off the stool and rushed to comfort him. Kneeling by his side, she cradled his head to her bosom, her maternal instincts sweeping away any thoughts she might have had of impropriety. They both wept together, words seemingly unimportant at that time. She kissed the top of his head without thinking and they remained like that, rocking gently, neither attempting to break the embrace.

'You are like an onion, David Neander,' she whispered into his hair. 'Beneath every layer that you peel I find another David Neander underneath.

CHAPTER 22

Dortmund 1821

Bernd Hartman was a hard taskmaster in his academy. He lived up to his name and no one dared challenge his words; this was his domain. Even the young gentlemen that he taught knew better than to bring with them their superior attitude into the academy; they were just as deferential as everyone else. I felt like an apprentice and Bernd treated me as such. The training was hard; he worked on my lung power which, in truth, I didn't find difficult because I seemed to have that naturally, but not so the strength training. The lifting of weights and medicine balls was endless and my muscles ached—from the repetitious exercises he put me through. I started to bulk up quickly though, helped by the diet he had written out for me.

The gym smelled of sweat, but it was a manly smell and I quickly began to find it pleasant, however illogical that may seem. I looked forward to going and spent some part of most days there. I was an outsider and I knew it: the other professional pugilists in Bernd's string were from the lower classes. They all had a fighting spirit and that was born out of hunger. When your belly cries out for sustenance it fosters a fighting spirit in a young man, gives him the urge to use his fists to fight for what he needs. I was unusual in that although I was from a middling-class background, I also had that fighting spirit, but mine had been honed on quite a different anvil.

And so I learned the art of pugilism: Bernd taught me to block and parry, to take my opponents' punches on the arms, to protect my face and my chin, to pull in my elbows to protect my midriff. It all came easily to me and I learned quickly. I was in demand as a sparring partner. Bernd Hartman liked to use me to spar with the young gentlemen. He taught them a style of fighting that was based on the noble art of self defense, to protect themselves at all times. I seemed to know exactly what he wanted of me; I would flick out punches that were not too stinging if the young gentlemen failed in his attempt to parry. Some of the other professional fighters, however, traded on strength and power and they found it difficult to pull their punches. They were less keen on sparring with me, however; that was because I was a lefty. I was the wrong way round, I led with my right hand and right leg and kept my left hand back for the potent punches. Bernd tried to turn me round but he soon gave up when he realised that it was natural for me and not just a bad habit. My wrong way round stance seemed to confuse some of the others. Added to that I was Jewish, yet surprisingly, over time I was accepted into the fold and treated as one of them. There was a mutual respect amongst the string and that seemed to override these negatives.

In a little less that two months I had put on nearly seven kilos but I had lost none of my speed. Bernd Hartman matched me with another professional fighter, for a modest purse. My first fight, but I showed little fear, I was entering a brutal profession, but I did not realize it. To me it was an opportunity to prove myself and I did not contemplate losing. Bernd told me that my opponent was Wolfgang Schmidtlein. He had been a great fighter, a local champion, but he was now thirty-eight years old and way past his best. He would outweigh me by fifteen kilos, although three centimeters shorter than me. He was a powerful man, but I should be too young and fit for him. I went into the fight without any real game-plan, I was just going to best him – it was as simple as that.

The fight took place in the city park on a bright sunny Sunday afternoon. The excellent weather had brought out a large crowd, which supplemented the keen sporting fans who regularly went along to see the fights. As I entered the park I saw the bill-poster advertising the pugilistic contents. There were to be four of them and I was surprised to see that I was third on the bill and not bottom. This had little to do with me, I was an unknown, and was probably because my opponent was a past champion and a favourite with the crowd; but nevertheless, I took some reflective pride in the billing. I resolved to give the spectators a show of my skills. The fight was billed as being between 'Wolfgang Schmidtlein, the past champion and Loeb the Jew'. I shrugged my shoulders when I saw that; I hadn't thought about a fighting name but decided that 'Loeb the Jew' was as good as any.

I remember that when I walked through the gates, the sights, the sounds and the smells accosted my senses, and for the first time since that tragic day of riots it felt good to be alive. The place was vibrant; there were ball games and animal baiting; peddlers selling their wares, the whole of their stock carried on their backs. Food vendors called out their customary cries, selling everything from hot tea to oysters, pies to spiced ginger, and, of course, traditional sausages of all kinds: *katenrauchwurst; mettwurst; cervalet; bierwurst; kochwuerste.* The smells filled the air and I wandered around taking it all in.

I changed in a tent with the other fighters from Bernd Hartman's string. I was second fight on after Boris Walter, the last on the billing going first, but I was ready well before the first fight. I wore only a pair of breeches and stockings with a light pair of sporting shoes – aside from that I was stripped to the waist. Bernd had tied my hair in a pony tail at the nape of my neck and then encouraged me to oil my skin to give me some protection if my opponent tried to grab or wrestle me. I didn't think that I needed it, but I did as I was told and set about the task. I was only part way through when Boris Walter was carried in through the tent flap, followed by Bernd Hartman, and put on the treatment table. He was unconscious and Bernd set about reviving him. Water was thrown on his face but it had only limited success and then smelling salts were put before his nose. Again at first there was little reaction but after a second or two Boris responded, pulling his head away fiercely from the powerful smell. They sat him up rubbing his hands and arms in an effort to get his circulation working, all the time asking him questions to make him respond. The fight had lasted only two-and-a-half minutes, yet his left eye was closing and blood was streaming from several cuts across his forehead, his nose and particularly around the bruised mound that had been his left eye.

I suppose that I should have been alarmed, should have realised the danger that the ring had in store. At that time Boris was probably a better fighter than me, but if I remember correctly, even then I had confidence in my ability. It makes me seem arrogant now, but I was so sure of myself back then.

I was called to fight and I climbed into the ring accompanied by Bernd Hartman who was to act as my second. The ring was an unfenced platform with several rows of seating for the gentlemen, separated from the platform by a gap where the middling classes stood, their eyes on a level with the ring floor. There was no cheering for me, no more than an apologetic ripple of applause and for the first time that day negative thoughts entered my head; despite it being a public place I suddenly felt very alone. When my opponent entered there was a resounding cheer for him that took some time to die down and it was clear that he was a crowd favourite. I looked across at him and was stung by what I saw. I don't know what I had expected, but I wasn't expecting what I saw; he looked a brute of a man. Knowing his age, I suppose I had imagined that he would not be an athletic specimen. There were certainly signs of wear. His hair was close shorn so that he almost looked to have a shaven head, and this emphasised the scar tissue on his face and forehead. His skin seemed to be pulled tight over his skull giving him a gaunt expression and he had cold, steely blue eyes. But this was an immensely muscular man with huge forearms and biceps and a deep, powerful chest, the only weakness that I could see was an accumulation of fat around his midriff.

I turned to Bernd. 'I thought you said he was an old man, out of condition?'

'He smiled sheepishly, 'He is; look at his belly - you will outlast him.'

I gave him a worried look. I had no strategy worked out and now my mind went into overdrive. 'How should I fight him?' My stupid confidence born out of ignorance began to ebb away.

'Remember what I have taught you; beat him to the punch and parry everything that comes back.'

I wasn't so sure that would be enough, but then Bernd was called over to the referee and I saw a heated exchange with him and my opponent's second. He came back with anger writ all over his face, 'They have objected to you,' he said.

'Me! Why?' I was nonplussed, but then anger rose within me, "Cause I'm Jewish?'

'No – no lad, 'cause of your beard.' I was now a practicing Jew and I had my full beard.

'What's that got to do with fighting?'

'It's supposed to give you an unfair advantage that's all. Fighters come to the ring with several days' growth because it's supposed to give them punch resistance, but there's a sort of unwritten rule that they don't come to this ring with full beards.'

'Well tell them to go to hell,' I said, 'I'll not be dictated to by them.'

'I have, but the problem is that the referee has agreed with them. If you don't shave it off then you will be disqualified and that means you will forfeit your purse.'

I stared across the ring and was met by the cold blue eyes of Wolfgang Schmidtlein. There was a smirk evident at the corner of his mouth as if he had won a small battle. I realised that the intention was to undermine me; to destabilise my preparations, but then another thought occurred to me. If he was prepared to do this then he must fear me. 'Come on Bernd,' I said as I jumped down from the ring. I strode quickly to the changing tent and asked for a razor from my fellow fighters. They looked at me blankly and then Bernd came through the flap. Fighters shaved their bodies sometimes and then oiled themselves so that it would be harder to be thrown if their opponent tried to wrestle them; there are few rules in fighting, and what rules there were,

were mainly to make it absolutely clear who the winner was so that the gambling debts were clearly established, the wagers could be paid out and the losers knew their debts.

A cut-throat razor was produced when Bernd reinforced my request. I hacked away at my beard without any attempt to lather my face; that would have been pointless anyway as the beard was too long, probably three months' growth by then.

'Steady lad!' said Bernd. 'If blood is going to be spilled, then the ring is the place to spill it, not here.' He took the razor from me which, looking back; was probably for the best. He tugged at each clump of beard and then sliced at it with the honed blade. It was much less painful than my angry hacking and I was grateful. When he had done I called out for some lather but Bernd said that I could go and fight the way it was. A looking glass was given to me and I looked at myself through the cracked dirty mirror; it was no barber's handiwork, but it would do. I looked as if I had about a week's growth of stubble. I climbed back into the ring to the sound of boos from the crowd, who had had their entertainment interrupted. The referee came across to inspect Bernd's handiwork; grimaced to register his dissatisfaction but then grunted his acceptance, which evoked an ironic cheer from the impatient throng.

My dander was up, and I saw a satisfied look on Bernd's face. He patted me on the back with his huge bear-like hand, but that paw then came up and cupped my head–pulling me towards him. He slapped me roughly with his other hand and it made my face sting. His eyeballs were only and inch from mine so that I was uncomfortable; he was invading my natural space, but he was cutting through my anger and trying to channel it. He spoke low and conspiratorially, each word emphasised by his piercing eyeball-to-eyeball gaze.

'Aggression is good, young Loeb, but so is strategy. I have taught you how to defend yourself – now *don't* you forget that.' He slapped me hard again and released my head then he took me to the mark in the middle of the ring, and Wolfgang Schmidtlein's second did the same with him. The referee repeated the rules of engagement we were to fight under, they were fairly simple, but I wasn't really listening. The seconds retreated and the bell sounded almost immediately. We both took up our attitude, our fighting stance; Wolfgang Schmidtlein with his left hand and left leg forward and me the other way round. He weaved from the hip and let fly with a powerful left round punch, but he was slow, as Bernd had predicted, and I easily parried it with my right hand. We stood toe-to-toe and I became more confident with each blow he tried to throw. If he threw with his left I parried with my right. If he threw with his right I parried with my left. My arms were rapidly turning red with the force of the punches but I was growing in confidence that I had the skill and speed to beat him. I threw my first meaningful punch, but he too showed that he was a master of the art of self defense, parrying the shot on his bulging arm. But then I stated to throw the punches in quick succession; he parried the first three but he was not quick enough to evade the fourth, which went home with some force to the side of his head and a trickle of blood started down the side of his face.

The crowd fell surprisingly quiet. They expected their favourite to beat this young Jewish upstart easily, but a different fight was unfolding. For the next few minutes I went on the attack. Wolfgang Schmidtlein stood his ground as I rained quick punches down on him. That was the pattern of the fight; he would expertly defend most of the punches but a significant number were getting through. His face began to cut up so that he looked back at me with an expression of scarlet surprise.

The noise of the crowd then entered my mind; a fair proportion of it was now cheering my performance; I had turned some of them by my spirited display. When a good punch went home through my opponent's defense I could hear a cheer.

But then came oblivion.

The first thing that coalesced in my mind was the canvas floor of the ring; I was looking down at it; tasting it, it was stuck to my lips. Then Bernd's mighty hands pulled me up and I walked unsteadily back to my corner supported by his ample frame, my arm clamped around his neck for in truth if he had let me go then I would have fallen down. He had thirty seconds to revive me and take me to the mark at the centre of the ring ready to fight on. He sat me down on a stool and threw water on me and then slapped me.

'What's your name?' he said.

'Huh!'

'Just answer, Mister Know-it-all.'

'Loeb Ephraim.'

'Well your wits are not scrambled but that punch will still be in your legs.' He thrust a small bottle of smelling salts under my nose and I pulled my head away at the pungent, overpowering vapor. He knelt down before me so that he was looking up at me and started to rub my thighs to get the circulation going 'Now you listen to me young Loeb Ephraim. If you carry on like that I'll have to carry you out of here.'

'Like what?'

'Fighting to the crowd and forgetting what I have taught you.'

'I was not,' I said indignantly.

He reached up and slapped my face. 'Shut up and listen. When you go back just concentrate on parrying everything he throws at you until the effects of that punch leave your legs.' I noticed that the hand that had slapped me was red with blood – my blood. I touched my face and winced at the bruise that was swelling around my left eye. 'That's right, you're bleeding and your eye will start to close. When that happens you will not be able to see the punches coming.'

Bernd pulled me up onto my feet and wiped the blood from my face with a white towel that now was stained scarlet. I walked back with him to the scratch mark unaided and I saw the look of contempt on my opponent's bruised features. My arms came up before my face instinctively and I had taken my attitude seconds before the referee called, '*Fight on.*' Wolfgang Schmidtlein was so contemptuous of me that he did not assume his fighting stance; his face was unprotected; he knew I would not try to punch him, but only try to parry him. In his mind the fight was won and the next punch he got through would finish me.

His arms came up and the blows started, but I did as I was told and just parried them on my blue-black forearms. He was now swiveling from the hip to get full power into his punches and they were beginning to knock me off my stance even though I was parrying them as I had been told. I decided that if was going to be defeated then at least he would know he had been in a fight. He was wide open in his contempt for me so I unleashed a straight left that homed in on his many times broken nose. I saw the look of amazement on his face, but it only prompted him to take up his full fighting stance.

Nevertheless, I was still able with my speed to beat him to the punch and the fight returned to the way it had been and the accumulation of my successful punches added to the damage that years of fighting had done to his face. I was in the ascendancy and was again beginning to enjoy myself - and then oblivion again and I was once more sucking the canvas.

Bernd carried me back to the corner and dropped me on the stool like a sack of potatoes. 'I'll pull you out now lad,' he said.

'But I can fight on,' I protested.

'Aye, you can but the result will be the same. You have learnt your lesson now I think.'

'What's that supposed to mean?'

'It means what I say. You had a lesson to learn.'

'And what was that?'

'That you cannot do this without me,' he said, 'and that you have to listen to what I have to tell you and not think that you know it all.'

'Did you expect me to lose then?'

'Oh yes – I over-matched you deliberately. I knew that you would lose, but I wanted to see if you had a fighting heart when it came to it, and to show you that I will decide on the strategy that you should follow.'

He was right, but I didn't see it that way. I saw only a form of betrayal. I saw him nod to the referee that I was not capable of continuing, and that made me even angrier with him. I wanted to show him he was wrong. I jumped up and walked back to the mark on my own to the surprise of the referee and my opponent. I stumbled slightly but that did not affect my resolve. Bernd walked easily after me and pulled me back by the arm, but I shrugged him off me. Wolfgang Schmidtlein walked to meet me, he would have liked nothing better than to give me a good beating, and then the referee called '*Fight on'*, and he had his opportunity.

But this time I was not going to fight the way Bernd had taught me. Standing toe-to-toe may have been the accepted way, but that did not suit my style. I was tall and lean and agile; I did not bring raw power into the ring. My instinct now was to defend myself against an early assault and I did this by being mobile. I circled my opponent instinctively to my right, always moving away from his powerful right hand. I knew if that landed again then it would probably be the end. The crowd started booing me; it was seen as manly to stand toe-to-toe, to defend yourself the way a fencer does, with thrust and parry. I had listened to Bernd who had tried to teach me this method, but by instincts told me to do something different; he had seen this inclination in me and wanted to get rid of it once and for all. His ruse had had the opposite effect on me to the one intended. I had learned a lesson, certainly, but it was a life lesson: it is wise to take advice, I told myself, but ultimately, Loeb, you have to be your own man.

Bernd had gone back to his corner expecting the obvious; that whatever I did a powerful punch would land and that would be the end of me. But as I moved everything seemed to come together. My opponent stayed out of range making little attempt to come after me and I felt the strength come back into my legs. All my fighting instincts came together and my fighting guile coordinated them. I started to flick out punches, not powerful ones to start with, but I had realised that his counter punches were slow and I could easily stay out of range. I watched the arc of his failed punches scythe through the fresh air, all the time draining his reserves of stamina. But I reasoned that I needed to get those old legs to carry him about, to make him blow even more so I started to taunt him.

'Come on old man,' I said, 'can't you keep up?' And then I moved in and hit him with a combination, a straight right followed by vicious left hook that hit him about the right ear, and then I quickly moved backwards out of range again. It was the most powerful punch I had thrown in the whole fight. I knew that his ears would now be ringing, but I also saw the anger rise within him. This upstart Jew was making him look bad. He set off after me throwing punches wildly, but I just backed away, snapping out punches that started to make his face look like a vermillion mask. I was like a matador with a rampant bull in front of me and I continued to taunt him, always staying just out of range. It was totally natural to me and it was easy. I couldn't believe how easy it was and it was getting easier - and I realised that those old legs were failing quickly and he was gasping for breath, sucking in great gulps air to compensate.

My God! I thought to myself, *he's gone, he's got nothing left.* Nothing, that was, except his fighting spirit; that remained intact. I knew I must respect that but the fact was that he was there for the taking. He had stopped coming after me; not from the realisation that his strategy was wrong but because he had run out of reserves. I planted my feet to increase the power of my punches. I sank low and brought an uppercut through his defensive guard; it hit with percussive effect and his head rocked viciously back throwing mucus and snot into the air. That fighting spirit engaged and he threw a punch back at me, but I was long gone out of range and I knew that he no longer presented any danger for me.

Bernd looked on from the side of the ring and as I glanced across at him I could see he had realised this at the same time.

He must have had mixed feelings; pleased that I would win, but he would also know I was lost to him as the diligent apprentice he wanted me to be. I would now be a maverick in his stable of fighters.

I moved in and out on an imaginary diagonal line unleashing heavy punches, and now they all started to go home until at last even his fighting spirit failed him and there were no punches coming back. As a fighting force he was spent, but his pride kept him upright and that pride would cost him dear: it would cost him a beating that his second should have stopped. There was disbelief all around: this young Jew boy was beating the old champion and beating him badly. The ring is a dangerous place and there is no place for compassion in the fighter's mind, and I have to confess that there was no compassion in my mind that day. I gave him a terrible beating, aided by the man's fighting pride. He stood for a full minute taking all my punches until his addled brain was finally separated from his battered body and he sank to his knees. The bell sounded and his second hauled him off to his stool; they threw water over him and thrust the smelling salts under his nose; it had no effect. They poured brandy into his mouth but most of it just dribbled back out and his eyes remained tight shut. The thirty seconds came and went and the referee raised my hand. There were mostly boos from the crowd but there were also some cheers.

Bernd walked over and put his mighty paw across my shoulders. 'Well done young Loeb,' he said, 'though I'm not sure if you realise just what you have done.'

I shot him a puzzled look, not sure what he meant. Bernd shrugged his colossal shoulders in a gesture of resignation. I realised then that I was to be my own man and that he saw that as limiting my prospects.

'Go on then, accept the acclaim,' he said, adding grudgingly, 'you have earned it.'

I raised my hand, unaware of the pain I would suffer after the fight: my arms bruised and sore; my left eye swollen and closed; my knuckles raw and shredded. But at that moment, as I accepted the cheers, all I felt was elation.

CHAPTER 23

London 1823

The passageway between Newgate prison and the Old Bailey Courthouse was enclosed within brick walls. The gaoler had released the prisoner into the custody of one of the court's dock officers. David Neander's feet had been shackled and he now trundled uncomfortably down the passageway, his staccato steps and jingling chains echoing back at him from the historic brickwork as he laboured against his restraints. He was in irons as if he was a common criminal, but that was the way the judicial system was treating him. Today was the day of his retrial, charged again with the felony of theft. His emotions were mixed: there was the denigration of being considered a criminal, knowing he would face the scorn and condemnation of the public gallery - a belittlement that stung his pride - but he also felt relief that the day had finally come. All his hours of studying the English legal system had been for this. He took a deep breath and puffed out his chest defiantly as they emerged from the passage into the Courthouse. It was an anticlimax for he was transported straight to the prisoners' quarters in the basement to await his hearing. His adrenalin subsided as he continued to wait.

The waiting room of the new second courtroom at the Old Bailey was wood-panelled and reeked of a combination of polish and stale sweat; the smell of polish, though heavy in the air, losing its battle against the stench of body odours. The room was three-quarters full and there was a collective air of anxiety. Julia sat with her father, waiting apprehensively, speaking in inconsequential undertones, cradling a large brown paper parcel on her lap and trying in vain to distance herself from this oppressive place, which she had come to hate after only a few minutes. There was a total lack of privacy, yet they were forced to talk privately in so public a place. Their dilemma was mirrored by everyone else in the room so that the collective hushed conversations merged and buzzed like a swarm of honey bees in search of nectar. That hum was punctuated at intervals by the sounds of the court business going on outside the room as the ushers called out the names of the plaintiffs, respondents or witnesses.

And then David, still shackled at the ankles, was brought to them by one of the dock officers. Julia stood, resting the parcel on the vacated seat. 'Will you cast off the shackles please?' she asked forcefully.

The Dock Officer looked at her and shifted his feet uncomfortably. A tall, powerful man, employed for his brawn rather than his brain, his hair was thinning and greying. Now in his late forties he had been doing this job for many years so was used to showing deference to people of rank, but he knew his duty. 'Can't do that, ma'am,' he said.

'Well can you leave us then to discuss Mr Neander's case in private?'

'I'm afraid that I can't do that either, ma'am,' he said apologetically. 'I have to stay with the prisoner. It's my duty to deliver him to the court for trial.'

Julia knew that, of course, but she still made no attempt to hide her irritation from the Dock Officer. 'Well then, perhaps you can step back a few paces and give us some privacy?'

The Dock Officer looked at George Carmichael for guidance, the lawyer's black robe and wig being the nearest thing to court authority for him to consult. George's gesture with his head in the direction of *over-there*, told him to do as he was bid and he shuffled back reluctantly.

'It's alright,' said David, 'he's only doing his duty.'

'I know.' Julia sighed as she spoke, 'It's just that…' She didn't finish the sentence when she saw in David's eyes that he understood. 'Did the barber I sent arrive at the gaol?' she said instead.

David rubbed his clean-shaven chin. It was obvious that the barber had been and done his duty. 'Yes, he came,' he said.

'When you go into court today you will look like the gentlemen that you are.' She turned to the seat beside her and the brown paper parcel that lay upon it. She undid the string, opened it carefully and took out David's jacket. 'I've had it cleaned and newly pressed,' she said.

'Thank you my dear,' said David before he could stop himself then, seeing the disapproval on her father's face, hastily corrected himself, 'Thank you Miss Carmichael.'

He started to put on the newly neatened jacket. 'No, not yet,' Julia said, turning again to the parcel and taking out a new linen shirt, 'Put this one on; that shirt will not do, it's filthy.'

Looking around the room and noting the lack of privacy, David was undecided what to do. Taking the shirt, he smiled, 'Thank you again. Err… would you mind…?'

Julia took the cue instinctively and turned her back, but could see David's reflection in the glazed picture of the King that hung on the wall directly in front of her. She saw him pull the soiled shirt over his head and shoulders revealing his torso. Since she had known him he had lost weight, but he was still toned and muscled. She saw her father's look of admiration and hid a grin. She saw also that David took no notice, his mind clearly on the retrial that was about to take place. Aware of warmth creeping up her neck, she lowered her eyes from David's reflection as he began tucking the shirt into his breeches. Finally she turned back to him and took the last item from the parcel: the stock. She wound the muslin necktie around his shirt collar and tied it off neatly. 'There,' she said, patting it straight and standing back to admire him, 'that should make an impression.'

'And I'm afraid that is going to be important today,' said George, not altogether happy about his daughter's familiarity with the prisoner, but appraising David's appearance with a critical eye. 'Anything we can do to enhance your standing is vital.'

'Oh?' David looked at him, one eyebrow raised in query.

'At your original trial the prosecutor, Herbert Bond, did not employ a lawyer in the prosecution of his case; he would not have had the funds. But the court has appointed a prosecuting counsel for this retrial, which is probably in response to my acting for you – otherwise they would not have seen it as sufficiently important a case.'

'Do you know this prosecuting counsel?' asked David.

'Yes, it is Josiah Heath. He's a good man and also a fair one, but he is not the problem.'

'The problem?'

'I'm afraid the Judge is to be Judge Cardew.'

'But isn't he...?

'Yes, he's the Judge that sentenced you to death at the first trial.'

Julia shuddered at that word 'death' and exchanged an apprehensive glance with David. He looked back at George, 'Is that normal in a retrial.'

'No it is not,' said George, 'it is not normal at all.'

'So why...?' asked David.

'Why indeed,' George cut across him. 'I think he must have pulled a lot of strings to get himself appointed.'

David nodded, 'I suspected he would feel aggrieved that the original verdict was set aside and a retrial ordered, but I did not think he would go to these lengths. Perhaps we should have expected it though. Is there anything we can do?'

'At this point in time, not much, though it may be grounds for an appeal later, but you have already made the system lose face in obtaining a retrial and there will be little appetite to overturn another verdict. This Judge will know that and it will strengthen his hand if he has a mind to take revenge on you.'

'I see that,' said David.

'I'll not hide this from you, Mr Neander,' said George, 'but this is a bad thing, a very bad thing indeed. We have to revisit our strategy for the case, for there will be no help from the Judge today.'

'So we put our faith in the jury?' asked David.

'Yes, we put our faith in the jury,' agreed George.

Julia took her place in the gallery looking down over the vast courtroom. The large brass chandeliers hanging from the ceiling obscured her view of some of the auditorium, but she could see clearly the Judge's seat, the witness box and the prisoners' bar. She also looked down at the large semi-circular mahogany table provided for the prosecution and defence counsels to plead from, but her father was not yet there. The earlier cases as they were called seemed endless, although in reality justice in each case was being dispensed in a matter of minutes. And then the commission for David's case was read out by the Clerk to the Court.

Back in the basement David had sat with the other prisoners, incongruous in his clean, smart clothes. The dock officers as well as the other prisoners had stared at him, but he had looked directly back into their staring faces, into their inquisitive eyes. Despite the fact that he had entrusted his case and his life to George Carmichael, he still clutched his own preparatory papers; written during nights of endless candlelit study deep into the long, lonely hours before dawn. He found patience from somewhere and sat quietly awaiting his fate. And then the name 'Neander' echoed down the stairway to this subterranean holding place, and he stood as the Dock Officer approached him.

'Time to go,' said the Officer, 'steady now,' he added, with something approaching sympathy. It was a show of compassion that David had not encountered for months, apart from that shown by Julia and her father, and it almost unmanned him.

As David and the Dock Officer entered the courtroom, Julia looked instinctively across at the Judge's face and caught his expression of contempt. His lip had curled, there was an expectant gleam in his eye and he was rubbing his hands together, as if gloating at the prospect of this retrial. Julia transferred her gaze to David, who now stood shackled at the bar. She looked down on him with tempered pride, smiling at the sight of him. Her apprehension was undiminished, but he looked every inch the handsome and respectable man he was, not a dirty ragamuffin to be tossed easily aside by an uncaring judicial system.

As he stood by the bar his shackles were removed, but his eyes needed time to adjust to the bright light. Months in Newgate prison and hours in the courtroom cells had made his eyes sensitive to the light, but this was now forced upon him. Looking up at the gallery he searched frantically for Julia's kind, supporting face. And there it was, smiling down at him. His heart leapt at the sight of her and he smiled a confident smile back at her, as much to reassure himself as her, for he could see the apprehension in her eyes - he knew he was not alone in his fight for justice and it was that which gave him reassurance.

The Judge turned to the Clerk to the Court, 'Is the interpreter present? I cannot see him,' he said matter-of-factly.

George Carmichael stood. 'That won't be necessary, My Lord,' he said, 'the prisoner has used his time in gaol to learn English.'

The Judge's eyebrows rose in a look of surprise, which was then followed by a sneer. David glanced again at Julia and caught her pointed look; knew it had occurred to her, as it had to him when he saw that sneer, that the Judge would somehow use it against him.

Twelve jurors were to be sworn from the panel provided by the Sheriff. George Carmichael again addressed the Judge, 'Your Honour, if the court will oblige, I'd like to petition for a jury of six Englishmen and six foreigners.'

'Is that really necessary, Mr Carmichael? By your own admission your client now professes to speak English.' The Judge's tone was disdainful.

'He is still a foreigner, My Lord, whether he speaks English or not. And if I may remind you, you did allow it at the original trial?'

In the gallery, straining to hear, Julia held her breath hoping her father would not antagonise the Judge. She saw Josiah Heath get quickly to his feet, heard him say with a slight bow, 'I have no objection, My Lord.'

'Oh, very well, if we must,' the Judge gave an exaggerated sigh and turning, nodded his assent to the Clerk to the Court. A new jury was sworn and they started to examine the bill of indictment against

David as produced by the clerks. He was indicted, as before, for feloniously stealing, on the 10th of December last, a wether sheep, value forty shillings; the property of Herbert Bond.

David was asked to plead. 'Not guilty,' he said loudly, his richly toned voice ringing across the courtroom.

At that point, the Clerk called for witnesses for the Crown who were to give evidence against the prisoner, and those who came forward were sworn in to tell the truth.

CHAPTER 24

Dortmund 1821

I was elated after that fight with Wolfgang Schmidtlein. It's hard to understand why something as physical and brutal as a pugilistic pitched battle could help me come to terms with the mental turmoil that had been eating away at me for the months since that horrible day in Frankfurt. I thought I was a sensitive man, a man with a poet's soul, yet here I was revelling in what I had achieved in the ring. But it was more than that; it meant that I was my own man – the fight was somehow a metaphor for that. I was not Bernd Hartman's man; I was me, Loeb Ephraim. If that meant that I would not attain my full potential as a fighter, then so be it.

Away from the ring I had come to love Rabbi Baum as a second father. This man of diminutive stature had become my personal tree to lean on, but I also realised that I was not *his* man either. That fight had made me understand that the answer to my turmoil lay not in Orthodox Judaism and that however knowledgeable the Rabbi was, he could not deliver me from my own personal hell. That was something I had to do for myself or not at all. But he helped me to come to terms with the fact that I *was* a Jew. I continued to go to the synagogue on the Sabbath, but I shaved off my beard, put away the sombre black coat and established my own statement of belief.

The day after the fight I wrote to Uncle Meno. I sat down at the solitary table in my rooms and picked up the quill. It was physically painful; both my hands were blue, scarred and swollen around the knuckles, my fingers stiff and tender. My arms had turned blue-black as the bruises deepened, but when I started to write, the long held back words just flooded out of me as though a dam had burst. I had sent him a short note soon after I had arrived in Dortmund, but it had said little more than where I was. He had written to me several times but I had never answered, and I realised that this was a terrible omission on my part. I was the only family he had left and I had just walked out of his life. The least I could do was to keep in touch with him, but in that I had failed. All I can now say in my defence is that poor, lonely Uncle Meno was a part of my past life, and my past life was something I wanted to avoid – he was a casualty of that. After the fight, however, I found I was able to tell him about my new life; how I had found it difficult to come to terms with things - and as I wrote, suddenly, things seemed to just come together, to coalesce in my mind; to make sense.

Wolfgang Schmidtlein had been a substitute for all those mob-crazed people in Frankfurt who had violently revelled in the riot - those anti-Semitic thugs that had caused the wicked death of my family. Bernd had seen in me a fighting spirit, but mine was not born out of hunger, using my fists to ensure that my empty stomach would never ache again, or that my children would never go hungry. Revenge is not the most noble of emotions, but I accepted that this was the source of my fighting spirit. I was not afraid of that realisation; I recognised that it was cathartic. It was the counter balance to the rage that had been eating away at me for the months since I had arrived in Dortmund. Fighting would become my release, my therapy, and I realised something else; I *liked* the adoration of the crowd, it released new emotions within me. As a Jew growing up you learned to be invisible to the German people, to always keep your head below the parapet, to never get above yourself, to know your place. But now the cheers rang out when I threw a good punch; my Jewishness seemed to be invisible in the fighting ring – I loved it.

I was not yet twenty, but I saw a good living as a translator and as a pugilist however incongruous these two professions, on the face of it, seemed. But in writing that letter, a third profession crystallized in my mind. My father was a writer, a professor of German literature; it was my inheritance. I started to write poetry. It was initially an indulgence, but because I liked that adulation in the ring so much, I wanted it for my poetry too. I wrote in German, it was my first language, and with that my hatred of all things German began to dissipate. I needed a publisher; I began to write long rambling letters weekly to Uncle Meno and he dutifully wrote equally long ones back. I asked him about my father's publishers and I then sent them some of my work for consideration. They liked it but could see little commercial interest in it. They were aware that my father's work had become unfashionable after the defeat of Napoleon and the rise of German nationalism. People wanted great German writers, not great Jewish ones. I took little persuading: I saw myself as a new man. So I changed my name, and David Neander the poet was born. Loeb Ephraim the fighter also became David Neander. I knew who I was; I thought that I had found myself.

My second victory in the ring came easily to me. My opponent was young and strong but he had nothing of the skill and guile of Wolfgang Schmidtlein. But this was not Loeb the Jew he was fighting. This was David Neander, the new man. Having shaved off my beard I once again looked German. I had no stigma to overcome by my fighting spirit. In the crowd's eyes I was starting off from the same place as my opponent. In my mind I was now my own man and everything Bernd taught me I adapted. Bernd was exasperated at times: if his coaching helped me then I accepted it, if not I rejected it. It was a dangerous precedence and he allowed no such freedom to his other fighters, but he reluctantly accepted me as a nonconformist – I was an intellectual, I was Jewish, I was not from the street; I was his stable's rebel.

On that day my opponent had no answer to my strategy, my new way of fighting, moving around the ring, using my athleticism to avoid being hit. Many of the traditionalists in the crowd did not like it, they wanted to see the gladiatorial toe-to-toe brutality of time-honored fighting, but once I had my opponent bested I gave them the all the brutality they wanted – then even *they* began to cheer.

The local tavern was crowded after the fight that evening; it was loud, the clientele boisterous, fuelled by their consumption of beer. The sun had gone down and the lighting in the saloon was subdued, lit only by candlelight punctuated by the occasional burst of burning tobacco in the bowl of a pipe. German songs were being sung, it was a typical German watering hole. I was drinking with Helmut and Rudi, two of the other fighters in the stable. They were the nearest to my age, both being twenty-three, almost four years older than me, but immature. I was positively grown-up compared to them. I was a willing partner, however, and happy to accept their invitation; I had a victory to celebrate. Since shaving off my full dark beard I was more acceptable company for socializing. Helmut and Rudi's company was shallow in the extreme – they had only three topics of conversation, fighting, money, and *fräuleins*. I may have been well educated, multi-cultural and well rounded socially, but I found I could come down to their level easily – in truth I enjoyed being with them.

They were both afraid of Bernd; he had total dominance over them. I think they were a little jealous because they could see that he had no such control over me. I was perceived by them as a bit of a mutineer and I think a little respect came with the jealousy because of it. Helmut was a short, powerful man with brilliant red hair; his face was a wide expanse of freckles that cascaded down his neck, his arms, his back, his chest. When he fought, his upper body from the face down all turned scarlet so that he was reddened even before any blood was spilt. His arms were freakishly long, leading to huge bucket-shaped hands, which also displayed the freckles on the back of them. I suppose that he was not the most handsome of men, but that had no effect on his ever happy personality and he could belly laugh at the slightest invitation. He was the joker in the stable.

Rudi was always his partner in crime. He was the typical blond, blue-eyed German, his particular incarnation of the breed was as tall as me, but more heavily muscled standing on two tree trunks of legs. If Helmut was involved in mischief then you could be sure that Rudi was at the back of it. Helmut was always an open book, but Rudi had guile, a deviousness that should have been unattractive but he was one of those people who could just smile his handsome face and flash his mischievous eyes and it was hard to stay mad at him for long. He had probably been doing that since he was a naughty child and was still getting away with it as an adult.

Drinking beer was not part of our training regime. Bernd told us what to eat, what to drink, when to sleep. Despite being afraid of him they were both here in the tavern; why? The answer was simple: *fräuleins!* We had minor celebrity status and Rudi in particular, with his devious cunning, was intent on capitalising on it. We were all wearing our best expensive frock-coats bought out of our winnings to accentuate that celebrity, to show off our affluence. He called over the serving frau and she bent over and filled our tankards from the large beer jug she was carrying. She was a pretty young girl in her traditional costume, a low cut bodice, worn with a blouse, a full skirt and an apron. But as well as filling our tankards she also filled our vision with the sight of her large and overflowing breasts, which seemed to be trying to escape from her bodice. She knew, of course, and lingered so that we could drink our fill of them before we drank our fill of the beer she was dispensing. Rudi was more cunning more adventurous than us; he brought his hand up and placed it on her rear end fondling her buttocks gently as he did so. She turned around slightly whilst still bending over and slapped his hand away, but there was little admonishment in the gesture.

Rudi beamed a roguish smile, knowing that he had, once again, got away with his mischief. 'And what do they call you then?' he said.

'*You* don't call me anything,' she said to him, and then Helmut and I took our cue and jeered at the put down, but she looked across the table at me; gazed hard into my eyes, said, 'But your friend can call me Marita.'

I shuffled uncomfortably in my seat and felt my face suffusing with colour. Rudi was clearly put out, but Helmut oo'ed in a juvenile sort of way. I wasn't sure what to say. For some reason my eyes were drawn to Marita's red shiny lips. They seemed for some moments to be disconnected from the rest of her face. My mind replayed that sensuous mouth speaking those words, *'but your friend can call me Marita.'* I was a writer, but at that moment no words came to me and in fact her words had made me rigid. I disengaged my stare from her mouth with some difficulty and looked into her eyes again; they were encouraging, enticing and then she came to my aid.

'And what's your name then?'

Helmut answered for me, 'He's called David, and I'm Helmut and this is Rudi.'

'Hello David,' she said looking directly at me and deliberately ignoring the others. Then she just bobbed a curtsy and walked away with all our eyes gazing riveted after her. She must have known that for after a few paces she looked over her shoulder, but again her glance was only for me. She smiled a come-on smile at me – I was in no doubt about that.

We were all speechless for a few moments at the frankness of what had just happened, but then the noise gushed from Helmut like water from an opening sluice gate. 'You're in there, David Neander.' Then he followed it up with a belly-laugh. He put his powerful arm around my neck and pulled my head down and close to him, ruffling my hair in some odd manly mixture of friendliness and admiration.

Yes, I knew *I was in.* I had absolutely no experience with women, but I clearly knew I was about to get some! I was a young man and my thoughts should have been filled by thoughts of the opposite sex, but the terrible events of the past year had suppressed them to the point of non-existence. I had not thought of *fräuleins* at all: but I did now. The picture of those red,

156

enticing lips was somehow burned into my brain; it was as though that image was superimposed on the current scene before me. My problem was that I had no idea what to do next. For the next hour Helmut and Rudi gave me the benefit of their own experience in such matters. They teased me, cajoled me, nudged me, tried everything they could to get me to go and talk to the young woman.

'You can't let this opportunity go by, you dunderhead,' said Rudi. 'You're in. All you have to do is go and talk to her – go on, go on.'

He pushed me to the end of the bench but I stayed resolutely stuck to it, squirming at the same time. But although I did not know what to do, that involuntary suppression of everything sexual was being dismantled with every second that passed, it was being eaten away by those words, *but your friend can call me Marita*. It was as though those words were corrosive acid devouring my senses. I felt a stirring in my loins; I was alarmed yet overwhelmingly exited at the same time. I felt my heart start to pound, thumping so loudly I thought everyone would hear it. I was more nervous than before any of my fights. I had gone from sexual dormancy to intense desire in a matter of minutes. I knew nothing of this girl at all and yet, at that moment, she was all that I wanted. And therein lay my problem. I needed to do very little to have her, yet I was totally incapable of doing even that. That realisation began to take me; I knew that I was not going to do anything about it. There was not going to be a Napoleonic conquest of this girl, merely an ignominious retreat in front of an imaginary self-created foe.

Helmut and Rudi could see that as well, and the admiration they felt for me for being able to stand up to Bernd Hartman was now draining away like grains of sand falling through the isthmus of an egg-timer. But if I was going to let this opportunity go by, Marita was not. As she passed our table again, she stooped slightly and pressed a note into my hand before resuming her duties. I was surprised, it happened swiftly and unexpectedly, but then I saw the beaming faces of Helmut and Rudi gesturing at me to open and read it. I did so and opened the crumpled paper; the note was written in an uneducated hand using a thick graphite stick. It read simply - *I finish at thirty after eleven, Marita.* I looked round and saw her staring at me waiting for my answer. I nodded in her direction and she turned away to serve at another table.

I sat there in a daze saying little, nursing my drink, my hands sticky with the sweat of nervous anticipation. I must have been poor company for my two friends, but their high spirits seemed never to flag as the raucous evening dragged on.

'Shall we go, David?' The words made me turn around; I had not seen Marita approach me. Helmut and Rudi were again sniggering like two adolescent schoolboys and I wanted the floor to open up and swallow me - but there was no going back now. She reached out with her hand and I took it obediently. We walked to the tavern door and stood hesitating in the doorway, lit by the light from the tavern. Releasing my hand she turned to me and smiled and I noticed that her lips were even more enticing, she had refreshed them, reddened them with stained beeswax. How I, ignorant of the ways of women, knew that I have no idea. Someone somewhere in my past must have explained it to me.

'What shall we do?' she said.

I had no idea. I just stared gormlessly for a heartbeat, shivering, then said simply, 'Shall I walk you home?'

'That would be difficult.' There was mischief in her eyes.

'Why?' I said naively.

'Because I live here,' she gestured upwards, 'above the tavern.'

'Ah,' I said and there was another uncomfortable pause, but then she took pity on me. She reached up and kissed me gently on the lips. It was the briefest of kisses but it was my first and it had intensity out of all proportion to its substance. I tasted the beeswax; it had sweetness and clearly something sweet had been added as well as the plant stain. It was a delight and I longed for another, but then I heard the jeering again from back in the tavern where Helmut and Rudi were observing us. I closed the door quickly behind us. 'It's a nice evening,' I said, 'shall we go for walk?'

'That would be nice.'

I seemed to have unknowingly said the right thing; she took my arm and we started to stroll. Acutely conscious of her hand on my arm, for a time I couldn't think of anything to say; my thoughts were transfixed on the image of the two pointed shadows that walked before us, cast by the bright full moon that had emerged from rolling clouds. But after a time we started to chat more easily.

'Is the landlord your father?' I said.

'No, I come from a village just outside the city. My papa is a farm worker; well he was until he became too ill to work. My cousin lives in Dortmund and she works at the tavern; she wrote me about a job here and the money I send back is needed by my mama. And you?'

'I'm from Frankfurt originally, but all my family are now dead so I came here to Dortmund.'

'They're all dead? – you have no one?'

'No - no one at all.' I didn't elaborate any further and I did not tell her about Uncle Meno – I don't know why. I didn't tell her that I was Jewish either. The kindest reason I can give for my denial by omission is that I didn't want anything to spoil things, but looking back I was probably just being devious or maybe it was just that I am naturally inclined to reticence. We walked for some time; it was still only late spring but the weather had been kind; the evening was balmy and the walking pleasant. She held my arm tighter and snuggled closer as if to comfort me for being alone in the world.

'Those other two are fighters aren't they? What have you to do with them?'

'I'm a fighter as well,' I said proudly. I thought it would impress her.

She stopped walking, let go of my arm and turned to look at me intently. 'I'm not sure I would have come with you if I had known that.'

'Why not?' I was genuinely surprised; listening to Rudi I thought the *fräuleins* were impressed by young fighting men.

'Fighters are arrogant; they throw their money about. They assume that the serving *fräuleins*, are... well, you know?' I didn't know and she saw that from my expression. 'They think that we are all going to...,' she paused, choosing her words. 'They feel they can have any woman they want,' she said finally, exasperated by my apparent lack of understanding.

I knew from listening to Helmut and Rudi that she was right, of course. 'Is that how you see me?'

'No, you don't seem arrogant at all; and you don't look like a fighter – you are too handsome for that.'

'Me – handsome?' I was genuinely taken aback that she thought I was handsome. I had also fought that day and it was a miracle that I was not marked to pronounce me as a fighter.

'Don't give me all that false modesty. The girls must have told you that before.' There was concern in her face - I think she was beginning to think that she had made a mistake with me.

'No, not really,' I said honestly. The fact that she didn't like the arrogance of fighters had put me at ease; I felt that I didn't need to try and impress her. 'I've not really had much to do with girls,' I confessed without much thought.

I saw her brow furrow. 'You are telling me that a tall, handsome young man such as you doesn't have a string of lady friends?'

'Well yes, I suppose I am. How old do you think I am?'

She looked me up and down, at my new smart frockcoat, my clean white breeches, my new shiny shoes – and then at my face, 'twenty-four, twenty-five?'

'I'm just turned nineteen.'

'You look older, David,' she said, surprised. 'You are younger than me.'

'Does that matter?' There was apprehension in my tone; I thought I had spoiled things.

'No, of course not, I'm only twenty; there is not much difference in our ages. I'm glad that you are not older. You haven't had time to learn all that conceit: and that handsome face of yours has not had time to be mashed around. But why boxing?'

We resumed walking as I said, 'By accident I suppose. I was set upon in the street, and when I bested my attackers I was offered a chance to fight for money.'

'Is the money so much better than what you were earning before; what were you doing?' she said, her fingers curling into my hand.

'I wanted to go to the University, but I couldn't get a place so I was working as a translator.'

Again she stopped and turned to look at me, disbelief evident in her features. 'Are you playing games with me David? Do you think I am some simple country girl to be taken advantage of? Someone to tell lies to, 'cause if you do, let me tell you that lies do not impress me. '

Alarmed I protested, 'No – no!' I thought I had really ruined it then - and I had done that by telling the truth! 'I really am a translator, my father educated me. He was a teacher of German literature.' I was making it worse. She let go of my hand and moved a pace away from me.

'I was really wrong about you, wasn't I?' she asked.

My thoughts whirled crazily in my mind; I could not think what to do. Without thinking it through I spoke to her in French; then in Latin. I could see that she was still unconvinced. 'Is it so difficult to accept that I am telling the truth?'

She frowned, looked at me intently for a heartbeat, but then I saw her expression soften, 'I suppose not,' she said, reluctance lingering in her tone. 'But you could be still making it all up; I don't speak these languages.'

I could see that the suspicious frown was leaving her features when she added, 'I think it might have been better if you had just been a fighter; I think I'd know how to handle that. But if you are an educated man then we have nothing in common,' she said flatly. 'I'm a simple country girl.'

'But perhaps you can be *my* simple country girl.' I reached out and this time I took *her* hand. Remarkably I had said and done the right thing. She snuggled close into me and I felt the concern drain away from her. She allowed herself a smile. I wanted so much to kiss her but my courage deserted me, so once again we resumed walking. 'I'm from a poor family as well, even though I was educated,' I said, 'we are not so different.'

We walked for a long time and the conversation became easier. And then we were walking down the street where I had my lodging – it was accidental, I had not planned it. Helmut and Rudi came into my mind and what I would say to them the next day. They would want to know if I had... if we had... well, they would expect that I had – done it. Helmut's words came back to me: '*You're in there, David Neander.*' I stopped. Looking back on it now, I think I was motivated more by what I thought Helmut and Rudi would say than what I really wanted at the time. I looked up at the window on the first floor above us. 'This is where I lodge.'

'Oh; is it expensive?' she said.

'No... and I suppose that I could afford something better now. But it suits me and I can write here without being disturbed. I had not told her I wrote poetry. I shuffled my feet uncomfortably. 'Would you like to come up and see?' I said sheepishly.

Marita stepped in close to me, reached up and kissed my lips. It was longer than the first kiss in the tavern doorway, though was not a long, passionate kiss. It lasted for perhaps a couple of seconds and was warm, but not lustful, yet the effect it had on me was immediate. She smiled up at me and did not answer, just squeezed my hand and started to walk nonchalantly forward. I walked with her taking her lead automatically. She had felt intimidated by the fact that I was an educated man, but she was clearly the one in control of this first liaison and it was I who was intimidated.

CHAPTER 25

London 1823

The first witness, Herbert Bond, was called and sworn. A short but powerfully built man, who had the physique of one who lugged animal carcasses around for a living. Josiah Heath called upon him to give his testimony and he did so forcefully, his manner in concert with his appearance. He testified as before, almost word for word, that he was a butcher in the Strand, and that he had lost a sheep on the 10th of December, out of a field at Mary-le-bone. He swore to the skin of the sheep that was found on David; that his mark was across the loins, a cross with red ochre, and that the salesman's mark was also on the carcass, meaning that it was to be sold that day.

George Carmichael stood to cross examine. 'Mr Bond,' he said, 'is theft a problem for a good honest tradesman such as yourself?' His words were chosen carefully to gain the witness's confidence.

'Aye, 'tis that,' he replied, the question giving him chance to get something off his chest. 'Sometimes it's worse than others. The watchmen will eventually catch somebody and it will die down for a time but then it starts up again. There are not enough watchmen you see.'

'Yes, I do see,' said George Carmichael, 'it must be a great problem for you?

'Aye, 'tis true enough.'

'Mr Carmichael!' interrupted the Judge, 'is this relevant? Move on if you please.'

George Carmichael bowed to the Judge. Turning back to the witness he said, 'And was it bad at the time of this particular theft on the 10th of December?'

'Aye sir, I was losing a carcass a week.'

'That must have been very difficult for you?'

'Aye sir, I have a wife and four children to feed.'

'Mr Carmichael!' said the Judge again, making no attempt to hide his irritation.

George, with a fleeting apologetic glance at the bench, continued with his cross examination, 'When did that particular spate of thefts start?'

'About three months before, about September, I think.'

'So you must have been relieved when the accused was apprehended?'

'Aye sir, that I was.'

'So business is better now?'

Herbert Bond was silent for a few moments. 'Well not exactly sir,' he said finally.

'Why not? Have the thefts continued?'

'Aye sir, they have...' his voice tailed off as he spoke.

In the gallery Julia smiled. Her father had told her many times that the first rule in a courtroom was never to ask a question that you did not know the answer to beforehand. She had already established through her own investigations that the crimes were continuing. She brought her attention back to her father, who was speaking again.

'Do you think that the prisoner is the culprit for the spate of thefts?'

Bond paused to consider, said, 'Well, I thought so at the time sir, but it can't have been him, can it? Not the others.' His tone was contrite but then more animated, 'but he had the carcass on him that particular day sir, didn't he?'

'Yes he did Mr Bond, and that fact is not in dispute.' George turned to the Judge, 'No more questions, Your Honour.'

Next, John Henry was sworn and gave his story. He looked as if he had come straight from his shop; still wearing his apron he came into the witness box as if to demonstrate his irritation at losing custom. He told the court that he was a shopkeeper on Oxford Road and that the date in question was in the period when he was required to act as the Watchman for the area. He had met the prisoner between seven and eight in the morning, at the top of Oxford Road, towards the fields, and saw that he had a bundle on his shoulder. He followed him for about two hundred or two hundred-and-fifty yards, but when the prisoner realised he was being followed, he threw down the bundle and endeavoured to escape. John Henry's story had not changed from the first trial.

'What did the accused say when you apprehended him?' asked George Carmichael.

'He told me he had been promised a shilling to take the bundle from the country to Oxford Road. He was only to deliver it.'

'Did you ask him why he threw the carcass away and tried to run?'

'I did, sir.'

'And what did he say?'

'He said that he couldn't speak English. He was speaking in some foreign language, French I think.'

'Do you speak French, Watchman?'

'No sir.'

'Do you speak Yiddish or German?'

'No sir.'

'Then how did you know that he said he had been paid a shilling to deliver the carcass from the country to Oxford Road?'

'Well, it was…' the Watchman faltered. He did not know what to say to the question.

'Were things confusing because of the fact that the prisoner was a foreigner?' asked George, prompting the witness.

'Aye sir,' he said with some relief, 'things were a bit confusing; him not being able to speak English.'

'That's understandable Watchman,' said George, 'the prisoner had only a few words of English.'

'Aye sir, just a few words.'

'When the prisoner was taken to the watchtower was an interpreter then called for?'

'Aye sir.'

'After how long?'

'It was about six-of-the-clock.'

'So he was in custody from about nine in the morning to six in the evening before you were able to hear his side of the story.'

'Aye, I suppose so sir.'

'Now; you have testified that the prisoner had said he had been paid a shilling to deliver the carcass from the country to Oxford Road?'

'Aye sir.'

'So why did you not investigate the prisoner's story?'

'I…,' John Henry hesitated, 'err, I don't know sir.'

'Now is that not quite a detailed explanation to be given with just a few words of English? And you have also testified that you do not speak a foreign language.'

The Watchman's face coloured at the question. It was clear he understood for the first time what his questioner was suggesting. 'I'm not sure, sir,' was all that he could say.

'We all appreciate that it was confusing at the time, Watchman, but could it be that you did not understand what he was saying until the translator advised you some hours later?'

The Watchman looked around the court. He shuffled uncomfortably. 'Maybe that is right sir.'

'So you did your duty, on that day. The reason you did not investigate that story was that you did not understand at the time?'

'Aye sir, that's right. I did not understand what he was telling me. If I had I would have investigated it.'

'And that is also the reason why you did not try to apprehend the other man running away; the man who had paid the prisoner the shilling?'

'Aye sir, it is,' said the witness.

In the gallery, Julia smiled at her father's skill. He had introduced to the jury the concept that another man was responsible for the theft. Eagerly she leaned forward to look down at their faces, but her good spirits were short-lived for at that same moment the Judge had realised the prisoner's acquittal was a distinct possibility and it was clear that this was the last thing he wanted.

As a Judge, Cardew was a man entrusted with the upkeep of the law, but all that was now downgraded in his mind. What was more important to him was his reputation and he reasoned that acquittal would be a slight on that reputation. To hell with the law; this was personal; his judgement was as much on trial here as the prisoner!

'Mr Carmichael!' he interrupted smartly.

'My Lord?'

'You have not established either that this other man or even that the alleged shilling existed.' Frowning, he turned to the jurors and said, 'The jury will disregard that last evidence, and you...' he wagged his finger at George and stared sternly at him, 'be careful if you please, Mr Carmichael.'

George bowed in acquiescence covertly looking round at Josiah Heath, who gave him a knowing smile as if to say, *my fees will be earned easily today*. With a twinkle in his eye, George acknowledged Josiah's smug smile with the briefest of nods before turning back to the witness.

'Mr Henry, did you search the prisoner?'

'Aye sir, we searched him when we had him back at the watchtower.'

'And did he have any money on him, when you searched him?'

'He had a shilling and a few pence, sir.'

'There is no evidence that that shilling came from this mysterious other man, Mr Carmichael,' interrupted the Judge. 'A shilling is a shilling.'

Julia sat up with a start. He can't say that, she thought to herself, he is a Judge not a prosecutor. She looked down anxiously at her father, but he seemed unperturbed. Glowering at the Judge, she settled back in her seat, her fingers clenched tightly in her lap.

'Mr Henry, did the prisoner have a weapon when you searched him?' George continued.

'No sir, he did not.'

Once again, the Judge entered the fray. 'But if you did not search him until you got back to the watchtower,' he turned to the jury, 'then the prisoner had every opportunity to throw it away.'

Ignoring the interruption, George cast a sideways look at the Judge, *I'll show the old bastard*, he thought. 'And who carried the carcass back to the watchtower?' he asked the witness.

'We placed the carcass on the prisoner's shoulders, sir, and made him carry it back to the watchtower.'

'And did the prisoner need both hands to keep it there?'

'Oh yes, of course sir', said the witness with a grin, 'they fat wethers be heavy beasts.'

'Quite so,' George said smoothly. 'So are you saying that the witness did not have a hand free from the moment you apprehended him?'

The witness wrinkled his brow, 'Aye, that's right sir,' he confirmed. As he spoke there was a rustle of movement amongst the jurors.

George thought about asking the next obvious question. *Did the prisoner have the opportunity to throw away a knife?* He decided that he did not need to. He just turned to the Judge, bowed compliantly. On the surface it was a bow of respect that he had done many times before, but there was a small triumphant smile on his face as he murmured, 'No further questions, My Lord.'

The Judge leered back at him and George met the full malicious force of that leer. There was now no doubt in his mind that Cardew had abandoned all pretence of impartiality. Murmurs broke out in the court as various officials whispered to each other and a member of the jury leaned towards another to discuss what he had heard. They had all seen the small victory that George had made over the Judge

Judge Cardew saw what was happening and his face flushed an angry red. 'Silence!' he raged. He took up his gavel and thudded it down several times, each time harder than the last. 'Silence, silence in court,' he bellowed.

Silence fell almost immediately; the court officials looked to the Judge with fearful eyes, they knew how powerful a figure he was and how malicious he could be; he was not a man to cross.

Herbert Ackroyd was next called to the stand, his name ringing in the newly established silence. A rotund bald man got to his feet and waddled to the witness box. He was sworn to tell the truth, gave his name and then confirmed his occupation as Harbour Master.

'Do you recognise these documents?' George Carmichael handed him a sheaf of papers. He looked at them intently over a large bulbous nose, his brow furrowed in deep concentration, the creases going right up to his bald pate.

'Yes sir,' he wheezed, and then prompted by his questioner's raised eyebrows added, 'it is the passenger manifest for a ship called the *Wilhelmina,* which docked on the 8th December 1822, from Hamburg. It was logged with the Harbour Master's office on the same day.'

'So you have seen this document before?'

'Oh yes, it has my signature of endorsement upon it.'

'I have underlined a name on the second page. Will you be so good as to tell the court that name, Mr Ackroyd?'

'Yes sir, the name is David Neander.'

'So David Neander arrived in London from Hamburg on the 8th December 1822 – is that right?'

'That's exactly right sir,' wheezed the Harbour Master.

'Thank you Mr Ackroyd, there will be no further questions,' George bowed.

Josiah Heath stood and said that he had no questions. The witness struggled to turn his overweight frame through a half circle so that he could leave the witness stand, but before he could a voice boomed from above him.

'Just a minute sir,' said the Judge.

Herbert Ackroyd looked up at the belligerent figure staring down at him, put his hands on the rail of the stand and squeezed himself round again.

'Are you able to recognise David Neander in this courtroom sir?' the Judge asked. 'Have you ever met him?'

'No, My Lord,' Ackroyd wheezed again, prompted by his exertions this time breaking into a rasping cough.

'Then how can you testify that he arrived in England on that day?'

The large man paused to reflect: he did not know this Judge personally, but he had seen enough to know he did not want to antagonise him. 'Well I – well I suppose that I can't sir. I can only testify to the manifest and that it shows his name.'

Judge Cardew's expression changed almost immediately. He smiled at the witness; a smile that said he had got the response he wanted. 'Thank you Mr Ackroyd. That will be all,' he sat back in his chair and waved his hand dismissively towards the witness to emphasise his words. He was the master in this court and everyone should know that.

In the gallery, Julia's emotions were running wild. She was immensely proud of her father's skill, but at the same time fearful of the Judge's vindictiveness. Whatever the jury felt, she feared they were too in thrall to Cardew to go against his obvious wishes. She looked down at David by the bar. He seemed to know that she was doing so and turned his head to meet her gaze. They exchanged glances. He gave her a satisfied smile; nodding his head slightly to show that he was pleased with the way the case was going. She returned the same smile, nodding a gestured agreement as she did so. For both of them it hid the apprehension within, an apprehension that ran like an icy wind blowing over a cold ocean

CHAPTER 26

Dortmund 1821

That summer in Dortmund was the summer of my first love. Marita and I had very little in common, but somehow that did not seem to matter. She'd had very little education and although she could read and write she did so very rarely. My poetry was philosophical and political and not unnaturally she showed very little interest in it. The literary world did not exist to her, and yet I wrote some of my best work while I was with her – it was, I suppose, less intense, some of the anger was dissipated by my feelings of love. The world was somehow a less bleak place and that gave me a different perspective, curbing some of the more one-dimensional introspective writing I was prone to deliver. I even started to write poetry for *her*. Little love poems, verses that she found embarrassing and impractical. She said that they were bits of nonsense and not for the likes of her, but I could tell from her eyes that she treasured them as she tucked them neatly into her purse.

The early spring turned into a long hot summer. We walked for miles some days, easy with each other talking about inconsequential things. We spent hours down by the river, sat on the riverbank picnicking as the cool water flowed languidly past. I carried my portfolio and took the opportunity to write, and she seemed happy for me to do so and was comfortable just to relax and let me do as I wished. We even walked to her village one time and I spent a delightful day with her mother and younger sister. Her father was consumptive, and the sound of his coughing filled the little cottage, but it was still a happy house and it brought back bitter sweet memories of my own family. I had brought a hamper of food to take with us; it needed all my persuasion to get her father to accept it, his pride being bruised. I think that his inability to work and support his family weighed heavily upon him.

Helmut and Rudi thought that we were lovers because that was what they expected of tavern girls, but we weren't. She had occasionally been back with me to my lodgings, but our intimacy was restricted to kissing and fondling. I wanted her desperately, but I was brought up to believe that sex came with marriage and I just accepted that she was not 'that sort of girl'. I don't think that I actually contemplated marriage to her, but similarly I did not dismiss it either. There was no sense in my mind that she was beneath me, nor did I think that I should only marry a Jewess. I had told her in the second week that I was a Jew; I was a little nervous, but she hardly batted an eye. She had never met a Jew before; there were none in her village and she just accepted me for what I was – I was just 'David' to her. Once, as we strolled through the streets of Dortmund, a Jewish man walked towards us, dressed in traditional black, his beard full and with side ringlets in his hair. He stepped into the road as he approached us and without thinking I nodded an acknowledgement to him. I saw the look of puzzlement on his face; to him I was a German and Germans did not do that.

'Was he a Jew?' Marita asked me.

I smiled at her naivety. 'Yes, he's an Orthodox Jew,' I said.

'But you do not look that way?'

'No I don't,' I laughed, 'but I *have* dressed that way in the past.'

That was enough explanation for her. She seemed happy with just that and never mentioned it again.

That day, as we walked back from her village the hot summer sun beat down on us. It was six-of-the-clock, but there was no let up in the sunlight's intensity and it was accompanied by a fierce humidity. We had been walking for an hour and a half and the sweat was dripping from the end of my chin. Marita's face was suffused with the heat, despite hiding under her parasol as we walked. We were following the river and we stopped to rest. I bent over and cupped a handful of the clear cold water and drank profusely to quench my thirst. At that moment it was like an elixir, as sweet a drink as I have ever had. I trickled the cool liquid through my hair and allowed it to run down my back and my chest. It was just wonderful. I stood up with another cupped handful of the revitalising liquid, trying not to let too much run away between my fingers, and offered it to Marita. She drank it eagerly. I bent down and gave her another cupped handful and that too was taken fervently. I flicked my fingers playfully so that the last drops splashed her face. She laughed out loud, raising her head so the splashes could have full effect, then she undid the top button of her *dirndl*, the dress was sleeveless in the fashion of the summer and the effect to my masculine eyes was delightful. Then she took my cold hand and put it on the top of her chest, holding it there just below her throat, her head still looking skyward enjoying the cool sensation.

To Marita, there was nothing sexual in what she did, my hand was nowhere near her breasts, and yet I reacted sexually. I felt intense desire for her and reaching forward I kissed her full on the lips. She pulled away slightly and initially I was concerned, but then she took my hand away and moved back to me, reached up and re-engaged the kiss. It was long and lingering, but soft and gentle; it was wonderful. As difficult as it was for me, I subdued my lustful thoughts and got myself under control.

'Thank you,' she said.

'For what?' I was puzzled.

'For liking my family.'

She was grateful; something as simple as that, and she was immensely grateful to me for it. She must have been concerned about the visit. My concern had been their reaction to my Judaism, but hers had been simpler; would I look down on them? She need not have worried; it was not in my nature to think of myself as 'better' than they.

We sat and talked easily before continuing our journey home. We took off our boots and stockings and found a good spot on the side of the river bank where we dangled our feet in the fresh, invigorating water. Birds were singing and gnats danced in the evening sunlight all along the river bank. We watched the swallows swooping to skim the water and I held her hand and stared at the river as it ambled appealingly by. It looked so inviting.

'Go on then,' she said to me. She must have read my thoughts.

'What?' I asked.

'Go on, have a swim. That's what you want isn't it?'

I nodded, smirking sheepishly to acknowledge that she was right. I stood and pulled my linen shirt over my head and shoulders. I saw her look at my torso, at my new found rippling muscles standing out after the months of training, and I could see she was impressed. I pulled down my breeches and she giggled at the sight of my drawers. I looked down and saw how comical I looked, but I was not offended – nor was I embarrassed - and I laughed with her. I stepped awkwardly knee-deep into the water trying not to lose my footing when she called out to me.

'You'll get your drawers wet and have to walk all the way back like that.'

'But I can't...'

She interrupted me, 'Yes you can,' she said, turning her back on me as she did so. 'Come on, get out and take them off – I wont look.'

I stumbled out, removed the comical drawers quickly and then dived full length into the cold water. As it closed over me a tingly quiver took my body from the top of my head to the tip of my toes. But after that first shock the water felt enchanting against my skin. When I surfaced I whooped my delight and saw her looking longingly back at me.

I swam and dived and frolicked for ten minutes or so, enjoying the swim as the hot sun continued to bear down. I must have made Marita very envious. I had swum toward the far bank, when I heard the sound of another splash behind me. I had had no notion of her disrobing, but when I turned there she was swimming towards me. She was uninhibited, out of control; her nakedness was all there for me to see, and yet she didn't care. Her torso was milky white compared with her deeply bronzed arms. Her ivory breasts rose and fell as she jumped and frolicked in the water and I could not help but look at them. She saw the look of pleasure in my eyes; I was revelling in her nakedness and she was exhilarated by my reaction. I suddenly found myself frolicking in the water with her. This was something I could never have suggested to her, and in any other circumstances I doubt if she would ever have committed such an act of abandonment, but that longing to take a cooling swim had let the genie out of the bottle and there was now no way that it was going to go back.

We swam around each other touching at first inadvertently, but then more purposefully, each time a little bolder than the last. Then we stood at the shallow water's edge, up to our waists in the river, facing each other. Marita took a small step towards me and embraced me. She raised her hand to the side of my cheeks and then standing on her tip toes she kissed me gently but lingeringly on the lips. The kiss seemed endless – it was by no means our first kiss, but this was an immensely powerful one. My arms went round her, I felt her breasts firm against my chest and we both felt each other's hearts beating powerfully within us. But more than that, I felt my arousal standing erect between my legs. It was a kiss that had aroused us both to fever pitch and I pulled away in alarm, alternately embarrassed and ashamed. I splashed back into the middle of the river putting distance between us to give my clamouring body time to subside, and laughing to mask my confusion. Marita laughed with me; I do not think she was aware of what was happening to me nor the effect of her nakedness against mine - and so she waded out to join me and we frolicked some more.

When we emerged from the water at last, we just lay on the grass and allowed the sun to dry us – we had no towels and it was the sensible thing to do. There seemed little point now in being coy about our nakedness. Her chest rose and fell energetically after her exertions - the cold water had stimulated her nipples and they stood erect in the late afternoon sunshine emphasising each exaggerated breath. She noticed me looking and glanced down at herself to see what was attracting me. When she saw their hardness she smiled a knowing smile at me, but then she tried to put her arm across her breasts as a stray feeling of embarrassment suddenly took her. I grasped her arm and stopped her, shaking my head and gazing into her eyes to reassure her. 'You are very beautiful,' I said and she responded with a tremulous smile.

Deep inside me my upbringing told me this was all wrong, but somehow it did not seem so. It felt natural - it felt *right*. Most relationships take time to develop, but in those few short minutes that we had spent in the water together our relationship had taken a vast leap forward, blossoming spontaneously. It was more than just lust, although I have to confess that lust was the dominant presence spurring me on. I desperately wanted to take that next step – I wanted to embrace her, to kiss her, to make love to her. I was aroused by her nakedness. The river bank was deserted; it had a profound effect on both of us. It was idyllic, it was deserted – it was removed from the real world that we inhabited. Whatever we felt for each other, back in the city the day-to-day conventions of life, of loyalty, would have kicked in to prevent us from cascading head long into uncontrolled passion. But this deserted river bank somehow masked those everyday constrictions. We were like caged animals suddenly set free. It was a freedom that we were to embrace.

My arousal became obvious to her; I couldn't disguise it. I rolled on my side instinctively and she rolled on her side to meet me. I couldn't believe it. We leant into each other naturally and I caressed her breasts gently as I kissed her, until she let out a small cry of pleasure. We made love sensuously without fear. It was the first time for both of us, and it was how the first time should be: filled with innocence, tenderness and passion. Afterwards we lay easily in each other's arms, the majestic river flowing effortlessly passed our idyllic haven. We spoke no words of love, the silence between us shouting our love loudly to this deserted place. I dozed away, but I don't know whether Marita followed me. All I know is that we stayed in our unconcerned nakedness indifferent to the world around us, until the sun eventually began to go down. It seemed the most natural thing in the world to us.

We walked home slowly in the last rays of the summer sun, until darkness surrounded us. Then I stopped as my gaze was drawn, intuitively, upwards to the sky. We were beneath that canopy of stars. I remembered the night I had been sleeping rough and the emptiness I felt, I was a shell without emotion or purpose; adrift with not even the stars to give me direction. That shell now had some content. Love; love had entered my life and it was as though the stars were acknowledging that.

We didn't care about the darkness; we held hands and picked our footsteps carefully all the way back to Dortmund.

Ah, that summer of sun and first love; would I could turn back the clock.

CHAPTER 27

London 1823.

'Call David Neander to the stand,' the Clerk to the Court's shout reverberated around the courtroom.

David was unshackled and stepped forward, but he remained at the bar from where he would give his evidence; as the accused he was not sworn. He looked up momentarily. Above him was a mirrored reflector whose purpose was to reflect light from the windows onto the faces of the accused so that the jurors could examine their facial expressions to assess the truthfulness of their evidence. It was bright to his eyes and he blinked, squinting whilst his eyes adjusted.

From the gallery, Julia looked down at the man she loved - a love she was reluctant to admit to herself - and her heart missed a beat. The bright light illuminated his appearance that she had been so diligent in arranging. Her chest rose in pride at the sight of him and unconsciously she put her hand on it as she gazed down at him. There, spotlighted by the reflector, was a tall handsome man, clean shaven, resplendent in a smart frockcoat and new linen shirt. This was not the guttersnipe criminal that the Judge would have the jury believe.

He gave his name and his profession as poet and translator; there was momentary laughter from someone in the gallery, but that died down quickly when the perpetrator saw the angered face of the Judge look up at him. Cardew turned back to the defendant, studied him as he did so. 'So, you speak English after all, Mr Neander,' he sneered.

'I have used my time wisely in gaol,' answered David. 'I have had plenty of time, sir, to learn your wonderful tongue.'

Oh well done, well done, David, Julia thought, leaning forward over the gallery rail. *The jury will like that.* She looked across to her father, but he had eyes only for the Judge.

'Or perhaps the answer is that you could speak it all the time?' Cardew said bitingly. 'Perhaps it was convenient for you to feign ignorance of the tongue, eh?'

George Carmichael jumped to his feet, 'Your Honour! There is absolutely no evidence that my client could speak English when he arrived in this country.'

'Oh do sit down, Mr Carmichael.' The Judge waved his hand up and down to emphasis the words, 'The jury can make up their own minds as to the truth of the matter.' He turned and smiled at them, an insistent smile that conveyed his unspoken message.

With a big hint from you, Julia thought to herself, sighing with frustration as she watched her father. His expression mirrored hers and she saw his jaw clench as he gritted his teeth, forcing himself to smile and bow respectfully to the Judge as he sat down again. He exchanged glances with his daughter, grimaced and shrugged his shoulders with resignation. Julia dipped her pen in the ink-well and not for the first time, jotted down the observation: *judges do not pronounce on a question of fact and juries do not pronounce on a question of law – that is a basic requirement of court procedure!* Again she sighed; her father knew that all too well, but what could he do about it?

George Carmichael got to his feet again. 'Mr Neander, will you tell the court where you are from, and how you arrived in England?'

'I have lived in several of the states in the German confederation, but because I am Jewish I have no rights of citizenship in any of them. I travelled from Hamburg to London on the ship *Wilhelmina*, which docked on the 8th December last year.'

'That was only two days before your arrest; is that right?'

'That is correct, sir.'

'What is the purpose of your visit to England?'

'I came to start a new life. England has a reputation for tolerance afforded by the law. I cannot get that in my own country.'

Poor David, Julia thought. What he had said may be so on paper, but she knew the law did little to enforce those rights. Jew baiting was as rife in London as anywhere - and it went unpunished.

'So,' George continued, 'you came without knowing the language and without knowing anybody in this country?'

'Yes sir.'

'Wasn't that a bit foolhardy?'

'In retrospect may be so, but I have a talent for languages and I am well able to support myself. I have moved around Germany to earn my living. I had no apprehension that I might not succeed in England. And of course I came with funds – I had been saving for some time. '

'And what was the value of these funds – err, how much did you bring?'

'I brought two hundred and fifty thalers, sir.'

The Judge looked up sharply, 'And what precisely is a *thaler?*' he said with a smirk. 'I'm sure the jury and I would like to know what a *thaler* is worth against a coin of the realm.'

David turned the jury. 'A thaler is a German coin that is pure silver so that it can be used across borders in many of the German states. Its value can be easily established by its weight of silver.'

'And so how much is two hundred and fifty thalers worth in pounds sterling, Mr Neander?' said George, ignoring the interruption.

'The money exchangers offered a rate of five thalers for the pound, but they told me that I had to return with the coins so they could check the weight to establish that there had been no *clipping*, and to assay them to ensure they were pure silver and that they had not been adulterated.'

Once more the Judge cut across him. 'Are we supposed to believe that this man, who was arrested with a stolen sheep, was…' he paused whilst he did the arithmetic, 'was worth *fifty* pounds! That would indeed make him a rich man.'

'What I am *trying* to establish, Your Honour, is that this is a hard working man capable of earning a good living from his education and skills and that he did not come penniless to this country.'

'I think that you will find that quite a task,' sneered the Judge, smirking at the jury, who tittered dutifully.

George Carmichael turned back to David 'And had you arranged lodgings in advance?'

'No sir. I left my belongings on the ship with the intention of finding lodgings as soon as I arrived.'

'Did you do so?'

'Yes, but it was not easy not knowing the city.'

'So where did you take lodgings?'

'In St Giles, sir.'

'St Giles!' interrupted the Judge. 'Ha! A fine district for a man of means,' he said sarcastically, adding, 'I think he could have bought the whole place for fifty pounds.' The court laughed at his prompting; the area was noted for its slums.

'Were they good lodgings?' asked George as the mocking laughter died down.

'No sir, they certainly were not. But it was getting late and the daylight was fading. I took them temporarily and then went back to the ship to get my trunk and carried it back to the lodgings, meaning to find somewhere better the next day.'

'So what happened to your money?'

'I went out the following morning to look for a suitable place where I could take permanent lodgings and also from where I could run my business as a translator.'

'Did you find such a place?'

'Yes sir, in Threadneedle Street.'

'Ha!' The Judge interjected. 'Mr Carmichael, is your client suggesting that he intended to move from St Giles to Threadneedle Street?' There was mock incredulity on Cardew's face.

'Exactly so, My Lord.'

Judge Cardew turned once more to the jurors, 'Then the jury will no doubt find that as ludicrous as I do.' He laughed out loud at his own quip and one court official broke into a nervous laugh in response. When the court saw that the Judge did not disapprove and in fact could see this was the response he had wanted, the laughter ran around the courtroom like a children's game of tag.

George Carmichael knew he had to stifle this outburst. He turned back to David and raised his voice. 'So what did you do then?'

'I needed money as a bond to secure the lease, so I went back to my lodgings to get the thalers so that I could take them to a money broker and exchange them for pounds and shillings, but when I got there my room had been broken into and my trunk was empty; everything had been stolen. I know that it was the landlord; he was the only one who knew I was newly arrived in England. I think he broke in just to make it look like an opportunist thief.'

'So what did you resolve to do next?'

'For the rest of that day I was distraught. All my plans depended on my being able to establish a business. I knew that I couldn't do that from St Giles. I had a bad night's sleep but then I reasoned that I was a young and strong man, that the theft may have been a set back, but that I had earned the money once and that I would do it again. I am a skilled pugilist and that gives me access to funds.'

The Judge sat up in his chair. 'Pugilist! Is this another one of your client's fantasies Mr Carmichael?'

'No Your Honour,' said George, producing a document from his papers, 'I'd like to introduce this into evidence. It will confirm what the accused has said.'

The Clerk to the Court took the document and read it, in as much as he could since it was written in German. He then walked across the courtroom and handed it to the Judge.

'What am I supposed to make of this,' sniffed Cardew, turning the paper over in his hand as if it was somehow contaminated. 'It's in some foreign language that I am not acquainted with.' He then returned it to the Clerk and gestured for it to be taken to the jury.

George Carmichael saw the look of puzzlement on David's face, but he ignored it and turned to the jury to address them. 'This is a bill-poster from Dortmund, a free city in the German Confederation. It advertises a pugilistic extravaganza that was to take place in the city park and lists the contests to be fought. Your Honour, I have had it translated and I would also introduce into evidence the translation and an affidavit from the translator.' George paused while the documents were taken by the Clerk to the jury. 'If the jurors will look at the third contest listed on the poster; the named contestants are Deidrich Wotan and the accused, David Neander.'

David flashed a look at George and then up at Julia in the gallery, but she looked quickly away avoiding his gaze. He would know this was her doing and would guess she had been back to see Nathan Rothschild, who had agents in Dortmund and had been able at her request to find out about pugilism in that city.

The translation passed around the jury and George Carmichael heard the murmurs of acceptance by many of them. 'So,' he said, 'the jury can see that the accused is no *fantasist.*' He emphasised the word and looked up at the Judge.

'Oh no Papa, no,' Julia murmured apprehensively under her breath. 'Don't antagonise him further.' But George Carmichael, unheeding, his eyes glittering in triumph, was smiling up at the Judge.

CHAPTER 28

Dortmund 1821

There was still warmth in the late summer sun, but the leaves on the trees had begun to change their hue from green to gold so that the woodlands looked majestic in their finery. These autumn colours were, of course, a harbinger of change: a signpost towards a new season; a herald announcing the coming of winter. It was a metaphor for my relationship with Marita, but, of course, I did not see that at the time. It was in late September and my life was to change again.

Our love affair had lasted the whole of the summer. It had been easy, without conflict, neither of us asking anything of each other. We just accepted it for what it was and accepted each other for what we were. We knew we were in no way a matched pair, though we made a handsome couple, I think, but other than that there was no obvious connection. A Jew and a Christian, a city boy and a farm girl, an academic and a tavern wench, but none of that entered my mind and I was sure, at the time, that it was the same for her. It was to prove a misconception on my part, however. We did not make any plans; she was just my girlfriend and I was her boyfriend, it was wonderful. How naive we were.

In early September tragedy struck Marita's family. She was called away to help her mother look after her younger sister, who had taken a fever. When Marita arrived home it became apparent to her that her mother was just as sick as her sister. She put them both to their beds and nursed them, but the fever took hold and showed no signs of breaking. They were not the sort of family who had access to doctors, and despite her father's protestations I paid for a doctor to visit from Dortmund. He quickly diagnosed what everyone suspected: diphtheria. He prescribed a physic, but he knew it would have little effect. I had seen that same expression on Uncle Meno's face many times before that I now saw on the face of this doctor – the physic would not neutralise the toxic poisons introduced into the body by the disease. The fever would have to run its course and all we could do was to hope the patients would be strong enough to survive it - the danger was from suffocation as the airways were obstructed. A week later her mother succumbed, but her sister survived thanks to Marita's nursing.

I was caught up in the tragedy; I liked her family so very much. What I did not realise at first was the change it was to wreak on Marita's life and as a consequence on mine; there was now no family breadwinner. After the funeral, I went back to Dortmund leaving Marita behind and returning to my work as a translator and my training as a pugilist. I missed her of course, but it was obvious to me what had to be done; she was needed at home and I needed to earn a living. What was not so obvious to me were the responsibilities she carried and the weight of those responsibilities upon her.

Two weeks after the funeral I received a note asking me to visit her. I had fought again on the Saturday evening, winning a gruelling fight, but my ribs were sore and my face still swollen. On Sunday morning I set out on the long walk to her village; it was a painful trek my ribs causing me pain that got worse with each step and I was in agony by the time I got there. Two dogs were fighting in the dirt road in front of her cottage and I kicked out at them to get them out of my way, but that only served to jerk the bruised muscles on my rib-cage. A stabbing pain brought me to s standstill and I had to bend over until the spasm eased. As Marita met me at the door her face registered her shock at my battered appearance. I leaned in to kiss her and our lips met briefly, but she broke it off quickly so that our kiss was no more than a peck. I was disappointed, but put it down to my bruised, swollen face. I accepted that it was just a kiss of greeting and that her grief - or my appearance - made a more passionate kiss inappropriate. We all took a meal together, Marita and I, her father and her sister, but there was an atmosphere in the room and few words were spoken. I shuffled in my chair constantly, trying to ease the pain in my chest. I was uncomfortable, but it was more than the pain that was causing that feeling. Marita cleared the plates away, and when she sat down again raised an unconvincing smile. I saw her shoot a look at her father and gesturing compliance almost imperceptively he withdrew to his bedroom, taking the younger daughter with him. It was at this point I realised that something was not right.

'I need to tell you something.' She avoided eye contact, fiddling with a table knife as she spoke.'

'What is it?' I said apprehensively, my palms suddenly sweaty.

'I'm getting married,' she said.

She then looked up at me. She must have seen my utter bewilderment. I stared at her, trying to make sense of what she had said. 'But we haven't even spoken about it,' I said foolishly.

She sighed, I think she realised that this was going to be more difficult than she had thought.

'No – not us, I'm getting married to someone else.'

'What?' My mouth fell open; 'When, Who?' I stuttered, even more bewildered.

'In three weeks; that's as soon as the Church will allow.'

'Who is he?' I was angry now; I thought she had been deceiving me. 'How long has this been going on?'

'Nothing has been going on. His name is Joachim Hinkel. He is a farmer and he will take me as his wife and take my younger sister and my father into his home.'

'And do you love this Joachim Hinkel?'

'He is a good man.'

'That is not what I asked, is it?'

'It's not about love.'

'Then *I* will marry you, and I will look after your family, and you can have love as well.'

'If only that were possible,' she sighed.

'Of course it is possible. Do you not know me well enough to know that?'

Marita nodded, 'Yes, I do. I know what a good man you are,' she reached out and cupped the side of my swollen face. 'I know you would marry me and look after my father and sister, but...'

'Then I don't understand.'

'Our love was never going to be about marriage and family; I've always known that, and I think that deep down you have always known it as well.'

I was not prepared to admit that, though on reflection I knew it to be true. 'What I know is that these past few months have been the best in my life. I know that I love you.'

'And I have loved you too, David. You are so different from anybody I have ever met.'

'Then what... what is it?'

'It's *you* David, I don't want you to grow to hate me, and I know that you would if we married.'

'But I could never hate you,' I protested, 'I love you.'

'But *you* will prosper David Neander, I know that. You will improve your station in life.'

'Then you will share in my prosperity.'

'Maybe: but you will meet people far above me; and you will become ashamed of me. I won't be able to stand by your side and be accepted. I am an uneducated farm girl whom you met in a beer tavern.'

'That does not matter to me, you must see that.'

'Oh yes, I see that now, but what in the years to come. Dear David, I will turn out to be a disappointment to you, and that will lead you to hate me.'

'I could never hate you...' I repeated the phrase, my voice falling away as I spoke; I looked at her forlornly.

She saw my sadness and her eyes welled at the sight of it. 'Oh David, dear David, you are such a kind-hearted man.'

'Is that not enough for us to wed?'

She straightened herself in her chair and breathed in deeply. 'No, I must be strong. It would be easy to think that love will make everything right, but it won't, you know it won't.' Again Marita sighed, 'I know what I must do to make a good life for my family.'

'And what about a good life for you,' I said, 'is that not important as well?'

'Yes it is,' she said. Her posture remained upright and rigid like a tree standing against a winter gale, as if to relax would be to give in to her temptations. 'But Joachim Hinkel will give me a good life as well. I have known him since I was a small child; I know what a good man he is. He asked me to marry him before I went away to Dortmund so I know he has affection for me.'

There was silence for a while; I could see that she was determined on this course of action. She looked down as if she was afraid that eye contact would break her resolve. She started fiddling with the knife again then snapped it down on the table when she realized she was doing it.

'Does he know about me?' I also then looked down, afraid of the answer she might give. If he did not know then there was still a chance for me; he may not want to take her if he knew. I held my breath, but let it go dejectedly when she spoke.

'Oh yes, I could not marry him based on a deceit. He knows about you; he was at the funeral and saw us together. This marriage is his idea.'

'So he has seized his opportunity has he; he is a clever man.'

'You can choose to see it that way, and yes I suppose there is some truth in that, but it is still a generous offer.'

There was something final about that last statement. I could see that I had lost, and it was far more painful than anything that I had encountered in the ring. It was like a bereavement all over again. I stood and looked down at her but she averted her gaze, afraid to meet my eyes. I walked to the door; looked back, but still she did not look at me. I opened the door and left. No more words were spoken and we did not even say goodbye. I have never seen her again from that day to this.

In retrospect, of course, I can see that she was probably right and much wiser than I. Love alone is not enough on which to base a successful marriage. In the long term she would be happier as a farmer's wife, the intellectual difference between us would have surfaced at some point. I realise now that intellect is something I would want in a wife and it is quite probable that I would have ended up resenting her as she suggested. But my love for Marita was as powerful as it was real; I hope that she has many children and has found the happiness she deserved.

CHAPTER 29

London 1823

The court was reassembling after the lunchtime recess. Judge Cardew was seated several feet higher that the defendant and from David's vantage point, very little could be seen of him since most of him was obscured by the high bench before him. David assumed courtrooms were designed this way deliberately to emphasise the Judge's power. As Judge Cardew took his seat, all David could see of him were the top of his shoulders and his head, from which his long, powdered wig hung down from his temples to disappear from view behind the frontage of the oak bench. To David's eye he looked like a Basset Hound, his wig resembling ears that trailed from side to side with each movement of his head. David suppressed a smile at the thought as Judge Cardew, glancing down from on high, sneered at him malevolently.

In the gallery, Julia's apprehension was mounting. She knew that the most damaging indictment against David was simply that he was a Jew and, as everybody knew, Jews could not be trusted. More importantly, it was apparent that the Judge shared this common view. '*Jew*' triggered thoughts of deception, dishonesty and lies. The very word had undertones to it. In the eyes of the general public, it meant money lending, extortion, or mistrust. It did not matter that historically so many professions had been barred to the Jew that by dint of need they had been forced into certain businesses. The Jew was perceived as a merchant growing fat on other men's toils, squeezing the last penny from an honest man in his time of trouble; a view manifested in Shakespeare's *Merchant of Venice*. In the Judge's mind David was effectively charged with being a Jew as well as a thief.

As Julia studied the Judge another apprehension took her. She looked at Cardew's face - a face that she was beginning to hate - those two cold eyes sitting in judgement, those saggy, ruddy cheeks, criss-crossed with red snake-like veins. But now there was something else; what was it? And then she realised. He was flushed, his face suffused, reddened from the point where his forehead emerged from his wig to his neck as it disappeared into his scarlet robe. She knew that he must have dined well and she wondered if he had stopped at one bottle of claret or had devoured a second along with his ample victuals. He clearly thought he was immune from censure in this case, the judicial system would never overrule his judgements again. Now the odious man was fuelled with alcohol and a full belly, Julia feared that all restraint would be gone. She peered over the rail to look down at her father, who was at that moment preparing to address the court.

George Carmichael stood and turned to face the jury. 'Members of the jury,' he said, 'this is an unusual case...'

'Mr Carmichael!' interrupted the Judge. 'You know the rules. You address the court, not the jury.'

'*And a stupid rule it is too,*' said Julia under her breath. It was increasingly apparent to her that the Judge, this pompous bigot who had so much power over David's fate, intended to undermine her father at every opportunity.

George Carmichael bowed respectfully to the bench and turned to face the assembled members of the court. 'On the face of it,' he said, 'it seems that the accused was caught red-handed in the act of stealing a sheep. We have heard from the owner that this is a common crime, a crime that is prevalent in his trade of butchery. What I would ask the jury to consider is what type of person commits this type of crime. Is it not a crime committed by the lower classes, those who prey on good honest traders by observing their movements and waiting to pounce when the opportunity arises? Is it not a crime of the *street*, committed by the ruffian, the street blackguard? Is it not a long established venal street racket committed by the wily? Is it not a roguery of the low-life native Londoner preying on his hardworking fellow citizens?'

George Carmichael paused for breath, his gaze sweeping the attentive faces in the courtroom, noting those who nodded in agreement. 'I would ask the jury to take a look at the accused; does he look like one of these delinquent people? What we can clearly see is that here we have an educated man capable of earning his living from a variety of his accomplishments.'

The Judge leaned forward, 'Are you suggesting that an educated man is not capable of committing a crime, Mr Carmichael? For if you are, I can site many instances to the contrary.' The judge wheezed a laugh and sat back in his chair, his crimson robes scrunched up around his shoulders and his full-bottomed wig partly obscuring his face, but still unable to disguise the satisfaction he took from his comments, beaming loud across his flushed countenance.

'Not at all, My Lord,' said George, 'but any thief-taker will tell you that they go looking for the perpetrator of a crime in the places where they expect to find them. If a robbery takes place in an alley way of Southwark then they do not look for the culprit at a coffee house in the new affluent West End.'

'But the Watchman didn't have to go looking at all, Mr Carmichael,' barked the Judge still leaning back in his chair. 'The accused was caught red-handed – as you say so yourself.'

George knew the Judge could see the point he was making, he was just not going to admit it. Cardew's aim was clearly to lead the jury astray. George turned to them, eager to eliminate the Judge's negative comments. 'Members of the jury...' he held his breath for a heartbeat in fear that Cardew would again object to his addressing the jury directly, but the stupid man was momentarily preoccupied, still basking in the glow of his last rejoinder. '... I think you will agree,' George said quickly, 'that I have demonstrated that there is far more to this case than the accused being caught in possession of a stolen carcass.' As he spoke, George saw that heads in the jury were nodding. He flashed a look up at the gallery and exchanged glances with his daughter. She nodded back to him and smiled; she too had noted the jury's positive response. It was clearly a good sign.

Encouraged, George continued, 'My client is an accomplished translator capable of earning his living by this means,' he said, returning to the point he had been trying to make before Cardew interrupted him, but once again the Judge was to undermine him.

'Not much of a business, wouldn't you say Mr Carmichael, setting up as a translator in England and not being able to speak English, eh?' There was heavy sarcasm in the Judge's tone. He smiled in satisfaction then guffawing at his own wit he turned to the court officials, raising his eyebrows at them and nodding his head. They knew immediately that they were being asked to join in. They obliged, nervously at first, but then the laughter was taken up by onlookers in the gallery, who now were revelling in the entertainment.

Julia was distressed, she turned to shush them, but they would have none of it. For the gallery spectators, this was as good as going to the theatre. They were a rowdy audience and not in the habit of listening in silence to what happened on the stage. The Judge had invited their participation by giving them licence to laugh and they were intent on doing just that.

George Carmichael's patience snapped; a judge simply did not say such things. It was Cardew's responsibility to remain impartial, to counter the naivety of the accused and to protect him so that justice could be done. But here he was doing the exact opposite; he was in effect acting as a prosecutor. 'Your Honour, this is outrageous! You cannot...' George had been going to say, *you cannot say that*, but before he could finish the Judge stopped him.

'I cannot what, Mr Carmichael?' The expression on Cardew's face had turned instantly from one of humour to one of malevolence and George felt the full force of his icy stare. 'This is *my* court, and I can say what I like in it. Your client believes he doesn't have to answer to anyone, but he has to answer to *me* and this court.' He transferred that icy stare to David at the bar.

'The only thing my client is guilty of is being an honest, hard working citizen,' protested George.

'The jury will make up its own mind about that, Mr Carmichael. Now continue if you please and don't presume again to tell me how to run my court.' He waved his hand dismissively at George, who bowed with the outward appearance of respect, but inside a rage was growing, one that he had to fight to control; he had not one jot of respect for this Judge. He looked round with raised eyebrows at the Prosecuting Counsel.

Josiah Heath returned a self-conscious look at him; the Judge was making his day's work easy, but Josiah Heath appeared nonetheless to be embarrassed by Cardew's outrageous behaviour.

George turned again to the jury, he looked down at his papers for a moment as if to find his place, but in reality he was taking control of his emotions. 'The members of the jury have heard evidence given by the Watchman that, in the confusion, he did not investigate the real perpetrator of this crime.'

'No, no', interrupted the Judge yet again, the words spitting from his mouth. A large globule of saliva formed on his bottom lip and clung there, but then started slowly to descend under the force of gravity. He was unaware of it, however, and continued talking, each word adding to the momentum of the spittle so that like his wig, it began to swing like a pendulum. 'You have not established that someone else committed this crime, Mr Carmichael, and you know it.'

Yes I know it, thought George, *and you know all about the rules of court procedure but that's not stopping you, you arrogant bastard. If you can disregard them then so shall I.* Ignoring the interruption, he turned to the jury, 'Members of the jury; consider if you will the likelihood of someone else committing this crime - a street-smart ruffian who had duped the accused into delivering this carcass on his behalf, transferring the risks of being apprehended to a trusting, newly-arrived person.'

'I'm not having that either, Mr Carmichael.' The Judge looked down at the jury. 'We have heard all this sort of thing before, many times: "I didn't do it, somebody else did". What you have to ask yourself is whether this is just another of these fabrications.' He turned to David standing at the bar, 'Did you have the permission of the owner of the carcass to take it to Oxford Road?'

David shook his head, 'No, not from the owner, Your Honor, but I thought...' Before he could say that he'd had permission from the person he thought was the owner, the Judge cut him off. He turned back to the jury and said triumphantly, 'There! By his own admission he did not have permission from Herbert Bond, the owner. That's very plain for all to see is it not? Pray continue Mr Carmichael.'

George was now at a loss. If the Judge was intent on undermining every point he tried to make then things were very black indeed – there was nowhere for him to go with this defense. He looked up at his daughter and saw from her infuriated expression that her apprehension was now running out of control. She looked to be on the point of standing and screaming invective at the Judge. He gave a small, anxious shake of his head and trusting that she would interpret it turned back to the courtroom and looked at David, expecting to see that same apprehension. Instead he was met by an expression of such defiance that it had the effect of recharging him. George cleared his throat, determined to try again.

'I have demonstrated that the accused was not armed and was not trying to escape. The Watchman could not speak French and the accused could not speak English; because of this there was confusion and the Watchman did not investigate my client's account of the facts. I ask the court to take at look at him; this is a much wronged man, not a petty criminal.'

There was silence for a few moments. George Carmichael held his breath expecting the Judge to interrupt – but he didn't. He looked up from his papers and saw that the Cardew's eyes were closed and flickering. The bastard was nodding off! George, astonished, directed his gaze at the Clerk to the Court, who smiled and shrugged his shoulders, a gesture that indicated this was nothing unusual.

'I'm sure Your Honour will agree?' George raised his voice, almost shouting the words that bore no relation to the previous discussion.

'What! What?' The Judge opened his eyes with a start, said testily, 'Yes, yes, of course?'

Laughter broke out in the gallery and Cardew looked up at the perpetrators unsure of the source of their levity but clearly suspecting it might be him. 'Silence; silence,' he bellowed, thumping his gavel down on the bench as he did so.

'You're too kind, My Lord,' said George continuing the charade and playing to the gallery. Laugher broke out again and once more the gavel thudded on oak.

'Will you be calling any more witnesses, Mr Carmichael,' said the Judge. He did not wait for an answer. 'Never mind, I think we'll leave it there for today. We will adjourn until ten-of-the-clock tomorrow.'

The Clerk took his cue: 'All rise,' the sonorous tones were drowned out by the eruption of movement as the court obeyed his command.

Cardew struggled to his feet, but fell back into his chair; his wig now askew began to slip over his face. There was a shout of renewed laughter from the gallery and the Judge, straightening the errant hairpiece, looked up at the culprit and sneered with a look of icy contempt. Chastened, the onlooker fell silent. Cardew, now more purposefully, rose once again to his feet, clearly attempting to keep as much dignity as he could. He did not succeed and stood swaying for a moment, clutching at the bench for support. There was silence as he glared around him, looking to see if anyone was brave enough to get on his wrong side. Nobody was. Satisfied, he left the courtroom by his own private door. As it closed behind him, one man's laughter from the gallery broke loose again like a wild animal escaping from a cage. The man's unrestrained hilarity was infectious and triggered laughter from the other spectators.

This time Julia did not attempt to quiet the noise; *the old sot deserves it*, she thought grimly to herself. She looked over the gallery rail down into the courtroom and saw that even the court officials were smiling at the Judge's antics of unintentional buffoonery. David had seen it too and catching her glance, raised a smile in concert with them, but it was a brief, bittersweet moment that disappeared like a figure vanishing in the mist.

The carriage ride home was infected by conflicting emotions. Julia was taken with anxiety at David's possible fate if he was, again, found guilty. She bit her lip without thinking, and tasted blood as she stared, unseeing, out of the window. She had not even had a chance to speak to him; as soon as the trial was adjourned he had been taken by the Dock Officer back to the cells at Newgate Prison and given into the custody of the gaoler. A lump in her throat Julia brushed away a tear that ran slowly down her face. The afternoon session had been unbearable; she pictured David, shackled, shuffling down the passageway from the courtroom to the prison and then to his cell, a pile of straw for a bed and no other comforts, unable to sleep as the slow hours to morning dragged by mercilessly. She fought against weeping, tried to hide her distress form her father, but it was beginning to take her; she could no longer fight off the anguish.

George Carmichael was seething with anger. 'Vindictive old bastard!' he blurted out and then realised what he had said. He looked up at his daughter, 'Sorry my dear,' he said, apologising for his language. Only then did he notice her despair; those large green eyes were awash with tears, the light from the carriage window glinting in them. 'Now, now,' he leaned forward to comfort her and then the dam broke and the salty fluid cascaded down her face, her shoulders quaking as she sobbed. 'You really should not get so involved, you know,' George said. 'You have to stay detached.' He then realized that his words were inappropriate, insensitive, they were not for now. He was not an unfeeling man; being detached was part of his profession, but now he felt that he was being just that; unfeeling. He sighed heavily to himself. He felt ill-equipped to deal with his daughter's unusual display of grief; he was also perturbed that her affections had clearly been engaged far more deeply than he would have liked. For all that David Neander was a likeable, educated man he was also a Jew and stood accused of theft. George sighed again; he had given his daughter far too much license in this case. 'We will have to call him as a witness,' he said, distractedly.

'David will never forgive me,' she said, wiping away her tears on her handkerchief and scrunching it in her fist.

'Better that than a hanging.' He saw her visibly recoil at the word. His own emotions were ambivalent. He did not want his daughter to fall in love with this man but at the moment it was obvious to him that she had done just that. 'We have to,' he repeated.

'Yes, we have to – I know. He is expecting it.'

'We'll need the interpreter.'

'Yes, we will. He's on stand-by; I'll get a message to him tonight.' The words trembled out of her mouth.

195

'So one last throw of the dice tomorrow,' said George Carmichael.

'Yes; one last throw of the dice.' A new tear emerged from the corner of Julia's eye. It meandered down her cheek, but she did not notice it.

CHAPTER 30

Hamburg 1821

I yanked the strap and lowered the window, put my hand on the sill to steady myself and noticed the other passengers doing the same. The iron-clad wheels struggled as they rumbled over the cobbled street making it uncomfortable for us within the coach, shaking us about as they rolled over the uneven surface. The jolting had caused the bonnet of the lady facing me to be partly dislodged. She struggled to put it straight with her left hand whilst holding the hanging leather loop with her right. She gave me an embarrassed look, but I could think of nothing I could do to help that would not be considered impertinent - the gentleman's standard flourish of his silk handkerchief seemed irrelevant in the circumstances - so I returned her look as sympathetically as I could, then leant forward to gaze passed her and out of the window. We had gone through the main harbour gate and now I saw my first glimpse of the River Elbe and the city that was to be my new home: the deep water port of the *Freie und Hansestadt* Hamburg – the Free and Hanseatic City of Hamburg.

I had been attentive when my father had taught me history and geography. I knew that Hamburg had grown to prosperity as part of the medieval Hanseatic League: an alliance of trading cities that maintained a trade monopoly along the coast of Northern Europe. This was a large and prosperous city, a gateway to Europe and that is why I had come here. It was part of my ultimate strategy to make for England. I felt a sudden surge of excitement at the sight of the hustle and bustle of the people going about their business. The port looked so vibrant to me, so alive, despite the fact that - as Papa had told me - it was still recovering from the battering it took at the hands of Napoleon, who had annexed the Free City briefly for France. I looked up at the multi-storied warehouses on the wharf; at the loaded packhorses and the heavy wagons, each harnessed to four or six carthorses and all of them carting goods over the cobblestones to and from the wharves. This was a prosperous place indeed, I thought, leaning out of the window to gaze at the bustling scene; a place for me to prosper also.

I had been melancholy for some weeks after the break up with Marita. I had been extra difficult with Bernd Hartman in the training gymnasium, challenging his advice at every opportunity. I had been the victim of his wrath on many occasions before and the fearful eyes of the other fighters would often search me out as if to warn me of my folly. I don't know why I was not afraid of him as the other fighters were, but I wasn't. I suppose that if you have seen your family murdered then everything else life throws at you is less daunting. But I had become particularly difficult in my miserable spirits. He even took a swing at me one afternoon when I was constantly disregarding his advice, but I was too quick for him and I just pulled back out of his reach so that the punch flew past my chin. If it had hit me, all that power would have sent me over, but the strength of it was his own undoing. As his great right hand flew past me its momentum pulled him off his feet and he fell forward to his left, his hands reaching for the ground just stopping him from going over full length and sprawling onto the floor in front of me. He had taught me well though, despite my obstinacy, and I instinctively moved forward to take advantage of his defenceless position. As he came up and righted himself, his hands were not before him to defend himself. Quick as thought I recoiled to release a punch to the side of his head, but Helmut and Rudi saw my intention and rushed forward. Helmut seizing me by the torso and shoving me backwards whilst Rudi grabbed my arm stopping the punch before it could be thrown.

When the hullabaloo had all calmed down, it was decided that it would be better if I left. I think Bernd had nurtured a secret respect and admiration for me, even though I did not want to fight the way he wanted me to, but I was a bad influence on the other fighters so he readily let me go. He had repeatedly told me to fight toe-to-toe and learn how to defend myself from that position, but I wanted to use my athleticism to stay out of punching range. He believed audiences would see that as somehow cowardly and would not accept me as a champion even if I continued to win fights. A parting of the ways was agreed and when his anger had subsided he even gave me letters of introduction to promoters in Bremen and Hamburg.

Bremen had been my first stop, but my stay there was brief. It was a noble city, also part of the Hansiatic League for a time, but I was too intent on getting to Hamburg. I saw my immediate future there, which is how I came to be in the jolting coach.

'HEADS BACK IN THE CARRIAGE PLEASE,' shouted the driver as he manoeuvred the team through an archway barely wider than the carriage itself and then brought the team to a standstill.

I ducked hastily back into my seat. A happy smile of expectation must inadvertently have crossed my face, for I saw the lady with the crooked bonnet, which was still not totally straight, smile at me in response. I strained to subdue my excitement and when I stepped down from the carriage I offered her my hand. She took it and nodded graciously, bobbing the smallest of curtsies. I smiled inwardly as I handed her down, wondering if she would have done so had she known I was a Jew.

Leaves swirled around our feet in the late November wind and I felt the icy chill of it against my face. The lady clutched self-consciously at her bonnet, this time to stop the wind taking it. Her pretty face was suffused, most probably from a combination of the icy wind and a little embarrassment. There was the slightest hint of practised diffidence about her that is common in young available women when in the presence of a potentially available man. I had assumed that to be travelling alone she must be married, but from her manner towards me I now wondered whether perhaps she was single. I responded with a stiff bow and turned away from her lest she think I was interested in her charms.

I had taken the coach to Hamburg rather than walking because I now had belongings purchased from my prize-fight winnings. I had three frock-coats and numerous pairs of quality breeches; new linen shirts and I had books; lots of books. My trunk was hauled down from the coach for me and it thudded against the cobbled street, the coachman being taken aback by its unexpected weight.

'Hey, be careful there!' I yelled.

The coachman knuckled his forehead, 'sorry sir,' he said apologetically.

I rushed over and took the handle at the other end of the trunk and between us we managed to haul it to the sidewalk. I straightened up and looked about me. As people passed, the better-off doffed their hats and nodded or the ladies just gestured with a polite movement of the head. The lower classes kept their hands in their pockets and shuffled respectfully passed, giving me the right of way that they perceived my status required. My new frock-coat proclaimed me a man of means. I had gone for a sober look to suggest that I was a man of commerce rather than the more peacock look preferred by young gentleman of leisure. Not for me colourful waistcoat and stock.

We had been set down at the pay toll. This was where the post coaches set down their passengers. I had to state my provenance and pay the toll. I did not declare myself a Jew; that would have required a different toll or I might even have had my access denied. I did not mean to be fraudulent; it just seemed the natural thing to do.

My first requirement was to find lodgings and I looked about me on the street, but the wharf was clearly not a place of residences. I needed some help and that must have been evident to the wily on the open *Strasse*. I became aware of a shuffling of feet to my left and I turned to see who it was.

'Need a carriage *Junge herr?*' The voice addressing me as 'Young sir' was low and guttural and accompanied by the tapping of a cane on the sidewalk, its owner shabbily dressed in what looked like the remnants of a soldier's tunic. It was probably once blue but the colour had faded with age and dirt to be predominantly a dirty grey. It hung off his scrawny shoulders suggesting he was no longer the physical specimen that he used to be. I assumed he was a man of the street, wily and constantly on the lookout for an opportunity to make a few marks or gulden, hanging around the toll post for that purpose. That assessment of mine turned out to be correct, but any other assumptions I may have made about the man were to prove erroneous. As he came closer to me I saw that he was blind, his eye sockets like small pieces of coal on a snow-covered landscape; lifeless and unseeing.

'Yes I do, but...' I said. I was unsure what it was he was offering.

'I'll be back in a minute, young sir,' he said and with that just turned and scurried away, rounding the corner with all the certainty of a sighted man and at a speed that an agile young street urchin would have been proud of. Within that promised minute a carriage raced around the corner with the blind man standing on its running board. He jumped off as the carriage came to a stop and walked unerringly straight up to me. 'Where is it to be then, young sir?' he said. I waved my hand in front of his face to reassure myself that he was actually blind.

He must have sensed the movement for straight away he said, 'Yes, that's right, young sir. Old Musketeer can't actually see, but I know Hamburg like the back of my hand. Anything you want I can get for you.'

'I need lodgings,' I mumbled, unconvinced by his story and wondering if he was having me on.

'Will that be in the Juden quarter of the city, young sir?'

'What!' I exclaimed, the disbelief evident in my voice. 'How did you know I...?' I stopped myself from completing the sentence.

'So I was right then, young sir? You are Jewish? I hear and smell more than other folks you see.'

'So what did you hear and smell about me?' I was offended, yet intrigued. How could he, a blind man, possibly know I was a Jew? To all the sighted people on the street I was a young German of means.

'Confusion at first; your voice is above me so that means you are tall – yes?'

'Yes.'

'You speak well so that you have an education – yes?'

'Yes.'

'That suggests German, probably Frankfurt?'

'This is unbelievable,' I said, 'but why Jewish?'

'Because you smell wrong for a German, there was something not quite right. You have bathed within the last twenty-four hours. Now that could have made you a young Prussian Officer who has been duelling and has showered to wash away all his sweat. But there is no smell of German or Prussian food on you. The last meal you had included melted chicken fat, and that suggests that you are Jewish.'

'That's remarkable,' I said, both surprised and bewildered. Despite Papa being a reformer, Mama was Jewish at heart and she had fed us on a traditional Yiddish diet. I had left most of that way of life behind me and had been eating mainly German food, but last evening I had dined on Matzah ball soup – a Jewish dish consisting of dumplings in chicken broth – and this blind ruffian had still been able to detect something of it. I thought, *yes;he's right!* ' I gaped at him, bewildered, 'How did you learn to put all those things together?'

'Upon the command "PRIME AND LOAD",' he bawled out and stood to attention. I started at his loud words, which made me jump. I looked about me nervously to see the reaction of the people in the street, but it seemed that he was known to them. 'Necessity, young sir; when the powder in the priming pan of my musket exploded in my face it took my eyes. I needed to earn a living or starve so I taught my other senses to recognise signs that sighted people don't always see.'

'What's your name? What do I call you?' As impressed as I was by him, I was still unsure.

'Everybody calls me "Musketeer" – I'm Old Musketeer, young sir.'

'But that's French. Hamburg is your home town I take it?'

'HANDLE CARTRIDGE,' he yelled out again and stood to attention before responding. I realised that he always spoke as if he was still a soldier on parade before his commanding officer. He went on. 'Yes sir; came back to Hamburg after my accident. I fought against Napoleon at the Battle of Jena and was taken as a prisoner of war, but later, when Hamburg was annexed, I joined Napoleon's infantry. I was the best shot with a musket in his whole damned army. So everybody calls me Old Musketeer. Everyone knows Old Musketeer,' he repeated. 'Just ask for Old Musketeer if you want me and you'll easily find me.'

'Well, err... Old Musketeer,' I said hesitantly, looking into his mobile face. The absence of his eyes made it difficult for me, at first, to see any emotion there. His hair was thin, but still dark without any grey; it was heavily greased and hung down lankly at the back, but was swept back severely from his forehead exposing his full face, blackened around the eye sockets where the burned gunpowder had embedded itself in his skin. And then I realised his facial expressions were the canvas on which he painted. It must have been to compensate for the loss of his eyes that those facial movements were exaggerated. I had paused to think, and his face seemed instantly to turn into that of an inquisitive jackdaw, his head twitching from side to side as he tried to pick up the merest sound or movement that would be informative to him.

'Well, Old Musketeer,' I said eventually, 'no, not the Jewish quarter. I am a man of commerce; I am looking for lodgings that are near the commercial quarter that I can also use to pursue my business.'

'UPON THE COMMAND PRIME,' he yelled, making me jump again at the severity of his tone. I was to learn that he had been a sergeant in the infantry and had spent many hours calling out the commands required for loading a musket: 'PRIME AND LOAD - PRIME - ABOUT - HANDLE CARTRIDGE - DRAW RAMRODS – RAM DOWN THE CARTRIDGE – PRESENT – FIRE,' he yelled then dropping his voice to an ordinary tone he continued as though unaware he had shouted. 'Specific requirements indeed, young sir, but Old Musketeer can find the target.' He called out an address to the driver, who muttered a few words incomprehensibly before coming down. With a struggle, still grumbling under his breath, he wearily loaded my heavy trunk onto the back of the carriage and strapped it securely.

I was taken to lodgings on the *Bleichstrasse*, which I later came to realise was a street that straddled respectability and low living. It was not an address I would have chosen had I known the city, but surprisingly it turned out to be an inspired choice. I had a room on the ground floor with access to the street from which I could meet my prospective customers, and a room upstairs that was to be my sleeping quarters. I was pleased with Old Musketeer's choice and I nodded in his direction to show my satisfaction, but then I realised my folly.

'This will do fine, Old Musketeer,' I said instead, 'and tomorrow I will purchase a desk to work from and I will be able to go about my business immediately.' I reached into my waistcoat pocket and produced a full gulden and pressed it, perhaps over-generously, into his hand. I saw him rub it between his fingers to ascertain its denomination and then he bit into it to check that the coin had not been adulterated. I smiled to myself; I had seen this done many times and never believed that anybody could actually tell from that, but if anybody could then perhaps Old Musketeer could.

'THANK YOU SIR!' he yelled pulling himself up to an exaggerated attention, 'I'll be here at eight-of-the-clock, tomorrow morning with your desk.' With that he turned and disappeared through the door, his cane tapping expertly before him. I had not asked him to find me a desk, but I had no doubt that he would be here at eight sharp with his task fulfilled.

CHAPTER 31

London 1823

'CALL MENO EPHRAIM! The Clerk to the Court's words rang out and echoed round the courtroom. Sitting once again in the gallery, Julia steeled herself for David's reaction. She saw him go rigid, shoot a look to the Clerk and then to her father, grabbing the bar in front of him and squeezing until his knuckles gleamed white. He then looked up at Julia and painfully she met the full force of his shocked stare. Their eyes locked in an agony of unspoken words and she could see in his, the look of betrayal. She mouthed '*Sorry*' back to him, but she knew how inadequate this was. Without informing him, she had some time ago made contact with Meno Ephraim via Nathan Rothschild's business organisation in Frankfurt, his family still living just a few streets away from Meno's home. She had written a letter running to several pages telling David's uncle of his nephew's desperate predicament - a predicament David had kept from him - and Meno had made the long journey willingly at her request, even though it was difficult to see what help he could be.

His face pale and drawn, David broke eye contact with Julia and swung round to watch the tall figure of his uncle walk to the witness box where he was sworn in via the interpreter. Meno looked professional in his black frock-coat and a white linen stock at his collar. He seemed to have aged considerably in the past few years. Those large, slightly sunken eyes were deadly serious and not the mischievous eyes that David remembered.

As Meno took the stand, George Carmichael stood to address him. 'Will you tell the court your name, address and profession please?'

Uncle Meno listened to the interpreter and then turned to the jury. 'My name is Meno Ephraim, I live on the *Nonnengasse*, in the Free City of Frankfurt. I work there as a physician.'

'Can you identify the prisoner at the bar?'

'Yes sir; he is David Neander, but I know him by his former name of Loeb Ephraim.' A murmur of muttered comment went around the courtroom as he spoke.

George Carmichael knew that his decision to call Meno was a dangerous stratagem for it had introduced the notion of a deception;

David could be seen to be hiding behind a false identity. George now had to establish that the previous identity had been a wronged person rather than the wrongdoer and that there had been no intention to deceive.

The Judge leaned forward and George steeled himself for the inevitable interruption. If Cardew now asked what relevance this witness's evidence had to the crime committed in London it would be hard to counter. George's sole strategy was to create sympathy for David in the minds of the jurors, and he knew that this was open to attack from the Judge. To his surprise, the interruption did not come; Cardew, apparently happy that the witness was having a negative effect, had let it go. George breathed a sigh of relief and continued with his questioning.

'And what is your connection with the prisoner, Mr Ephraim?'

'I am his uncle; he is my only living relative,' answered Meno.

'And why is that?'

With that question, George had led Meno Ephraim into telling the story of the tragedy in David's young life. In terms of its relevance to the case its significance was suspect, but as George had hoped, when Meno described the horrific murder of David's entire family, even the need to translate every sentence did not diminish the power of his story. Everyone in the courtroom was transfixed and the only noises to be heard were muffled words filtering into the courtroom from outside as the rest of the court went about its business. Even the Judge seemed temporarily engrossed in the story that was unfolding.

David alone was not gripped by his uncle's evidence. Forced yet again to relive these horrors, he moved like a caged beast, agitated, up and down before the bar. Julia watched him, tears starting to her eyes. As Meno continued to speak, she looked anxiously around the gallery. She had been to the premises of several newspapers, among them the *Times*; the *Globe* and the *London Morning Penny Post*. She wanted the case to be reported, reasoning that if David's story was taken up by the press, there would be a tide of sympathy that may help his cause. At first it seemed the journalists had not responded to her information, but then she spotted a small, shrew-like man on the end of her row, so self-effacing she had almost missed him. She watched him for a few moments, scribbling away in a notebook, long bony fingers appearing to propel his charcoal across the page as if some spider was the scribe. He seemed engrossed it what was unfolding and it brought a temporary lightening of her spirits.

Uncle Meno told his story quietly, but it was not devoid of passion. He left nothing out; a young man destined to complete his education at the university, who was called back to find his family slain; butchered as if they were animals at the whim of the slaughterers. He told the story methodically, like a skilful novelist, sketching out the chain of events, his words gaining in power in the telling and losing little in the translation. The courtroom was unusually quiet, even the industrious clerks stopped what they were doing to listen.

It took a long time for Meno to tell the whole story, including his intimate knowledge of his nephew's intelligence and his fine, upstanding character, and he needed little prompting from George Carmichael.

The Prosecuting Counsel, Josiah Heath, stood at the completion of the testimony. He opened his mouth to speak but then thought better of it. He paused, unsure, then said, 'No questions, Your Honour,' and sat down again.

'You may step down now, Herr Ephraim,' said George Carmichael finally, turning to the Judge to gauge his reaction. Cardew lay back in his chair, his hands clasped together before his face and George was initially hopeful that he had succeeded in establishing in the Judge's mind a different persona of David; not one of a dishonest Jew intent on robbing the honest citizen, but an upright young man who had been the victim of mindless brutality. The Judge met his look and George held it and smiled politely, trying to detect any change in Cardew's demeanour and willing him to acknowledge this new image of the accused, but the Judge's gaze was implacable.

'We will adjourn for lunch,' was all he said.

Julia entered the wood-panelled waiting room in a fever of anxiety and was once again accosted by the combined reek of polish and stale sweat, but that was quickly relegated in her thoughts by her mounting agitation. Her father sensed her fears and put his arm around her shoulders, ushering her through the busy throng to a free space half way down one side of the room. She waited, the pounding of her heart creating a rhythmic pulse in her ear. She saw the door open and the Dock Officer enter, followed by David, his shackles now back in place. He shuffled to where they were standing, but his eyes remained downcast. He stopped before them and George gestured with his head towards the Dock Officer, who dutifully moved a few paces away.

And then David looked up at Julia, his stare burrowing deep into her psyche; there was no hostility in the stare, no belligerence: just betrayal – her face flamed; she felt treacherous.

'It was my idea,' said George quickly. It was a lie, but he was motivated by the distress he saw on his daughter's face.

'No, Father,' Julia placed her hand on his arm and smiled to show that she was all right, then she turned her attention to David. 'I know that it was painful for you, David, and I am sorry, but it had to be…' She was not allowed to finish.

'*Painful!*' the word spat from his mouth. 'You cannot know how painful. It was horrible. And it was unnecessary. What had any of that to do with the case?' He was trembling with anger.

Julia felt the tears well up in her eyes, but she fought to hold them back. 'It has nothing to do with the case; you are right. But it has to do with the picture the Judge is painting of you. We had to show the jury the other side of the coin; show them what an honourable man you are and how wronged.' She met his angry stare with all the intensity he had shown to her. A solitary tear escaped to run down the side of her face, but she now felt in control and dashed it away as if it were some irritant; a fly to be swatted.

For what seemed an age they held each other's gaze in silence, but their eyes spoke volumes. She had tried to explain and he had tried to understand, but neither of them had succeeded. Then something else intervened; his love for her broke through his anger and suddenly there was a nuance to his gaze. It softened at the simple sight of her. She saw it and relief coursed through her veins like an elixir. Words temporarily deserted her. Heedless of watching eyes, she did the only thing she could; she stepped into him and embraced him. He stood rigid for a heartbeat and her fears resurfaced, but then his arms came up and gently encircled her.

George Carmichael looked on and his thoughts were torn with ambivalence. He had come to respect David Neander, but he was acutely aware of the man's predicament. There was a very real chance he would have to face the noxious stare of the hangman, to be despatched in a line of other poor wretches, hanged piecemeal before a voracious, baying crowd. His daughter's feelings for this man were now unmistakable and should this happen he knew the pain would be unbearable for her. The only way he could protect her from this was to get an acquittal and he was unsure whether he could do that.

Preoccupied with these gloomy thoughts, George glanced at the door as it swung back on its hinges and a bewildered Meno entered the dismal room and looked around it in total confusion, unable to ask for assistance in a tongue that was foreign to him. George raised a hand to attract his attention and was met by a relieved look on the doctor's face. He came over, unseen by David, who was still locked in a delicate embrace. George gave a loud cough and then repeated it when it had no effect. The second cough broke into their awareness and they disengaged.

'Somebody to see you, David,' said George Carmichael gently as, with a tremulous smile, Julia stepped away from the embrace.

David looked round, then his gaze rested at last on his uncle. The kindly face was burdened with unease, but deep within Meno's eyes was the merest hint of mischief as, with a slight lift of his eyebrows, he seemed to say, '*I'm pleased to see you, my boy.*' The familiar gesture spoke a thousand words in David's mind: it was a reminder of better times, a reminder of a loving childhood with his family. He took a hesitant step towards his uncle, his face lighting up in a rare smile. Then he stood tall and nodded a stiff Teutonic greeting, to which Meno reciprocated in kind. They had lived amongst Germans for so long that it had become second nature to them both, but the twinkle in Meno's eyes became more pronounced and after the briefest moment he held out his arms in welcome. 'Come my boy, come and embrace your old uncle,' he said in German.

David stepped into the welcoming arms and Meno patted his back again and again. 'Good to see you my boy, good to see you.' Meno repeated the phrase time and again, reluctant to let go. When eventually he did, he stood before David and grasped his nephew's biceps. 'My word, Loeb, you have filled out into a strong young man,' he winked, 'I bet all the *fräuleins* are chasing you, eh?'

David blushed at the comment, which had brought a smile to their faces, but then the horror of the situation resurfaced and took them both like a spiteful visitor who would not be ignored. 'Why didn't you write and tell me, my boy?' That mischievous look was gone from Meno's eye.

'Why burden you with all this when there was nothing you could do about it?'

'I am strong enough to shoulder that burden, young Loeb. I have buried all the rest of my family; I think I deserved the right to fight for the last of them, don't you?'

David opened his mouth to speak, but no sound came out. Uncle Meno's words had emasculated him; their truth now seemed self evident. Seized with shame he looked down at the floor, but Uncle Meno cupped his face lifting his chin as though he were still a small boy, and then slapped it gently, affectionately. 'So, what do we do now?' he said, that mischievous smile returning.

David translated the question to George and Julia, who had stood silently watching the reunion, both smiling, Julia with tears in her eyes.

'The Judge will send out the jury this afternoon,' said George, 'and then we wait - and hope that they are swayed by us and not by that old bastard - sorry my dear,' he turned apologetically to his daughter as David translated his words to Meno.

'That's alright, Father,' she smiled, 'were I a man I would call him a worse name than that!'

At two-of-the-clock the court reassembled. There was an expectant buzz of murmured conversation in the courtroom as people took their places. After some minutes this began to die down - the Judge failed to appear. By fifteen minutes after two, George Carmichael exchanged a look with the Clerk to the Court, who raised his eyes in a gesture that seemed to say *'Here we go again!'* The minutes ticked slowly by. In the gallery, Julia's anxiety, already high began to run out of control. She knew, as did her father, that the Judge was again lunching to excess and she wondered again how many bottles of claret he had already drunk this time. When the court clock struck the half hour past two-of-the-clock, there was still no sign of him. She looked down at the jury, who were now talking openly amongst themselves to pass the time, and then she exchanged fretful looks with David and her father. Uncle Meno sat beside her in the gallery and she tried to explain unsuccessfully what the delay was.

At fifteen minutes before three-of-the-clock, the door to the Judge's rooms opened and Cardew at last appeared.

'ALL RISE,' shouted the usher.

There was another buzz; a shuffling of feet and chairs. Julia put her hand to her mouth at the sight of the Judge; his condition was far worse than even she had feared. His sagging, ruddy cheeks were suffused red, his gait on those few steps to his chair unsteady to the point that he was forced to support himself, clutching at the bench one hand over the other, and then he crashed inelegantly into his chair like sack of potatoes stacked against a wall. Laughter broke out behind Julia at his condition and the Judge took up his gavel and walloped it violently against the bench, shouting, '*QUIET! QUIET!*'

The court came to order and Judge Cardew turned to the jury, 'Members of the jury,' he said, his words slurred and accompanied by a shower of spittle, 'it is now your duty to consider the evidence before you.'

George Carmichael jumped to his feet; he had no idea what he was going to say, but he did not want the jury retiring to consider their verdict, with the last thing on their minds being the Judge's drunken antics. What he had wanted was for them to retire with the gravitas of Meno's story in their minds; the image of David as a wronged man who was a victim of circumstance.

'Your Honour; Your Honour,' he blurted.

'What is it now, Mr Carmichael? Cardew said testily, attempting to focus on George.

'Your Honour has obviously been delayed on important court business, and…'

'Yes, yes,' agreed the Judge.

'And this is such a difficult case...'

'Yes, yes, what point are you trying to make, Counsel?'

'Well, My Lord, in the circumstances, perhaps it would be better if the case is adjourned until tomorrow morning so that the jury has ample time to consider its verdict?'

Judge Cardew strained to look at the wall clock above his head. He needed very little persuasion. 'Oh very well then,' he said, striking his gavel. 'We'll adjourn until ten-of-the-clock tomorrow morning.'

In the gallery Julia sighed with relief, but then a new fear took her. She did not want the newspapers to report the Judge's inebriation; the levity of the court at his drunken antics overriding the serious nature of David's case. Nor did she want Cardew coming to the court with vengeance on his mind having read of his own shortcomings. She sought out the small, shrew-like journalist and suggested he leave out that fact and report it the following day. He seemed amenable to the suggestion and he also identified the reporter from the *Times,* who was in the process of putting his pen away, a broad smile on his face. Julia hastened to introduce herself and she made the same suggestion to him. To her relief, he too seemed agreeable.

Satisfied that she had done all she could Julia left the gallery. By ten-of-the-clock tomorrow, she hoped that David's case would have the support of the people.

CHAPTER 32

Hamburg 1821

Settling into my new lodgings, I whiled away the afternoon unpacking my many books and then spent an hour or so writing poetry, my notebook open loosely on my lap, but the absence of a desk made me irritable and it broke my concentration. The autumn light began to fade early. I realised I had not brought any candles with me and the oil lamp was empty, so I resolved to dine early and set off to find the nearest tavern before it was full dark.

I was given immediate attention by the landlord who, the moment I came through the door, dispatched a serving girl to take my order. I was pleased that my new frock-coat was apparently proclaiming me a man of substance to be given special consideration. I ordered a local favourite on the recommendation of the waitress: *Aalsuppe* - a sweet and sour soup of meat broth, dried fruit, vegetables and herbs - together with a tankard of beer and settled into a cubicle to await my victuals. The tavern was quite full and there was a welcoming log fire, but the place was of a lower order than I had first thought: the tables and chairs robust, but with little style or workmanship and the stone floor looked as if it could do with a good brushing, not that I could see much of it since the small bubble windows let in very little of the fading light that was left of the day. However, my beer arrived almost immediately and I took a long deep swig to quench my thirst. I was looking about the place idly, in anticipation of my meal, when the door swung open and a blast of fresh autumnal wind blew into the core of the room. The sudden draught made the fire roar; it flickered and danced, but did little to compensate for the sudden chill. Groans now began to arise from the disgruntled customers as they looked round to the door. It remained open, the newcomers standing at the entrance unsure whether to enter. There were five of them, young blades out on the town with drinking and wenching their objective. Dressed finely they stood out like peacocks from the rest of the clientele, but it was clear they cared not and had other things on their minds. And then two more of their party arrived: the sixth man was another young blade, dressed just as dandily as the others, but it was the seventh that took my attention: he was a brute of a man, barrel-chested and standing several centimetres above his companions. He was not dressed shabbily, that is to say, he was wearing a passable frock-coat, but the cloth and the tailoring were not of the quality of the others.

They all piled into the room, slamming the door shut behind them, to everyone's relief, then ordered beer and schnapps for themselves, but just beer for the large man. The tavern settled down again; my *Aalsuppe* arrived with a large chunk of black rye bread and I tucked into it heartily. Eyeing the young men as I ate, I was intrigued at what was afoot here for something clearly was. And then one of them stood and addressed the clientele and I realised what these young blades had in mind: it seemed that gambling was to spice their evening's entertainment.

'Stand up Willy,' he bellowed, and the large man stood and folded his arms before his massive chest. The young blade grinned up at him, 'Wilhelm says he can best any man here in under a minute.' He looked around the room for any reactions, but everyone was quickly losing interest when they looked on the size of the brute. 'Come, come gentlemen,' the young blade went on, 'are there no sporting gentlemen here?' His patter was well rehearsed and I was fairly sure he had done it several times already this day. I smiled to myself, guessing what was coming.

'Perhaps twenty thalers will entice a brave young buck to try his hand?' Heads now turned back to the young blade as he had known they would. 'Yes gentlemen; that's right, *twenty* thalers and all you have to do is to still be standing at the end of one minute.'

I dipped my rye bread into the soup and bit off a large chunk, savouring it; it was surprisingly very good. I smiled to myself at the entertainment that was being offered as the noise levels rose; twenty thalers was a substantial sum - that was 160 marks and represented several weeks' work for a labouring man. It was causing quite a stir and a young man was being cajoled into accepting the wager. I could see he was reluctant, but his companions had confidence in him. The ringleader of the young blades, as Wilhelm's champion, clearly, knew how to exploit this.

'Twenty thalers to the brave contender just to stand for a minute and we'll offer odds of five-to-one to anyone who wants to make a sporting wager.'

The young challenger was pushed reluctantly to his feet by his companions. He was tall and broad of shoulder and probably a docker by trade, which had developed his natural strength. He was still in his work boots and shabby clothing, several days of thick blond whiskers on his chin. I nodded to myself; he looked a good athletic specimen and worthy of his friends' confidence, but I also knew that it would all count for nothing if he had not been taught any fighting skills, for I was fairly sure that 'Willy' was a seasoned fighter. The bets were taken by another of the young blades, and then the whole of the tavern took to the yard outside where an impromptu ring was formed by the bodies of the onlookers. I gobbled down the last of my food then went to watch the spectacle myself.

The brute of a man removed his jacket and shirt and folded his arms across his huge, bare, muscled chest, to the dismayed eyes of the onlookers who had their money on their companion. I looked at Willy with a profession al eye. He was immensely powerful, but he carried much of his weight around his ample middle. He would bring muscle and probably skill into the ring, but not athleticism and endurance - but I knew he would not need either. The challenger took off his jacket and prepared to fight in his shirt, but I could see instantly that the restrictive ring - measuring little more than four metres square - gave him little room for manoeuvre and favoured the trained fighter; everything was set against him. At the command of 'Fight', the brute took up his fighting attitude and the young workman followed suit.

They both approached each other, the young worker rotating his fists before his face and looking for an opportunity to throw a punch. The brute just stood in the centre waiting like a spider drawing its prey into its web. The young worker threw a straight left hand, but Willy just parried it away making no attempt to throw a punch back. This emboldened the young worker; he came forward and threw a left followed by a right. Again both punches were parried, but without out any attempt to reply. Now the young worker's companions began to cheer at the prospect of him standing the full minute and taking their winnings. He came forward again and recoiled to throw a right, but the brute now saw an opening for a right punch and duly delivered one with full force.

The young worker went down like a felled tree, his senses temporarily detached from his body. His companions were momentarily quieted and then they started to yell at him to get up. He got to his knees and shook his head but he did not, I think, see the blood dripping from his broken nose onto the dirt floor. He staggered to his feet and instinctively brought both his hands before his face to protect himself. He now had only one thought in his befuddled mind and that was to survive; he backed away from his opponent, but the young blades were not going to allow this. Standing at the front of the crowd, they thrust the young worker back into the centre of the ring at each opportunity. The brute was there waiting for him. One more punch was all that was required to finish him off and it was delivered mercilessly; an uppercut up through the young worker's guard. His head was knocked back savagely and he sank to his knees and then fell forward unconscious.

There wasn't even a '*Well fought'* from the young blades and that annoyed me. They just patted their man on the back and went straight back to the tavern to finish their drinks and collect their winnings. The others followed, leaving the young worker to two of his friends. I went over to him and produced my new silk handkerchief and offered it to him. He was coming round and I sat him up, pushing his head down between his legs for some moments. I wiped the blood and mucus from his face and as his senses returned, his first thought was that he had ruined a young gentlemen's smart handkerchief.

'Don't worry about that,' I said, 'you fought well my friend. A handkerchief is the least of you rewards for your sport.'

'Thank you sir,' said one of his friends, who seemed nonplussed by my kindness.

I went back into the tavern, sat in my cubicle and ordered another tankard. I am not a gambling man by instinct. I knew of course that gambling was the chosen vice of the fashionable in society, but my origins were poor and it seemed foolhardy to me. Nevertheless, a notion took me. I think I was motivated more by a notion to take these young blades down a peg than the wager, but it took hold of me. I could see that they were getting ready to move on, believing that now everyone had seen the spectacle no one else would be brave enough to challenge. I called after them.

'Will Wilhelm take another challenge?' They turned and looked at me. I could see they were unsure who I had in mind to fight. My attire did not set me out as a man to brawl in the street. 'Me,' I said. 'I am offering to fight your man, to stand against him for one minute for twenty thalers. What do you say?'

They looked at each other smiling broadly surprised at their good fortune, 'Will your companions be prepared to wager on you?' said one of them.

'I have no companions, no friends,' I said, 'I am newly arrived in Hamburg today.'

That seemed to deflate them; their expressions changed immediately. However sure they were of their man, it was twenty thalers against nothing if no-one was prepared to lay a wager. 'Sorry young sir,' said the ringleader, 'but we are away to a tavern that will produce better wagers.'

He nodded respectfully and turned to go. I yelled after him again, 'I will wager on myself; will you give me five-to-one also?'

He turned back; there was puzzlement on his face. This was a well practiced routine for them and I did not fit the profile. 'How much?' he said.

I knew that I needed to make it worth their while; I did quick calculations in my mind, 'Twenty thalers!' I called out.

'Twenty thalers against our hundred thalers?' he said.

'No; twenty thalers against your hundred and twenty thalers. There are twenty for just remaining standing are there not?'

'Aye,' he said, 'and you can produce twenty thalers now?'

'Within minutes sir; can you produce one hundred and twenty?'

He turned to his companions. One hundred and twenty thalers was a lot of money to have about one's person, but they quickly decided they could raise this sum between them and it did not occur to them for even a moment that they might lose. 'Yes sir, we can,' he said, his smile now broadening at the thought of a single large wager to match all the wagers they had expected from their evening of revelling.

'Then can I suggest that it be deposited with the landlord to hold the stakes,' I turned to the landlord and called out to him, 'is that all right with you landlord.'

'Gladly sir,' he confirmed sensing some spice in the air.

The young blade didn't like this suggestion; his expression darkened. He turned to his companions; they were unused to being treated this way - their honour being challenged by the lower classes. I did not give them the chance to dispute my suggestion, however. 'If I am to prove that I can meet the wager, then it seems that it is only right you should do the same.' This produced a cheer from the tavern; this young gentleman was standing up to the privileged class in a way they dared not, and they liked it. I could see the anger in the faces of the young blades, but the first of them reluctantly nodded his approval, his expression darkening further.

I stood and bowed politely to him forcing him to reciprocate in order to display his own good manners. 'I will be back with my stake in a few minutes,' I said.

I returned to my rooms and started to unpick the lining of Uncle Meno's frock-coat that I still used to hide my money. I released twenty thalers and tried to put them into my waistcoat pocket, but it would not accommodate them and I had to put the balance in a second pocket. I returned to the tavern with my pockets bulging, but not once did I stop to think that I was being foolhardy. Looking back now, I think I know what motivated me. Although I wanted to prosper it was not the money, nor even the opportunity to right a wrong. These young blades were arrogant, sating their need to gamble by taking advantage of the lower classes and fleecing them with a loaded wager. But it was still only a wager; there was no swindle, nobody was forced to gamble. No – it was about me; it was about my right of passage. I was now turned twenty, but I was much older than my years in experience. I had been forced to stand on my own two feet, to survive in a hostile world. I had stood and fought two ruffians in Dortmund and now I wanted to fight again, but this time it was not my opponent that I was really fighting; it was the young blades. I was proving to myself that I was as good as they were.

I approached the landlord to deposit my stake, but before I could do so, Old Musketeer appeared at my elbow and intercepted me, tapping his cane as he approached and then barring my path. 'PRIME AND LOAD,' he yelled, drawing everyone's attention to us, but then conspiratorially, 'don't do this young sir,' he whispered.

'Where did you spring from? How did you find out?' My astonishment was evident in my tone.

'I know everything that goes on around here, young sir. Nothing gets past Old Musketeer.'

'Don't worry, Old Musketeer,' I whispered, 'I know what I am doing.'

'No you don't, young sir.' He pushed me into a corner away from prying eyes. 'The man you are fighting is Willy Netser, he's an old pugilist. You have no chance against him.'

I winked at him to show that I knew this all along, once again realising too late the foolishness of the gesture. 'And *my* name is David Neander, and I am a *young* pugilist,' I whispered back at him.

'But you are a man of commerce, young sir?'

'Yes I am, Old Musketeer, but that is not all that I am.'

He stared unseeingly at me for a heartbeat. The man prided himself on being able to deduce what people were; to know what was going on about him, but I had just thrown a spanner in that pride. He gripped my arm in his hand and pushed me backwards squeezing it with considerably more force than I thought possible from such a wiry figure. 'Make sure your confidence is not misplaced, David Neander,' he hissed. 'They do not wager twenty thalers for nought. They do this regularly and nobody has yet stood against him.'

'Then I shall be the first,' I said arrogantly. He released me and I turned from him and gave the landlord my stake. Old Musketeer followed me having appointed himself as my second, but surprisingly, I was pleased to have him with me.

In the yard of the tavern, the ring was formed by the onlookers. It was similarly restrictive and I saw where the young blades positioned themselves to intervene if necessary. I stripped to my breeches to reveal my physique, but although I was as tall as Willy I was clearly giving away much weight. Old Musketeer held my coat and my ruched shirt and found himself a spot at the front of the crowd. They were with me but I think they thought I had little chance. At the command of '*Fight*', Willy came ponderously forward to monopolise the centre of the ring, his huge tree-trunk legs holding up his powerful torso, but also all that excess weight about his middle. He waited for me to come to him, but I decided not to and I just circled him with my guard up in front of my face. The young blades didn't like this; they feared that I would last the minute by default and they started to push me towards their man. I saw him recoil to throw a punch at me as I was catapulted towards him, but I side-stepped to my left to avoid a powerful right hook aimed at my head. The punch missed wildly, but I was not to be left alone and I was immediately pushed back towards him. Again he recoiled to throw a punch; I think he had reasoned that I was no threat and I was just going to use my mobility to try to avoid him. I leant backwards and his large fist whistled before my face. I felt the waft of it and it temporarily brought fear to me, my heart racing at the danger. This was a powerful man who could drop me with that power no matter how skilled I was.

That punch, however, exposed his body to me as it turned him with its momentum. Before he could bring his elbows back in against his chest, I sunk a powerful left hook under that elbow to the side of his ribs. I heard him gasp; I knew that he was out of shape. He had brought his power to the fight but little conditioning. He needed some moments to recover but his companions would not give it him and urged him on. He tried to grab me by the throat, but I sank another punch in the same place and he released his grip enabling me to move back into the open. I circled him for some seconds and I heard Old Musketeer's voice shouting out, *one half minute* – how he was reading a timepiece I did not know.

The brute righted himself and took up his full fighting attitude again; left leg and left hand forward. He came after me and I noticed that the ring was shrinking as the young blades moved forward to deny me room to manoeuvre. I was forced to stand before my opponent and I said a belated thanks to Bernd for teaching me the skills that I would now need. The big man threw a left and then a right and I parried both shots. I saw the look of surprise on his face as the realisation took him that he was fighting another pugilist. I shot out a left as a range finder but that was parried in return, and for twenty seconds or so we stood toe-to-toe throwing punches and parrying, until I hit him cleanly to the side of his head. He stumbled back slightly, but the punch did not have enough force to drop him, though blood started to run down the side of his face. He came right back at me, but I planted my feet to get purchase and hit him a powerful blow as he came in. It hurt him, but he grabbed me in a bear hug. He held on for a few moments while he regained his senses; when he did, however, he started to squeeze and I knew that I was in trouble. My arms were pinned against my side and I was powerless to get free. I was lifted off my feet as he tried to throw me.

'ONE MINUTE,' yelled Old Musketeer, 'THE FIGHT IS OVER!'

But the young blades took no notice. I knew that if I was thrown they would claim their prize. I writhed and twisted frantically and managed to pull my right arm up and free, but I was still held tight. I punched Willy's left ear, it must have left it ringing, but still he did not release his grip. I was now desperate; I gouged my right thumb into his left eye .The rules of a professional contest would have barred that, but we were fighting under different rules; in fact no rules at all. Willy released me involuntarily, his hands coming up automatically to protect his eyes. I raised my arms to signal that I had won the wager and the crowd cheered me. The young blades circled their man and I think they would have sent him back in, but the crowd had now broken the ring.

The ringleader turned to stare at me and I'm sure he considered crying 'Foul!', but by now it was too late; the jostling crowd was laughing and jeering and in no mood to be gainsaid. I saw his hesitation and then the resignation that entered his eyes. He knew that he in his turn had been fleeced and there was little he could do about it. He came forward and offered me his hand in a gentlemanly fashion, 'Well fought, young sir,' he said. 'Who taught you to fight?'

I took his hand willingly, 'Bernd Hartman,' I said proudly.

'Ah,' he said nodding knowingly. 'He has taught you well, but I think Willy would have beaten you in a true fight.'

I shook my head, I suppose I should have been magnanimous, but I was in no mood to be. 'He is in no condition to fight me in the prize ring. I would reduce him to a state of exhaustion within minutes,' I said.

The young blade looked at me thoughtfully, but said nothing more.

I looked around for Old Musketeer, but he had disappeared as mysteriously as he had arrived. For the rest of the evening I drank free of charge, my tankard being refilled by the tavern's regular clientele. I had taken the toffs down a peg or two and for that they were grateful; I had become a minor celebrity.

That evening I felt good about myself. One hundred and twenty thalers was the purse of several fights. Tomorrow I would start my business; I was educated and prospering. I was no longer that young Jewish schoolboy who stepped off the road to let a German pass by. I would never do that again, I promised my self.

CHAPTER 33

London 1823

'You must eat something, Julia.' The atmosphere at the breakfast table was strained and Julia's mother fussed around her, not quite understanding the depth of her daughter's concern.

Julia had tossed and turned all night, slipping into a fitful sleep only a couple of hours before dawn. She barely heard her mother's admonishments, nor was she aware of her hair escaping from beneath her hastily donned cap, her curls falling in disarray onto her tense, tired face. If her mother had failed to understand her daughter's anxiety, her maternal eye did not miss Julia's dishevelled appearance and tutting she reached over and pushed the errant curls back beneath the cap. Julia hardly noticed, her concentration fixed on the newspaper before her.

The maid arrived with a tray and laid the table with a tea urn and bowls, chocolate pots and coffee cans, toast and butter. George Carmichael, his gaze similarly fixed on this morning's copy of the Times, absent mindedly tucked into his breakfast of hot buttered toast and honey, drinking deeply from the deep strong black liquid that was his morning coffee and spraying crumbs onto the paper that he studied so intently. He flicked them away hardly aware that he was doing so. He had expected just a single column reporting the case, but the reporter, recognising the human interest in David's plight had written an extended article running to several columns. More importantly, the story had been picked up by the Editor as part of his editorial comment. In his featured article he explored the questionable worth of the immigrant to London's affluent society, where the Irish and the Eastern Europeans brought with them criminality, but few skills, and so were a blight on honest citizens. Yet in this case, the Editor had written, here was an educated man who brought skills that the city needed, but had been immediately wronged by the theft of his own belongings. Despite this regrettable circumstance, this particular immigrant was prepared to work as a common labourer to get himself a new start.

Reading these words, George grunted with satisfaction and looked over the top of his paper at his daughter, but she was engrossed in her own copy of the London Morning Penny Post.

Julia's mother poured her daughter a cup of hot chocolate, her favoured morning drink; she ignored it. Her mother then buttered some toast, spreading some cherry jam liberally across it and placing the plate directly under Julia's nose onto the surface of the newspaper she was reading with avid concentration. Not looking up, Julia frowned, murmured her thanks and pushed the plate away from the section that held her attention. The story here was told in less lofty tones than the Times; it was not about the contributions of the immigrant to the great city, but dwelt entirely on the human interest of the case. The by-line was credited to Arthur Brandon, who she took to be the small shrew-like man she had seen scribbling his charcoal at great pace across his notebook. She had thought him an odd looking little man and was anxious at first that he might after all ignored her request to wait on some of the reportage, but now she warmed to him with every word she read. She picked up a piece of toast without thinking and then cradled the hot chocolate in her hands, eating and drinking as she read, her anxiety lessened by his story.

Her mother saw her expression lighten. 'Would you like some oatmeal, dear? Perhaps with some sweet cream; you like that?' She was ignored again. Pursing her lips and giving a small shake of her head, Mrs Carmichael looked from her husband to her daughter and with a sigh of resignation, helped herself to some oatmeal.

Reaching the end of the article, Julia smiled with delight. Nothing had been said about the Judge's drunken behaviour as she had feared. This was not so much a piece of objective journalism as a work of embellishment. It was the story of a hero; of a man wronged; of a man fighting to clear his name. It was the type of journalism she normally hated. She sat day after day in the court gallery seeing the poor and ignorant treated like fodder for the system, generally totally ignored by newspapers, whose reporters were intent only on pandering to the prejudices of their readers, so that the iniquities just carried on regardless and most of the populace were in ignorance of them. And yet this article was more than Julia had dared to dream. There was no restraint in the journalist's writing; he took liberties with the truth, embellished the facts; painted a one-sided picture and all in David's favour. It was wonderful, she thought.

Mrs Carmichael helped herself to coffee and replaced the pot on the table with a resounding thump, somewhat peeved that she was being ignored. The house was her domain; she was the Napoleon of it and she was not used to being treated as an invisible foot soldier. 'It's about time you found yourself a good husband, my girl,' she said waspishly.

It was a well worn theme and Julia normally met it with a dismissive, 'Fol derol' as the best defence she could muster, but today the words did not even penetrate her consciousness. 'Does the Times article help our case father?' she said, inadvertently ignoring her mother, whose mood darkened because of it.

'Rather,' he said enthusiastically.

'How - what does it say? Can we use it?'

'No, not really, there's nothing here that can be used as case law or court procedure. But Judge Cardew has already determined that this case is not to be about evidence. He has set the rules of the case and he now has to live by them. He'll be reading the Times this morning and realising that it is not about him in his courtroom - his domain – not about him being able to do just what he wants. You've put him in the public eye and he'll now realise that what he says has consequences. The old bugger will be choking on his oatmeal this morning all right - well done Julia my girl!'

'George!' his wife screeched. 'Oh, this in intolerable. Tavern language at the breakfast table and in front of your daughter too,' Julia's mother's mood darkened still further. Her face like thunder, she reached over once more to push the errant curl back under her daughter's cap, it had escaped again. This time Julia patted her away irritably.

George Carmichael finally looked up at his wife and saw the look on her face; a look that said more than words. He responded mildly, 'I am sorry my dear; you are right of course, my language is unpardonable.' He turned to his daughter, 'Will you forgive me, Julia?'

Julia looked at him nonplussed not having registered the profanity and not understanding what he was apologising for. 'Yes, yes,' she said anyway.

'I blame you for this, George Carmichael,' said his wife, 'allowing Julia to clerk for you. It's no position for a young lady. She should be learning more appropriate things.'

'Needlecraft, you mean.' Julia's interjected scathingly.

'Yes, among other things. And what is wrong with that, my girl? No respectable young man will want to take a wife who doesn't even turn a hair at such language! It is disgraceful.'

'And no respectable young man will want to take a wife who is as tall as I am, so it doesn't really matter does it?'

'Now stop that at once Julia,' her mother retorted. 'There are plenty of suitable young men; there's the Howard's youngest boy, Bartholomew, he's nearly six feet tall. He'll be just right for you.'

'Just right?' Julia looked at her mother flabbergasted, 'Simply because of his height! He's a dunderhead, Mother. He lags so far behind the conversation he's like a hound with no sense of smell! He probably keeps a note in his frock-coat pocket with his address written on it so he can find his way home - well with a bit of help anyway. She sighed with exasperation and with a contemptuous 'Pah!', returned defiantly to her newspaper.

Mrs Carmichael, her anger mounting by the minute, gave a shocked cry, 'How can you speak to your own mother like that?' She reached out and poked the back of her husband's Times. 'George! Aren't you going to say anything to that girl of yours?'

'I do beg your pardon, Mother,' Julia murmured not looking up, but realising that perhaps this time she had gone too far.

George put down his paper temporarily and looked at his wife for some moments. There was resignation in his eyes. 'We have discussed this already, my dear. I fear that Julia has already lost her heart, she is sweet on somebody else and there is no point in pushing any young men at her, tall or otherwise.'

Julia was prompted to look up from her paper, surprised that her father had realised this when she had hardly dared to admit it to herself. She stared at him and he gave her an affectionate smile, one that hid the fear within him that his daughter was going to be terribly hurt.

If his own fears were subdued his wife's were not; she gasped, said, 'The Jew boy? Well that's a pretty state of affairs! It cannot be, of course. But Julia will soon get over him.'

It was, on the face of it, just a statement of fact, but Julia heard the nuance in the tone; the nuance that tapped into the general feeling that a Jew was not socially acceptable. She shot her mother a fiery look and Mrs Carmichael, meeting the full force of it, opened her mouth to speak again, but no words came out as if they were too afraid to venture forward, scared away by her daughter's hostile stare.

'That Jew boy has a name,' said Julia. The words spat from her mouth.

Her mother had never seen her this way before and had certainly never been spoken to like this. But the intensity of that stare stifled any words of dispute that she thought about uttering. 'Yes, I know, dear,' she said instead, her tone much more appeasing. 'But this David Neander – well you surely must see that he is not a suitable match for you?'

'This David Neander is the most remarkable man that I have ever met. He is educated, intelligent, poetic, and honourable,' the words of admiration flowed from Julia without restraint. 'It is me who is no match for him.' She turned to her father for support, 'He is remarkable isn't he, Father?'

George Carmichael looked at his daughter and saw the pleading in her eyes. But then he looked at his wife and saw that she expected quite a different response to the beseeching expectation of his daughter. He knew he could find no response to satisfy both of them. He shuffled uncomfortably in his chair for what seemed like an eternity, contemplating his dilemma. It was the dark side of love when you know you must disappoint someone you deeply care for. He thought about changing the subject to deflect away the impasse, but that would only result in upsetting them both. Then it suddenly became clear to him what he should do. At that moment his daughter was in need of his support much more than was his wife. She would be piqued for a few days, but he was in danger of losing his daughter's love for ever.

'Yes, this David Neander is a most remarkable fellow all right.' There, I have said it, he thought, and having said it he also realised the plain truth of the words. He turned to his wife, 'Jew or not, my dear, he is everything that Julia says he is. It is true; he even seems to have retained a dignity despite having spent many months in that filthy prison.'

His wife stood and threw down her napkin onto the table. 'Oh, this is intolerable, George. You can't possibly be…' She did not complete the sentence, her exasperation getting in the way and stifling the words so that they died in her mouth. She looked at him and then at her daughter and saw the bond between them. 'Argh!' was all that she could say; she stormed off holding her head aloof, her chin leading the way.

After she had gone they both held their breath for a few moments then looked at each other. 'Thank you Father,' Julia said kindly, realising what he had done for her sake.

'Oh, your mother will get over it. She'll come round; you wait and see.' The words were as much to reassure himself as his daughter.

'Do you really believe what you said?'

'Yes I do, I believe David is the most honourable of men. He seems to have the wisdom of someone much older, but then, of course, he has had to face a lifetime of difficulties in his short life.'

'The murder of one's family is hardly a difficulty Father!'

'No, no, you are right of course; but it has forged what he is, and it could have forged someone much different, someone much more feral. But even though I acknowledge what a good man he is, that doesn't mean I approve of your losing your heart to him. He faces the gallows my girl, and if the worst should happen it will not be merely difficult for you. Oh Julia,' he sighed, looked into her eyes, his gaze softening, 'I am so afraid for you, dear girl, more so than I am for David Neander.'

Cold dread seized her at the truth of his words and she shivered. All the fears that had been temporally eased by reading the newspaper came flooding back to her. She was in an ever-shrinking place and it was becoming overwhelming. But then her courage surfaced as if in response to those fears. 'Then we have to be on our game today,' she said emphatically, looking squarely at her father. 'Today we have to be as good as we have ever been.'

CHAPTER 34

Hamburg 1821

That winter was a bitter one in Hamburg. My rooms were good but they always seemed to be terribly cold and I was forced to burn fires continuously. I wore mittens in my translation work, but my fingers were constantly numb and I sucked them regularly to get some warmth back into them. Thick snow fell frequently and the streets were difficult to pass at times. The heavy wagons struggled over the slippery cobbles, sometimes skidding sideways, and more than once I was obliged to use my athleticism to avoid being hit; others were not so lucky. The traffic turned the crisp snow into sludge, which then refroze at night only to be covered by fresh falls next day, adding to the danger in the streets.

Through all this bitter wintry weather, however, the daily life of the port continued with its usual bustle. Ships docked and were unloaded and the new cargoes then filled the empty holds as the trading of nations continued with as little interruption from the weather as was possible. Plumes of steam left the mouths of the dock workers as they toiled, their warm breath mixing with the freezing air, much like the steam that whistled from my boiling kettle. But the weather brought little sign of depression to the good Lutheran citizens of Hamburg. Trade was this city's lifeblood as it emerged from the battering it had taken from Napoleon's last campaign in Germany. So long as this continued, so did the prospect of affluence returning to its citizens. This was evident in the hard labour of its dockers, the commerce of its merchants and the guile of its bankers.

I too joined in that prosperity. The one hundred and twenty thalers I had won in the tavern on my first night in the city gave me a breathing space. I had an overall plan in my mind, which needed a fund to finance my eventual move to my final projected destination; a sort of war chest for 'campaign England'. The winnings took me almost there, but I also had my personal pride to overcome; I wanted to be successful in Hamburg and my pride would not let me leave until I had become so. I had cards printed up and I toured the commercial parts of the city handing them out. With the help of Old Musketeer, I turned the ground floor room of my apartments into a fine business premises. He found me bookshelves and leather seats, which proclaimed me a skilful and successful translator, and amazingly, he also showed unsuspected skills as an agent, procuring valuable work for me. Quite how he did this I found bewildering. Aside from the fact that he was blind – which was remarkable in itself - he was essentially a man of the streets, scruffy in appearance, and yet he seemed to know everything about everyone. I had initially defeated his perceptions, his powers of non-seeing observation. I think that was why he took a shine to me: I was not supposed to be a fighter and the fact that I was somehow seemed to create a bond between us. Whatever the reason, I was happy to reciprocate that bond. I grew to like that inquisitive jackdaw face, his head twitching from side to side trying to pick up any *soupçon* of noise that would be informative to him. His exaggerated facial expressions always brought a smile to my face. When I offered to pay him a retainer, this exceptionally self-reliant man, who had been forced to establish a life for himself after being blinded, was suddenly dumbfounded. No charity had ever been shown to him before and a moment of rare emotion took him. I saw his prominent whiskered Adam's apple bob in his scrawny throat as he fought back a sob. But it was not charity on my part. He was my passport around the city, far more valuable to me than the calling cards I had distributed.

Old Musketeer's reflex habit of barking involuntary military orders was, of course, a draw back in a commercial situation. 'UPON THE COMMAND, PRIME,' barked at full volume was hardly the most professional of images that I was trying to purvey to a prospective client, but there were far more positives than negatives, and so I tolerated his eccentricities. He became my constant companion. I bought him a new suit of clothes; sober grey livery jacket and a new linen shirt and clean breeches, but it only had limited success. The sockets around his non-existent eyes were stained permanently black from the gunpowder blast and together with his greasy lank hair they conspired to challenge my attempts to smarten him up. He wore the new suit to begin with, but I began to notice the return of that dirty old, worn military uniform, until once again it became his street-badge for everyday use, though he obliged me by changing into the new suit when I prompted him or whenever he accompanied me to meet a client.

1821 turned into 1822 without any let up in the freezing weather, but it was an opportunistic time for me. The jobs were coming in fast and I was gaining a reputation for fine and speedy work. I started writing poetry again and re-contacted my publisher, who liked what I was writing. Spring was late in coming, the winter lingering well past its allotted time, but then in April, winter finally gave up its obstinate struggle and within days it was gone. The spring sunshine had warmth that had been missing for so long and life for me seemed better than it had been since my break up with Marita.

I started training again, winning three fights in the city park. My style was not always appreciated; the sportsmen of Hamburg were no different to those in Frankfurt preferring the traditional toe-to-toe style rather than my athletic dodge and weave. But I knew how to give them what they wanted once I had exhausted my opponents after they had chased me around the ring for several minutes. These set-tos were not won until one of the contestants was bested and unable to come up to the mark within thirty seconds of being floored. It was not sufficient to merely out-manoeuvre them – I had to finish them off - and the bloodier the besting, the more the onlookers liked it. As I was getting older I was filling out, my power was increasing and the finish began to come more easily to me; I was also able to find more power punching at range as well as at close quarters.

In late summer I turned 21: but I was far older than that in terms of my maturity. In my short life I had battled prejudice, discrimination, bigotry, and intolerance, all of which had left me lonely and isolated. Riot and murder had scared and disfigured my adolescent life and yet all that experience had somehow sculpted who I was; it had chiselled away the pieces to reveal the new David Neander. It also gave me a driving force; it steered me in a direction that had a force of its own. All those terrible things that had happened to me had initially made me bitterly angry and given me a thirst for revenge, but in Hamburg this started to transform into something else. I had been brought up in a home where principles existed. Mama and Papa had taught me the meaning of living a life of honour and integrity. I had suppressed all that, but now it re-surfaced and my anger was channelled into something else: a need to be successful and prosperous. And first and foremost I needed to succeed and prosper in the German states where I was denied citizenship. That was a goal that I had set myself.

I surprised myself with the poise I had acquired. My success both in business and in the ring had imbued me with self-confidence, it permeated everything I did. Old Musketeer knew I was Jewish, but nobody else knew my secret; in fact I no longer saw myself as a Jew. I was neither German nor Jew; neither Lutheran nor a follower of Judaism. I was simply me, David Neander. I did not turn my back on God; I merely felt no need for either church or synagogue.

I started to make plans to go to England, my war chest was now filling nicely; but what of Old Musketeer? I felt that I would be abandoning him. Our relationship was not one of master and servant; he was obviously too self-reliant to ever be a servant. I determined to take him with me. I had fought my last fight of the year in the park and Old Musketeer had, as usual, been my second - he was surprisingly good at that as well. The fight had been difficult. My success had meant that I was being matched with increasingly bigger men and my last opponent, Manfred

Shoen, outweighed me by fifteen kilos, which was a huge disadvantage. If he had been carrying that weight around the middle then I would have bested him easily, using my skill and athleticism to drain him of his stamina and then used my increasing power to pummel him to defeat. But Manfred Shoen was a young man of only twenty-four, and that weight advantage was allied to conditioning and no little skill. My only advantage was my speed. He seemed like a colossus to me as I looked across the ring at him. He had the power to beat me and I knew that. This was not new to me, of course, but try as I might I couldn't drain this man's stamina. The fight was long and it was me who faded first. Shoen had let me skip around the ring for thirty-five minutes, taking the centre of the ring, parrying my shots and counterpunching whenever I came into range. The crowd did not like it and they bayed for action. I took his shots on the arms, using my own parrying skills, but as I slowed he began to come to me. This was what I had wanted, but I was now too tired to take advantage. At first I had success. I beat him to the punch several times and this raised my spirits. I remember recoiling to unload a power punch, but in doing so I must have left myself open.

I was down; blackness. When consciousness returned to my addled brain I was staring at the dirt floor and a rivulet of my own blood. Old Musketeer pulled me to my feet and carried me back to my corner, his wiry body straining with my uncoordinated weight. It was expected that pugilists fought to the very end, until there was simply nothing else left to give. The seconds ticked by being shouted by the timekeeper and they started to resonate in my brain as my senses came back to me. I turned towards the centre of the ring, ready to continue with the fight, but as I did so, Old Musketeer's right leg swiped at my unsteady left leg and down I went again.

Most of the crowd thought I had collapsed again from the effects of my opponent's concussive punch and those who had gambled on Manfred Shoen cheered their support. Others booed as they saw their own wagers going down with me, while the neutrals booed at being denied a fight that satisfied their blood lust – for there was always blood lust on these occasions. For the more sporting gentlemen who saw what my second had done, there was a lack of honour apparent in what was happening. Pugilistic contests were seen as honourable encounters; a man stood up and fought like a man. Retiring hurt was never an option. You lost in the act of fighting, not sitting on a stool in your corner. If you knew you were bested, honour demanded that you walk to the centre of the ring and take your beating. I knew that and I was prepared for my fate every time I entered the ring, but it seemed Old Musketeer had other ideas.

I looked up at him, initially unsure of what was happening, but it quickly became apparent to me what he had done. The timekeeper's counting entered my consciousness again. I was furious with Old Musketeer, but that would have to wait. I had only seconds left to come up to the mark. I scrambled to my feet, my legs still unsteady, but before I had righted myself fully, that scrawny leg swung again. This time I did not fall, but I staggered to my left and I had to grab the ropes to stop myself from going over. That had added perhaps another five seconds. I looked back at Old Musketeer, my anger emblazoned on my face; he could not see me of course, but I'm sure he knew for those exaggerated facial movements proclaimed some sort of begrudging admission of guilt, though without any request for forgiveness. I saw his shoulders shrug to reinforce his facial gestures.

I righted myself and took a couple of unsteady steps like a newly born foal. But I was too late: I heard the timekeeper call '*Thirty*'! The Referee waved his hands in my direction to show that I had been counted out of time. I had not *come up to scratch* and for me there were only boos of derision from the cheated crowd. It stung me - stung my honour. I felt that Old Musketeer had let me down. In the dressing room I sat forlornly on my stool, the sweat dripping off my chin, a mixture of perspiration and blood forming a pink puddle between my legs.

'Why did you do that?' I asked, bewildered. He did not speak. He was towelling me down vigorously, the towel acting as a sort of buffer between us. 'Well?' I pressed, but again he did not speak. The towelling continued, more vigorously than before. 'Well?' I pressed again, my voice rising in anger.

'We'll talk in the tavern,' he said and turned to walk away, but then turned back and spoke over his shoulder at me, 'I'll collect your purse and see you there.' He tapped his way to the door, expertly avoiding the other fighters and disappearing quickly from sight, leaving me to ponder on what had happened.

In the tavern he was in a booth waiting for me. There were two tankards of beer on the table, one before him and another for me, together with a money bag with my purse in it. I took my place opposite him and just sat looking at him for some moments. His face was expressionless, but his head continued to twitch from side to side.

'Well?' I said eventually, as though no time had elapsed.

'Well what? You were bested, why take a terrible beating?'

'How do you know I was bested?' I barked at him, 'You cannot see.'

'I carried you back to your corner; your legs had gone.'

He was right about that of course and I knew it. 'But that was not your decision to make,' I said.

'You were in no position to make that decision, so I made it for you.'

'So you decided to make me look like a coward.'

'No, I decided that as a loser you would get one third of the purse. You could take that ten thalers and be fit to fight again before winter comes, or you could take the ten thalers and a heavy beating and not be fit to fight again for many months, and you'd probably never be the same fighting force again anyway.'

I breathed a deep frustrated breath. I was still angry with him; I did not like being booed. I liked the adulation of being a winner, but deep down I knew he was right. Fighters were never the same force after a heavy beating; I knew that. I reached across and gripped the knuckles of his hand on the table to show that everything was all right between us; that I understood he had acted in my best interest. He smiled a smile so wide that it seemed to cut his face in half.

'I will not be fighting in the park again this season,' I told him. There was resignation in my tone, I think.

His head twitched more distinctly than normal, those eyeless sockets seeming to look directly at me, demanding an explanation. 'You intend to look for fights at the athletic clubs then? That will be good, David, fighting indoors before the sporting gentlemen; they will be more appreciative of your style, they are more knowledgeable.'

He had jumped to an understandable conclusion, but it was not a correct one. 'No, my friend; I mean that I will not be fighting again in Hamburg.'

He was quiet for some moments, but his heads twitched as he assimilated what I had said. 'Then you will make for England already?' he concluded; I had told him of my plans some time ago.

'Aye,' I said, my head nodding to his unseeing eyes. I had never really got used to the fact that he could not see me.

'But you are on the way to being rich, David; Hamburg has been a good city for you, you are prospering here. I had assumed you had thought better of heading for England; there is no guarantee that you will be successful there.'

''Tis true that I am prospering in Hamburg; but as a Jew I am a non-citizen. There is nothing to keep me here... well, perhaps one thing,' I added.

'One thing?'

'Yes, just one: you, Old Musketeer. You, my friend.'

His head stopped twitching at my comment. I believe it was the first time I had actually seen him motionless, outwardly calm. I think the word 'friend' affected him for his mouth trembled slightly. 'I have a proposition for you,' I went on. His head twitched into life again to gesture his interest. 'You have looked out for me since I arrived in Hamburg, I know that.' I hesitated, unsure how to broach the subject, but then just went straight to the heart of the matter, 'Will you come with me to England?'

The twitching suddenly became exaggerated, as if the question had taken him unawares, as though it had never even crossed his mind that I should ask him such a thing. 'As what?' was all he said.

I was taken aback; it was my turn to be bemused by a question. 'As my employee,' I said eventually, 'as my companion, as my friend; well... exactly as what you are now,' I added.

He reached out and without fumbling took the tankard of beer. His hand seemed to know instinctively where the handle was; a casual onlooker would not have known it was the action of a blind man. He took a long swig, swallowing it down in one gulp, his Adam's apple leaping as it went down. He was thinking deeply. I let him get on with it and took a long drink myself. I watched him as I did so.

He cradled the tankard in both hands on his lap, rocking backwards and forwards slightly. 'I have a map in my head, David,' he said after a long silence, 'and I know exactly where I am at all times on this map.'

'And that's why you have been so good for me.' I said with a smile of relief, thinking I was encouraging him to come to England with me.

'No, you don't understand,' he said, shaking his head in emphatic refusal. 'I know that I am good at what I do. I know that I am useful to you. But that map in my head is a map of *Hamburg*. Take that away and I'm just another blind man, begging for alms on the street.'

'You will never be just that,' I said honestly, but I knew he was right. He was special because he knew this *his* city inside out. I was disappointed, but I respected his view and did not press him to come with me. That was perhaps the greatest mistake of my life. I should have used every counter argument that I could have honestly come up with; and then I should have lied and invented bogus arguments to reinforce my case. If Old

Musketeer had been there to cover my back, then perhaps my life would not have taken such a catastrophic turn. But hindsight is a wonderful thing and at the time I had no inkling of the horrors that lay in wait for me. And so I acquiesced to his refusal.

CHAPTER 35

London 1823

Julia did not really notice the guard at the door to the Old Bailey; he was always there. She knew people paid to come in and watch the proceedings as entertainment. It had never bothered her before, but for the last two days it had upset her tremendously that David's fight for his life was reduced to mere entertainment. Today, however, she was blind to everybody: to the activity that characterised the assizes; to the crowds that wanted to come and fill the public gallery.

Barely aware of where she was Julia walked down the corridor her thoughts sliding even further away from her surroundings, her fears circulating rapidly in her head, her brain manufacturing various outcomes to the day's proceedings. The noise, a loud hum of sound as if she were about to enter a hornets' nest, took her by surprise and burst the fearful bubble of her thoughts before she opened the door to the gallery. For a moment she froze then tentatively pushed at the large, imposing oak door, first peering round it then more boldly stepping inside. That hum then exploded into her consciousness; not hornets, but a cacophony of expectant voices. She looked around the gallery in disbelief, it was packed, not an empty seat to be seen. The court had been obliged to dispatch an usher to take control and he had allowed many to stand at the back, but even that space was now full.

The usher saw the look of bewilderment on her face as her mind struggled to come to terms with the scene that beheld her. 'Sorry, miss,' he said, 'but we are at capacity. You will have to wait outside until somebody leaves.'

Julia looked at him in disbelief. She was temporarily unable to take in what was happening, unable to find the words that she needed. And then she became aware of a hand waving at her from a front seat of the gallery; it was the bony, crab-like fingers still clasping a piece of charcoal that first drew her attention. She nodded, turned to the usher and pointed at the little shrew-like reporter. It was a nonsensical response and the usher just looked at her nonplussed, but then she found her voice.

'I am clerking for my father, George Carmichael,' she said forcefully. 'I am not allowed in the courtroom, so I must do it from here. You will need to find me somewhere to do this.'

The court usher was now even more confused. He recognised her and knew of the improbable arrangement, which was the source of some mirth amongst the court officials: the silly girl who wanted to be an attorney at law just like her father. But this silly girl had given him an order and her father had standing in the court, therefore, by association so did she, and the usher was used to obeying orders from his betters.

'Very well, Miss,' he responded doubtfully, concerned as to her sensibilities. 'But there are no seats available; you will have to stand at the back with the others and I'm afraid that some of them are the more common sort - not really for the likes of a gentile young lady such as yourself.'

Julia forced an appreciative smile to acknowledge the man's concern but it was the least of her fears this day.

'Miss Carmichael! Miss Carmichael!' A high-pitched voice called out her name and she turned to see the little shrew-like man scurrying up the gallery towards her. 'Arthur Brandon at you service, Miss Carmichael. You must come and sit next to me, if you would be so kind. You can help with my story, fill in the gaps.'

'Thank you, Mr Brandon, but there is no seat available that I can see.'

'My colleague will vacate his seat for you; he's a sketch artist, he is used to sketching standing up.'

Relieved, Julia smiled. 'You are most gracious, Mr Brandon; thank you, I will accept.'

Arthur Brandon led her to his own seat and looked pointedly at his colleague, who vacated the next seat somewhat less willingly than Brandon had led Julia to believe, a full day's standing not being what he had anticipated. Nonetheless, he removed himself to the back of the gallery, grumbling inaudibly as he did so.

Julia smiled her gratitude at his departing back and looked about her, bewildered. 'There are so many people here,' she said, sitting down.

'They have all read my article in this morning's paper,' Brandon said, without any hint of modesty, adding with a grin, 'they have come to see the entertainment.'

Cringing at his words, Julia gasped, her hand straying to her cheek.

'Forgive me, Miss Carmichael, but I can see that your connection with the accused is rather more than I had realised; you are not here simply to clerk for your father, are you?'

Julia blushed, shook her head, whispered, 'I confess he means a great deal to me, Mr Brandon.'

The reporter's tone softened, 'Ah, and we must not forget that a man's life is at stake here, must we? But I promise you, my dear, all this attention will be good for his cause. The jury will be swayed by the enthusiasm of the gallery.'

'Thank you, Mr Brandon, for your kind words. I hope you are right.'

'I am, I promise you,' he repeated, intuitively putting his bony hand on hers in a gesture of comfort then quickly pulling it away as if scalded.

He had, of course, broken the rules of society. Julia was far above him and it was not for the likes of him to touch her. But he had meant well and she smiled to show she was not offended. 'You are most kind,' she said again.

He edged away from her and returned his attention to his notebook. Julia peered down into the courtroom and saw her father enter and take his place.

George Carmichael spread his papers out on the mahogany table before him as he had done so many times before, but he realised that today was different. He was a professional barrister and had trained himself over the years to be detached from his clients. Today, however, he realised that in this case he had been unable to summon that detachment. The enormity of the task before him suddenly hit him with such force it took his breath away. An obvious thought manifested itself that somehow had not registered before; this was the first time in his long career that he was defending a man who was facing the gallows. Only the rich could afford attorneys and he was not usually engaged to defend capital charges. He felt the weight of responsibility on his shoulders as he had never felt it before. And then there was the expectancy of his daughter, which added further to his burden and he felt his heart race at the thought of her. '*Familiarity breeds contempt*,' he muttered to himself, amazed at his own reaction. The courtroom was his domain and normally he was entirely comfortable within it. He told himself to take a few deep breaths to calm his nerves. And then he felt Julia's watchful gaze and looked up at the crowded gallery. He was met by a sea of faces, but nevertheless he was drawn immediately to hers. She smiled back at him and he tried to convey optimism to her, hoping she would not read in his eyes the self-doubt that racked him.

'HUZZAH!' Unbelievably a cheer had rung out in the gallery. George Carmichael turned back to the courtroom in astonishment to see that David had been brought into the courtroom by the Dock Officer, who was in the process of removing his shackles. This was bizarre, he had never seen anything like it; the courtroom was beginning to resemble a variety theatre. For some moments even the court officials were stunned, but then an usher walked across the floor of the courtroom to address the gallery.

'SILENCE IN COURT!' he yelled and when this had little effect, repeated his words, 'SILENCE, SILENCE! OR I'LL HAVE THE COURT CLEARED.'

David's face registered as much disbelief as the court officials. He looked around wondering if this hullabaloo was normal in this country. He too sought out Julia. She was in the process of removing her bonnet, but he saw that the bewilderment on her features matched his own. And then the court clock struck ten-of-the-clock, its striking hardly audible above the noise. Today there was no delay and the Judge's door opened on time. Cardew, attired in full-bottomed wig and scarlet gown, entered brusquely as if he had business he wanted to conclude quickly.

'ALL RISE,' yelled the Clerk, and the court dutifully obeyed as they did every day, but everybody knew that this was no ordinary day at the assizes.

The Judge took his seat and Julia searched his features for a sign of his mood; had he read the *Times* and if so, how was he reacting? Those two cold eyes were stern, but other than that they revealed so very little. There was a residue of mumbling from the gallery and he banged his gavel down belligerently to bring them to order. Julia broke out in a cold sweat as she now saw that his mood was black. She heard him say to the jury, 'Before you consider your verdict...' and glanced in alarm to see her father leap with a clatter to his feet, interrupting Cardew in mid-sentence.

George knew there was no requirement under the law for the Judge to sum up the case for the jury, but clearly that was what he was about to do. The last thing George wanted was for the jury to start their deliberations with Cardew's vindictive words ringing in their ears. He wanted to address the jury himself before the Judge spoke, but he also knew that there was no requirement under established court procedure for *him* to sum up either; something that he thought ought to change.

'Your Honour,' he said.

'What is it now, Mr Carmichael?'

'Before you address the jury with your wise words,' he said obsequiously, 'and with your kind permission, Your Honour, I wonder if you would allow me to *also* address the jury?'

Cardew, his eyebrows raised, looked across at Josiah Heath, who, with a surprised glance at George, raised no objection but simply inclined his head.

'Oh, very well Mr Carmichael,' Cardew exclaimed testily, 'if you must.'

George tried frantically to put his thoughts in order whilst at the same time moving his papers around the table to find the notes he was looking for - he had spent many hours the previous evening writing briefing notes for every possible eventuality. At last his fingers found them and his thoughts immediately arranged themselves at the prompt of the written words before him. He turned to the jury. 'Gentlemen of the jury, you have a grave responsibility to discharge. A man's life is dependent on your good selves and the decision that you come to this day - you must not approach it lightly.' George Carmichael paused for effect. He wanted them to dwell on his words, to recognize the enormity of what was being asked of them. He wanted them to feel the burden that he felt. Judge Cardew, however, broke into those moments of retrospection.

''Pon my soul, Mr Carmichael!' he said, his tone condescending, 'it is for me to point out such things to the jury, not you. Kindly confine yourself to putting forward your client's case.'

George Carmichael bowed to the Judge, 'As you wish, Your Honour; my apologies; I should have left these wise words to yourself, of course, but as you will appreciate, with a man's life at stake, this case is extremely grave and I have clearly allowed the burden of responsibility to affect my sense of propriety.'

Judge Cardew face turned from sour grapes to one of arrogant satisfaction that he had made his point and re-established his authority, not realising that George had cleverly used his apology to reiterate his point to the jury. The Judge would almost certainly have omitted such words and George was quietly satisfied.

His next task was to review the evidence and he set about doing so purposefully. The Watchman could not speak French and the defendant could not speak English; they did not understand each other; there was confusion. David Neander had not been armed and did not resist arrest; he did not try to escape. The Watchman did not investigate

David's story nor ascertain that he had arrived in the city only a day previous to the offence, as had been evidenced by the Harbour Master. The thefts had started before his arrival and had continued thereafter.

This rebuttal of the case against David was strong, but George knew he needed more than that to counter the effect of the Judge's opposition. He needed to get the jury on David's side; he needed to get them to associate themselves with David; to put themselves in his shoes. He had a small start in that half the sworn jury were foreigners.

'Gentlemen of the jury; some of you will know what it is like to arrive in this country as a foreigner. How strange the people and their culture must have seemed to you; a different currency to contend with; not knowing your way around the city, and yet you have prospered. You must have done so to be called here as a juror. You will know, therefore, how David Neander must have felt on his first day. But he had come prepared with skills and money to start a new business; he aspired to prosper as you have done. And I'm sure that you had to overcome many obstacles along the way. The obstacles placed before this man, however, were extraordinarily cruel. He was robbed of his life savings on his very first day, and yet he was prepared to lower himself to offer his physical labour, to start again at the very bottom. This is the sort of man this great city needs, a man who would prosper along with it. And yet fate has conspired so maliciously against him; this honourable man was duped by one of the rogues that live amongst us.'

'SHAME, SHAME!' The words rang out from the gallery as one of the onlookers shouted out. This was taken up by many others who had come to be entertained.

'SILENCE, SILENCE.' The Judge banged his gavel again and again, and continued until all were silent. He looked back at George Carmichael making no attempt to hide his displeasure. 'Continue, Mr Carmichael - and make it brief if you will.'

'Your Honour,' he bowed as he spoke the words. He turned back to the jury, 'And to those members of the jury who are natives of this city, as I am myself, I would say that you must not convict this man simply *because* he is a foreigner; I think we all know what sort of a villain really committed this crime. This was not an opportunist crime. This was a well worked out, long-term transgression committed by a scheming thief, wily enough to protect himself if things went wrong. I'm sure you recognise what has happened here just as much as I have. This scoundrel had a good thing going and he had the craftiness to cover his tracks so that if discovered, someone else would take the blame.

Gentlemen, that man could have duped any one of you; it could be you at the bar today. Gentlemen, what evidence is there of this man's guilt? I tell you there is very little. And remember, gentlemen, you have to be sure beyond all reasonable doubt before you convict. I urge you to bring in the only verdict that you know, deep down, applies in this most difficult of cases. And that is a "not guilty" verdict.'

George Carmichael bowed to the jury to reinforce his words and then turned to the Judge and bowed again, this time, however, out of protocol rather than respect. Then, adjusting his gown, he sat down.

A round of applause sprang up spontaneously from the gallery and Julia looked round at the throng. The sketch artist was busy at work with his charcoal, holding his sketch pad in the crook of his left arm whilst drawing with his right. He had been looking George Carmichael up and down all the time during the summation to the jury and she assumed he had been sketching him. She was so proud of her father, he had done well and delivered his speech so eloquently, but at the same time she was apprehensive about the Judge's reaction to the antics in the public gallery. She looked back over the rail and down upon Judge Cardew. His scowling features reinforced her fears.

'Gentlemen of the jury,' said the Judge. 'You have heard Mr Carmichael protesting with noteworthy eloquence that his client is a wronged man, innocent of the charges brought against him,' he paused, his lips lifted in a sneer. 'What you have to decide is whether the facts put before you support that contention.'

'*So far so good,*' Julia thought; Cardew seemed to be staying within his legal boundaries thus far.

The Judge glanced around the court and then continued addressing the jury, 'What you have to consider is if there is any evidence to support the existence of this phantom thief, this apparition cited by Mr Carmichael.'

Julia sat up straight in alarm and put her hand to her mouth in disbelief. She turned to the journalist beside her, 'He can't say that, he *can't.*' She saw the look of confusion on Brandon's face and knew she needed to explain further. 'He should only pronounce on matters of law, it's for the jury to decide if they believe in this other man's existence. By calling him a phantom he is putting himself in the jury's place, he's saying that the other person doesn't exist.'

The bony hand scribbled down her words, 'Don't worry, my dear; he'll pay for that in my column tomorrow.'

'It may be too late by that time Mr Brandon.' Her heart pounding in agitation, Julia's voice quivered as she spoke.

The Judge went on, 'The plain truth is that the accused did not have the permission of the owner to take this carcass, at the very least he was in possession of stolen goods. That fact is indisputable.'

'He's doing it again,' Julia mumbled softly, and the bony-handed charcoal recorded her words.

'Gentlemen of the jury, this is not the difficult case that this clever lawyer's eloquent words would have us believe.'

'What!' exclaimed Julia, expressing her thoughts out loud, unable to contain herself in sheer disbelief at the Judge's words.

Cardew did not so much as glance up at the gallery, but continued addressing the jury, 'This is actually quite simple. The defendant was caught in the act of stealing this sheep. Do not lose sight of that fact in your deliberations. It is now,' the Judge looked to the clock, 'ten minutes after eleven-of-the-clock. The court awaits your verdict.'

Julia, taut with anxiety, looked down on the jury. The journalist did the same, his charcoal poised. A hush fell over the packed gallery as the tension mounted. In the full view of the court the jury started to deliberate, talking amongst themselves, first in twos and threes and then the Foreman began to speak to each juror in turn. Despite the silence, Julia could only manage to pick up the odd word and could not gauge how the deliberations were going. Her father was closer and she sought out his face to see his reaction.

George sensed her looking for him and turned to meet her eyes, but she saw no encouragement in them. The jury had been deliberating for only a few minutes, but each second seemed elongated like the dawdling tick of a pendulum clock in the middle of a long sleepless night. And then the actual tick of the courtroom clock entered Julia's consciousness; it had been there all along, ticking its secret non-stop countdown of time, unheard, anonymous, but now each tick was audible and seemed louder that the last.

And then the Foreman stood.

'Do you have a verdict?' asked the Clerk to the Court. Julia's heart seemed to stop.

'No sir, we have a disagreement as to the verdict.'

A lone 'BOO!' rang out from the gallery. It was spontaneously taken up by the throng until there was a chorus of boos.

'SILENCE' yelled the Judge, his gavel smashing down as he did so.

'Do you wish to leave the court to deliberate further?' said the Clerk.

'Aye we do' said the Foreman.

The Clerk set them to do so and they all shuffled out of the benched seats following the Foreman's lead. As they left a chant started in the gallery. '*Not guilty, not guilty, not guilty, not guilty...*"

CHAPTER 36

Hamburg 1822

My first glimpse of the good ship *Wilhelmina* was not the most inspiring. She was no passenger package ship with facilities for the traveller. She was a plain working vessel with a number of berths that supplemented the owner's profits. That thought seemed to reassure me and I exhaled a satisfied sigh – she was a good honest vessel and would be an adequate craft.

It was the last day of November 1822 and the city was deep in the first grip of winter. The sky that day, however, was cloudless and the low sun skimmed the horizon as it arched across the azure sky. I pulled my muffler up around my face, the icy wind biting into my exposed skin; a reminder that the season had well and truly changed. Old Musketeer, my companion to the end, had arranged the berth and my transport to the dock. I got down from the carriage and leaving the driver to undo the straps that held my luggage safely on the luggage rack, I looked across the harbour. It was a vista of wooden masts, hundreds of them, all pointing skywards like medieval church steeples, their sails folded away so that the boats seemed naked to the world. The wooden hulls were weatherbeaten, some with their holds open; some disgorging their contents onto the dockside; others re-gorging themselves on the new cargos that disappeared quickly down below. The dockers busy like ants over a dead carcass, hoists swinging backwards and forwards to satisfy the ever-increasing hunger for cargo and trade. Row boats crisscrossed the open water finding alleyways between the vessels wherever they could, so crowded was the harbour. And above them all, gulls were flying, wheeling and squawking, ascending and descending, somersaulting, fighting each other for scraps, determined, it seemed, to be the noisiest and busiest of all. It was the first time I had stopped and really looked at the business of the harbour since that first day of my arrival in the city a year ago.

Just a year and I was already moving on. I was ahead of my schedule, that loose plan in my mind to prosper and make for England where I would build a new life for myself. I knew I had done well financially, my income as a translator being significantly added to by my professional fighting, and I was feeling self-satisfied as I turned back to the carriage to take charge of my luggage so that I could arrange for it to be taken on board. I took a silver mark from my waistcoat and gave it to the driver. His face lit up at my generosity and he knuckled his forehead again as he jumped up to his lofty perch. The carriage quickly sped away leaving me there, alone but for Old Musketeer standing guard over my luggage, his unseeing eyes as sharp as any predatory falcon. I was suddenly stung with a pang of painful conscience.

As I came to him he stood to attention. 'UPON THE COMMAND DRAW RAMRODS,' he bellowed and saluted.

I smiled at him involuntarily. 'My old friend...' I said, the words drying in my mouth.

He stood at ease, but his military bearing was not diminished. He was waiting for me to continue, to give him his orders, but I did not see the situation that way. To me it was a painful parting. I looked into his face to see if he was as emotional as I was, but that normally excessively expressive face was unusually bland and impassive. I was unsure of what to say; he was the only true friend I had in Hamburg, but I knew he did not see our relationship in the same way as I did.

'There's still time to change your mind, Old Musketeer,' I said eventually. 'I'm sure the Captain can find a berth for you; if not you can share mine.'

He was silent for some moments. 'Not my place sir!' He bellowed the words, snapping back to attention as he did so. Looking back, I think this was a defence mechanism for him. I'm sure he was as emotional as I was at our farewell, but by bellowing his words it was easier for him to cover any possible waver in his voice. He paused as if sensing my discomfort, then added in a quieter tone, 'Hamburg is where I belong sir.'

'Then will you take my hand old friend, to acknowledge our comradeship together?' I put out my hand boldly, the way I had done so often in my commerce. He could not see me of course and at first he did not respond. Then, tentatively, his hand rose, hesitant at the start like a child's first uncertain steps. The hand seemed too large for the rest of his body, I had not noticed that before, but the old dirty tunic that hung off his shoulders was testament to his having once been a much bigger man. His finger nails needed cutting, they were too long and black with dirt. The sight of this brought an agreeable smile to my face. Of course, I thought to myself, he would not know that they were black. I moved in and took that wavering hand without hesitation, and then my left hand came over and I cupped it, squeezing it to express my affection for him.

'Take care, my friend,' I said and then I felt him shudder. I did not want to embarrass him, and now my own embarrassment mounted because of that. A thought took me; I had never made physical contact with Old Musketeer before, and if *I* hadn't - well it probably meant that nobody else had either. That such a simple pleasure was totally denied him was pitiable and that hand shake was, in all probability, very potent for him. I sensed that, but I also sensed that it would be unacceptable for this ultimately self-reliant man to be a victim of his own emotions, so I turned and walked briskly away. When I reached the gang plank I looked back over my shoulder. Old Musketeer had not moved. His head was bowed, his body bent over, there was pain emanating from his stature, but then to my relief his self reliance reasserted itself.

'UPON THE COMMAND, PRIME AND LOAD,' he bellowed to nobody in particular. He turned and walked briskly away, tapping the ground with his stick as he did so like some frantic woodpecker. That agreeable smile returned to my face. He would be all right, I thought to myself. I turned and walked up the gangway to arrange for my luggage to be taken aboard.

Captain Johannes Neeskins was an easy man to like. My first meeting on the deck of the *Wilhelmina*, however, was brief in the extreme. He gave me little attention, his focus being on the business of the ship as it prepared to sail; he did not deviate from that; catching the tide seemed to be the only thing on his mind. I was despatched with one of the ship's hands, who showed me to the little room that was to be my cabin and who then some minutes later brought me my trunk. There was room for little more than the bunk, which was nailed to the floor and was the length of the cabin, somewhat less than my own height. Other than that there was just a railed stand, holding in place a tin pitcher and bowl for washing.

The rest of the day, I spent writing poetry, my portfolio resting precariously on my trunk, there being nothing else in the tiny cabin that would double as a desk. When we set sail I went up on deck to take in the sights, but it was clear that I was in the way so I retired back to my cabin, but the writing became even more uncomfortable as the ship began to roll. Later that evening, along with the three other passengers, I dined with the Captain and was taken by the straightforwardness of the man, allied to no little intellect and wit.

He was an impressive figure physically. His black captain's tunic was like him: weather-beaten, but by no means past its best. On deck he wore a black cap, but now this was removed there was displayed a shock of white, wavy hair that was swept back from his forehead and tied in a short pigtail at the nape of his neck. Long bushy white sideburns grew down the side of his face, his cheeks and chin heavy with white bristles from several days' growth. We spoke in German; Neeskins was Dutch by nationality, but he switched easily to English when talking to one of my fellow passengers. He had a natural air of authority about him, and I surmised that this must have come from his position as Captain. He was the master aboard his own ship, there was no doubt about that, he had right of life and death over his passengers and crew whilst at sea. But he had a countenance to match that manner. He was one of those men who seemed to have acres of face when they look at you, wide of jowl, undiminished by his sideburns. That great expanse of face shouted honesty, openness and integrity - I liked him immediately.

We ate well, a stew of mutton and potatoes with some herbs that I did not recognise accompanied by thick crusty bread, which was used to soak up the broth. Red wine flowed copiously and with its consumption the natural restraint of strangers soon dissolved like sugar in hot chocolate and we became loud and bawdy in our conversation. The Captain explained that we were expected to take eight days to reach London, subject to weather and tide, but that would include a two-day stop over in Amsterdam to unload and then take on new cargo. Hamburg, Amsterdam, London was his usual trading route, he explained, and that brought a good profit to his principals.

Initially I was disappointed with the two-day delay, but I reasoned that it would give me time to write my poetry, notwithstanding the discomfort that would bring. I had been so busy this last year that opportunities to write had been few and far between, so in some respects I welcomed this hiatus.

Later that night in my bunk, I began to regret my overindulgence. The wind freshened and the roll of the ship intensified. I awoke feeling bilious, a wave of nausea rising up from the pit of my stomach. I staggered to the deck certain I was about to vomit, which certainty manifested into reality as my stomach heaved. I threw myself at the side and leaned over just in time, spewing my over-filled stomach into the black rolling sea below me, only for much of it to be thrown back at me by a spiteful wind, so that there was vomit on my face and in my hair. I retched again and the obnoxious procedure was repeated.

I felt a powerful hand take hold of the back of the collar of my linen shirt. I was lifted upright and frog-marched across the deck to the other side. 'Not *into* the wind Mr Neander,' said the Captain, his voice cutting through the howl of the wind like a knife through butter. 'You'll get your sea legs in a few days.' I didn't resist and with a sympathetic pat, he leant me over the side to get on with my retching.

Between the retches I turned to thank him and at my muttered 'Danken', I saw the look of amusement on his face. I felt humiliated, I had not been beholden to anyone for such a long time, yet here I was covered in vomit like a helpless child waiting for his mama to clean him up.

'You're not the first and you won't be the last,' said the Captain, but it did not make me feel any better. 'I'm away to my bunk now Mr Neander, I'll leave you to it.' I watched him walk away; I started to shout after him, to try to resurrect some of my lost dignity, but as I opened my mouth I retched and had to turn back over the side again.

The rest of the night was horrible. The full effects of the sea-sickness took me; it wasn't just overindulgence. I was constantly nauseous and I couldn't relieve the feeling by sleep. I made repeated journeys to the deck and although I retched, my stomach had emptied long ago. My stomach muscles ached from the constant heaving and I just felt miserable. The only consolation was that the wind and spray soaked my face and washed away the clinging vomit. I was cold, shivering like a beaten pup, my knuckles white as they gripped the rail and I guessed my face was equally as pallid. Every time I sought the warmth of my bunk, I was forced back to the deck and the rail to vomit again. As the hours went on it seemed like every muscle in my body began to tremble at the same time; I was quaking from head to foot.

The following day was little better and I was unable to keep anything down, but by the third day I was, to my relief, beginning to get my sea legs. I remember going on deck that third night; I had come to hate that place having spent many hours vomiting there, but now the wind was gentle, almost tender on my face. That old lady *Wilhelmina*, was not such a bad old girl after all. I looked to the sky, cloudless with that canopy of stars. My sprits rose at the sight of it as if those stars were aligned just for me, to guide me towards a new country a new life, where I could prosper and put the terrors of my young life behind me.

By the time we put in to Amsterdam I felt much better, but I was desperate to get out of my vomit-smelling cabin and I resolved to spend the two days available to me looking around that historic city.

The harbour had the same flavour as Hamburg, a myriad of wooden masts piercing the skyline, and industry all around as the work of the port went on at a pace. The city itself, however, was so different; it was not like the German cities that I knew. I remembered Papa telling me that this had become the richest city in the world in the Seventeenth Century, its merchants sending ships to all corners of the known world, whilst its bankers made it the world's leading financial centre. My father had taught me about Amsterdam; how this city built on reclaimed land was famous for its tolerance and had offered safety to the Jews of Spain and Portugal as well as to the Huguenots from France. Holland, however, had been absorbed into the French Empire and with that had lost much of its power, but now, like Hamburg, it was rebuilding itself after the establishment of the new Kingdom of the Netherlands.

As I walked into the city I was taken with wonder like an expectant child on his birthday; so much so that I considered revising my plans and making a home here. Despite what Papa had told me I was unprepared for what I found. Amsterdam was eye-catching and elegant, made for men of culture such as me. I walked around the *Grachtengordel* , the Canal Belt - a semicircle of manmade waterways - and marvelled at the wealth that had built the adjacent canal houses, those impressive gabled mansions that fronted the canals. I visited the vast open spaces of the Dam Square; it looked enormous to me, its lofty buildings standing several stories high surrounding the plaza.

The fresh air had banished my feelings of queasiness; I was suddenly ravenously hungry. I took a meal at a tavern which had an uninterrupted view of the square. I ate voraciously like a ravenous dog, my body demanding nourishment to replenish what had been lost over the side of the *Wilhemenia*. My vigour returned as I ate, together with my spirits, elevated by a mixture of the sustenance and the beautiful vista before me. I was inspired to write and I made notes in my notebook to be transcribed when I returned to the ship. As the afternoon wore on I knew that the late autumn light would soon fail, so I reluctantly started to make my way back to the harbour.

The tavern landlord had given me directions as to the quickest way back to my ship, but this route took me through a much less stately part of the city. The alleyways narrowed as I moved beyond the fine merchants' houses where wealth abounded. Amsterdam was a port and that meant it also had a much seedier side to it. That was a universal truth: ports meant vice, gin houses, brothels - wealth and squalor living side by side.

That feeling of openness and space deserted me. I felt that I was walking back to the *Judengasse* in Frankfurt and I shuddered at the thought. Much to my relief the alleyways widened into commercial streets as I neared the harbour. Up ahead of me I saw the substantial figure of Captain Johannes Neeskins striding authoritatively along the road, his black cap and brass-buttoned black tunic proclaiming him to the world as a ship's captain. I quickened my pace to catch him; the thought of accompanying him back to the ship seemed enticing. He turned a corner ahead of me and I started to run so that I would not lose him.

When I also turned the corner I saw that Captain Neeskins was heading away from what I had thought was the direction of the harbour. I looked around me. Amsterdam was not my city, of course, and I started to wonder if I had lost my bearings. Added to this I noticed that the Captain was carrying a satchel, clutching it tightly to his chest as if it were the most cherished thing in the world to him, and I realised that he was probably engaged on business and not returning to his ship at all.

Disappointed, I was about to retrace my steps to where I thought the harbour must be, when it happened. As the Captain walked past the entrance to an alleyway, two men who had been walking behind him bundled him into it.

It had happened in the flickering of an eye and I was momentarily shocked, but then, without thinking, I found myself running to his aid. When I reached the alleyway I looked down it and saw that Captain Neeskins was standing up fearlessly to one of his attackers. He was still clutching his satchel with his left hand whilst trying to fight the man off with his right. Even as I ran towards them the second man came at Neeskins from behind, a cudgel raised high. It came down forcefully on the back of the Captain's skull. He was floored like a felled tree. Brutally that cudgel came down again and again as the Captain lay there, his nerveless fingers still clutched tight to the satchel as though his life depended on it.

'HEY! HEY!' I shouted down the alleyway, my bellowing and pounding feet echoing back from the high walls. I was shouting in German but they clearly understood my intentions. Whilst his partner tried to wrench away the satchel from the Captain's grip, the man with the cudgel stood, legs apart, to confront me. He spoke to me in Dutch and I think he was telling me not to interfere, waving the cudgel in my face to emphasise his words.

I was within a few metres of him when the second man barked something to his partner and I saw that he had succeeded in wresting the bulging satchel away from Captain Neeskins, splitting it in the process. It had burst open and he was frantically picking up the spilled contents and stuffing them back into it. He then started to run away. The man with the cudgel jumped to follow, looking back over his shoulder and shouting at me as he ran. I did not understand his words, but the expression on his face was telling me in no uncertain terms not to go after him if I knew what was good for me.

Concerned for the Captain I let them go and sank panting to my knees to help him. Remarkably, he was conscious, but very distressed. Blood was now flowing down the side of his face so that his white sideburns were turning crimson, and I saw that two of his fingers were broken, probably when he had endeavoured to protect his head from the cudgel's blows.

'You're safe now,' I said, attempting to comfort him, but he was still highly distraught. I quickly realised that it was the loss of the satchel that was distressing him more than his injuries. He reached to grip my lapels, pulling himself up as he did so then wincing from the pain of his broken fingers.

'You have to follow them,' he grunted through the pain, 'I can't go to my principals without the money. They will think I was in collusion with the robbers; no one else will employ me after that. I will be a pariah.'

I looked down the alleyway and saw the two men were turning the corner at the end of it and disappearing from sight. Gently releasing the Captain's grip I set off after them. When I too reached the corner I saw that the alleyway was a cut-through to a wider street that led back to the harbour. Loaded wagons taking goods to the docks were rolling noisily over the cobbles. The robbers were not in sight and must have turned away from the harbour. I stood and looked up the street in the direction I thought they had run. They could only have been about a hundred metres ahead of me, but there was no sign of them. I set off running, not really knowing where I was going. At the next crossroads I looked up and down both the intersecting streets. I had drawn attention to myself and I noticed people staring at me, their curiosity aroused by my apparent anxiety. A young lad came towards me and spoke. I did not understand him, of course, but he was pointing to yet another alleyway up ahead, leading off this main road. It seemed likely that the two men had run past him moments before and he realised I was chasing them. I blurted a 'Danken', at him and set off again.

As I rounded the corner I saw them. The light was fading quickly now, but here in the alleyway it was even more gloomy, the height of the buildings blocking out much of the winter's light.

Nevertheless, as my eyes adjusted I saw that they had stopped and thinking they were safe from pursuit were looking into the torn satchel to see what pickings they had stolen. I ran towards them and they looked up in alarm at the sound of my boots echoing back to them down the alleyway. As I neared them I stopped and held out my hand, gesturing that they should give me the satchel. The first man looked up and down the alley and seeing that I was alone he laughed, doubtless thinking my gesture absurd. He then produced the cudgel from up his sleeve and still sniggering, walked towards me, his intent obvious to me from his body language if not from his face, which was in heavy shadow.

I had been in this situation before, of course. I moved to my right and backwards slightly so that we were all three in a line and I had isolated him from his partner – I remembered the tactic, an action of instinct. He raised the cudgel high, but instead of backing away as he expected, I moved towards him so that I was inside the arc of the intended blow. He tried to adjust, but I quickly moved further in against him, turning my back and sinking at the knee so that the blow went high over my shoulder. I then gripped his wrist with my right hand and his upper arm with my left and using my shoulder as a pivot yanked his arm against the elbow joint. I did this several times in quick succession until I heard a crack. Yelping in agony he released the cudgel. In one rapid movement I bent, picked it up and turned to his partner, who threw down the satchel and ran at me his arms raised as if to grab me by the throat. I simply aimed the cudgel and swung it at his knees, hitting him a powerful blow. He crumbled before me. They were both down now and at my mercy, but I backed away, the cudgel waving aggressively in my hand, circling them as much as the narrow alleyway would allow and inching ever closer to the satchel that lay on the ground. I was offering them the opportunity to run away and I was relieved when they both took it, one nursing his arm, the other limping as they retreated to the safety of the open street.

There were coins and paper all over the alley. I groped around in the gloom stuffing everything back into the ragged satchel, all the time anxiously looking up and down the alleyway in case the ruffians came back with their cohorts. I made my way back to the scene of the robbery. I was unsure of where it was at first, but eventually I found it. As I turned into the alleyway I saw the outline of Captain Johannes Neeskins. He was attempting to get back onto his feet, his hands clawing at the brickwork for support. I heard a yelp of pain as his broken fingers rebelled against his own ample weight.

'CAPTAIN! CAPTAIN!' I yelled out, 'I HAVE IT.' He turned in my direction. I could not immediately see his features, my eyes not yet adjusted to the gloom, but as I reached him I could see enough to notice that he was confused. I placed the satchel in his uninjured hand. Swaying on his feet he looked down at it for a heartbeat then clutched it to his chest as if he were embracing a prodigal son returning home.

CHAPTER 37

London 1823

Julia stared at the courtroom clock. It was four minutes before noon, but the minute hand did not seemed to have moved for a very long time. Her father was sitting at the table on the chamber floor. She looked down at him and watched him take a pinch of snuff as he too waited for the jury to return. A peal of laughter came from behind her and she looked back and saw that the onlookers in the gallery were now amusing themselves with banter to pass the time. It sent a shiver down her spine; she found their casual attitude odious and repugnant. At that moment she felt nothing but abhorrence towards them. It was an emotion that was alien to her normally friendly personality, but today in her anxiety it rose up and gripped her until she was trembling with suppressed anger.

She looked back down at her father and met his gaze as he scanned the gallery. He smiled a reassuring smile at her, but she knew, as must he, that the delay was not a good sign. Juries were normally required to bring in several verdicts in a single day and usually took little time to deliberate. Even with a verdict such as this where the case had been unusually long and the jury, unable to agree, had been forced to retire, they were kept without fire, food or drink until a verdict was reached. This tactic of starving the jury into agreement meant they rarely failed to come to a quick conclusion, so why this interminable delay? Julia was convinced her father had succeeded in showing that David was unlikely to have committed the crime of which he was accused, but she knew his strategy of introducing reasonable doubt into the jurors' minds could easily fall down on the one indisputable fact that David had been caught in possession of the stolen carcass.

This thought came back to her time after time as she sat, pulses racing, watching the minutes struggle by. And then an awful vision claimed her mind, terrible in its clarity: David, taken outside the prison to Newgate Street to be displayed before a large crowd of gawping spectators; the law-abiding citizens of London. There to be hanged, struggling and swinging in a line of others, a grotesque entertainment; a spectacle for the masses on a public holiday. She saw his contorted face turning blue as he tried to breathe, his black tongue, engorged, protruding from his mouth, his legs kicking and his beautiful eyes bloodshot and bulging as the life went out of him. The vision racing through Julia's mind was so real the gorge rose in her throat. With a soft cry she put a hand to her mouth and fought for control, afraid she was going to vomit or faint – or both.

The clock struck noon and prompted an outbreak of conversation, a spike in the noise level as that minor fact was discussed and then died down again. It brought Julia back to the present; back to this dreadful place and the anguish of uncertainty, but it gave her a level of resolve. She owed it to David to be strong for him, whatever happened. The waiting continued. She looked at some movement below, saw her father stand and walk across the court and talk to the Clerk. She wondered what he was saying, her eyebrows furrowed unable to guess. He came back to his chair and took out his snuff box from his waistcoat pocket, pinching some of its content onto the back of his hand and then snorting it up each nostril leaving a brown stain on his nose. He took out his silk handkerchief and shook it flamboyantly before his face as he always did. It was a little affectation of his and as she watched him, Julia knew she loved him for it. He seemed to sense her gaze on him, her tender smile. He turned to seek her out in the gallery and finding her, smiled. She sat forward in her chair; there was something about that smile, a nuance that was not just a return of her affection; it seemed to infer that he had done something that satisfied him, but what?

Julia puzzled for a while, looking from her father to the Clerk; it was something to keep her mind off things, wondering what had been said, but the monotony soon returned. The clock struck a quarter-after-noon, but little notice was taken of it and the sound hardly registered to Julia over the pounding of her heart. Nausea bunched in her stomach, she could feel the blood pulsing in her throat; in her ears. Beside her Brandon was scribbling again. Her eye was taken by that bony hand; the charcoal spinning its spidery words in the journalist's notebook. She started to read them and saw that he was setting the scene in the courtroom, emphasising the rising anxiety as the tension mounted. As she read, that feeling of abhorrence returned but was now directed not at the spectators in the gallery, but at the newspaper's readers who would read these words as entertainment over tomorrow's breakfast.

And then she became aware of activity in the chamber below her. An usher was delivering a message to the Clerk to the Court. Was the jury ready to return? But no; the Clerk just followed the usher out of the courtroom on some unknown business. Julia's father turned and gave her that same smile again, the one with the nuance – what was he trying to tell her? She was confused. Once more she puzzled over it and it banished temporarily the awful vision of David's body; hanging, swinging, lifeless. Julia covered her ears; the crescendo of anticipation was becoming unbearable.

And then it popped. All at once, without any forewarning, the courtroom burst into life. David was being brought back to the court, his shackles being removed. Julia looked up and saw the jury filing back in, taking their seats on the benches. She searched their faces for any sign of their verdict, but could see nothing to encourage her. Their faces were blank and none of them was looking at David. She feared the worst. She saw the flash of scarlet out of the corner of her eye and turned to see the Judge's robe as he entered from his door. She had wanted the interminable waiting to end, but now that it had she feared the outcome and wanted desperately to turn back the clock.

She watched, trancelike, as the Clerk to the Court called upon the Foreman to stand and give his verdict. He stood purposefully, a ruddy-cheeked man with long white side-whiskers and a brown snuff stain on his ample fleshy nostrils. His jacket had probably been fine once, but was now worn and ill-fitting so that he seemed to be bursting out of it, his prosperity manifesting itself in his increased girth. This comical looking man held David's life in his hands. His beady eyes remained fixed; his gaze on the Clerk, avoiding the prisoner, and in a blinding flash of horror, Julia knew what the verdict would be.

'GUILTY.'

The word rang and echoed back at her in the vastness of the chamber: GUILTY GUILTY GUILTY GUILTY GUILTY. It invaded her mind, repeating over and over, so that, for a heartbeat, everything else was cast aside. The gallery exploded behind her, but she was cocooned in silence.

The Judge leant forward impassively, resting his elbows on the oak bench in front of him. He let the gallery have their moment and kept his overworked gavel resting on its base. A satisfied look crossed his features as though he was sipping a fine brandy. Julia guessed why: he had got exactly the same verdict as the original trial. In his mind he had been vindicated and he was savouring the moment. Catching sight of his smug, odious face as he turned his attention to David, now standing dejected at the bar, Julia could see that the Judge was revelling in it. Only then did she become aware of the cacophony of noise behind her, the cries of 'BOO! and 'SHAME!' that were being yelled by the spectators in the gallery. Shrill whistles pierced the air as they gave full vent to their emotions. They had wanted an acquittal and they now wished to make that fact known to the court in no uncertain terms. The Judge's gavel now rattled down in response again and again, but with little effect until, finally, he called for men-at-arms to be sent for to clear the gallery. That threat had the required effect and the outbreak died down to a low murmur of outrage.

All through this, the Foreman had remained standing. He raised his arm tentatively to get the Clerk's attention and eventually succeeded. The Clerk nodded his approval for him to proceed.

'Sir...,' the Foreman said, turning to the Judge. He hesitated, his voice uncertain, fading away completely as he met Cardew's stern, attentive gaze. He cleared his throat and tried again, 'Sir, the jury wish to convict on the lesser offence of stealing a wether sheep to the value of twenty shillings, and strongly recommend the defendant to His Majesty's mercy.'

The people in the gallery responded by stamping their feet. Cries of 'HERE! HERE! ALLOW HIM THE KING'S MERCY,' echoed the Foreman's words.

The Judge's eyes narrowed, his face hardening still further as once more he reached for his gavel and shouting 'ORDER!' thumped it down.

Julia's heart skipped a beat; she knew what this lesser offence meant. Defendants found guilty of stealing goods worth forty shillings or more were subject to the death penalty. By reducing the value of the goods below that, the jury had avoided the statutory penalty; it meant that David's life would be spared. And then Julia realised what her father had done – her wonderful and brilliant father. He had guessed the delay was because the jury wanted to convict, but equally did not want the death penalty, and he had reasoned they would send for the Clerk to gain advice and clarification, as was often the case when the jury was stuck. When she had seen her father talking to the Clerk, he must have been reminding him that the jury had the option to bring in a lesser verdict. He had planted that seed in the Clerk's mind and thus in the minds of the jurors. Her clever father had given them a way out of their dilemma before hunger overcame their reluctance and they brought in a full guilty verdict.

The Judge turned to the Foreman, his rage exploding into words, 'the indictment is for a theft of a sheep valued at forty shillings. Why bring in this lesser verdict?'

The Foreman shrank at the onslaught directed at him and looked round at the Clerk for reassurance. The Clerk, no less intimidated than he, managed a feeble nod, on the strength of which the Foreman continued, 'But it was only half a sheep, Your Honour,' his words were barely audible, 'surely forty shillings is too a high a valuation for just half a sheep?'

'You were not asked to value the sheep sir,' Judge Cardew shouted, 'but to pronounce on the crime that has been committed.'

The Foreman now totally cowed by the Judge's intimidating words sought to deflect the blame, 'But we were so advised, Your Honour. The Clerk to the Court told us that...' he did not complete the sentence. Cardew put up a hand to stop him in mid-flow, glowered and turned to the hapless Clerk, who now took the brunt of the Judge's rage.

'May I remind you that this is my court? I will not have you colluding behind my back to subvert the full process of the law!' he thundered.

There was a moment of stunned silence; Cardew's vindictive displeasure was obvious to everyone, but the clerk's advice had been correct in law, and that fact began to seep through his anger. He opened his mouth to protest, but at that moment the Judge glanced up at the gallery, cleared his throat, waved his arms about and said, his face purple with impotent rage, 'Ahem; that is to say, you should have sought my advice before interrupting the deliberations of the jury with your advice, however correct it may be.' His mouth closed slowly, a sneer replacing the anger on his face.

In the gallery, Julia read the implications of what was taking place; it was clear to her that the Judge wanted the Clerk to submit to his will at all times, and his will in this case was to bring a maximum sentence to 'the Jew' at the bar – not for David's supposed crime, but for what he stood for. It was equally clear that the Judge knew he had overstepped the mark and that there was at least one reporter in the gallery avidly scribbling his words. She watched the scene play out below her, her sense of justice and her knowledge of the law crying out in outrage.

The Judge now turned his head to the bar and glaring at David intoned, 'Prisoner at the bar, do you have anything to say before I pass sentence upon you?' He waited impatiently for a brief moment - clearly for form's sake since his expression inferred he was not expecting a response - but as he turned back to the court, David cleared his throat and made to speak.

Since the awful verdict had been brought in, David Neander had been lost in terror, his panic barely contained as the full horror of his predicament was brought home to him. Now, looking down, he saw that his leg was noticeably trembling and he reached out and grasped the bar before him to steady himself. He did not understand why people seemed to be in disagreement about the value of the sheep – as if it mattered! He had barely followed the Judge's admonishment of the Clerk, nor understood the reason for it. But even though the significance had been lost on him and he fully expected to be hanged, he suddenly felt calm. He had spent three days holding back his words so as not to antagonise the Judge, but now he was to hang he had nothing to lose.

'Yes, Your Honour, I do,' he said, his voice as straight as a musket's ramrod. 'I have stood here observing the famous English legal system for three days now...'

'And it is the best in the world sir,' sneered the Judge.

'Yes it is a fine system; I have studied its workings by reading in my cell each night. And yet I have watched my Counsel trying to use his considerable legal ingenuity, rather than the substance of the law, to get me an acquittal.'

'You are very perceptive sir,' sarcasm dripped from the Judge's every word. 'The decision should rightly followed the substance of the law. That should prevail, not legal ingenuity.'

'But you have not followed the substance of the law, Judge Cardew, have you?' There was a sharp audible intake of breath from the officers of the court followed by a collective gasp from the gallery. Nobody challenged the actions of the Judge in his own court, least of all a convicted prisoner at the bar. Julia put her hand to her mouth in alarm, 'No David; don't, please don't,' she whispered to herself.

On the floor of the courtroom, George Carmichael leapt to his feet, but was waved down by the Judge, who, his jaw dropped and his eyes gleaming with malicious intent, allowed David to continue digging himself into a hole.

'You must ask yourself the question, Your Honour.'

'And what question would that be sir?'

'In my study I have read that it is a fundamental principle of your fine legal system that the Judge pronounces on a question of the law and that the jury pronounce on a question of fact. You must ask yourself sir, whether you have done that,' he looked directly at the Judge inviting him to respond, but he didn't. What David saw on Cardew's face was anger and incredulity in equal measure, a face almost vermilion with rage so that it matched the colour of his gown. He had given David the opportunity to speak and now this convicted prisoner was using that opportunity to challenge him to justify his actions - in his own courtroom. The original appeal had been a slight on him professionally, a loss of face before his legal peers, but this was now a slight before his own court officials, before the press and tomorrow it would be before the general public. His rage was palpable, but it remained impotent; what could he do? He was being invited to debate his actions with the defendant, to justify them – and he knew that here he could not do that. But it was about to get worse.

'Can you enlighten me sir,' David continued in a polite tone, 'and advise me on which principle of English law allows a judge to act as prosecutor?'

That sharp intake of breath from the court officials now rose to an audible 'Aaw!' 'Please stop, David, please stop, this man holds your life in his hands.' Julia spoke to herself, but her muttered words were overheard by the journalist.

Brandon stopped scribbling and looking at her, saw her anxiety and momentarily felt her personal distress, but then his journalistic guile kicked in. This was pure gold for him; this story would work on so many levels – human interest, a rogue judge to be brought down a peg or two, perhaps a campaign to have the man struck off and disbarred. Yes; pure gold! He turned away from Julia's distress and started scribbling again.

And then there was silence; a hush that descended on the court like an autumn mist as all eyes turned to the Judge to see what he would do. It was only a few seconds but it seemed to last for a hundred years. And then it was punctured; a voice rang out from the gallery, 'TELL HIM JUDGE; COME ON, ANSWER HIS QUESTION!' And then there was pandemonium as the call was taken up by the whole gallery: 'TELL HIM, TELL HIM, TELL HIM,' the words rang out again and again, 'TELL HIM, TELL HIM, TELL HIM,' rhythmically they chanted, 'TELL HIM, TELL HIM, TELL HIM.'

CHAPTER 38

Amsterdam 1822

In the gloom of that Amsterdam alleyway, Captain Johannes Neeskins appeared at that moment far from the impressive physical specimen I had first encountered on the deck of his ship. The beating had somehow diminished him. Leaning unsteadily against the brickwork he looked utterly bemused, his eyebrows knitted above eyes that peered confusedly at me through the shadows. Gradually his confusion began to lift and he looked back at me with immense gratitude.

'Thank you, thank you, my boy, I am in your debt.' The words had hardly left his mouth when his legs gave way and he started to fall. I caught him, instinctively pulling his weight towards me and putting one of his arms around my shoulders to support him. I noted that his other hand still clung tightly to the remains of his satchel and its precious contents.

I shrugged off his gratitude, 'Let's get you back to the ship.'

'No, No, Herr Neander,' there was alarm still in his voice; 'I have to get these papers to my principals at the shipping company.'

'That will have to wait Captain,' I said firmly. 'We need to get you cleaned up. Lean on me.' He nodded assent and we inched slowly, unsteadily, down the alleyway, his arm across my shoulder, my arm around his middle taking as much of his weight as I could, but his legs were very wobbly. On the main road they gave way completely and he sank to the ground. I hauled him back to his feet, but each time I did so he took only a few steps before he collapsed again. It was a struggle and I knew it would not be easy to get him back to his ship. He was too heavy for me to carry any distance so I hailed a young boy who was loitering in the street gawping at us and I sent him to find me a carriage.

At last we were within sight of the *Wilhelmina* and at my shouts, the crew rushed to help me get Neeskins to his cabin. The ship's cook, who doubled as the ship's doctor, came with clean water and linen and cleaned up the Captain's wounds. All the time he clutched his satchel to his chest and his anxiety did not diminish.

'You're safe now, Captain. Isn't that right Herr Cook?' I looked up at the cook and realised from his blank expression that he did not understand my German.

Captain Johannes Neeskins looked at me intently and I could see his wits had returned to him. He opened his mouth to speak, but then winced as the cook pulled at a broken finger to set it, taking a wooden peg from his pocket to use as a makeshift splint and tightly bandaging the two broken fingers to it, the Captain all the time cussing him for his actions. I did not know the Dutch words, but profanities seem to have the same sound in any language.

When it was done, Neeskins looked back at me. 'Do you know what is in this satchel?' he said in a fierce whisper.

'I can guess,' I replied, not wanting him to think I had been prying.

'What would be your guess then?'

'Well I assume it contains money, bonds, bills of exchange; letters of credit and so forth. I could not help but see the nature of the contents when the satchel came asunder,' I confessed.

'That's right,' he said. 'You understand commerce Herr Neander. My principals have agents in London and Hamburg, but I am still authorised to negotiate shipping contracts in both cities. Returning with an empty hold is not good business, so I do all I can to fill it.'

'I can see that.' I said, but at that moment I was more interested in ensuring that the cook knew what he was doing than worrying about the Captain's business. But clearly this was mightily important to him. He grabbed my arm, wincing as he did so.

'Yet you did not steal it from me, even though you knew its value.'

'I am no thief!' I snapped back at him, angry at the suggestion.

He saw the resentment in my face, said, 'I apologise, my boy. I did not mean to imply... well, let us say that I am doubly in your debt - my life *and* my career.'

My anger eased away quickly at his apology. 'Then we shall say no more of it,' I said.

'But I must, my boy. What time is it?'

I pulled out Uncle Meno's watch and glanced down at it, thankful that it appeared to have suffered no damage. 'It is a half past five-of-the-clock,' I said.

'Then I have time; if I rush.'

'You are going nowhere Captain. You are concussed.'

'But I *must* deliver these papers before six-of-the-clock.'

'Not today I'm afraid, you would not get there.'

Concussed he may have been but his eyes were far from vacant. I could see he was musing on some alternative plan. 'You have shown yourself to be an honest man, Herr Neander. Will you deliver these papers for me?' For the first time he released his grip on the satchel, easing it away from his chest and offering it to me. 'Ask for Mann Herr de Jong; give it to no one else.'

I looked down at the precious cargo with which I was being entrusted and then back at him. Words of refusal formed on my lips, but then I saw the pleading in his eyes. Reluctantly I took the satchel from him. 'It would be an honour, Captain,' I said. 'To where must I deliver it?'

CHAPTER 39

London 1823

Judge Cardew looked up at the gallery, his ears ringing with the cacophony: 'TELL HIM, TELL HIM, TELL HIM.' Humiliation sat heavily on him; this was his courtroom and he was used to being the master of all he surveyed, but some how it had been stolen from him by this ... foreigner; this ... Jew. For a heartbeat he froze. In his entire career as a Judge nothing like this had ever happened to him before. His gaze darted around the courtroom as his mind struggled to come to terms with it, but then his cunning kicked in. He realised that it gave him the opportunity he wanted. At the very least he could get rid of that rabble in the gallery.

The gavel came down hard, again and again, hammering against its base, echoing around the chamber, 'I WILL have order, I WILL have order,' he shouted. 'Clerk, send for the men-at-arms and have the gallery cleared. A runner was sent and the soldiers quickly arrived. A pistol was brandished and order was rapidly restored at the sight of it. The spectators began to file out of the gallery at the command of the soldiers, those standing going first and then those who were seated. Julia did not move; she stayed seated, looking forward and not even acknowledging the men-at-arms. She was not going to be deprived of seeing what was going to happen to David. Her anxiety was so high that she had complete disregard for her own safety. She saw her father looking up at her, alarm written all over his face. She ignored it.

'You too miss,' said the soldier. There was no aggression in his voice; he could see from her attire that she had status and he was respectful.

'I shall stay here sir,' she said.

'I am sorry miss, but you can't. I have my orders to clear the gallery.'

'I know you have, soldier,' she paused to look him up and down, 'but nevertheless I am staying here.'

'I would prefer not to remove you by force, miss.'

'Thank you, soldier, but I will stay here.'

The man-at-arms felt the eyes of the court trained on him, especially those of the Judge. He was on the horns of a dilemma. The last thing he wanted to do was manhandle a fine young lady, but there was expectancy channelled towards him from below; it burned into him. What could he do? He froze unable to reconcile the problem. But then the usher came to his aid.

'I will personally vouch for Miss Carmichael,' he said, 'I will sit next to her and supervise her.' The soldier nodded his relief at the solution. He withdrew leaving just two figures seated at the front of the gallery, at which the Judge seemed satisfied.

There was now absolute quiet in the courtroom and with one last stare at the gallery the Judge turned back to the chamber, his gaze sweeping over the heads of the court officials and coming to rest on David. 'Will that be all, prisoner at the bar?' he sneered, not waiting for a response. He was certainly not going to answer the impertinent question the prisoner had dared to put to him. 'Then it now falls upon me to pass sentence,' he said.

'Before you do, Your Honour,' the Clerk to the Court interrupted nervously, 'if I might be permitted to speak?' It was the last thing he wanted to do, to provoke the Judge's wrath still further, but he felt keenly his responsibility to uphold the process of the law, so with an obvious effort he ignored the venomous stare directed at him from the bench and continued speaking. 'There is a Captain Johannes Neeskins in court. He says he has only just arrived in England today, but he has evidence to give that is highly relevant, My Lord.'

'He is too late,' snapped the Judge, 'you have explained that to him, I trust?'

'I have, Your Honour, but he was most insistent.' The Clerk shrank at the Judge's possible reaction to his temerity, having already angered him, but he continued doggedly, 'I have also explained that should a guilty verdict be brought in by the jury, he may - with your permission - be allowed to plead for clemency on behalf of the prisoner.'

In the gallery, Julia silently cheered the brave little Clerk to the Court, who knew his responsibilities under the law and was intent on carrying them out. She could see his agitation as he rocked from foot to foot apprehensively awaiting the Judge's response.

Judge Cardew could see it too. He sat back in his chair and steepled his hands to his chin in contemplation. He did not want to admit that David's words had stung him. He supposed it was just possible that he had allowed his justifiable repugnance of Jewish immigrants to get the better of him. For the first time in this trial he realised his handling of the case might be questionable and he resolved,

273

not least for the benefit of the press, to be seen as fair. He contented himself with another stern glare at the meddling Clerk to the Court and after a moment he gestured a curt, reluctant nod of approval and Captain Johannes Neeskins was duly called.

The tall, powerfully built frame of Johannes Neeskins entered the courtroom, his weather-beaten countenance proclaiming his profession. He walked in military fashion to the stand and was sworn, taking the oath in a heavy Dutch accent, but his English was good and he had about him that air of authority that proclaimed he was accustomed to being obeyed. The Clerk to the Court invited him to state his name and occupation.

'My name is Johannes Neeskins and I am a ship's captain.' His voice was strong and guttural and reached every corner of the court chamber. His years at sea, barking orders over the sounds of surf and wind, had strengthened his vocal chords to the point where his voice had an intensity not given to ordinary men. His face was wide and open, not handsome, but purveying honesty and straightforwardness. He was invited to make his plea by the Clerk and he faced the Judge to do so.

George Carmichael, bewildered, watched this unexpected turn of events with interest. He did not know who this man was. He glanced up at his daughter, caught her eye and saw that she was equally bewildered. He swung round to David. He was staring fixedly at Neeskins, his face alight with recognition. Clearly the two men were known to one another. George settled back in his seat eager to hear what Neeskins had to say; whoever he was, he would make a good witness.

'I only docked last night, but I read of this trial in this morning's paper and realised that I know this man. I captain the good ship Wilhelmina and we docked in London on the 8th December, 1822, outward-bound from Hamburg via Amsterdam with a cargo of wines, tin and silks from the Dutch East Indies. I also carried four passengers who had paid for their berths. David Neander was one of them.' He turned his head to smile reassuringly at David as he spoke those words.

'It was to be a routine voyage, a trip of eight days,' he continued, 'and we put into Amsterdam on route to London. It was there that the full calibre of Herr Neander's courage and honesty were brought home to me.' He went on to relate the incident that had occurred in Amsterdam, telling his story purposefully, the drama intensified by the power of his voice. He could have been an actor propelling his voice to the furthest reaches of Drury Lane Theatre. Expectancy hung on his every word, his tale one of honour and principle. Even the Judge seemed to be taken with it.

He concluded, 'I make this submission to you in earnest, Your Honour. This man demonstrated his honesty by his actions that day. He saved my life. He had every chance to take the valuable contents of my satchel and nobody would have ever known, but he returned them to me, thereby saving both my reputation and my career. What is more, he took them to my principals for me while I was incapacitated. He showed that he is sincere and truthful; he is a man of integrity. I cannot believe he is guilty of anything other than a misunderstanding; a misunderstanding that has now resulted in a grave miscarriage of justice. Sir, his noble actions in Amsterdam deserve to be recognised as the actions of an honest man. He has earned the court's clemency, and I recommend such clemency to you.' Johannes Neeskins gestured to the Judge with a nod to show that he was done. An acclaimed barrister could not have delivered his plea with more eloquence.

Judge Cardew sat back in his ample chair in contemplation, again making a steeple of his fingers in front of his face. His body language acknowledged the strength of the plea. The courtroom was hushed, waiting with bated breath.

In the gallery, Julia sat with the usher; two isolated figures, both saddened. The story Johannes Neeskins had told was typical of the man Julia had come to love. A tear welled in her eye, overflowed and ran down her cheek. She heard the kind-hearted usher gulp as he too swallowed back a sob. Hardened as he was to hearing guilty verdicts and their consequences, he now knew beyond doubt that this man was innocent.

CHAPTER 40

London 1823

The Judge's steepled fingers began to drum together as his contemplation deepened. An uneasy silence had descended across the courtroom; uncomfortable, yet spiked with an atmosphere of expectation that seemed to crackle, as if dry wood was burning on a camp fire. His thoughts were oblique. On the one hand he was motivated by revenge. This man, this David Neander or Loeb Ephraim, whatever he called himself, had not only had the audacity to have the original verdict challenged - and he, Judge Cardew, had lost face amongst his peers because of that - but now the wretched Jew had the gall to challenge his actions in his own courtroom.

The silence continued. Cardew contemplated ignoring the jury's plea for clemency and passing the death penalty anyway. As a judge, he was well within his rights to do so. But his cunning, rational mind strove to overrule that urge, reasoning that such a course of action would be an invitation to another challenge. If that happened, it would be all too easy to have the death penalty overturned since that damned jury had brought in the lesser charge of a theft of less than forty shillings, for which the death penalty was not the prescribed punishment.

A scornful look crossed his features as thoughts of his own folly seeped in, gaining ground in the contest taking place in his mind. Too late he began to realise that he had been sawing off the branches he had been sitting on. David's question about his acting as a prosecutor had stung him. He had left himself open to ridicule in the press and from his colleagues. He had always been able, in the past, to disregard any criticism; to treat it with contempt. The power he wielded in his own court enabled him to do that, but that irresistible truth had been suddenly wrenched from him and had proved to be illusory. He was uncertain now; there was an undoubted shift in his perspective and he was unsure how to respond to it. It was as though his mind was playing the same piece of music it had always played, but it was now in a different key, such that it sounded so very different to him.

The words of Johannes Neeskins were suddenly very powerful in his mind; they now began to colour his view of this David Neander.

Retrospectively he began to judge the evidence in the light of that plea for clemency and when he revisited David's words, from the perspective of an honourable man those same words now seemed to have a different meaning. Despite himself, Judge Cardew's view of David was transforming. Candidly, begrudgingly, a truth was manifesting itself in his mind. Had there really been a miscarriage of justice? It began to seem likely. Had he failed to regard Neander as innocent until proven guilty? Maybe so. And yet there was the indisputable fact of the possession of stolen goods - and people *could* and did change. His belligerence raised its head again as this thought leaked back into his mind. *What to do, what to do.*

At length, Judge Cardew leant forward and rested his elbows on the bench in front of him. He looked around and saw the expectancy in the eyes that were all trained upon him. He chose his words carefully and deliberately, knowing that they would likely be repeated in tomorrow's papers.

'This has indeed been an unusual and difficult case - for the court and in particular for the jury.' He turned to them, nodding as he did so; for the first time they heard no rancour in his voice and saw no sourness on his face. It was as if the rancid smell of the Thames had suddenly left his nostrils. Too late he wanted to give the impression of an even-handed man. 'You have brought in a guilty verdict, and I think it is the correct verdict, bearing in mind that the defendant was caught with the stolen carcass in his possession. On the other hand, it is also clear that he is no street ruffian, but an educated man with the means to earn a good living. This does not, of course, mean that he is above the law.'

In the gallery, Julia held her breath, her gaze fixed intently on Cardew's unforgiving face. She was rigid with fear, her hands sweating profusely. She looked down on David's bowed head. *Courage my love; courage,* she thought. At that moment, as if her unspoken message had reached him, he squared his shoulders and stood tall, looking up at the bench as the Judge continued.

'Nevertheless, gentlemen, I am minded to accept your plea for him and grant His Majesty's mercy.' The inference was that he had been *persuaded* to grant that mercy. He made no mention of the lesser charge the jury had brought in. He now turned to David.

'Prisoner at the bar; it is now my duty to pronounce the sentence of the law, which must follow the verdict that has just been recorded. You are sentenced to be transported to a penal colony in New South Wales for a period of seven years. Dock Officer, take him down.'

With those fateful words still resounding into the stunned silence, the Judge pushed himself to his feet. The court officials followed suit, nodding respectfully to him as he left the bench. There was an air of anticlimax in the courtroom, but after a few moments a muffled roar could be heard from outside as news of the sentence filtered out. The Dock Officer refitted the shackles to the prisoner's legs and began to lead him away. David looked up at Julia as he shuffled out. His features were serene: the spectre of the hangman had been lifted; he would no longer have to face him.

George Carmichael sat back in his chair at the sound of the roar, breathed a long sigh of relief, took out his snuff box and arranged a pinch on the back of his hand. He snorted it deeply as a sort of reward to himself for a job well done, and then looked up at his daughter whilst he fluttered his silk handkerchief affectedly across his face to remove any stain. He saw tears now flowing profusely down her face, her shoulders rising and falling in silent sobs of relief. He sat up with a start, he was overwhelmed by a need to go and comfort her, but she anticipated his reaction and gestured to him with merest wave of her white-gloved hand that she was alright, that they were tears of joy.

It was the best possible outcome, thought George with satisfaction. An honourable man's life had been saved. He was aware that his satisfaction was tinged with another, less noble thought. Transportation would take David Neander away from Julia. She would be upset, but he was clearly not a suitable match for her and she would get over it - eventually.

The gaoler opened the cell door, the keys jingling as they turned in the lock. He stepped aside, knuckled his forehead and gave his black-toothed grin of expectancy, but there was no coin for him this time. Julia rushed past him and into David's arms. For her at that moment the gaoler did not exist. His grin turned to a sneer when he realised there was nothing for him today. He turned and repeated the knuckle to George Carmichael, the grin reappearing temporarily, but he was met with a nodded gesture that said clearly, '*Go away.*'

George followed his daughter into the cell and watched her openly embracing the man she so clearly loved then, discomfited, he looked away.

All the rules of society that Julia had been brought up to adhere to were overruled in her mind by the sheer weight of relief that she felt. Had she thought about what she was doing she would not have done it, but as it was her head rested on David's clean linen shirt that she had bought for him, her arms circling his midriff. She increased the pressure of the embrace and he reciprocated, his own constricting arms squeezing her to him. No words were spoken for some moments.

Helpless to interfere, George Carmichael waited a few moments. He could assert his rightful fatherly outrage at this openly wanton behaviour, but that would have denied his beautiful daughter this natural moment of relief. After a while he merely coughed loudly and pointedly to reinforce his presence.

Julia released her grip and looked up at David, discomfort taking her briefly at the realisation that they had embraced in front of her father. She stepped back, but David took her hand as she did so and did not let it go. She looked down at their two hands and decided not to pull away.

'Seven years is not so long, my boy,' George Carmichael's words were said as much out of embarrassment as they were an observation. 'After a few years of probation you will be able to apply for a Ticket of Leave.'

'A Ticket of Leave?'

George Carmichael saw the look of confusion on David's face. 'Yes; it is given in cases where the convict has shown good behaviour. It will allow you certain freedoms; you will then be able to seek employment in the colony.'

'But David is no convict Father,' Julia retorted hotly, 'we both know that.'

'He is in eyes of the law, my dear. I have taught you such things, have I not?'

Julia looked down at the dirty stone floor in contemplation. She had been so elated that David had eluded the hangman that the consequences of penal transportation had not fully penetrated her mind. Maybe there *would* be opportunities for him to build a new life for himself in New South Wales, after he had served his sentence, but it was still *exile*. She gasped, shuddering as that thought took her. *He would never come back to her.*

CHAPTER 41

From Newgate to Chatham, 1823

My first view of New South Wales was on the misty morning of 18th June, 1824. The cry of 'LAND AHOY' rang down from the crow's nest, shouted with enough gusto that the wind, try as it might, could not carry it away. Dawn had not long lifted that curtain of pitch blackness that was the ocean night. First light always raised the spirits of those on board, but those two simple words mightily eclipsed that feeling; they signalled an end to those never ending months at sea. People scrambled to the side of the boat, cupping their eyes to peer into the mist, but they could see nothing, the spray and the haze denying them their first glimpse of the other side of the world. The sighting was overdue and had been expected for so long a time and yet nevertheless it still seemed to take us all by surprise. Everybody, from the non-sailor to the saltiest of old sea dogs, was taken by the cry and wanted to catch that first glimpse of something he had not seen for so long: land.

It was another forty-five minutes before those on deck could see what was visible from up in the crow's nest. Our prison doors had been opened at daylight so we, the prisoners, were on deck for our morning exercise and were allowed to the side of the ship to look. I peered intently; my first sight of my new home was in reality an insignificant sight, no more than a scar on the horizon, yet it represented so much more to everybody on board, including me.

But I am getting ahead of myself in my story and must relate what happened after my trial. I was now a married man. I had nothing, of course, to offer Julia: a one way ticket into exile was my immediate future. I could never have proposed to her on that basis. She was a young woman with her whole future ahead of her and the last thing I wanted was to be the obstacle to that future. But the decision to marry was hers. Much as I wanted her, from the moment she first mooted the idea I declined - constantly - and, of course, her father and mother were vehemently opposed to it. They even threatened to cut her off if she went through with it. My wonderful Julia would have none of it; she had made up her mind and had a will of iron to see it through.

She had a plan; she turned up at the gaol on my 22nd birthday in 1823. I had forgotten it was my birthday, so that was surprise enough, but the present she brought me took my breath away. She had a minister with her; we were to be married on the spot – then and there in the gaol.

'What about your mama and papa?' I said when I had recovered sufficiently to utter a few words.

She was matter of fact about it, 'Well even if we marry in a church, my mother and father will not come, so we may as well marry in here,' she said whilst taking off her bonnet. The minister hesitated in the cell doorway, looking from one to the other of us, a spark of amusement in his eyes.

'You can't do this to them,' I pleaded.

'I have made up my mind David,' she said firmly, looking me in the eyes so that I got the full force of her gaze, and all the time still holding her bonnet. It was new for the occasion and she didn't want to put it down to be contaminated by the grime of the gaol. The purchase of a new bonnet was illogical, of course, but somehow it made sense to Julia.

I met her stare; my thoughts were racing away in all directions, exploding like firecrackers in the night. 'But...but...' was all I could come up with. Glances were exchanged, but I was struck dumb: what could I do?

'You do want to marry me, David, don't you?'

'I want nothing more,' I said vehemently, 'but not like this.'

'I know, my love,' she said putting her white gloved hand on mine, 'but fate has determined that it must be this way.'

I was not of the faith of this minister, of course, but that did not matter to Julia, the only important thing in her mind was for it to be legal: a marriage under Church of England Canon Law. She had thought of everything: she had a special licence and she had made the necessary declarations, the marriage allegation, swearing that there was no just cause or impediment why we should not marry. It had to be legally binding because that was part of her plan. She intended to petition the Home Office for permission to accompany her husband on his penal transportation, and such was her fervour that against my better judgement she swept me along with her plan.

After the brief ceremony, that was that. We were man and wife. Before Julia left we embraced and kissed, but there was to be no wedding night for us. I sat in my cell, bewildered and yet somehow my spirits running high – higher than they had been since this whole sorry mess had started. I was married. It had all happened so quickly that I had to keep repeating it to myself to believe it. It was my birthday – I was twenty- two years old and married to the most wonderful of women. I had a life to look forward to. The fates had, after all, been kind to me.

Some days later I was transferred from the gaol to a prison hulk, the Dolphin at Chatham. It was an old man-o'-war with its rigging and other fittings removed, moored on the River Medway that flowed into the Thames Estuary. George Carmichael had told me that transportation was a humane form of punishment; it avoided execution or a whipping, but I think he had been making light of it to calm my fears for this holding ship was the most dreadful place imaginable, far worse even than the gaol at Newgate. It was a floating dungeon filled to bursting point with over six hundred poor souls; filthy, contaminated and infected with disease. This was Dante's Inferno made real on Earth. Many died of dysentery, many more of gaol fever, or 'Typhus' as it has come to be known. I was spared both these dreadful afflictions. I was also spared an outbreak of the pestilence – I believe they call it 'Cholera' now. It was regarded as the deadliest killer, the victims' bowels turned to water accompanied by constant vomiting and agonising stomach pains until death came as a blessed relief. I was lucky; the worst I suffered from was 'the itch,' but almost everybody suffered from that since the place was a haven for fleas and lice carried by the rats that abounded in that hellhole.

I was put to work in the dockyard whilst on the hulk awaiting transportation. I spent my time driving in posts to protect the river banks from erosion. My companions and I were cheap labour for the contractor, but the little food that we were provided with on the hulk was so poor that most of the men had little strength for this demanding physical work. Frequent bouts of dysentery weakened them still further. It did not look like a good deal for the contractor to me; sickly workers, however cheap, were not productive.

The hulks housed many bewildered souls, sentenced to transportation for the most minor of crimes. But there were also hardened criminals, thugs that bullied and preyed on these bewildered souls. Sometime it was just belligerence on their part, but many times they stole victuals from their fellow convicts happy to see them starve to death for a few extra mouthfuls of the poor quality scraps that were provided. There was one brute in particular, named William Slater, but he called himself Bill Slaughterman for that is what he had originally been, a slaughterman at Smithfield Market, known as 'Ruffians' Hall' to Londoners. There was no bigger ruffian on the hulk than Bill Slaughterman. One evening he tried to steal my food. I'd had a gruelling day driving posts into the mud and I ached all over, but I stood up to him... well, as much as I could below the decks. We were both stooping and in leg irons, but I brought my fists up before my face, much to his surprise. He worked his mouth and spat at me; a stinking gob of foul mucus flew at me and landed on my face.

'You'll do well not to make an enemy of me, posh boy,' he said through rancid breath.

I smiled at the thought that I was a posh boy, but that confused him. He was used to people cowering before his intimidation. He swung a large hairy fist at me but I simply pulled back and the punch just scythed through the foul air. I knew from experience what would happen now. His own momentum threw him off balance and he sprawled on the creaking deck before me, much as Bernd Hartman had done in his gymnasium. Because of the irons I could not swing my leg with full force, but as he tried to get up I put my boot as hard as I could against his raggety-arsed backside and sent him sprawling again. At first there was only stunned silence about the place, disbelief, but then laughter began to break out. It was not what I wanted, I knew that this was humiliation for him and that would gripe in his guts until he had revenge. That meant that I had to knock all such thoughts from him. I needed to leave a mental scar on him; he needed to know that he could not best me for if that was not the case, I knew I would forever need to watch my back.

Each time he tried to get up I repeated the kick to his backside. He sprawled time and again, and each time the laughter rose. His humiliation was total. He twisted his prone body on the deck and then scrambled to his hands and knees, the shackles making that simple task more difficult. He lurched forward at me from that crouched position, but I just dropped my right knee as Bernd had taught me, transferring my power and meeting his charge with a right uppercut, the man's own momentum adding to the force of the punch. He fell at my feet like a sack of beets, his head bounced hard on the deck and he lay unconscious, without a friend to come to his aid. I turned back to my corner, sat and ate my meager rations that I had fought to protect.

Slaughterhouse lay there for a few minutes until consciousness returned to him. He looked around at all the condescending eyes and then at mine. I disdainfully waved him away to a far corner, but initially he did not move, not until I made to get up and then he scampered away like a beaten pup, as far as his irons would allow. I knew that I would have no more trouble from him.

That scrap had unexpected consequences, however. I became a sort of Pied Piper. I first noticed it when we lay down to sleep that night, or more precisely, when I awoke next morning. It was like a manifestation of Herr Isaac Newton's theory of universal gravitation that Papa had taught me about. I was surrounded by sleeping bodies; they had all apparently just been drawn to me in the night, that is to say, as far as men in irons could be drawn. They felt vulnerable I suppose and they probably saw me as a protector. There were two young boys in particular who latched on to me. They were around fourteen or so I would say, though neither one of them knew precisely how old he was. Their names were Harry Thomas and Thomas Harris. I found it amusing that they seemed to have the same name, only backwards, but it had not occurred to them until I pointed it out. Harry was a country boy from a village near a town called Halifax and he had been convicted of stealing turnips, whilst Thomas was from a town called Manchester and he had been convicted of stealing a sack of charcoal. Both had been sentenced to death, but it had been commuted to transportation in view of their ages. At their age I, who had been well nourished, was well on my way to manhood, but they were little more than children, undersized for a lack of good food on their parents' tables, which had led them to thievery in the first place. They looked on me for protection and I was happy to give it. They told me their heart-wrenching stories, their misery of separation from their loved ones, the families they would never see again. I had no family, of course, not any more. I had only Uncle Meno to leave behind and I had the heartwarming prospect of Julia coming out to New South Wales to be with me, but I could well understand their sorrow. It made me think of Uncle Meno. He had returned home to Frankfurt soon after giving evidence at my trial and I longed to be able to write to him, but it was not allowed. I resolved to do so at the first opportunity when - and if - we reached New South Wales. At that time it seemed a distant prospect.

Harry and Thomas were alone in a terrible world, this awful hulk of a ship their vicious, stinking home. They were lost and terrified and their plight was reflected everywhere. People lived in a welter of misery: fathers who would never see their wives and children ever again, knowing that in their absence, their families would starve for want of a breadwinner. There were mothers whose babies had been plucked from their breasts and children who would never see their parents and siblings again. We helped each other to endure it, but sometimes I could not help but wonder if those who died were the more fortunate among us.

CHAPTER 42

Passage to New South Wales, 1823-1824

The fleet left London on the evening tide on November 5th 1823. There were fireworks lighting up the sky and I wondered if it was some form of celebration at the departure of the country's criminals, but young Thomas told me it was for something called 'Guy Fawkes Night'; an English festival to celebrate the foiling of a plot to blow up parliament two hundred years or so ago.

I learned from our prison warder that ours was one of eight ships in the fleet. There were six transport ships and two naval vessels with over a thousand aboard in total, of which 730 were convicts, both male and female. I was astounded at the number of personnel: there were 180 marines and 20 marine officers, 30 marine wives and 20 marine children. Then there were the ships' captains and their wives, the chaplains and their wives and the surgeons and their wives. There were also 36 free settlers, of which my wonderful Julia was one. I sailed on the *Albion*, whilst Julia had passage on the *Porteus*, a women's convict ship, and for the duration of the journey I was in constant anxiety as to her state of health. Being so near to my beloved wife and yet so far, was agony.

I sensed that every one of the convicts aboard the *Albion* was fearful. We knew little of our destination and rumours circulated about man-eating natives and the gigantic voracious creatures that awaited us. Stories abounded; everyone had heard about the first fleets that had set sail for New Holland in the 1780's and how many had died on the way. Starved, beaten, abused; of those who survived the voyage it was said that most could hardly walk when they disembarked. There were stories of New Holland itself, of the terrible, brutal colonies of Van

Dieman's land and Norfolk Island, where treatment of convicts was harsh and cruel. Our fear of what awaited us haunted us all.

And yet, as the voyage unfolded it was not as bad as I thought it would be. That was mainly down to a remarkable young man named Matthew Henshaw. He was the Surgeon-Superintendent appointed to the *Albion* and he was remarkable not only for the position he had attained at such an early age, but also for his unusual attitude towards the convicts. Matthew took his responsibilities very seriously and had vowed that he would get us all safely to our destination. We lost only one person on the way, to dysentery, but the man was already weak with the disease when he came on board.

Our enlightened young surgeon arranged for fastidious washing facilities for the prisoners. Every day he also made a tub of a solution of lime-juice, water and sugar and each prisoner was dosed with a tin measure of the gooey fluid. It kept us well and stopped our teeth from falling out, or so he told me. He took charge of our diet and oversaw the victuals. He had the marine captain post a guard on the stores so that the crew could not steal the provisions intended for the convicts. By the time we had reached Rio de Janeiro, some fourteen weeks later, most of the complaints presented to him on a daily basis had virtually disappeared because the convicts were clean, nourished and living in comparatively sanitary conditions. Matthew was a stickler for cleanliness: every day immediately after breakfast and before morning prayers we prisoners were required to clean the prison deck and a solution of Chloride of Lime was issued against the stink.

On route the ship stopped at Santa Cruz de Tenerife. We were there for three weeks while the ships were restocked with water, fruit, meat, grain and wine. The week before we arrived, Matthew had petitioned Captain Caleb Palfremen to allow the convicts free access to the deck, when we were not at work or at school. At first he was horrified; mutiny was never far from a captain's mind. I think he was a good man, but he was a veteran of eight such fleets, initially as a first officer and then, on the last four, as a captain. He knew the dangers of discontent aboard a ship thousands of miles from any form of police enforcement or justice, with only a few marines to call on. His experience told him that strict discipline was what was needed to maintain safety, but young Doctor Henshaw was nothing if not persistent. He eventually persuaded the Captain to a trial period when the prison doors were opened for an hour each afternoon and convicts were allowed on deck. To the Captain's apparent astonishment there were no disciplinary problems, and the convicts were delighted to be free of the stale air and stifling heat that was prevalent below decks, particularly now the weather was getting warmer.

At Santa Cruz the crew was given some staggered shore leave and the marine officers and their wives took lodgings in the town. Young Doctor Henshaw had met up with his fellow ship's surgeon on the *Porteus* and on his return gave me a letter from Julia and offered me paper and ink to reply. It was such a joy to me to be able to exchange long letters every other day during our stay there. Our contact had been minimal whilst I had been on the prison hulk, but now, uninhibited, we wrote many pages to each other as though we had a lifetime's news to catch up on. I found out how she had got passage. She had petitioned the Home Office to accompany me, but she knew that only a few were accepted no matter how heart-wrenching the circumstances, so her tactic was not to petition for a *free* passage. She agreed to pay her own way, which had eventually cost her twenty guineas, an exploitative amount and she knew it, but one that she was happy to pay. What she did not know until later was that her father had also petitioned the Home Office expressing the sober and industrious character of myself.

She also told me of the terrible ship that was the *Porteus*: how the crew for the most part comprised drunkards who stole from the stores. How the marines and even the marine officers looked to the women convicts for sexual favours, many of whom were happy to give them for the promise of an easy assignment when they arrived in New South Wales. Many had been prostitutes back in England and it was no hardship for them, it was only the form of payment that was different. For others it was a difficult and conscious decision to offer their bodies, their prettiness the only thing they had left to barter. If they were not pretty enough or were old, haggard or ugly, they had a pathetic existence from one day to the next. In many ways, she said, their plight was worse than the men's. A woman was prized by society for her chasteness, her honesty, her vulnerability. To see these brazen, corrupt, fraudulent creatures was an anathema, an abomination. They were seen as deserving of no compassion, yet compassion is what Julia still had for them.

I learned that she had volunteered to help the ship's Surgeon-Superintendent - that brought a smile to my lips, it was just the sort of thing she *would* do. I admired her tremendously, but I was concerned for her. Lacking Matthew Henshaw's knowledge and enlightenment the surgeon on the *Porteus* was overwhelmed with disease made worse by the filth of the ship's convict quarters. I was worried sick that my wife would contract some illness, but I could see from Julia's letters that her strong sense of injustice continued to motivate her. It was there in every word, and every word I read reinforced my love for her. My letters began to change: I started to write my poetry to her. It just poured out of me spontaneously. Not the sort of poetry that I normally wrote, just my way of expressing my love.

All too soon we set sail again and the letters came to an abrupt end - it would be several weeks before I could write to her again, but that gave me something to look forward to and in the meantime, even though I knew the words by heart, I re-read her letters every day. They became increasingly crumpled as our journey progressed.

Our next leg was across the Atlantic to Rio de Janeiro, an eight-week journey. We became aware of the extreme heat of the tropics on the way, it was unbearable below decks. Young Matthew Henshaw again became a thorn in the side of Captain

Caleb Palfremen. Matthew was such a small, insignificant man physically, standing no more than one metre, 62 tall. Narrow of shoulder, his blond hair was already thinning in one so young, for he was but twenty-six years of age, but he was like a terrier hunting an animal down a burrow. I admired him greatly and he sought me out after learning of my predicament from Julia. He had willingly acted as our postman at Santa Cruz and now he befriended me on the voyage. I think he liked the intellectual company that I offered him. He told me that he was the son of a governess, who had educated him alongside her master's children. He inherited a good education, but little else, yet his academic achievements won him a scholarship to study medicine. He told me that the position of ship's surgeon was not regarded as a particularly advantageous one. Most were failed doctors, mainly because they were drunks addicted to John Barleycorn, but some, like him, did not have the funds to buy into a partnership so it was the best they could do. Nevertheless, if fate had cast him as a ship's surgeon, then he was going to be the best ship's surgeon that he could be.

He persuaded the Captain to extend our time on deck. Firstly by another hour, but after a few days he was back asking for more. By the time we were six weeks out of Santa Cruz, the prison doors were open at daybreak and were not closed again until dusk. We convicts were immensely grateful for this. To escape the stifling atmosphere below decks that the extreme tropical heat was bringing, and to feel the cooling breeze on our skins, was wonderful. The whole atmosphere on the ship lightened as the voyage continued. No one was more delighted than Captain Caleb Palfremen, and no one was more amazed than he either.

I remember vividly the day we crossed the Equator. I had no idea that it was such a special day for mariners. Those who had never gone south of the Tropics before faced an initiation into *the mysteries of crossing the Equinoctial Line, and entering the dominions of Neptune*, as the crew put it. Again, Matthew Henshaw petitioned the Captain to allow us on deck to watch. He was reluctant at first, fearing that some of the more roguish of the convicts might take advantage of the lax security, but the young terrier surgeon went back to him accompanied by the Captain of Marines, who said he would personally vouch for order. And so Captain Palfremen acquiesced and in the event we had a wonderful day. An experienced seaman was selected to act as Neptune and he sat on a large barrel at the head of his 'court'. He wore an immense grey horsehair wig, long enough to reach well down his back, together with a grey beard that was almost as long. A tin crown and a trident completed the regalia. His legs and arms were blacked, his cheeks painted vermillion. Next to him sat a sailor dressed as Aphrodite in women's clothes, mostly under garments, and I wondered where on earth he could have got them. I suspect that some ladies in Portsmouth might be looking for them now! They were indeed the most comical of sights. A sail was then suspended, secured from various parts of the deck, and the sailors put to work in bailing an immense quantity of sea water into it until it formed a large pool, which I swear must have been six feet deep.

The initiates had been ordered below, and the gratings put on. Each initiate was then called individually to Neptune's Court and he emerged blindfolded, and then had his head shaved. The barber had filled a bucket with all the cleanings of the hen coops and mixed with it a due proportion of tar. A large paint brush was dipped in this stinking bucket, and with his razor now sheathed the barber stood awaiting the signal. Neptune's first question was 'What is your name my man?' to which the fearful sailor answered, 'John Shaw, Your Honour,' but at the instant he opened his mouth the brush went across it. We all laughed so loudly at the face he pulled.

'Phoo, what do you call that? What do you call that?' asked Neptune again.

'John Shaw,' repeated the sailor and the brush stroked across his mouth again. Neptune then asked how old he was. 'Eight and twenty Your Honour,' he replied, at which point the foul brush was plunged into the initiate's mouth once more and we all fell about laughing. Then Neptune said he meant to put the man overboard and would call for a good rope for perhaps he could not swim? This terrified the fellow as indeed he could not and he cried out in panic, 'I cannot swim, oh, I cannot swim!' The foul brush crossed his mouth as he spoke and he tried to say it again through his panic, his teeth clenched tightly closed.

Now, amid a roar of laughter, two men tripped the handspike on which he sat and sent him backward into the sail full of water where, believing he was overboard, he splashed about for a few moments shrieking with fear. He soon recovered, however, scrambling out of the sail to stand dripping on the deck, his blindfold removed. Then he stood by to see a succession of his shipmates share his fate, laughing at their terrified antics just as wildly as the rest of us.

It was a wonderful experience and a wonderful day that I will remember for the rest of my life. Strange that; we were convicts on a penal ship being transported to... well, who knew what, fearful of what awaited us, and yet for a few joyous hours we were able to forget about our predicament. But there was another day, or in particular another night, that I will also remember for the rest of my life, but for such very different reasons.

The words *storm at sea* trip easily off the tongue. We read about them all the time in the newspapers, but the reality of being in the middle of one was a frightening shock to all of us. We came upon this tropical storm just after noon. There was a slight freshening of the wind to begin with and some black clouds in the distance, but over the next few hours the clear blue skies turned sinister. Blocks and halliards began to rattle as the wind strengthened and above our heads the main topsail roared like a kettle drum as the wind took it. The crew was put to lashing down everything as firmly as they could before the worst of it arrived. We convicts were sent below to the prison deck and the prison doors were locked. Although our quarters below deck were much better than on the hulk, they were still dank, dark and damp and lacking in ventilation, but now the waters began to steep through so that our meager bedding was quickly soaked. We had become used to the putrid smell of the wet and rotting timbers combined with the packed bodies of the prisoners all around us; now added to this was the rank smell of vomit, gallons of it as no one escaped the nauseating effect of the ship's exaggerated roll. But it was to get much worse as darkness fell.

At about ten-of-the-clock the wind was so strong that the ship, pitching and tossing in the vast seas, was lying over on her sides alternately and the water leaking through the deck timbers had risen almost to the very hammock nettings. It sloshed from side to side alarmingly and in no time we were all soaked to the skin. For us in our locked prison the sensation of rocking was horrific, but it was the noises that were the most terrifying. The ship's straining timbers creaked and groaned like lost souls yelling out their agony in purgatory. Added to this were the intermittent sounds of objects crashing, thumping and rolling, whether it be on deck or in the cabins, where they had not been lashed down or had worked themselves loose in the fury of the storm. And above it all was the constant howling of the mighty wind. I needed all my young strength to hold on and avoid being tossed about like a rag doll. This lasted for hour after dark never ending hour. The swinging lanterns made small circular pools of light, but most of the prison deck was in deep shadow. One by one the lanterns went out, the wicks being soaked by the cascading water. We attempted to keep candles lit, holding down the candle holders as otherwise they would be thrown about and snuffed out by the sea water that was still accumulating as it seeped through the deck and down to our pit of terror.

The malevolent wind blew and blew and blew. The ship tossed and pitched, rolled and groaned. The rasping din of the storm and the creaking noises of the ship were occasionally punctuated by the frantic sounds of the crew as they manned the pumps, trying to keep their feet steady as they did so. All through the night they toiled, the wearying, drudging effort of pumping hour after exhausting draining hour was evident in their cries. Yet I longed to be with them; at least their gruelling toil would occupy their minds whereas my troubled mind had nothing to do but dwell on the watery fate that I expected to befall us all. My fears for Julia were paramount, but I thought also of my father, and then of Mama and Moses and Henriette, but I could find no shred of comfort in the thought that I would meet them all again before the night was done.

We all believed that the good ship *Albion* was going to the bottom and that this dark locked prison was going to be our cold wet coffin; Davy Jones's locker our godless watery grave. Men fell to their knees in the salty water to pray for mercy, quaking from a mixture of fear and cold, their teeth chattered as they prayed. Some tried to read their Bible, but were hampered by their lack of reading skills or were denied its comfort when the lights were constantly extinguished. Hour after terrifying hour the storm raged and the ship was tossed on the vengeful waves like some child's play thing. Men prayed for it to end; but it did not. The torrent continued to blow and the ship to creak and roll; water continued to break over the sides and then seep down below decks, and men continued to cry out in fear and to pray; while somewhere in the bowels of the ship the crew in desperation manned the pumps without ceasing. It seemed that it would never end.

And so the night passed, and even now, years later, when I think of it I break into a sweat of remembered terror. But by morning we were still miraculously alive and the ship still afloat, though it had not stopped rolling and pitching to the malicious dictates of the heinous wind and sea. Some, welcomed, stray rays of daylight had perculated down through the gratings and a partly opened hatchway. Just knowing it was daylight outside – even if we could see little of it in our dark prison – somehow lessened our fear.

The wind finally began to ease a little after noon, more than twenty-four hours after it had started, and as we felt the rolling of the ship become less violent, we dared to begin to hope. We held onto that hope as if it were the most precious thing in the world and when eventually we knew the storm was over and we had survived it, the prayers turned from pleas to thanks. I too thanked my God; not just for sparing me, but also Julia, for I knew by then that my beloved wife was safe. Doctor Henshaw had lost no time in passing the news to me that the *Porteus* had been sighted and had also survived the storm intact with no loss of life. Exhaustion then took us all, and we gave ourselves thankfully to sleep. We were wet and uncomfortable but our fatigue was so total that we all slept for the remainder of the afternoon and through the following night as if we were frightened children snuggled up to our mothers after a vicious nightmare.

Afterwards, the crew tried to make light of the storm to us; it only lasted twenty-four hours they said. They told us tales of storms at sea lasting for seven or even ten days. Well, that's as may be; all I know is that for those twenty-four hours I was consumed by abject fear – it is not something that I would want to repeat. Not ever.

When I was on board that terrible hulk in Chatham, I found it very odd that there was such an emphasis put on religion. To avoid *The Profanation of the Lord's Day,* as they called it, Sundays must be dedicated to prayer and preaching. I think the reasoning behind it was the hope that convicts could be redeemed by moral instruction; that the gospel of Christ would somehow turn them away from their wickedness. The problem was that most of the convicts were not in fact wicked; their crimes for the most part were driven by despair and extreme poverty. Harsh punishment went hand in hand with this religious instruction, and of course it failed because with few exceptions, wickedness was more manifest in the brutal guards than it was in the unfortunates they guarded.

On board the *Albion,* the ship's Chaplain, Joshua Herbert, had the same idea: that he could redeem us convicts with moral instruction. Doctor Henshaw had told me that Herbert had tried this on three previous fleets but with absolutely no success. Despite this, his belief in himself was undiminished, so sure was he that a combination of harsh treatment and religious instruction would turn sinful men away from crime. He had brought with him a copy of the Book of Common Prayer, one for each prisoner, and a Bible for every sixteen prisoners – he was going to save these men. Of course, no one had been interested in this form of redemption on Joshua Herbert's previous voyages any more than they had been interested in the Chaplain's efforts on the hulk, but on this voyage in the aftermath of that terrible storm something remarkable was to happen.

Whilst a few of the convicts only went through the motions, most actually did take refuge in religion, singing hymns with gusto and listening to the sermons. Surviving the storm accentuated this new religious fervour. Joshua Herbert told anyone who would listen of the wonder of Christ to work miracles, but he couldn't see what was obvious to everyone else. The miracle worker was actually young Doctor Henshaw. He had again petitioned the Captain, but this time he wanted to give schooling to the convicts. Knowing that the hours of boredom endured by convicts was the root cause of dissent on a long voyage, the Captain needed little persuasion. Anything that kept us convicts occupied was to be encouraged. That's why he put the prisoners to unskilled tasks whenever possible, swabbing, laundering, holystoning the decks, but education had not been on his agenda until Doctor Henshaw put it there.

A programme was worked out and the literacy skills of the convicts assessed. We were divided into four groups: those who could read well, those who read tolerably, those who read imperfectly and those who were illiterate. I was press-ganged into being an additional teacher, along with the Doctor and the Chaplain and one or two of the more literate officers. I also gave lectures on Napoleonic history, astronomy, poetry and the circulation of blood, which I had learned from Uncle Meno.

Doctor Henshaw had created an environment on board this prison ship that was far less harsh than I had expected - much less so than on the hulk - and I began to hope that this would also be the case when we arrived in New South Wales. There were hard core ruffians, of course, who were untouched by what was happening, but most of the convicts prospered under it; they learned to read and write or improved their reading skills, and in consequence stopped turning their backs on religion as a comfort. Joshua Herbert failed to see all this, of course.

We stopped off at Cape Town and then came the final long haul eventually dipping below the 40th parallel to New South Wales. Our voyage had taken eight months. We were allowed on deck on our approach to Sydney Cove and we all rushed to the side to see a shoal of flying fish, and wondered at this amazing sight. As I watched in awe, I resolved to write to Uncle Meno about it. And then a shoal of fish seemed to be escorting us to our new home. A crewman told me that they were actually not fish at all; dolphins he called them and I wondered at these creatures as their smiling faces repeatedly broke the water's surface. The name '*Dolphin*' had scarred my mind for it was the name of that awful hulk, but now, in contradiction, here were these wonderful creatures that were welcoming me to my new life and helping to dispel the horror of the past.

We viewed our new home with a combination of fear and, believe it or not, excitement. I was certainly glad to be here, if only for the thought of seeing Julia again, but it was more than that. I was not allowed on deck after night fell and I lamented that I could not see that canopy of stars that might give me some reassurance, to confirm that I had a place in this universe. But I *was* enthused, there was no doubt about that and I'm sure I sensed an excitement in the other convicts as well; a new life beckoned us all and the privations of our past lives seemed very far away.

CHAPTER 43

New South Wales, 1824

As the fleet approached Sydney Cove on Port Jackson the sight of it took my breath away. It was not what I expected; then I really don't know what I did expect, some primitive uncivilized place I suppose. But this initial view was idyllic: the water brilliantly blue, the shores high and wooded running gently down to the shore line, a scattering of islands, sandy beaches, the trees shimmering under the sun. It was a sight that brought a brief peace to my troubled mind, and it made me want to write a poem about it. Doctor Henshaw told me that Sydney town itself, despite being less than fifty years old, now had a population approaching 35,000 with banks, markets, well-established thoroughfares and an organized constabulary, or so Captain Palfremen had told him.

I well remember that first day after the ship tied up in the harbour. We had arrived at our destination of New South Wales, fit and healthy, most far fitter and healthier than when they had left Chatham. What awaited us was bewildering, however; we needed to be processed by the colonial officials before disembarking. I was surprised at what they wanted to know; they recorded our literacy our religion, our previous occupation, our place of birth and age. When it came to my turn there was much head scratching and it was clear they did not know what to do with me or how to record me. Poet, translator and pugilist were not occupations they had come across before. They also recorded our physical descriptions, our build and hair colour, birthmarks, scars and tattoos. The English seemed as thorough as the German states in that respect.

We were then handed over to the Governor of Hyde Park Barracks, which became my temporary home for the next two months or so. The penal system required us to labour and I was put to work as a 'government man', working on public works - we were never referred to as convicts. In England at Chatham Docks I had been put to work driving great posts in the mud to protect the river bank. Now, here in New South Wales, I spent my time driving in great posts to make breakwaters. The government men, as we continued to be called, were a regular sight to the good citizens of Sydney Town. We could be seen being marched in single file through the streets to and from our work detail, wearing the distinctive grey and yellow jacket, daubed over with broad arrows.

The Colonial Office operated what was known as the *Assignment System*, where a convict could be lent out as a labourer to a private citizen. After two months I was assigned to work for a free settler, who then became responsible for my clothing, food and shelter. I went to work for a Jacob Shoesmith, who had a farm along the rich plains of the Hawkesbury River, north-west of Sydney. He farmed a grant of 75 acres on land claimed from the Bush. I learned that there were now many free settlers, who had come to start a new life and prosper here in New South Wales and had been given grants of land. Most had indeed prospered, but it was clear that Jacob Shoesmith was not one of them; he was struggling on his personal road to advancement. His farm was badly run despite the man himself working from daybreak to sunset.

I was his fourth assigned man, but it was clear that the other three were taking advantage of him. The harder he worked the less time he had to supervise his men and the less work they did as a consequence, and so he had to work harder to cover for them. I could see this after only a few days on his farm. I liked him though; physically he had the look of my old stable fighter, Helmut, barrel-chested with bright ginger hair. The sun had made his face red and freckled, but he was a trusting soul, unlike that rogue Helmut who was neither trusting nor trustworthy. Jacob Shoesmith blamed his lack of prosperity on the shortage of supplies from which the colony suffered: farming materials, livestock and essential provisions, but in reality it was down to his own shortcomings as a farmer.

My letters from Julia were a great comfort to me. She wrote most every day, but now I was at the Hawkesbury River the delivery was spasmodic and sometimes I received several on the same day. I remember devouring them in the evenings and I asked Jacob Shoesmith for pen, ink and paper so that I could reply. I asked nervously if he would also cover the cost of the postage until Julia could reimburse him. He was a generous man, however. Not only did he agree, he even invited me into his home to use his bureau rather than take the writing implements into the barn, where we four assignees slept. It was then that I discovered the ink had dried in its well; he cannot have been keeping up to date with his ledgers, I thought.

Julia's letters told me that back in Sydney she had been busy on my behalf, but then, knowing my lovely wife as I did, I knew she would have been. She had somehow got herself an invitation to dine with the Governor, and my story, as told by her, had been part of the after-dinner conversation. The Governor and his guests had listened intently to her words and her enthusiasm, and with not a little wonder at her bravery in following me out here. She had put on a charm offensive and the Governor had indeed been taken by her charm. He had listened with interest to her thoughts on the New South Wales legal system, which she encouraged him to believe was more enlightened than that back in England. On the back of this connection she had made to him an audacious suggestion.

I read with increasing delight her vivid account of what had then occurred, and she has since related it to me in person: 'Sir,' she said, 'can I beseech you directly with a proposition for your consideration?' The Governor had nodded politely for her to continue. 'My husband is a convict with a sentence of seven years transportation, and that makes him eligible for the Assignment Programme; is that not right?'

'That is correct, Madam,' the Governor had again nodded politely.

'Is it not also true that convicts can be assigned to be domestic servants in the households of the higher members of Sydney society?' had asked my intrepid wife.

'That is also correct, Madam,' said the Governor. 'Do I take it that you want me to use my influence to find an assignment position for your husband as a domestic servant?' He had paused awhile as he thought about it and then said, 'I think that might be arranged.'

'Not quite, Mr Governor, I already have a position in mind.' At this point in Julia's letter, I found myself laughing out loud.

'Pray tell, Madam, and who is to be your husband's master?'

'Why, I am sir,' said my wonderful Julia. I could imagine her eyes looking straight at the Governor and never wavering – and I knew full well the power of that gaze.

The Governor had laughed robustly at the notion and shared his amusement with the rest of the dinner party.

'I am in earnest sir,' Julia had said, continuing to fix him with her steely gaze.

'I can see you are, Madam,' said the Governor, still wheezing at the capriciousness of the suggestion. 'You want me to authorise your own husband as your assignee, as a domestic servant?' His comments provoked another round of laughter from the dinner party.

My amazing wife had then realised that she needed to change her tactic. '*I lightened my stare and made sheep's eyes at him instead*,' she had written. I could imagine her holding her head aloof, shooting him a sheepish look and saying through a demure smile, 'Is that really so outrageous sir?'

'Well, Madam, if your suggestion is not *outrageous* it's certainly *audacious*?' He had laughed at his own wit, prompting his guests to do likewise. They had clapped politely and my Julia had joined in with the applause, but her smile and stare indicated that she awaited his answer.

Julia's wiles proved successful for after coughing in embarrassment beneath her relentless gaze, the Governor had given ground, 'I will take it under-advisement, Madam,' he said eventually. And with that Julia had to be satisfied, at least for the time being.

In the event he declined. He sent her a brief personal note saying that it would be a precedent, one he did not feel able to grant. I think he must have feared an invasion of wives wanting to do the same thing. I smiled for a long time after I had read her letter. I think on balance I probably agreed with the Governor that she was indeed being audacious. She was not to give up, however.

Prompted by Julia, I set about improving my situation on the farm. I offered to keep Jacob Shoesmith's ledgers for him. He readily agreed, but when I started I quickly found that his ledgers were not only behind, they were in fact virtually non-existent: page after blank page, the last entries over five years ago. What business records he did have were kept in his head, and that meant in reality that there was no control over his business and in particular no control over his billing. We spent three long evenings trying to put down what he could remember, specifically who were his debtors. His recollections only went back a few months, of course, and it quickly became obvious that much of the monies owed to him could not be quantified and would never be recovered. I suspected that the word had gone around and that his debtors were deliberately withholding payment. Nevertheless, I issued invoices for all the debts that he could remember and some funds did start to arrive, and I followed up the others vigorously. It was also clear that I was lifting a burden from his mind and we became sort of friends.

He told me that his parents were wool merchants from a place in England called the Cotswolds. He was the eldest son and had been well educated, but despite this he could still not really read and write; somehow, no matter how hard he tried he just couldn't do it. He had been taken into the business at the age of sixteen years but his lack of literacy had been disastrous and by the age of twenty-one things had not improved. His father had been in despair, fearing that after he was gone, his son would run the business into the ground. It had then been decided that the business would pass to Jacob's younger brother, who was then only fourteen, and he would be groomed to take over. Jacob knew this was the right thing for his father to do, but it nevertheless bruised his pride greatly. He asked his father to provide him with funds to start a new life as a free settler in New South Wales. He had heard much talk of this place, and the family had reluctantly agreed. In effect he had taken these funds as his inheritance in lieu of his right to the business.

His lack of business acumen, however, was proving just as catastrophic here in New South Wales as it would have been back in the Cotswolds. I could see that he was facing ruin unless he turned things around. I saw an opportunity and decided to act upon it. Prompted by Julia's faith in me I offered to be his overseer.

'Can you do that Neander?' he asked, the suggestion taking him by surprise. 'You are a convict yourself; you are not a free man.'

'I don't see why not,' I replied encouragingly, not sure what that had to do with it.

'The assigned men will not like taking orders from you, another assigned man?'

I had not thought of that. 'No they won't,' I agreed, 'but you can leave that to me.' I could see he was wavering, so added, 'Give it a month's trial?'

He liked that suggestion, but he was right about my three fellow assigned men. One in particular was a surly man. He was lazy and his life here was far better than he had enjoyed in England. He was fed, clothed and housed and his work-shy attitude went unpunished. He stood up to me the first time I tried to give him an order to do some task. He saw me as an upstart chancer - a foreign one at that - who was threatening to put an end to his easy life style. He expected me to back down and when I didn't he threw a punch at me, sure that it would do the trick. I needed only one punch to chase any such notions from his thoughts: I stepped back as his fist flew wildly past my face and then I let fly a rounded left into his unprotected midriff. He sank to the ground wheezing for air and was unable to stand for fully ten minutes, his face a crimson picture of shocked surprise.

I convinced Jacob that this was the opportunity he needed to get rid of this troublemaker, who had broken the terms of his assignment by resorting to violence. I accompanied Jacob when he returned the fellow to the Hyde Park Barracks in Sydney. While we were there, I briefed him on a replacement; the farm sorely needed an agricultural labourer I told him. Jacob was offered all sorts of trades instead, but with my prompting he refused them all, in the process making himself a bit of a thorn in the sides of the colonial officials.

'There must be agricultural labourers or agricultural stockmen amongst the convicts?' I prompted Jacob to keep saying.

Indeed there were, and Jacob was bright enough to know that, but these were the prized convicts. Convict labour generally was the lifeblood of the colony, but some workers were much more prized than others. A lot of the best farms were run by gentlemen farmers, many of whom were serving marine officers. They employed farm managers and used their influence to get the best of the convicts; experienced farm workers and husbandmen were consequently in high demand.

The visit to Sydney gave me the opportunity to see Julia. I sent a message to her as our meeting at Hyde Park Barracks dragged on hour after hour. She eventually joined me there and the colonial officials looked dumbstruck at the sight of this fine lady consorting with an assigned man. Understanding the situation immediately she took her place beside me and weighed in to the argument on Jacob's behalf.

'I will be dining with the Governor this Friday evening,' she said, 'I wonder what he would think if he knew that your department is in collusion with certain farmers to keep all the best convicts for themselves.' She then gave the official a scornful look.

The Governor probably knew what was going on, but the official obviously thought it was not worth taking the chance. He relented and we left with a strong twenty-four year old, who had been a farm labourer in Devon. Julia and I had no chance of private conversation, but while our mouths spoke commonplace words that were fit to be overheard, our eyes revealed eloquently all the things we couldn't say – and just to see her again, and looking so well, gave my heart such a lift I was hard put to it not to sing all the way back to the farm.

Over the next month I worked out new work rotas to make the best of this season's crops and with the help of our new assignee, who turned out to be every bit as good as I'd hoped, we made plans for next year's farming. The problem was that Jacob had so little funds for seeds and supplies and his ability to get credit had been reduced by his history of bad payments. I wrote and told Julia all of this, asking if she would stand surety for him with the suppliers, but Julia had much bigger plans in mind.

One of the finest farms on the Hawkesbury River plains belonged to a Major Trumpter a retired marine officer. He had brought his wife and son out to New South Wales, and he was prospering with 500 acres of prize grazing land. But his wife and son had died tragically in an epidemic of the pestilence and he had taken to the bottle, spending most of his time in a drunken stupor as a way through his grief. His tragic story was the topic of conversation at one of the Governor's dinner parties, to which Julia was now regularly invited. She went to see the unfortunate Major Trumpter and in conversation with him, he told her of his profound loneliness and his longing to return to England to be with his relatives back there. She made him an offer there and then to buy him out. She offered him two shillings an acre; fifty pounds for the full five hundred acres.

At the time I did not know she had such funds; she had kept it a secret even from me, thankfully, for it would have been a source of considerable anxiety for me, which is why she did not tell me. She would most certainly have been at risk on the convict ship had it been known she was travelling with a hundred gold sovereigns secreted in the lining of her travelling bag! Her doting father had given her the money when it had become obvious to him that he could not stop her from travelling to New Holland after me. It was to help her set up a new life, but also to pay for her passage back if things did not go so well, or to pay for both our passages back at the end of my seven years of transportation. George Carmichael was nothing if not a fair-minded and generous man and he loved his daughter to distraction.

Julia then went to see Jacob Shoesmith and offered him a partnership if he would sell his fifty acres and move to the new farm, with herself and Shoesmith becoming equal partners in the business. On the face of it Jacob Shoesmith was getting much the better of the deal financially. He was bright enough to see that and he readily agreed. We all moved to the bigger farm and the two workforces were merged. Of course I was still legally assigned to Jacob, but my clever wife had engineered what the Governor had denied her, for in reality I was assigned to her. Her ingenuity and resourcefulness never ceases to amaze me. Julia was – and is - a most remarkable woman.

CHAPTER 44

New South Wales, 1825

Things were a bit chaotic when we first moved to the new farm. Julia shared the main farmhouse with Jacob Shoesmith, and even in this remote part of the Empire she was concerned about the impropriety of it, despite efforts being made to separate the two households. I have to confess that I was a bit put out since I was still expected to sleep in an outhouse with the other assignees, but Julia convinced me that our first priority was to put the farm in order. The livestock had to be got to market and the crops harvested. There was no immediate buyer for Jacob's acres and we needed to bring in his crops as well. I continued in my role as the overseer, but now at the new farm, and that too put noses out of joint. After a few months, when everyone had settled into their new routine, the farm was running as it should and the crops had been harvested, Julia put the men to work to build a home for us and at last I could look forward to the day when we would live together as husband and wife.

A whitewashed cottage emerged from the men's labour, complete with a shady veranda that we could sit on in the evenings. I accompanied Julia to Sydney one day to take possession of the furniture she had ordered for it. On a whim she purchased a caged cockatoo for the veranda and paradoxically we named it 'Freedom' to remind ourselves of our eventual aim. We also bought a new wardrobe for my use in our new home. In the eyes of the law I may still have been a convict, but once our front door was closed I would be the master of our house. And so we purchased new breeches and stockings for me, a muslin necktie, and a pair of light leather shoes so that I could wear something other than those heavy work boots that I had been issued with at the Hyde Park Barracks. Most welcome of all were the new shirts. In the shop I had fingered the softness of new linen before they were parcelled up and it brought back such pleasant thoughts; thoughts I had not allowed myself for so long. We went then to the hardware shop for the final purchase: a large enamel bath.

'A bath!' I said, 'What's that for?' I meant that I thought there were other priorities before such a luxury item, but at my ill considered words Julia gave me a hard stare.

'That is for us, David, but mainly for *you*. When you come to my bed for the first time you will not come with the smell of the farm still on you!'

And then the full significance of the bath hit me. It was obvious and I was ashamed that I had not seen it for myself. Julia had been so practical for these last few months that I had viewed the shopping trip in the same light. But now I understood; she was still planning, and what she was planning was our wedding night. Our marriage had never been consummated, and now it was going to be and she wanted to make sure everything would be right for us.

The 25th April, 1825 was the day that Julia had picked. I know because that is the day that we have since celebrated as our wedding anniversary, rather than that terrible marriage farce in Newgate gaol. When the day dawned, water was boiled to fill the tub outside the back of the cottage, and I was sent out to bathe with a bar of sweetly scented soap. My daily cleansing routine of stripping to the waist and sluicing myself under the pump would not suffice for that special night. While I pampered myself, Julia set to, preparing a fine meal for us. After I emerged from the tub I went into our bedroom and found the clean clothes she had laid out for me. I dressed in the new breeches, linen ruched shirt, silk white stockings and the new leather shoes. As I was fastening the muslin necktie, I noticed that the jacket, newly pressed was mine, it was not new. Julia must have brought it all the way from England with this day in mind. I remembered buying it in Bremen. It had been an expression of my new found wealth. I smiled as my thoughts slid away to that other place, that other life. It was no more than the silhouette of an emotion. It was brief and it passed quickly, yet it made me shudder at the direction my life had taken since then.

I put on the jacket; it was loose on me and I realised that I had lost weight during my incarceration, but I shrugged my shoulders and in the best of spirits went through to the living room. I was amazed; Julia had laid the table with a fine damask tablecloth, silver cutlery and slender wax candles, and glowing in their soft light was a bottle of burgundy and two wine glasses. It was a far cry from what I had been used to and I stared at it agape.

'Sit my love,' she said, taking off her apron. She sat beside me and poured me a large glass of the wine. 'Now you enjoy your wine while I go and change.'

I sat back in the chair and brought the glass to my lips. I wanted to savour it. I swilled the deep red liquid around the glass and put it to my nose. The aroma brought back other memories, some good, but some far from good. I took a deep drink, allowing the liquid to swirl around my mouth, but suddenly I could not swallow. It was as if I was afraid that the pleasure would disappear if I did so and that this wonderful night would disappear along with it. It was a moment of gut-wrenching insecurity. A page was turning and a story unfolding and I was fearful that the plot would once again spiral downwards and take me into peril. But most of all, I was terrified of losing my wonderful Julia. I had no need to be, it was irrational, yet I could not prevent that sombre thought from taking me and for a few moments I was in danger of falling into melancholy, just as Papa used to do.

When Julia came back into the room I sat up in my seat at the sight of her and swallowed the wine involuntarily. She was wearing a fashionable gown of the modern French style, silk, cornflower blue with opaque sleeves. The waistline was in the normal place for a waist, not the high-waisted Empire style made fashionable by the Empress Josephine. It showed off her slim figure wonderfully; to me she was the most beautiful woman in the world and I could hardly believe she was mine. All those melancholy thoughts were cast from my mind like rabbits diving into their burrows when the dog is let loose.

Julia took her apron again from the back of the chair and put it across her gown. 'Pour me a glass of wine, my love,' she said, 'and I'll serve our dinner.'

We ate a wonderful meal. To start we had a white soup of veal stock, cream and almonds thickened with bread, followed by a platter of baked fish. The main course was boiled mutton with dumplings and greens. To finish, a cider syllabub, sweetened and flavoured with nutmeg, milk and more cream. I'm not sure where she got some of the ingredients from, nor had I known she was such a good cook, but the meal was delectable, nearly as delectable as Julia herself. I sat back in my chair and looked at the candlelight as it flickered on her beautiful face. I was contented; the world seemed a better place than it had for such a long time.

I was gazing at my wife in appreciation when I noticed a flicker of apprehension creeping into her face. I could not immediately understand it and coming as it did on the heels of my earlier thoughts, it worried me. 'What is it, my love? Are you not feeling well?'

'It is nothing, David, I'm fine - honestly I am.'

I knew she was hiding something from me. 'No, tell me, please,' I begged.

She sighed heavily, choosing her words with care. I waited patiently until on another sigh, she said, 'For so long I have had only my tearstained pillow to keep me company through the night.'

'But no longer, my love,' I said, still not realising what was worrying her.

'Yes, dear David, no longer – but...' She paused and looked for a spark of understanding in my eyes, but fool that I was, I was unable to show it to her. 'This is our wedding night, David...' she paused again and when I looked at her, nonplussed, she whispered, 'I fear that I will disappoint you.'

And then realisation took me. What a dunderhead I was to be blind to her apprehension. She was a virgin; it was only natural that she should be full of doubts and anxieties. The strange nature of our relationship had denied her so much; denied her dances and balls, dresses and petticoats, ribbons and curls, stays too tight when youthful passions surfaced, the fumbling at tapes and buttons as those passions took hold - they had all been denied her. There had been no road for her to travel to arrive at her wedding night; those pages in her life had been ripped from the book.

Filled with relief, I rushed around the table, pulled her up and took her in my arms, kissing her gently but lingeringly.

'You will never ever disappoint me, Julia. Fear not, we will be apprehensive together, we will share that as we will share everything else from now on.'

I kissed her again and this time she responded and the kiss became more passionate. I lifted her in my arms and took her through to the bedroom. I sat on my side of the bed and began to disrobe and she sat on hers. We were back to back so that we did not look at each other. I saw that she had laid out two nightgowns, one on each side of the bed. I resolved that they were not to be used and naked, I climbed silently between the sheets. She had more to take off than I and in a state of pleasurable anticipation I watched her disrobing. She suddenly felt my gaze on her and brought her elbows in to the side of her body to cover herself.

'Don't look at me, David; please,' she whispered, a flush staining her lovely face.

I turned away onto my side and studied the wall, but in my head was the delightful image of her nakedness and my body clamoured for release. 'I won't my love,' I said, but...'

'But what?'

'But don't put on that silly nightgown.'

There was a pause and I wished I had not said that. I was happy for her to come to me in any way that she felt comfortable. And then I sensed her slide in beside me. I waited for her to... well, I am not sure what I waited for, I only knew that I had to take things slowly.

'I am ready now, David.'

I turned round keeping my movement slow and controlled. She lay on her back, rigid, motionless as though she were paralysed with fear. I moved towards her and kissed her gently on the lips. I felt her relax slightly, and that's all we did for some time, kiss gently. But then I sensed a passion rising in her, gradually at first, hardly noticeable, but increasing until it matched my own. We both acknowledged it and bit by bit abandoned ourselves to it.

My wedding night was all that I wanted it to be; delayed for two whole years, but just as wonderful for all that; maybe even more so.

In November 1825 I applied for and was granted my Ticket of Leave. It was no more than a piece of paper, but it represented much more than that. A piece of paper issued to convicts who had served a period of probation, and who had shown by their good behavior that they could be allowed certain freedoms. In some respects such freedoms were less valuable to me than to others, for though it allowed me to seek employment, my Julia had already arranged that for me. In effect I was already a grant farmer even though everything was in her name. I couldn't leave the district without the permission of the resident magistrate, but that was no constraint on me, I had no wish to. Similarly, a Ticket of Leave permitted a convict to marry and raise a family. Once again, thanks to Julia, I already had that privilege. But there was even so a significance to my Ticket that was quite profound for both of us. It was a signal that we were starting to live a new life; a *normal* life. When my Ticket was issued it became a double celebration for on that same day, Julia announced she was with child and I was to become a father. This news was perhaps the greatest joy in my life, eclipsed only by the birth of my son in May, 1826.

And so the years passed and in November 1830, my seven years of penal transportation was completed. I was 28 years old and I was now a free man again. We had two children: George Moses aged four, and named after Julia's father and my brother, and a daughter, Henriette Julia, aged 18 months and named after my sister and, of course, my wife. The farm had prospered; we now had 750 acres of the best grazing land on the Hawkesbury River plains and the partnership with Jacob Shoesmith went from strength to strength; in fact he had become my best friend. He was a hard working man, a man of integrity and as it turned out, a man of some intellect despite his inability to read and write. I wrote letters back to England for him, and I could see the immense pride in his dictated words telling his father and brother of the success that he was making of his life.

One of my first tasks as a free man was to stand as best man at his wedding. A cousin from England accepted his proposal and, like so many other women who followed their men to New Holland, or Australia as it had now been officially named, she sailed to be his bride.

The delight of his wedding in January 1831 hid a fear that was eating him. I knew of his anxiety, although very few words passed between us on the subject. To Jacob, Australia was to be his new life. For Julia and me it was always seen as a period of exile; we would return to England when my sentence was completed. Her father had given her money on the assumption that she would return when that time was over. I remember that we had many sleepless nights over what we should do.

One balmy evening we sat out on the veranda after Julia had put the children to bed; it was a cloudless night with a full moon, still, without a breath of wind. There was a peaceful silence punctuated only by the incessant sounds of the crickets and other insects, but then there was a loud and harsh squawk. It was Freedom, our cockatoo, his squawk was always loud and harsh. I turned to look at the white bird and his crest rose when he saw me smiling at him.

The bright moonlight illuminated the kitchen garden that Julia had planted and tended so diligently and I looked at the produce growing in neat rows and anticipated harvesting the result of our labours. A farmer's life was never one that I had aspired to; it was not the one that my education had prepared me for, and certainly my wonderful Julia had been forced to put her law training to one side while we made this opportunist life for ourselves. I looked up at the sky; that canopy of stars that populated the darkness from horizon to horizon. It made me feel insignificant, yet a thought took me and I wondered again as to my place in this universe. And then something profound struck me in those serene moments; I was happy; happier than I had ever been in my life. I turned to look at Julia and at that very instance she turned to look at me. No words were spoken for a heartbeat, but I knew that she had been thinking the same thoughts as I.

'This is our home, our *wonderful* home,' I said eventually.

'Yes it is, David,' she smiled contentedly at me. That was all the discussion entailed, no more words than that, hardly a discussion at all in fact, but the decision had been made.

'You will probably never see your parents again?'

'I know,' she said philosophically.

Our life in Australia was prosperous. I became one of the first ex-convicts to be appointed as a magistrate; I also became one of the first ex-convicts to dine with the Governor, which we now do regularly. Julia became one of the first women to be appointed as a magistrate. She became passionate that Australian law should be more enlightened than English law and such was her commitment and forcefulness that she went a long way towards making it so. Recently, my Uncle Meno braved the long journey to come and live with us, and he has quickly become the mischievous uncle to my children that he once was to me.

My life's journey has, to say the least, been an eventful one, the twists and turns of fate, of serendipity, which led me into the shadow of the gallows and then enabled me to escape that chilling brute by the merest scintilla of providence, has led me to a distant land and unimagined riches.

Has the final page now turned? Has my story been told? Has my life finally unfolded? Who is to say - but for now I lay down my pen.

EPILOGUE

The power of emotions can be overwhelming. David and Julia together endured so many vicious and spiteful emotions: anxiety, dismay, alarm and fear - even blind terror; trepidation, panic, horror and dread. Worry - endless worry, which had eaten away at their troubled minds like parasitic insects, burrowing deep, denying them the peace of undisturbed sleep in the long, long restless nights. Yet over and above it all there had been love to see them through it. But now; now there were kinder emotions, equally powerful: those of contentment, satisfaction and serenity, and these were all-consuming in their magnitude. They should not be at balance on the scales that measure such things, and yet they were.

Author's notes

1. The facts and the proceedings used for David's trial are taken from the Old Bailey record of the trial of Peter Shalley, REF: T17900113-17 that took place in 1790. It is therefore actually 30 years before the date of David's trial and the proceedings may have changed in that period. I have sacrificed some accuracy in period to maintain the accuracy of those proceedings.

   There were reforms to the judicial system in the 1820's when the number of crimes punishable by death was reduced. In addition in 1827 the threshold of the 40-shilling theft rule requiring a mandatory death sentence was raised to 100 shillings. By setting David's trial in 1823 it would predate these reforms and he would indeed have been on trial for his life.

   It is interesting looking at Peter Shalley's case that the sheep in question was valued at exactly 40s so making it a felony (not a misdemeanour) punishable by death but the jury in his case did not bring in a lesser verdict, but guilty verdict with a recommendation for the kings mercy.

2. The physical descriptions of David are based on Heinrich Heine, pale with dreamy blue eyes and long wavy hair, although I have made David a much more robust figure. Heine was also a German poet and a Jew. There are elements of Heine in the character I have drawn for David

3. David/Loeb's father Felix – the character drawn for him is that of a non-orthodox Jewish reformer. There is reference to other contemporary figures of the time as follows and he is an amalgam of them:

   • Ludwig Börne. (1776 – 1837) German political writer and satirist, born Loeb Baruch in Frankfurt son of a Jewish banker.
   • Henriette Herz. (1754-1847). Hosted a literary salon in Berlin where stimulating people of quality gathered to enjoy conversation and literary readings.

- Moses Mendellsohn. (1729 –1786) A brilliant German Jewish philosopher. Forerunner of the European Jewish renaissance.
4. Chapter 13. The reference to the new courtroom at the Old Bailey is in fact my licence. It was not actually opened until 1824 a year after the setting of the chapter.
5. There were multiple currencies in the German states. The thaler was an international coin in a fixed weight of silver. The guilder or gulden was an international coin in a fixed weight of gold. The many national coins were often debased and it has proved impossible to research conversion rates of these currencies. I have therefore used mainly the thaler in telling David's story using a conversion of:
   1 thaler = 2 gulden (a reliable conversion)
   1 gulden = 4 marks (not so reliable)
   1 pound = 5 thalers (not so reliable)
6. Up to 1837, a marriage ceremony was required to be performed in a consecrated building. Julia and David would not have been allowed to have been married in the gaol therefore. This inaccuracy has been allowed for dramatic affect.
7. David is accused of stealing a *wether sheep* – for all those who have asked, a wether sheep is a castrated ram.

Bibliography.

Modern Legal History – A H Manchester.
Punishment at the Old Bailey - Old Bailey Proceedings Online.
The National Archives' Library Bibliography
Bound for Botany Bay – Alan Brooke/David Brandon
The Fatal Shore – Robert Hughes
The Hep Hep Riots. - David Shyovitz (The Jewish Virtual Library)
The Pity of it All (A History of the Jews in Germany) – Amos Elon
Judaism for Beginners. - Charles Szlakmann
TV Drama. Is God Guilty?